I'm a stalker. The good kind...

We've all done things we aren't proud of, haven't we? Things we don't want to confess to friends or parents or children. My obsession with Joe Carpenter was one of those things. It was bad enough to have been secretly in love with a man for more than half my life, but resorting to stalking at twenty-nine and a half was really embarrassing. Still, one does what one must.

Millie Barnes has concocted a foolproof plan for winning the man of her dreams. Or is she just a fool in love?

KRiSTAN HiGGiNS

Fools Rush In

HQN™

ISBN-13:   978-0-373-77109-7
ISBN-10:   0-373-77109-6

FOOLS RUSH IN

Copyright: © 2006 by Kristan Higgins

To Ed Higgins, a great storyteller and great father
who loved Cape Cod above all other places.
Thanks, Dad.

Acknowledgments

Without my agents, Maria Carvainis,
Donna Bagdasarian and Moira Sullivan,
being published would remain an elusive dream,
like donating a kidney to Bruce Springsteen or
cooking Thanksgiving dinner. I am endlessly
grateful for their excellent representation.

Deepest thanks and appreciation to my editor,
Abby Zidle, a funny, kind and wicked smart
person whose suggestions and guidance
made this a much better book.

The people of Cape Cod have always
been gracious, welcoming and helpful,
kindly overlooking my lifelong love of the
New York Yankees. Thank you for making
the Cape our second home.

Personal thanks to fellow writer Rose Morris
for her immeasurably kind soul and helpful input;
to Carolyn Wallach for unhesitating honesty and
generous praise; to Heidi Gulbronson and
Pam Boynton, brave enough to read the first
draft and say nice things anyway; and to
my wonderful family: Mom, Hilary,
Mike and Jackie, my truest friends.

Fools Rush In

PROLOGUE

I'M A STALKER. THE GOOD KIND.

Well, I *was* a stalker. It's been a while. Even so, it's hard to admit that you've followed, eavesdropped, spied, lurked, skulked and bribed in the name of love. But I've done all of those things—rather well, I might add. Perhaps you know what I'm talking about. It doesn't matter how old you are, what level of schooling you've had or where you live— stalking is innate to the female psyche. We've all been there.

In my case, I stalked Joe Carpenter from the age of fourteen and a half until I went away to college. I knew where my subject lived. I knew his middle name, his mother's name, his sister's name, his dog's name. I knew what kind of truck he drove, his favorite color, the names of his past four girlfriends, his favorite beer, where he went to happy hour on Fridays, which songs he played on the jukebox. I knew where he worked, how he took his coffee and the grade he got in third-year Spanish. There wasn't much I didn't know about Joe Carpenter.

While I didn't quite meet the legal definition of stalking, I did drive by Joe's house once or twice. Maybe more. (It was more.) I'd been known to "run into" him, a calculated maneuver executed with military precision and made to look quite accidental. It took years of training to reach the level of "coincidence" I developed. I probably shouldn't be proud of that. Still, a talent is a talent.

It started in freshman biology at Nauset High School in Eastham, Massachusetts. Joe's seat was diagonally in front of mine, and in order to look at the blackboard, I had to look past Joe. And I couldn't. Not many women could look past Joe, even when he was fourteen years old. Then I discovered that his locker was three down from mine, and the stalking began.

Joe might mention to a friend that he was going to the beach after school, and I'd show up, too, crouching illegally in the terns' nesting area so as not to be discovered, watching Joe frolic with the in crowd. I'd see his mom's car at the store as my dad drove me home and suddenly blurt the need for tampons, knowing that feminine hygiene products would ensure that my father remained in the parking lot. I'd skulk through the aisles, hoping for a glimpse of Joe Carpenter. I'd ride my bike around town looking for Joe, stopping once I saw him to check the air levels in my perfectly inflated tires, carefully not noticing him, simply lurking in his golden presence.

Joe became, ironically, a carpenter, known professionally as Joe Carpenter the Carpenter. Thanks to my years of research, I knew what others, too sidetracked by his beauty, might have missed—Joe was honest, humble, hardworking and sweet. He performed anonymous acts of kindness, took pride in his work and treated people with benevolence and good cheer. He even adopted a three-legged dog. And yes, Joe Carpenter was gorgeous.

He had the kind of looks that made breathing irrelevant. A smile from Joe could cause waitresses to drop coffee carafes, sending splinters of glass skittering across a restaurant while they stared dreamily at my subject. Cars had collided when he jogged across an intersection; rooms had fallen silent at his entrance. And God in heaven, if he took off his shirt when he was outside working... Tourists had been known to stop and photograph the beauty Joe provided. Forget Nauset Light, take a picture of *that!*

Not a woman alive could remain unaffected by Joe's looks. Dark blond hair, streaked with lighter gold from his hours in the sun. Clean, strong bone structure. Pure green eyes framed by impossibly long, thick golden eyelashes. Dimples. A slightly lopsided, boyish smile. Perfect teeth. Of course, Joe knew he was beautiful—a person couldn't look like that and not be aware of the effect he had on others. But he never flaunted it. Usually a little scruffy, he didn't seem to care too much about his appearance. His hair was often tousled, as if recently from bed. He was frequently unshaven. Clothes rumpled. Effortlessly, magnificently appealing.

Joe and I were both native Cape Codders, both in the same school year. We weren't friends, though we might have said hello to each other a few times in high school. (It was three times, and these slight acknowledgments in front of our peers caused bursts of giddy joy and acne as my hormones surged with the thrill.)

And then came The Time—the monumental event that ensured Joe's status in my heart forever more.

In sophomore year of high school, our class made the trip to Plymouth Plantation required of all New England schoolchildren, by civic pride if not by law. With the curious mix of ennui and exuberance typical of fifteen-year-olds, we spent an hour on our rattling, fume-ridden bus before slouching through the streets of the historic village. Despite the fact that my peers were sullen and bored, I couldn't help but be charmed by "Obadiah," the period-garbed man who was roasting bluefish over an open fire. He offered me a taste. I accepted. He gave me another. I ate that one, too, delighted at his interest in me, ignoring the fact that he made his living by schmoozing tourists.

On the bus home, as kids tossed wads of paper back and forth, shrieking like enraged chimpanzees, that bluefish made itself known to me. My best friend, Katie, asked me if I was okay; apparently, I was more than a little green. I answered by throwing up on my shoes. Ah, bluefish. I've never been able to eat it since.

At any rate, the kids around me reacted with all the kindness you'd expect from teenagers—that is to say, none. I gagged a few more times to the taunts and disgusted cries of my peers as Katie went to the bus driver for paper towels. My eyes were tearing in the aftermath of vomiting, my nose prickling, face flaming. And then…and then Joe was sitting next to me.

"You okay, Millie?" he asked, pushing his hair off his forehead.

"Yes," I whispered, horrified, thrilled, nauseous and smitten.

"Shut up, guys," Joe instructed affably, and because he was Joe, they listened. He patted my shoulder, and even in my weakened state, I registered every detail—the warmth of his hand, the kindness in his beautiful eyes, the half smile on his perfect lips. Then Katie arrived with paper towels and kitty litter to absorb the mess, and Joe returned to the back of the bus where the cool kids sat.

Proof! Proof that Joe was more than just a pretty face. College and even medical school didn't help me outgrow my obsession; instead, I'd come home on break and pick up where I left off—find Joe. Run into Joe. Speak to Joe. Sure, I'd feel slightly ridiculous…until I caught a glimpse of him, when all embarrassment would evaporate in a cloud of love. He always had the same effect on me, his casual "Hey, Millie, how are you?" sending tremors through my limbs, heat to my face.

Now, at nearly thirty, I was still doing a pretty good imitation of teenage obsession. With my residency finally over, I had just moved back to the Cape, and here I was, in agonizingly close vicinity to Joe again. But this year would be different, I vowed. This was the year I would become Joe-worthy.

I didn't have any illusions about myself. I was a smart, nice person. Funny. Caring. A fine friend. Though I was still pretty new to the profession, I knew I was a good doctor. But in terms of physicality, I was short, chubby, with long, lank hair that I pulled into a ponytail more often than not. Straight enough teeth. Brown eyes. Overall, rather plain and ordinary. Being cursed with an extremely beautiful older sister had certainly not helped my self-image over the years. Nor had my residency improved on what nature had given me, though I had definitely mastered the pasty skin/dark circles/unshaven legs look.

In order to attract the attention of a man who embodied physical perfection, I knew I had to make the most of what I had. While I didn't imagine that I could become a swan, I was determined to become at least, oh, I don't know, a Canada goose? They're nice, right? Nothing wrong with a Canada goose.

My plan was simple, much like those of countless women who had set out to get their men. I would get a good haircut and makeover and shed the excess weight that gave me the Pillsbury Doughboy figure I now sported. I would buy a new wardrobe with the help of better-dressed friends. I would get a dog, as Joe was a dog lover, and become a better cook. And once I'd done these things, I would insert my newly forged presence into Joe's life and make my move.

CHAPTER ONE

ON THE FIRST MORNING in my new home, I awoke to the sharp, hopeful smell of fresh paint, the radiator ticking companionably against the cold March day.

Today held all the unsullied promise of a new school year. Residency finished. Home remodeled. Career soon to begin. And Joe...Joe was out there this cold morning, soon to find that I was the love of his life. Swinging out of bed, I looked around the room, noting with pride the bright, clean blue walls and antique quilt. I padded barefoot to the kitchen, admiring my gleaming counters and shining porcelain sink. Turning on the coffeemaker, I breathed a deep sigh of happiness and gratitude.

As the coffee brewed, I rummaged through a box that was yet unpacked. Finding what I was looking for, I returned to the kitchen as the coffeemaker emitted its last gurgles, poured myself a cup, sat down and turned my full attention to the object before me.

An eight-by-ten photograph showed Joe Carpenter standing silhouetted against the sky, shirtless, as he nailed a shingle on a roof. The crispness of the black-and-white photo showcased his perfectly muscled arms as he performed this seemingly mundane task, which, with Joe's easy grace, became poetry. He was slightly turned away from the camera, but enough of his face showed that you could see just how beautiful he was. The caption had read *Aptly named Joe Carpenter of Eastham works on the restoration of Penniman House.*

How did I get this picture? I'd called the paper and asked for it, thank you very much. It had been in the *Boston Globe,* and they'd never suspected that I wasn't Joe's mother, as I'd claimed to be. Sometimes having an old lady's name comes in handy. After all, they wouldn't have believed me if my name had been Heather or Tiffany…. Of course, I couldn't keep this picture out in the open, so I secreted it away for special times. Now was such a time, and I gazed at it with the reverence it deserved.

"It all starts today, Joe," I said, feeling pretty idiotic. Still, as I traced the outline of the man I'd loved for so long, the foolish feeling dissipated like early morning fog. "You're about to fall in love with me. Everything from here on is for you."

Resisting the urge to kiss the photo, I got up and strolled around my little house, cup in hand, basking in the thrill of simply being here. Home ownership on Cape Cod is a monumental achievement…one that I'd accomplished through no effort of my own. My grandmother had died just after Christmas. When the will had been read, I'd learned, with great shock and unsquelchable joy, that she had left her house to me—and only me.

The modest little ranch wore the requisite cedar shingles of the Cape, bleached a soft gray by the salt air and sun. There was no yard to speak of, just a scattering of pine needles, sand and moss. But the house was priceless because it was on protected land of the Cape Cod National Seashore. This meant that it would forever be free from development, I would never have a new neighbor, and I was pretty close to the water (three-tenths of a mile to be precise, though there was no view whatsoever). But I could hear the roaring surf of the mighty Atlantic, and at night the beam of Nauset Light swept across the darkness.

For months, I'd been driving up from Boston to work on the house, sanding floors, painting walls, sorting through my grandmother's things, and the end result was a nice amalgamation of old and new. Gran's needlepointed footstool sat next to my glass coffee table, bright new fabric covering her old beige love seat, a nice watercolor in the spot where a photo of John Kennedy at prayer had once hung. I considered the warm yellow I'd chosen for one wall of the living room, decided it was indeed fantastic, and walked into the bathroom to check on the pink flamingos my mother and I had stenciled on the pale green walls. Wait till Joe sees it here, I fantasized...he'll never want to leave. I stuck my head in the bathroom vanity to assess how much space I had. The small area still smelled pleasantly of lemon Pine-Sol, the fumes making for a rather pleasant buzz.

The phone rang and I jumped, whacking my head on the cabinet. I ran to the kitchen to answer my first phone call in the new house.

"Hi, Millie, hon," my mom said. "How was the first night? Everything okay?"

"Hi, Mom," I answered happily, rubbing my scalp. "Everything's great. How are you?"

"Oh...fine," she answered unconvincingly.

"What's up?"

"Well...it's Trish," Mom murmured.

"Ah." Of course it was Trish, the usual topic of family conversation. "So what's going on?" I opened the fridge and eyed the few occupants: oranges, half-and-half and, purchased in a moment of self-delusion regarding my baking ambitions, yeast. Clearly, I would have to hit the market later on. "Is Trish visiting?"

"No, no, she's still in…New Jersey. But the divorce is final today. Sam just called us."

"I'm sorry," I said. And I was. My parents adored Sam Nickerson, my brother-in-law. As did I. As did the rest of this town. Sam was the son my parents never had. He and my father often watched football games together and did manly things like dump runs and driveway patching. My mother loved nothing more than feeding him and my much-beloved seventeen-year-old nephew. "Well, it's not like we'll never see Sam or Danny again," I assured my mom. *"They're* staying put, at any rate."

"Oh, I know," she answered. "I just wish…I wish your sister had taken more time. I think she's making a mistake."

A sweet, guilty pleasure rushed through me at my mom's disapproval. Trish had always been Mom's favorite, and for years Mom had turned a blind eye toward my sister's behavior, always putting a positive spin on her selfishness. Even when Trish had gotten pregnant just after high school, my mother had defended her, taking comfort in the fact that Sam had immediately married Trish and taken her out to Notre Dame, where he'd been on an athletic scholarship.

I reminded myself that I should be over this sort of thing. Still, I couldn't help saying, "Well, of course she's making a mistake." Closing the refrigerator, I asked, "How are Sam and Danny?"

"They're all right. Sam seemed very sad, though."

"I'll go visit them later," I offered.

"That would be nice, honey. Oh, Daddy wants to talk to you. Howard, it's Millie."

"I know who it is," my father said. "I'm going to the plumbing supply store, punkin. Anything you need?"

"No, thanks, Daddy. I'm all set for now."

"Well, I need some pipe. The Franklins' septic system overflowed last night and their yard's a mess. I told them Scott tissue only, but who listens, right?"

"Serves them right, then. I don't think I need anything, but thanks, Dad."

"Okay, baby. Bye-bye."

"Bye. Have fun with the cesspool!" I answered, knowing he would. My father owned Sea Breeze: The Freshest Name in the Business, a robust septic service company, and he loved his job with the kind of zeal usually displayed only by missionaries or NFL cheerleaders.

Pleased with the sense of familial closeness, I hung up the phone. Then, with great moral fortitude, I readied myself for the next step of my plan to win Joe Carpenter.

As a medical doctor, I obviously knew that there is only one way to lose weight, and that is to burn more calories than are consumed. I'd put myself on prison rations, hence the dearth of anything good to eat in my house. My self-control lacked gusto. If I bought Ben & Jerry's Heath Bar Crunch, arguably the finest ice cream on earth, I would eat the entire pint in one sitting. With this fresh start of mine, I had resolved to improve my eating habits, and therefore I hadn't bought anything fattening or sugary or buttery—in other words, anything good. To facilitate the weight-loss process, to enter the golden realm of the physically buff, I had also decided to start running.

Running, I surmised, was easy. Just put on sneakers and go, right? Very little skill required in running. I had all I needed. Running bra, check. Nikes, check. Black running shorts, check. Not the spandex kind. Dear God, no! These were a nice, loose, breathable fabric. Cute T-shirt, check.

This one said *Tony Blair Is a Hottie.* Gaze upon Joe's picture, check. Sigh dreamily, check. And out the door I went.

I'd never really exercised before. At all. Oh, I played a little softball as a kid, as it was something of a religion around here, but I never did aerobics or Jazzercise or Pilates, as did, say, sister Trish. And the difference showed. Trish, who was thirty-five, looked about twenty-three, with toned, tanned arms, tiny waist, firm bottom. As an adult, I had been too engrossed in college, med school, etc., to spend any time on my physical well-being. Residents are notoriously unhealthy. We eat Twinkies and call it a meal. Sleep for four hours and call it a night. Exercise? That's something we advise for our cardiac patients. It's not for *us,* silly.

After a minute or two of vague stretches, I walked down my long dirt driveway and onto the road. Since the Cape was pretty deserted in March, I was fairly sure I'd be safe from unwanted spectators. It was overcast and cool, a good day for running, I thought. Off I went. Trot, trot, trot. Not bad. Easy, in fact. Mercifully, no coordination was required. Trot, trot, trot. It was pretty cold, and my bare legs and arms stung in the damp, raw air. I passed my neighbor's driveway and continued down the road, finding that I had to breathe through my mouth now. My stomach jiggled. I wondered how far I'd gone and glanced at my watch. Four minutes.

I tried to distract myself, get into the zone, by looking around at the pretty sights. Twisted locust branches clacked together in the salty breeze. I came up to the lighthouse, its bright red-and-white tower starkly beautiful against the gray sky. Ouch! A sharp pain lanced through my left side. *Run through the pain, Millie,* I coached myself. *Pain is weakness leaving the body.* My feet slapped the pavement. Nine minutes now. The cold air scraped my throat, and I was not encouraged to hear my lungs convulsively sucking air. *Agonist breathing,* we call it on the hospice ward. Had I run a mile yet? Was I doing something wrong? Was my oxygen saturation dangerously low?

I lurched to a stop, bending over and wheezing pitifully. *Just taking a breather,* I consoled myself as my heart thundered sickeningly in my head. After a couple of minutes, I regained my composure. Off I went again. Immediately, the wheezing was back. I tried to concentrate on breathing...how hard could it be? In, out, in, out, in, out, oh Jesus, I was hyperventilating! And now I could hear a car! I feigned athleticism and forced myself to lengthen my stride in case it was someone I knew. Smiling through the incredible pain, I waved, which caused my shoulder to spasm and cramp. The car passed. Crisis over.

No, not over. A hill loomed ahead. *Keep the feet slapping, Millie. Don't stop now.* This hill didn't look like a hill to the naked eye; it was more of a grade, really, but as far as I was concerned it was Heartbreak Hill. I imagined myself in the Boston Marathon, that pinnacle of all athletic events, often imitated, never duplicated...*and here comes Millie Barnes, that's* Dr. *Millie Barnes, ladies and gentlemen, from beautiful Cape Cod—*

Was I about to lose control of my bladder? And/or throw up? My watch said thirteen minutes. Clearly, it was broken. At the top of Heartbreak Hill, I turned around and started back. Ah, this was easier, except that I was hyperventilating again. *Calm yourself!* I commanded. The hill, so horrifically long on the way up, was far too short on the way down. My legs were as supple as oak beams, and my shins practically mewled in agony. The pain in my side had yet to go away, and my shoulder cramp had now spread to my neck, forcing me to tip my head at an awkward angle.

The lactic acid in my body was building up to toxic levels. I imagined them diagnosing me at the ER in Hyannis. "Christ, what happened to her?"

"She was running, Doctor."

"How far?"

"Almost a mile, Doctor."

Damn it! If I stopped now, I knew I would never again attempt this stunning torture. *Think of Joe,* I ordered my brain, *think of being naked with Joe and having a fabulous body.* "Oh, Millie, you're in such great shape," Joe will sigh reverently as he gazes upon my...my...my neighbor's mailbox! I was almost home! And yes, there it was, home sweet home, my own beloved washed-out driveway! I staggered into it and careened to a stop. Knees buckling, legs shaking uncontrollably, T-shirt soaked, throat dry and rasping, fighting off the dry heaves, I wobbled drunkenly into my house and collapsed into a kitchen chair.

Here she is, ladies and gentlemen! Dr. Millie Barnes, winner of the Boston Marathon! I looked at my watch again. Twenty-eight minutes, 1.7 miles. That was awesome! I had done it. My convulsive gasping took a while to stop, but after all, what a workout! After twenty minutes or so, I heaved myself out of the chair and downed a glass of water.

Then I made the large mistake of looking in the full-length mirror. My face was a shocking shade of red. Not pink, not flushed with the glow of a good workout, not even just red. A shocking shade of beet-red. The whole face, just one solid color. My eyes were puffy from sweat irritation, my lips chapped and flaky white, providing the only break from the Crayola crimson. My sweaty T-shirt clung to the doughy skin of my upper extremities and neck. My legs were red and wind-burned, better, I supposed, than the chalk that was my normal skin tone. Oh, well. I was a work in progress, after all.

I took a hot shower, forced out far too soon by the tiny water heater's shortcomings. As I made myself a pot of greenish herbal tea, I decided to call my sister. After all, her marriage officially ended today, and I thought I should be, well, sisterly. Still…Trish scared me a little. I remembered her hissing fury when Gran's will had been read. Trish had received several thousand dollars, a pittance compared to what this house was worth. That was the last time I'd seen her.

After a few minutes of sifting through papers on my desk, I found her number. The strange area code gave me a pang. She was pretty far from home, our Trish.

When I'd been in college, I'd called her fairly often for Danny updates, as I adored my nephew, but after he was six or seven, Trish would just put Danny himself on, knowing the true purpose of my call. Or I would talk to Sam, who would give me blow-by-blows of Danny's Little League games, parent-teacher conferences, clarinet lessons, etc.

"Hello?" As always, she sounded impatient.

"Hi, Trish, it's Millie," I said, immediately uncomfortable.

"Oh, Millie. Hi," she answered. "What's the matter?" I could picture her fidgeting next to the phone, no doubt with many better things to do than talk to her younger sister.

"Nothing's the matter," I answered, pouring my bilious tea. The aroma of herbal sludge filled the room. "I, um, I heard your divorce was final today and I wanted to see how you were doing."

There was a pause. I could sense her irritation coiling like a rattlesnake. "I'm fine," she said briskly. "Never better."

I gritted my teeth. Wishing I hadn't called, I nevertheless forged on. "Well, you know, you were married for a long time, and I just thought…"

"Millie, I'm happier now than I've been in years. Just because you belong to the Sam Nickerson fan club doesn't mean that we made each other happy, okay? This is what I want. *Avery* is what I want. Not Sam. Sam is boring." There was no greater crime in my sister's eyes than being boring.

"Right," I answered. "It's just that…I thought you might be down. Seventeen years and all. Thought you might be feeling a little melancholy, but I can see I was wrong."

"That's right."

"Okay, Trish, great talking to you. Have fun in the Garden State."

"How are you?" Trish asked unexpectedly.

"Me? I'm good. Great, in fact," I answered, immediately assuaged by the unforeseen attention. Such was the plight of a younger sibling.

"How's Gran's house?" she asked with only a moderate amount of hostility.

"It's getting there," I answered. "Is there anything you want? Maybe an afghan?"

"God, no, Millie. Please." We were back to normal.

"Well, I'm going over to see Danny later, and I'll tell him you said hi," I said, hoping to inspire some guilt. It didn't work.

"I called him earlier. He's coming to visit again next weekend."

"Oh." Our conversation was clearly over. We said our uncomfortable goodbyes and hung up.

Trish and I were as different as two who shared a gene pool could be. While I had battled crooked teeth and fat as a youth, Trish had floated through adolescence, untouched by eating disorders, pimples or bad hair choices. Trish had been captain of the cheerleading squad. I had been president of the science club. Trish had been prom queen. I'd taken honors biology. She'd dated the football hero. I'd dated not at all.

In order to dispel the feeling of incompetence and frustration my sister inspired, I next called Katie Williams. We'd been friends since kindergarten, when she'd thrown up on my desk, a bonding experience that has withstood the test of time. There's something irreplaceable about a person who's known you since you lost your first tooth, bought your first bra, had your first drink. Katie knew about my undying love for Joe, my plans, Trish, everything. Being the single mother of two little boys, she seemed to enjoy hearing about topics other than potty training and Bob the Builder. And of course, she got free medical care, courtesy of her sons' godmother (that would be me). At any rate, Katie was my sounding board as I plotted, ranted, raved and fantasized about Joe Carpenter. She had always been extremely tolerant of this.

Katie listened with false compassion and far too many laughs to the account of my first athletic attempt, sympathized about my sister and agreed to come over for coffee the next day with my godsons. After we hung up, I got dressed, hooked up my CD player and danced around to U2, pretending to be Bono for two songs. Then I finally stopped stalling and got into my car. Time to go see Sam and Danny.

They lived on the other side of town in one of Eastham's most picturesque neighborhoods. When my nephew was three or four years old, Sam's parents had died in a car accident, the result of a drunken teenager smashing into them on Route 6. Trish, Sam and Danny had moved into Sam's parents' house three weeks after the funeral. My sister had begun remodeling immediately. A year later, the house was unrecognizable. They'd gutted it almost completely, and in its place now stood a modern, angular structure with huge windows facing the bay. Sam had taken a second job to help pay the bills.

The modern house was not at all my taste, though I had to admit it was very impressive—large, open, lots of glass and deck space. But it was the view that made your heart stop. The house overlooked a tiny bayside beach. Water stretched out to the horizon, dotted with wooden rowboats and seagulls, cormorants, the occasional swan. You could hear their constant cries, a melody of sea birds, if you will, that blended with the omnipresent wind and gentle lapping of the waves. At low tide, you could walk almost a half mile out, and at high tide, the water was deep enough to swim. Sea grass waved gracefully, deep green in the warm weather, golden in the winter. People, even we hardened locals, came to the beach to get a glimpse of the sunsets that glorified the sky each night. This was what my sister had left for Short Hills, New Jersey, where I hear they have an impressive mall.

I parked my car in the crushed-shell driveway and ran up the steps. Sam was a cop, and when he was not making the world safe for the rest of us, he worked part-time for a land-scaper. His own gardens were spectacular. Even now in March, unexpected green things popped up to relieve the gray and brown of the dormant flower beds. In a few more months, people would be stopping on the street to admire my sister's former showplace.

I opened the door and shouted hello. With pounding feet, my nephew came bounding down the stairs like an excited Irish setter. I felt a rush of love and gratitude that even at the advanced and cynical age of seventeen, Danny was still so happy to see me. My nephew seemed, to me and just about everyone else, the culmination of what you'd hope your child would be. Funny, generous, extremely smart, tall and a bit gangly, he also excelled at baseball, truly the all-American boy.

"Hey, Auntie," he said, bending down to smooch my cheek. He'd become taller than I was about five years ago.

"Hello, youngster," I said. "What are you doing?"

"Calculus homework. Want something to eat? I'm starving," he said as we went into the kitchen. Stainless-steel appliances, granite countertops, stark white walls and an unforgiving black tile floor gave the room an imposing military feel. Clambering onto a stool at the counter, I watched Danny galumph around, slamming, rattling, sloshing. I refused his kind offer of sustenance, though my stomach growled, triggered by the smell of a toasting bagel and the sight of my nephew downing a glass of creamy whole milk in four swallows. Thousands of calories.

"Is your dad at work?" I asked.

"Nope. He took the day off," Danny said, peeling a banana and stuffing half of it into his mouth while he waited for the bagel to toast. "The divorce is final today, you know."

"Yes, I heard. How are you doing with all that?"

"Well, okay, I guess." He paused for a moment, looking out the window toward the bay. "I mean, Mom's been gone for a while now, so I'm pretty used to that. But Dad's taking it kind of hard."

"Did you talk to your mom today?"

"Yup. She's okay."

I waited, fascinated by the amount of food my nephew could force into his mouth at once. A third of a bagel. My, my.

"She said she's glad to be on to a new chapter of her life, a door closes, a window opens, that sort of thing. I think she's doing all right."

"Wonderful," I murmured, trying to be neutral.

"Oh, come on, Aunt Mil. You can't blame her too much." Danny continued with a shrug, swallowing like a python polishing off a goat. "She deserves to be happy. Just because my parents screwed up when they were kids doesn't mean Mom shouldn't be able to move on. I mean, yeah, the whole cheating thing really sucked. But I don't think she meant to hurt anybody."

Such generosity! How could this child be the product of my sister's loins? "You're the best boy in all the world," I said. "And they didn't screw up, having you. You're the best thing that ever happened to either one of them. Or to me, for that matter. Come here so I can pinch your cheek."

"You're not that old yet, Aunt Mil," Danny said. "Hey, remember my friend Connor? He said you were cute. He wants to play doctor when you open the clinic."

"That's terrifying," I laughed. "So, where is your dad, anyway?"

"He's walking on the beach." Danny turned somber. "He's wicked sad, Aunt Mil. Wicked."

Poor Sam, walking picturesquely on the beach on the day of his divorce. My heart tugged. I chatted with Danny a little more, asked him about his grades to remind him that I was the adult, and then left the house to find wicked sad Sam.

How Trish had landed Sam Nickerson—well, getting pregnant with Danny had worked its magic. But she'd never deserved him, that was for sure. Sam was the nicest guy around and always had been, and he'd always been especially good to me.

When I was eleven or twelve and Trish and Sam were hormonal teenagers, my parents had gone out, leaving my sister in charge. Katie was sleeping over, and Trish stuck her head into my room to inform us that she and Sam were going to a party. She warned us not to tell Mom and Dad or she would kill us, a threat we'd taken with the gravity it deserved.

At this moment, Sam came in and said hello to us, commented favorably on my Barbie and her Dream Van, chatted us up for a minute or two. When he realized that Trish was supposed to be babysitting, he told her that they couldn't just leave us alone. They ended up taking us to the movies to see some preteen-appropriate flick. Sam even bought us popcorn and soda and hadn't seemed to mind that Trish was fuming. Tragically, that night still held the title of Best Date of My Life.

That was Sam for you. Or that was Sam before seventeen years of marriage wore him into a "yes, dear" kind of husband, slightly defeated and always a little confused when it came to Trish. But once, at least, he had genuinely loved her, and when I caught sight of him, looking out over the ocean, shoulders hunched against heartbreak, he did indeed look wicked sad.

"Hi, zipperhead," I called merrily over the wind, my shoes crunching on the crisp, cold sand as I walked over to him. He turned slightly, wearily.

"Hey, kiddo," he responded listlessly.

"That's Dr. Kiddo to you," I said. My eyes felt wet; not from the wind, alas, but from seeing Sam so obviously miserable. I linked my arm through his. "How's it going?"

"Okay." He gave a halfhearted grin and returned his tragic gaze to the ocean. Sympathy and irritation bickered in my head. Sam was better off without Trish, though I knew better than to say this.

"Guess what?" I offered, determined to be upbeat.

"What?" Sam answered.

"I'm taking you out tonight! Come on, let's go back to the house. Man, that wind is murder! My ears are like hunks of ice." I began to steer him to the path that wound through the sea grass toward his house.

"Sorry, kiddo. I don't want to go anywhere," Sam answered, letting me propel him, though he had at least eight or nine inches on me.

"I know. That's why we're going out. It's too pathetic to sit at home on the night of your first divorce. As opposed to your second, when you can indeed stay home. It's every other divorce. Go out, stay home, go out, stay home." Shockingly, Sam was unamused by my feeble attempt at humor. I stopped to look up at him. "Really, Sam. Come out for a beer with me. I'm buying. You will not sit home alone tonight. I will chain myself to your oven before I let you."

"Millie…"

"Come on! Please?"

He sighed. "Okay. One beer. Nowhere local."

"Good boy!" As we climbed up the deck stairs, I turned to him once more. His face was so sad, so dejected, that my eyes filled. "Listen, Sam, I want to say something. Seriously." I swallowed. "I just wanted to tell you that I think you're wonderful. And I'm sorry you're hurting." My mouth wobbled. "I've always been really proud to have you as my brother-in-law." I wiped my eyes with the heel of my hand and gave him a watery smile.

Sam looked at me with a trace of amusement, then put his arm around my shoulders and started into the house. "That was pretty good, kiddo. Did you practice it in the car?"

"Yes, I did, wiseass. For that, you'll have to buy the second round."

CHAPTER TWO

TWO HOURS LATER WE WERE at a bar in Provincetown, drinking beer and waiting for buffalo wings. There are still places like this in P-town, though you have to know where to look. Otherwise, you end up eating things like grilled sea bass enchiladas with fresh cumin in a creamy dill sauce.

The bar was perfectly ordinary and nice, and chances were we wouldn't run into anyone we knew. I understood Sam's desire to get out of town. There wasn't a person around who didn't know about the breakup and winced at the fact that not only had Officer Sam been dumped, but for a rich stockbroker from New Jersey.

We sat quietly at our little table, watching the local color. Sam had been pretty morose on the way up, and I was getting a little tired of it. Trish had left last August, and though today was the official day, it seemed (to me, anyway) that Sam was enjoying his misery a tad too much. Determined to snap him out of his funk, I kicked him under the table.

"Guess what?" I asked in my adorable, merry way.

"What, kiddo?" answered Sam gamely.

"I started running today," I said. "As in, 'I will someday run in the Boston Marathon' running."

Now Sam, as an ex–Notre Dame football player, had obviously been something of an athlete and was still in good shape. He ran, played softball in the town league and probably did other physical things related to his profession. His interest, however, was muted, and he merely nodded and took another sip of beer.

"Want to hear how far?" I tempted, not above using my own degradation to bring a smile to my brother-in law's face.

"Sure."

"One point seven miles."

This caught his attention. "Really," he said, looking slightly less tragic. "How long did that take you?"

"Oh, gosh, let's see now," I answered. "Um, about twenty-eight minutes."

His laughter bounced off the walls, and I grinned along with him.

"Christ, Millie, I can crawl faster than that."

"Ha, ha, gosh, you're so funny, you stupid jock. I'm just starting, you know."

Our wings arrived, and I, who had worked so very hard that day, felt that surely I deserved at least eight of them. We slurped our way through the food as old pals can, and I watched him for signs of suicidality or vegetative depression. None so far.

Sam was pretty attractive. Not the masculine perfection that was Joe, who had been the subject of at least three catfights in which the authorities had been called. Sam was averagely clean-cut, American attractive, tall and lean, light brown hair going to gray, beautiful, sad hazel eyes with crinkles at the corners. Gentle voice, nice smile. He was such a kind man, so sweet and hardworking. And yes, I had a master plan to fix his life, bring him happiness and undo some of the misery my sister had wrought. But I had to do this gently, because, after all, the poor guy had only been divorced a few hours.

"How's your dad?" Sam asked as the waitress cleared our plates.

"Dad's okay. You know. He's still furious with, uh, Trish, but uh, you know how much he loves you." Whoops! I didn't mean to mention the *T* word. Sam grunted in response.

"So, Sam, how are *you* doing?" I asked in my best compassionate-doctor voice. He smiled sadly, tragically. I clenched my teeth hard for a minute.

"I'm okay, I guess." He took a deep breath and another swig of beer, then rubbed his palms on his jeans. "It's just that…well, I keep wondering what I did wrong. I never saw it coming."

"Really?"

"Well, I mean, I knew she wasn't happy. Neither of us was, but we weren't exactly miserable, either."

"Why wasn't she happy?" I asked curiously.

"I don't know! Don't you guys talk about stuff like that? Ask her. She's your sister." Sam shot me an irritated glance, then began picking at the label on his beer bottle.

"Well, Trish and I aren't exactly close," I murmured. "I didn't mean to upset you, big guy. It's just…I don't know, a marriage doesn't fall apart just like that, does it?"

Sam sighed. "Probably not. She complained about me working too much, but, well, we had lots of bills. And she was happy to spend whatever I brought in."

True enough. My sister *liked nice things,* a term she used to describe her spending habits. Others might use *foolish* or *irresponsible*.

"And…I don't know, Millie. We got to a point where we knew things weren't really working, but we didn't know what to do. It wasn't anything concrete, just this sense of things not being…right. I didn't know how to fix it, so I basically just ignored it until the boyfriend came along."

That was probably the longest paragraph I'd ever heard Sam utter, and he seemed to regret saying it. He took a long pull from his beer, then said, "It's weird not to be married anymore. I've always been married, you know?"

"Sure," I said. "It'll take some time." *Six months and counting,* I added silently. "And as for Trish, well, she's just…she's always wanted so much," I finished lamely. "She's kidding herself if she thinks she's going to be happy with Mr. New Jersey."

"Right," Sam said tersely. I winced and made a mental note to avoid mentioning Trish's lover.

"Guess what?" I said. "I'm getting a dog."

"Oh, really?"

"Yup. I think I'll name him Sam."

He smiled. "It's good to have you back on the Cape, Millie."

I smiled back, and we chewed our celery sticks without further discussion, listening to the music and watching a game of darts. Then Sam glanced up. "Oh, hey, Joe," he said casually.

My heart froze, my face froze, my mind—yes, you guessed it—froze. I looked up. And there he was.

It was like a play, when the spotlight shines only on the leading man. Joe Carpenter stood at our table, smiling down at us, dimples flirting, white teeth gleaming. Lust and panic flooded my veins in equal measure.

"Hey, Joe," I said, my heart suddenly pounding, mouth dry.

"Hey, guys. Mind if I sit down a sec?" Joe asked, pulling a chair around and straddling it. He wore faded blue jeans, a flannel shirt and work boots, and I swear to you, he was the most desirable and delicious man God ever made, thank you, Father, thank you, Son, thank you, Holy Spirit.

"Make yourself comfortable," Sam answered. "What are you doing so far from home?"

"Oh, just out on a date," Joe replied, turning his beautiful, smiling green eyes to me. "Hey, Millie."

"Hey, Joe," I said again, wracking my brain for a clever comment.

"What about you two?" Joe asked. "What are you doing up here? Arresting someone, Sam?"

My heart thudded so hard my chest hurt. Why hadn't I put on makeup? Why wasn't I wearing something other than a Holy Cross sweatshirt? Did I have on earrings? Was chicken wing stuck in my teeth? Trying to save Sam from having to explain that this was Divorce Day and also to say something adorably memorable, I fumbled for an answer.

"Oh, we heard this place had good food," I said.

Then, walking across the room, hips swaying, blond hair flowing as if in a shampoo commercial, came Joe's date. Tall. Skinny. Big boobs despite the skinniness, their cantaloupe-like roundness announcing them as store-bought. Unlike me, she seemed to know what to wear to a bar in Provincetown: she had on a wide-necked shirt and interesting earrings that matched the blue in her blouse and, no doubt, her eyes.

"There you are," she said, placing a hand on Joe's shoulder in a statement of ownership. Yes, I could now see that her eyes were indeed blue—Caribbean-blue, I believe Bausch & Lomb called them.

"Oh, hey," Joe said, grinning easily at the blond one, "let me introduce you. This is Sam, this is Millie, and this is Autumn."

"Actually, it's Summer," she said with a glare. Sam swallowed a smile and I bit my lip.

"Right," said Joe, unremorseful. "You're just so pretty, I forgot for a minute." Gross.

She bought it, gracing him with a tight smile. For us, she had nothing.

"Well," said Sam. "We'll let you get back to your night. Nice meeting you, Summer," he said, standing. "See you, Joe."

I sat frozen for a moment. Was I going to have to stand? This would mean Joe and Summer would see that I was still chubby, the day's run notwithstanding. But, no, gracious Joe also stood. He smiled down at me and I managed to smile back.

"Bye," I said.

"Bye, Millie," he answered. Summer apparently didn't think that a goodbye was necessary, for she just walked away, tiny little behind twitching.

I dragged my gaze away from Joe's perfect backside and looked at the table. *Say something,* I commanded myself, not wanting Sam to see the love I had for Joe written all over my face. Feigning normalcy, I asked Sam if he wanted another beer.

While seeing Joe with another woman never felt good, it was certainly not uncommon. For sixteen years now, I had watched him with other women, and I didn't expect that someone as gorgeous, sweet and hardworking as Joe would be alone. Of course, it bothered me a little. He was always with someone like Summer, someone very pretty and not really nice. These relationships never seemed to last.

I wholeheartedly believed that once I had Joe's attention, he would see in me all that he had been missing with other women. I was smart, nice, funny, undemanding. And let's not forget I was a doctor, for crying out loud, helping the sick, comforting their families, and, once in a while, saving a life! A pretty cool job, if I did say so. Once I became as attractive as I could become (short of plastic surgery and diuretics), Joe would finally see me as something more than an old class-mate and fall in love with me.

Maybe you're wondering where I got the *chutzpah,* the *hubris,* the *balls* to go after a guy like Joe. After all, the longest relationship I'd had was less than six weeks. The thing was, I'd spent most of my life in love with Joe Carpenter. I would be turning thirty soon. I figured it was now or never, and if I was going to try to get Joe, I was going to give it all I had.

I put the encounter with Joe in the back of my mind…another trick I'd mastered over the decades. Later I would examine every detail with excruciating fervor, rating myself, considering what I could do better, psyching myself up for next time. But for now, I put the incident aside. After all, I was used to pretending Joe was just an ordinary guy.

Joe and What's-Her-Name were occupied playing pool when Sam and I left a little while later. We strolled down to where we'd parked.

"So, Sam, you're not going to go home, listen to a Norah Jones CD, get drunk and cry, are you?" I asked as we got into the car.

"Well, I think I'll probably pass on that one," he said amiably. "Another time, maybe."

"You're a good boy. An excellent role model for my dog."

"Don't you dare name your dog after me," he laughed.

When we got back home, I felt warm and fuzzy, like a good sister-in-law, though officially, I wasn't one anymore. Sam kissed my cheek, thanked me and walked inside his big house, looking, I believed, not nearly so wicked sad as he had earlier. "Hang in there, buddy," I murmured, putting my car in reverse. "Life is about to get better."

CHAPTER THREE

THE NEXT MORNING, I GOT OUT of bed and collapsed to my knees. My God! What had happened to me? Every muscle south of my scalp had seized like a bad engine. Scrabbling with my quilt, I hauled myself up and lurched stiff-legged into the bathroom, swinging my pelvis like John Wayne to minimize any leg extension. Knives of pain shot up my Achilles tendons into my calves. I'd been hobbled. Whimpering, I bent to the faucet for a mouthful of water and gulped down four Motrin.

My pain turned to joy as I mounted the bathroom scale. I had lost not one but two, two whole pounds! Of course, I knew this was just fluid loss from my excessive perspiring yesterday, and that I couldn't really have lost two pounds of fat in one day, that the complex workings of the human body just won't allow that, but long before I was a doctor, I was an overweight American woman, and guess what? I lost two pounds, that's what!

Katie and her sons arrived a little while later. Corey was six years old, Mikey three. Like her sons, Katie had creamy blond hair and sky-blue eyes, making her my polar opposite. Her beauty attracted dozens of admiring men, but Katie...well, since her divorce, Katie had become a bit hardened. Maybe even before that, but since Elliott left her, she just didn't, as she put it, have a lot of time for crap.

And when exactly had Elliott chosen to leave her, you ask? Why, just after she'd given birth to Michael, after thirty-six hours of labor and three hours of pushing her nine-pound, six-ounce son into the world. Good thing I was there for the birth, because Elliott the Idiot was not. In one of those unbelievable, made-for-Lifetime-television scenes, he arrived a few hours later and told Katie that he wanted a divorce, that he "just wasn't happy anymore." And so, as Katie bled from her impressive episiotomy, as her breasts took on the texture of granite, as her newborn son mewled in her arms, her husband had dumped her for a younger woman.

Katie had become, unsurprisingly, suspicious of men. In addition, she had to work hard to support the boys. She lived in an apartment above her parents' garage and worked as a waitress at the Barnacle, and while she made ends meet, I wanted more for her. Though she swore the last thing she wanted was a relationship…well, I just happened to know a wonderful man who was recently divorced himself, a man who loved children, especially boys, had a fine son of his own, a man I was very fond of, who would make a perfect husband for my best friend. I had to tread gently here, because Katie would hate the thought of being set up. And Officer Nickerson was still smarting from my own sister's betrayal. Gently, gently, subtly, subtly…

"I saw Sam last night," I blurted as Katie and I sat at the kitchen table. The boys were in the dining room, engrossed in the Bob the Builder and Spider-Man coloring books I had bought for them.

"How's he doing?" Katie asked.

"Sad, for some reason. He's so much better off without her," I said, deliberately insensitive, though I did indeed think it was true.

"Oh, come on," Katie said. "They were together a long time. He must feel pretty crappy, poor guy." She sipped her coffee with an appreciative murmur.

"Maybe we could take him out some time," I craftily suggested. "Cheer him up a bit."

"Sure." Mission accomplished! "When do you start work?" Katie asked.

"April Fool's Day. A coincidence, I hope, and not an omen."

Though I wanted to go into private practice, the costs were prohibitive for someone just out of residency. I had approached Dr. Whitaker, our Norman Rockwell–style physician and my own doctor since birth, to take me on as a partner. He wanted me to get a little more experience first and suggested the Cape Cod Walk-In Clinic, which was a satellite of Cape Cod Hospital. Dr. Whitaker would then reevaluate the situation in the fall.

"Are you excited?" Katie asked.

"I sure am. Can't wait."

"And how's the Joe-hunt going?" Katie inquired, looking into the dining room at her boys, their fair heads nearly touching as they colored. A maternal smile of happiness warmed her face.

"Joe, Joe…" I crooned. I told her about how yummy he'd looked the night before, how sweet he'd been, how funny it was when he'd called Summer the wrong season. Katie listened as my voice took on the tone of a zealot. I could hear myself babbling inanely about Joe's virtues and charms, but like any good zealot, I found it hard to stop. Finally I reined myself in.

"So, anyway…that's Joe for you," I finished.

Katie chuckled and patted my hand. "You're a nut, you know that?" She put aside her cup with a regretful sigh. "But you make the best coffee. Come on, boys. We have to go to the market. You can have a muffin if you behave."

Corey and Mike cheerfully ripped out their masterpieces, proudly presenting the blurry, messy pictures to me for my refrigerator door, where they would hang for months. I received my kisses and hugs and helped buckle the boys into the back seat of the Corolla, waving as they trundled down my driveway.

Turning back to my little cottage, a small, familiar wave of loneliness mingled with my new sense of house pride. I knew Katie would have given her kidneys (well, one, at least) for the pleasure of a day alone, but it was different for me. When solitude was unrelenting, it tended to lose its shine. And so, onto the next step in my plan. Adopt a dog.

Oh, yes, a dog. Not a cat! No, having a cat says, "Hi. I'm single. For a reason. Because I love my cat. My cat and I have something special here." But a dog! A dog is a statement of humor, energy, fun. A gal who can get down on the floor and wrestle with her dog is wicked cool!

We'd always had dogs when I was a kid, but when I was a teenager, our last dog went to that great beach in the sky, and my parents hadn't gotten another one. Now, with a home of my own, I was all set to become a proud new dog owner. This dog of mine, my new best friend, my companion while I ran oh-so-gracefully, this dog who would adorably wake me with a cheerful nuzzle, who would collapse in paroxysms of joy upon my arrival home, who would protect me, no, *die* for me, who would undoubtedly love Joe and Joe's three-legged dog, was just hours away.

To the Cape Cod Animal Shelter in Hyannis I went. I first stopped at one of those mega-stores for pets, where I purchased an adjustable-length collar with day-glow reflecting colors to save my pup from an accident. Along with this went a leash, a comfy cedar pillow bed that had Sweet Doggy Dreams printed all over it, and a two-sided ceramic doggy dish with blue-painted paw prints in it. Throw in a bottle of shampoo, some tick repellent, heartworm tablets and a book on dog training, and I had spent $167 before even laying eyes on my new pal.

The animal shelter was surprisingly benign. When you picture *the pound,* death row usually comes to mind. Poor, abandoned animals in too-small cages, making their last confessions to the priest…but this pound was not bad at all. While I waited in the sunny foyer, I talked to the adoption counselor and explained what I was looking for. She told me to go ahead and look around, and so I went to where the dogs were kept.

A cacophony of barking, from savage snarling to high-pitched yipping, greeted me. The vast echoing room housed dozens of doomed doggies, each in its own cage. Tears welled in my eyes as I passed the inmates. It *was* death row. Doggy death row. Poor darlings. A huge black-and-brown beast snarled at me, and my sympathy faded as I leaped away from his cage. There were quite a few of this type of dog: huge, muscled creatures with terrifying, feral mouths excellent for killing the addict who tried to get to my stash. Of course, as I was not a drug dealer, I didn't really need such a creature. Now, there was a nice-looking pooch, a little mop kind of thing of indeterminate parentage. Whoops, large scaly patches on back. Not a Joe-magnet type of dog. In the next cage a Chihuahua mix, looking like a wingless bat, trembled and urinated in terror. Sorry, kid.

And then…there he was. My dog. As if waiting for me, he wagged his tail as he stood on his hind legs, front paws against the chain-link door. Mostly white with splotches of black, floppy ears, sweet, hopeful eyes…he looked like some combination of Border Collie and Lab. I put my hand up to his eagerly sniffing nose.

"Hi there, buddy," I said. He licked my hand. Sold.

Of course, we had to spend some time in the Bonding Room before I could leave with my new best friend, but it was just a formality. We were in love. I filled out the paperwork and coughed up some more cash. An hour after meeting, Digger and I were walking to my car. He was two years old, which meant he was fully grown, friendly, good with kids, and he was adorable. Wagging, wriggling, licking, Digger was my very own.

He loved the car. He was so excited that he peed on the passenger seat as we drove out of the parking lot.

CHAPTER FOUR

THE NEXT STEP IN THE Plan to Get Joe was the all-important makeover. This would serve two purposes: one, obviously, to make me more attractive to Joe; and two, to make me look more professional at the clinic. In Boston, I hadn't cared too much about how I'd looked, buying bland, comfortable clothes, favoring my ponytail for its ease and speed. But my attitude was different now. Some of the people I'd treat would become my clients, and I wanted to project a confident, professional demeanor. And of course, I wanted to be a babe. *Dr.* Babe.

Turning to the best possible source of a woman's beauty— a gay man—I called my dear old friend, Curtis.

"I'm ready," I told him.

"Thank God," he replied.

Curtis and I had been pals since freshman year of college. He was from Nebraska, of all places, and I'd taken him home for Thanksgiving so he could see the ocean for the first time. He'd stood there, stunned and lovestruck, and hadn't been back to the Cornhusker State for more than forty-eight hours since. At any rate, Curtis and his long-time partner, Mitch, had joyfully agreed to become my style consultants. These guys made the Fab Five seem like Neanderthals: Curtis's fair-haired, blue-eyed-angel looks set off his wicked sense of humor, while Mitch's dark, Byronesque beauty and upper-crust accent suggested generations of robber barons and too many Cary Grant movies. They looked perfect together, and, as far as I could see, they were. Their relationship was so blissful and solid and charming that everyone who saw them together felt happy inside, except for the zipperheads who beat them up periodically if they ventured too far from home.

Since college, Curtis and Mitch had lived in Provincetown, that mecca of homosexual freedom, beautiful gardens, charming shops and fabulous food. The boys owned and operated the Pink Peacock, a beautiful bed-and-breakfast that showcased their genius for interior design. And, true to stereotype, Curtis and Mitch adored women and absolutely reeked of good taste in all matters related to the female form. I had no compunction about placing myself in their well-manicured hands.

So it was that on a cold, blustery Wednesday, I drove up to P-town in my rapidly aging Honda. The drive was glorious, a straight shot up Route 6, the highway that runs down the middle of the Cape. I passed groves of stunted pitch pines and postcard views of salt marshes, zooming along in fourth—my overdrive had never worked—joyfully singing at the top of my lungs to "Rosalita" by my other boyfriend, Bruce Springsteen.

I turned off Route 6, passed the rows of cheerful beach-side cottages and navigated down Commercial Street, where galleries and cafés hugged the narrow road. Parking was no problem this early in the season, and I easily found the salon recommended by Curtis and Mitch. The boys themselves frequented this place, and they had gorgeous, lustrous hair, robust cuticles and no visible pores.

Inside, the walls glowed a gentle apricot, and the soothing tones of classical piano music drifted out of discreet speakers. The guys were waiting for me. Their friend Lucien was the owner of the salon and had agreed to "do" me personally, an offer that Curtis and Mitch viewed as quite miraculous. As soon as I walked in, the three gay men descended upon me, clucking as if I had just arisen from my deathbed. I couldn't blame them. A Boston University sweatshirt and jeans so old they were nearly white did not exemplify the height of gay male fashion.

Extremely tall and buff, Lucien had the ebony skin and dangerous cheekbones of Grace Jones. He also sported a fabulous British accent, which I suspected might be fake. "Fan*tas*tic to meet you," he said stonily. He grimaced as he pulled the elastic out of my ponytail, running an elegant hand through my heavy hair. "Better change, duckie. We'll be here all day."

Well, that's what I was here for, after all. Cut and color, makeup and manicure. I had turned down the pedicure, embarrassed at the thought of someone else cutting my toenails. As I pulled on the chic black robe, I could hear my pals discussing my situation with Lucien.

"She's set her cap for a man," Mitchell said in his trademark 1940s lingo.

"Who hasn't?" sighed Lucien. "Save the two of you, of course."

"She's going for a whole new look," Curtis volunteered. "Professional but interesting and youthful. She's a doctor." Here I smiled at the pride in my pal's voice. No friend like an old friend.

"Right, Cinderella!" barked Lucien. "Why don't we start with the facial? I'll need to work from the bottom up on this one. Let's see if we can do something about that wretched winter skin."

THREE HOURS LATER, I had been highlighted, brushed, teased, shorn, pumiced, waxed, detoxified, moisturized, astringentized and practically spanked. My cuticles throbbed from the orange stick abuse. My face still stung from the punishing, acidic toner. Scalp tingled, burned and itched from the hair color. Eyebrows screamed from waxing. Could they be bleeding? People really did this willingly? The boys wouldn't let me see how I looked…. They'd draped a sheet over the mirror so we could do the "reveal." I tried to remind myself that this was all for a greater good, but even picturing Joe's perfect face didn't make me feel better.

As the foiled highlights set in my hair, Lucien escorted me to the makeup area. "Time to fix that face!" he announced. Sitting me down, he began to apply cotton ball after cotton ball of paste-like foundation over my still-suffering skin.

"That color seems a little light," I commented as he opened another bottle.

"Just sit back, love, and we'll choose for you." Clearly, my opinion mattered not one bit. I let Lucien scrub my face with a rough sponge, coughing as he poofed powder onto my cheeks. "There's simply no cheekbone visible, is there?" he sighed. "Well, we'll have to fake it."

"I've always tried…" I began.

"Darling, don't speak. Just sit back and let me work. Mitch, precious, tilt that light just a tad? Brilliant. Now, Millie, is it? You're going to love me for this."

As Lucien applied every makeup item known to mankind, Curtis and Mitch began to look a little…concerned.

"Do I look okay?" I asked, trying not to move my lips as Lucien dabbed Product Number Four upon them.

"Ah…" began Mitch. Lucien shot them a heated glance.

"It's very…dramatic," Curtis attempted.

"Well, what did you want? Boring?" demanded Lucien. "I thought we'd *done* boring."

"I'm sure it's great," I soothed. "And you're right. I've done boring. Time for a little flair."

"See?" hissed Lucien. "Right-o, we're done here. Back to the sink." He began removing the foil wraps from my hair and rinsed my head. I yelped as the hot water hit my tormented scalp.

"Sorry!" Lucien sang out cheerfully. He adjusted the faucet so that the water turned ice-cold. Back at the cutting area, though, he settled in, brushing and drying my hair with a dexterity I knew I could never achieve.

"Ready?" he finally purred. Curtis and Mitch exchanged worried glances. With a quick, smooth move, Lucien tore the sheet from the mirror.

The first thing I saw was my eyebrows, or rather, the lack thereof. Granted, they were a bit unruly before, but now they were no longer recognizable as human eyebrows, so thin they looked like they were one hair thick or drawn on with a very, very sharp pencil. The skin around them was puffy from the waxing, and even the grotesque amount of makeup Lucien had applied couldn't quite mask the redness.

And speaking of makeup…my skin was now pasty-white except for angry slashes of brown ("cheekbones"). I looked like I had just drunk deeply and satisfyingly from the neck of a wayward virgin, thanks to the arterial red on my lips. My eyes, tightened by the minimizer/astringent therapy, looked tiny, ringed in thick black. I glanced in alarm to Curtis, who had the honesty to look away, ashamed for his part in this fiasco.

"What do you think?" cooed Lucien the Nazi.

"I…I…" I had no answer. My brain reeled.

"Your hair is lovely," Mitch said kindly, apologetically.

I forced my gaze north of those eyebrows, and…oh. My hair—thick, heavy, somewhat schizophrenic—looked fabulous! Now, layered, chic, at least eight inches shorter, it was lighter, too, a vibrant, glowing mahogany. Shiny waves floated about my face, sophisticated but casual. I loved it, thank God.

"Wonderful," I said to Lucien. Curtis smiled in relief, knowing he had been granted reprieve from certain execution. The makeup, after all, could be washed off. The eyebrows…well, eyebrow pencils had been invented for a reason, right? But hair was critical to good looks. You couldn't be adorable if you had bad hair, and I now had great hair.

A short time later, I walked down the street, having parted with an ungodly sum to pay for my degradation, wondering how to grow my eyebrows back while avoiding unsightly stubble. Once in my car, I checked myself out in the rearview mirror. Eyebrows still bald. Skin still shockingly white, lips still blood-drenched. My previously wonderful hair had been ravished by the salty Provincetown wind. The carelessly sophisticated look was gone, never to be completely reproduced, soundly replaced with the fourth-grader-asleep-on-the-bus look.

There was no singing along with the radio on the way home.

CHAPTER FIVE

FEELING THE NEED TO SHIELD myself from the stares I knew my naked eyebrows would evoke, I stayed home as much as possible for the next week, working diligently on sanding my deck. My sweet (though not very bright) dog followed me everywhere with energetic wags of his whip-like tail. He took to my house and yard immediately and had yet to stray, bounding immediately when called. His only flaw seemed to be a nervous stomach. He pooped at least five times a day, sometimes in the house. Luckily, I was well-armed with multiple cleaning products.

I enjoyed myself in my new home with kooky little Digger. Sure I did. The problem was, there was no one to admire my adorable, sparkling house, no one to ask "Do you like this chair here?" or "What do you feel like for dinner?" There was no one to care about how my day had been, no one to put me first. I wanted to be adored. I wanted to snuggle. I wanted to get laid.

I had dated a little, here and there. In college, dating wasn't really dating. It was more like go to a party, flirt with someone, go back to his/your room and make out. There were no dinners in restaurants, no phone calls, no gifties. Maybe an e-mail. Maybe you'd walk back from the dining hall together. Catch the movie on Saturday night, him, you and ten or twelve other pals. I might have had a boyfriend in college, but it was hard to tell.

The time I'd felt most desirable was the semester I'd spent in Scotland, the latter half of my junior year. I went to a remote school in the Highlands, took four easy classes and developed muscular calves from the startling hills. For some reason, the Scots found my American-ness very hot, and I was loath to disappoint. They weren't so hung up on skinny, perfect-toothed, androgynous Calvin Klein beauty, and I found myself making out in the back of pubs with Ians and Ewans and even an Angus, happily not understanding a rolling word out of their manly mouths, but who cared! I was popular! Of course, the lads all expected me to put out in the great American tradition of casual sex, and I had to send the majority of them back to the sheep meadow, their big burly hearts a wee bit broken. Once word spread that I wasn't easy, it was almost time for me to go back to the States, anyway. My brief popularity in the Highlands had been pretty damn wonderful. I missed those brawny Scots.

Back at home, there was the romance of medical school. What romance of medical school, you ask? Excellent question. We were all so busy learning so much in so short a time that it was impossible to have a date. Once, in panicky desperation born of fatigue, terror and caffeine, I ended up in bed with a classmate, only to pretend the next day that it had never happened. And we were so stressed and tired, it practically *didn't* happen.

On to the exotic sexiness of internship. If any resident I knew had time to burn flirting, kissing or shagging, he or she would have vastly preferred to spend it weeping in a closet somewhere or maniacally studying the question they'd botched during rounds. We hung in there grimly, learning, watching, assisting, guessing, chanting to ourselves, "Someday this will all be worth it."

By my third year of residency, I had a little more time to date. I even had a six-week relationship with a very nice neurologist. But then he accepted a position with a Cleveland practice, and that was it. I didn't really mind, to tell you the truth. We'd liked each other, and he was funny and cute enough, but it was nothing like what I felt for Joe.

But now I was ready to start life with the man who epitomized my every romantic dream. Thanks to my years of research, I was convinced that Joe would find what he'd wanted all of his life, too…the love of a good woman. Me. Joe's looks could distract a person, to say the least. It would be like dating Brad Pitt. But thanks to my years of stalking, I knew the true, secret heart of Joe Carpenter.

I knew about the time Joe, quietly and anonymously, had fixed old Mrs. Garrison's railing after she'd fallen and broken her hip. Thanks to an eavesdropped conversation at the post office a few years ago, I knew that he gave money to his sister on a regular basis to help make ends meet. I knew about his three-legged dog who hopped after him everywhere, adoration written all over his doggy face. How many times had I revisited The Time, replaying in slow motion that act of innate kindness on the school bus so many years ago? Of course I loved him!

And soon he would love me back.

As part of my Dalai Lama/Richard Gere relationship with Dr. Whitaker, I would be seeing his nursing-home patients once a week. The Outer Cape Senior Center, or OCSC, was located just a mile down the road from my house. Every Thursday, I was to visit Dr. Whitaker's patients and treat them as necessary. And the joy was that, in addition to the obvious benefit of gaining medical experience, I would also see Joe Carpenter, who had been hired to put on a new wing.

I spent an entire sixty minutes showering, applying

makeup and fixing my schizophrenic hair into a semblance of the style I'd paid a week's wages for. Dressed in black gabardine pants, a loose-fitting pink sweater and pink flowery earrings, I bid Digger farewell, ignoring his imploring howls as I got into the Honda, hoping he wouldn't soil the floor again.

The raw March wind tried to shove my little car off the twisting road to the OCSC as I mentally rehearsed what I would say when I "ran into" Joe. Something casual yet charming. Something that would stick in his brain. I had to remember to feign surprise that he was working here. "Oh, hey, Joe! What are *you* doing here? Me? Oh, I'm going to be covering for Dr. Whitaker here on Thursdays." Hence, I would impress Joe with my credentials, inform him that I would be a regular visitor and get to see him without having to create a coincidence.

As I turned into the OCSC, my heart leaped. Joe's truck, a worn, maroon Chevy Cheyenne with Joe Carpenter the Carpenter stenciled in white on both doors, was in the nearly empty parking lot. I girded my loins, if a woman could do that, and prepared to insert my funny, kind, generous and more attractive self into Joe's radar. The minute I stepped out of the car, the wind began ravishing my hair, but having learned about the effects of salt air and my new cut, I clamped my hands over my head and ran to the front door.

The familiar, not unpleasant (to me) smell of a health-care institution greeted me…low-salt food, disinfectant and that indefinable medical odor. I peeked down the empty hallways that led off the foyer. No Joe. There was no one at the front desk, either, so I walked over to the large common room on the left, noting the automatic locking doors at the entrance that would prevent anyone from leaving without notice. Ah, here was life! Clustered around a huge TV that showed Judge

Judy in alarming detail, a dozen or so seniors, some in wheel-chairs, sat mesmerized by Her Honor's shrill opinions.

One woman managed to tear herself away from the show. She wore scrubs, and I guessed her to be an aide of some kind, the type of person who does all the dirty work in a place like this. She approached and gave me a cool once-over.

"Yes?" she asked, hands on her hips, looking a little ticked that I had interrupted the good judge.

"Hi, I'm Dr. Barnes. I'm covering for Dr. Whitaker," I answered with a smile.

"Millie Barnes?" asked the aide. Her eyes narrowed suspiciously.

"Yes."

"You don't recognize me, do you?" asked the aide sourly. Thin, chin-length blond hair with an inch and a half of black roots framed a plain, worn-looking face. She had a truck driver's build—beer belly, big, strong-looking arms and pink-rimmed eyes.

"Uh, no, sorry…you look familiar, but I can't think of your name," I said awkwardly.

"Stephanie Petrucelli," she answered, irritated that I hadn't placed her. "We went to Nauset High together."

Oh, yes! One of the rougher girls in my class, tattooed, bullying, large-pored. An image of freshman Spanish class came to me, Stephanie snickering loudly as I tried gamely to imitate our teacher's accent. Memories of her waiting ominously for me in the bus line. Mocking me at the tenth-grade dance. Laughing as I barfed on the bus. Though she had never actually made good on her threats to beat me up, she had terrorized me nonetheless. Stephanie had been one of those less-gifted students who had hated everyone smarter than she was. And that was a lot of people.

"I remember now," I said, neutrally assessing her appearance. The years had not been kind.

"I heard you were a doctor," she said, sneering.

"That's right."

"So what are you doing here? Dr. Whitaker's our doc."

"I think I've already told you," I answered snippily—amazing how quickly old resentments flare up. "I'll be covering for him on Thursdays."

"Oh. So. What do you want?"

"How about the charts on his patients?" I asked.

"Fine. Go down that hall to the nurses' station. The charts are all there."

"Thanks," I said. "Enjoy your show." She scowled, and I hid a smile.

I walked down the hall, aware again that Joe Carpenter was somewhere in the building, and discreetly fluffed the chronically flat part of my hair. At the nurses' station, I introduced myself to the other staffers, only one of whom was a nurse, and spent about an hour going over charts. Most of the patients suffered from fairly standard senior-citizen complaints: coronary or vascular disease, Alzheimer's, stroke, diabetes.

Dr. Whitaker examined each patient at least twice a month, some as often as once a week. He was meticulous in his notes, his handwriting uncharacteristically neat. He'd left a list of patients to examine today and had given me some background information on each of them, which I appreciated immensely.

The first patient was Mrs. Delmonico, who suffered from morbid obesity and insulin-dependent diabetes. I chatted with her for a few minutes before starting the exam, congratulating her on her newest great-grandchild. She had a shallow ulcer as a result of her poor circulation, and I changed the dressing and wrote orders for whirlpool therapy. Next came Mrs. Walker, a dementia patient who was nonverbal and thin but otherwise seemed to be in good health. I checked her Aricept dose and asked the nurse about art or pet therapy for her, something that seemed to work well with Alzheimer's patients. Mr. Hughes, the father of one of my childhood friends, was ornery, itching to go home after a long recovery from peritonitis resulting from a ruptured appendix. I told him that I would talk with Dr. Whitaker about discharge and asked after Sandy, his daughter. He then apologized sheepishly for his bad temper and told me he couldn't believe I was old enough to be a doctor.

It was wonderful. This was exactly what I wanted to do with my life. And then came Mr. Glover…

Stephanie helped him down the hall to the tiny exam room. Only slightly stooped, he looked pretty hale, actually. Rather dashing in a way, with a white mustache and nicely ironed cotton shirt under a blue cardigan.

"Hi, Mr. Glover," I said with a smile.

"This is Dr. Barnes," Stephanie said in a clear, precise voice. "She's helping Dr. Whitaker. Is it okay if she checks you out?"

Mr. Glover looked at me, nodded and got onto the exam table without too much difficulty.

"Great!" Stephanie smiled as she left. I guess I'd been too harsh on her before. She clearly had a way with the old folks, and as for the work she did, well, you couldn't pay her enough.

"I'm just going to listen to your heart, okay, Mr. Glover?" I asked. He didn't answer, but smiled sweetly. I pressed the stethoscope against his chest and listened to the blood rushing through his ventricles. Faint but regular. Blood pressure excellent. I tapped on his back to auscultate his lungs, then checked his pupils for reactivity.

"Everything seems great," I said. "How are you feeling, Mr. Glover? Any complaints?"

"I feel rather hard," he said, gazing at me with a lovely smile.

"Pardon me?" I asked.

"I'm rather hard," he repeated.

I glanced at his lap, not quite sure if that was the hardness he meant. It was.

"Um…" I stalled, not sure if he was giving me a real complaint. After all, involuntary tumescence was a legitimate medical—

"Care to take a look?" he asked pleasantly. His gaze dropped to my chest, and he casually reached for my breast, arthritic fingers outstretched.

"Hey! No! None of that, Mr. Glover!" I stepped back quickly, bumping into the scale. "Uh, I think you might want to talk to Dr. Whitaker if you think—" *Sometimes dementia results in inappropriate sexual impulses,* my brain recited. It would have been nice if Dr. Whitaker had mentioned this in his meticulous notes—

Suddenly, Mr. Glover grabbed me by the waist and yanked me closer, wrapping his skinny legs around mine, pinning my arms at my sides, and lay his head on my chest.

"No, Mr. Glover! Please let go!" I tried to sound authoritative. It had no effect. I wriggled a little, trying to free my arms. He gave a happy moan and rubbed against me.

"Hey! Stop it!" I said, more loudly. "Mr. Glover, please!" Though he weighed no more than one hundred and fifty pounds, he was wiry. And humming. "Mr. Glover, please let go. Right now. This is very inappropriate." I tried to twist away, which only seemed to excite him more. He giggled. Shit!

I was the doctor, which meant I couldn't exactly knee him in the groin. "Mr. Glover!" My mind raced furiously, trying to think of how we'd been taught to handle this sort of thing in med school. *Call Security* was the best I could come up with.

My patient began to sing softly. "I saw her today at the recep-*tion...*"

"Mr. Glover, stop this right now! I mean it!" I managed to liberate my left arm, and gave him a tentative shove, trying to extricate myself without breaking his brittle bones. He didn't notice. Wincing, I tentatively pulled on a wispy strand of his thin white hair. The Hippocratic oath echoed in my mind. *First, do no harm.* Mr. Glover didn't notice, his song continuing, "At her feet was...a footloose ma-an..."

There was drool on my new sweater. Enough! "Excuse me!" I yelled. "I need some help in here!"

I heard footsteps squeaking down the corridor, and in came Stephanie, looking ever so pleased to see me in Mr. Glover's python grip. And right behind her stood Joe Carpenter. Of course.

"Is there a problem, Doctor?" Stephanie asked innocently.

"You can't always get what you wa-ant," Mr. Glover crooned.

"Give me a hand here," I ground out.

"Oh, Mr. Glover, you know you shouldn't be doing that," Stephanie said calmly. She pried his hands off me and calmly unwound him from my waist. I took a step back and tried not to shudder. Straightening my sweater, knowing my face was beet-red, I retrieved my stethoscope, which had fallen during the unorthodox exam. Joe looked on in amusement.

"Hey, Millie. You okay?" he said, not unkindly.

"Oh, sure, you know, just getting to know the clients here," I babbled. "Quite intimately, in fact." Not too bad for a woman with an octogenarian's saliva on her chest. Joe smiled.

"So sorry, *Dr.* Barnes," Stephanie said smirking as she helped Mr. Glover off the table. "Are you all finished here?"

"Um, yes. Thanks, Stephanie." She gave me an evil smile and led Mr. Glover from the room.

"Goodbye, my dear," he said, waving. "Thank you!"

"Uh, bye, Mr. Glover," I answered. To Joe I said, "To think, I get to do this every week."

"Oh, yeah? Are you working here?" Joe asked with his accident-causing smile. Finally, the reality of his presence rocketed into my nervous system, and warmth filled my body. God, his golden lashes were *so* long.

"Filling in for Dr. Whitaker," I answered, sounding a little breathy. "Today was my first day. What a wacky thing to happen. Old coot." We walked down the hall together, and I remembered to feign astonishment at his presence at OCSC. "But what are you doing here, Joe?" I peeked up at his glorious cheekbones.

"I'm doing some work here, didn't you know?" He gave me a sideways grin, and my loins fired up.

"No, I didn't."

"Didn't you see my truck in the parking lot? I thought I saw you park behind me." He pointed out the window to the parking lot, where my car was practically mounting his truck.

"Oh, of course!" I said, blushing. "Stupid of me," I muttered.

"Well, I guess I'll be seeing you around, huh, Millie?" He smiled again, and I forgot my stupidity.

"You bet, Joe. Take care. And thanks!"

I watched him walk away. The view was magnificent. And the plan was working.

CHAPTER SIX

ON APRIL FOOL'S DAY, I began work at the Cape Cod Walk-In Clinic. It was a small facility in Wellfleet, located right on Route 6, in a little strip mall with ample parking. Our neighbors were a T-shirt-and-gift shop, a video/liquor store and a take-out fried-seafood place. I would have to be wary of that last one.

I would be working at the clinic full-time, though my hours would vary. It was up to the other doctor and me to split the time as we liked; we would each cover a shift. The clinic was open from eight in the morning to ten at night, so even the late shift wasn't too bad. We'd have a nurse and an administrative assistant for the day shift; after six, it would just be the doc and a temp to fill out paperwork and deal with the phones. A nurse would be on call if things got really busy. With any real emergencies or critically ill cases, we'd ship the patients down to Hyannis. Aside from basic X-ray and ultrasound equipment and an electrocardiograph, we were pretty much bare bones.

I hadn't met the other doc yet but was looking forward to it. I had made some really good friends during my residency, but the closest one was in Dorchester, where she worked at an inner-city hospital. Hopefully my fellow clinic doctor would become a buddy, too.

The Cape Cod Walk-In Clinic was furnished in the same

generic, soulless design of thousands of doctors' offices. The waiting room featured bland blue chairs, six in all, covered in nubby, uncomfortable fabric. Sand-colored carpeting. Blurry floral prints on the walls to soothe our patients' strained nerves. Punishing fluorescent lights to agitate said nerves. Coffee table with fake plant on it. Children's corner, with cardboard box of cast-off toys. Counter where patient must stand and be ignored by receptionist for at least three minutes before being acknowledged. (That actually isn't protocol…it's just something I've noticed.) And beyond the counter, two exam rooms, the X-ray area and an office. Could have been on the Cape, could have been in Arizona.

We weren't actually open for business today; it was more of an orientation. As Cape Cod Hospital officially ran the clinic, a representative was there to fill us in on paperwork, procedure and protocol. The three Ps, as she'd said brightly on the phone. The other employees were already seated.

"You must be Dr. Barnes," an attractive woman in her forties greeted me, extending her hand. "I'm Juanita Ortiz from the hospital. We spoke on the phone."

"It's so nice to meet you," I answered. She wore a light gray suit, the skirt short and slim, showing off her long, toned legs. A pink-and-gray scarf circled her neck, and I made a mental note to try that. I myself wore a generic pair of tan slacks and a cream-colored blouse, which I had pulled out of the waistband a bit to camouflage my lack of waist.

"This is Dr. Balamassarhinarhajhi," she said, the endless syllables rolling effortlessly off her tongue as she indicated a very short, bald Indian man of indeterminate age. Bala…Bala…Balasin…

"Doctor," I said, extending my hand automatically. He took my hand and shook it gingerly, giving me a nod.

"I've heard you and Mrs. Doyle know each other," Juanita continued, indicating the plump, smiling woman next to Dr. B. I grinned and leaned over, giving her a kiss on the cheek. Jill Doyle was one of my mom's oldest pals, and I had been thrilled when I'd heard that Jill would be working here. She was chatty and comforting, organized and energetic…a perfect nurse, I would wager.

"And this is Sienna," Juanita finished, pointing to a young woman who looked no more than fifteen years old. *Ah,* I thought. *Some flavor.* Sienna had pink streaks in her brown hair, liquid black eyeliner and bloodred lipstick the likes of which I hadn't seen since my makeover. Her ears were studded with punishing-looking hoops and chunky metal fragments, none of which could really be called an earring. She smiled and idly kicked her Doc Martens against the chair.

"So!" Juanita said. "Let's get started."

For the next two hours, Juanita told us how to handle the three Ps. This was the most excruciatingly boring part of any job, and medicine was no exception. Insurance forms, test orders, referrals, transfers, treatment documentation, confidentiality regulations, malpractice…unfortunately, these things took up much more time than you might expect. In truth, Dr. B. and I would rely on our staff to handle a lot of these while we did the actual treating. Apparently, Sienna had a degree in health information processing.

After a few hours, Juanita and Sienna went out to pick up our lunch, leaving Dr. B., Jill and me alone. "I think I'll take a look around," Jill said, wandering off into the exam rooms. I trailed along, daydreaming.

I am working at the clinic, wearing much better, more sophisticated clothes than I have on currently. I have a waist. My hairstyle is symmetric. Suddenly, a battered maroon pickup screeches into the parking lot. Out staggers Joe, one hand bloody from the foreign body protruding so rudely from the soft tissues of his palm.

"Millie...Millie, are you in there?" he calls. Adorably, he is woozy from the sight of his own blood. (This is an actual Joe C. fact, filed away from the time he got cut during metal shop in eleventh grade.) *I come out, placing a friendly and firm arm around his waist, and he leans against me.*

"I had an accident with the nail gun," he murmurs. I guide him inside, competently reassuring him, numbing and steril-izing his hand. He gazes at me with clear green eyes, suddenly seeing me in a new light....

"Where did you do your residency, Dr. Barnes?"

It was the first time I'd heard Dr. B. speak. I turned to him, smiling. "Brigham and Women's in Boston," I replied. "And you, Dr.—I'm sorry, I don't think I've got your name down just yet." I smiled with what I hoped was charming self-effacement.

"Balamassarhinarhajhi," he answered in a lyrical, singsong accent. "I was a resident at St. Vincent's in New York City, though that seems a very long time ago."

"This must be a big change, then. Much quieter." Clearly, I was going to have to write his name down and study it before tomorrow.

"Indeed. A pleasant change."

"Have you lived on the Cape long?" I asked.

"No, not long," he answered.

"Do you like it here?"

"Of course." He stared at me expectantly, so I forged on.

"Are you married? Any kids?"

"Yes," he replied, his black eyes staring at me, no doubt wondering why I was grilling him. Okay. Not the chattiest guy. New friend would take some work.

THE NEXT FEW WEEKS WENT WELL. Although work was pretty
slow, it was fun to be with Jill, mostly shooting the breeze
while we waited for people to walk in. My parents' friends
were by and large wonderful people, and Jill was a particular favorite. She had several grandchildren she doted on, and
I listened happily as she reported on their amazing talents and
clearly much higher-than-average intellects. Sienna was a
hoot, filling us older folk in on her youthful exploits...
actually, she was only five years younger than I was, but I
didn't do things like go into Boston at eleven o'clock at night
to hear a band or sleep over at strangers' houses or date
multiple men. Sienna did these things and seemed happy to
burble on about them to us.

Dr. Balamassarhinarhajhi (it only took me twenty or so
tries) agreed to be called Dr. Bala when Sienna told him
outright she thought saying his entire name simply took too
much time. We met briefly during the half hour that our shifts
overlapped to fill each other in on the happenings of the day.
Otherwise, he remained polite and distant. Sienna had
managed to discover that his was an arranged marriage. How
she learned this was a mystery, but it didn't stop us three
females from talking about it a good deal.

And yes, there was an occasional patient. A Provincetown
chef sliced open his finger and needed three stitches. A child
slammed his finger in a car door and needed an X-ray and a
splint. Your everyday emergencies... We had no bomb scares,
no poisonous gas leaking into our air supply, no gang
members, no feral dogs, no helicopters crashing through our
roof, so it was nothing like TV.

The night shift was even quieter. Dr. Bala usually covered
this for mysterious reasons that I certainly didn't want to
question. Our temp was a college student, a very pleasant

young man named Jeff, who opened his books and studied diligently in the complete silence that often characterized the hours between five and ten o'clock. When I did work the night shift, I quickly learned to bring the *New England Journal of Medicine* or my laptop and spent quiet hours reading the latest medical news.

Here at the clinic, it was easy to help the patients who came in. I got to spend a lot of time with the few I saw, chatting them up and paying lots of attention to them, and it was this that I loved the most. My dream of being a family doctor seemed closer when I chatted with Mrs. Kowalski, who suffered from a rash after eating Chinese food, or gave Barbie stickers out to Kylie McIntyre, who'd gotten poked in the eye by her older brother. And I enjoyed being the doc in charge, because as a resident, I had always been supervised. I called Dr. Whitaker each week and filled him in, on both the clinic and the nursing home, and he seemed pleased with what I was doing.

When I wasn't at work, I toiled diligently away at my other life's mission, stalking Joe. Each Thursday during my hours at the senior center, I carefully staged an innocent crossing of paths between the golden one and myself, a casual hello, a friendly wave. Once Tripod, who accompanied Joe on all his jobs, hopped over to me, and I was able to stroke his head and tell Joe what a sweet dog he had.

I continued to run, and after a few weeks, my little jog didn't cause quite so much pain, though I still gasped like the largemouth bass my dad regularly pulled from Higgins Pond. I lost a few more pounds and tried to cook at least one decent meal a week, learning the hard way that most recipes call for the meat to be thawed before cooking.

On another front, the house was becoming more and more

mine. I painted the cellar floor and cleaned energetically. Occasionally I would pick up a picture frame or vase or some other little object and happily agonize over where to put it. Digger and I were quite content.

ONE SATURDAY AFTERNOON in late April, as my dog and I huffed toward the house, I saw Sam's truck in my driveway. He and Danny were getting something out of the back of the pickup.

"Hi, Mil!" Sam called.

"Hi, Aunt Mil!" Danny echoed.

"Hello, boys," I gasped, letting Digger off the leash. The silly dog forgot he was supposed to protect me from strange men and instead leaped over to Sam and Danny, collapsing with joy as they reached down to pet him. I took advantage of this moment to regain my breath and steady my trembling knees.

"How's the running going?" Sam asked with the annoying smirk of a natural athlete.

Ass, I thought. "Great!" I answered with feigned enthusiasm.

"You up to two miles yet?"

"Bite me," I whispered cheerfully so my nephew wouldn't hear. Sam laughed.

"You're looking good, Aunt Mil," Danny said, extricating himself from Digger's maniacal licking. He glanced at my T-shirt. "'Mean people suck.' So true."

I grinned up at my tall nephew. "What are you guys doing here?"

"Thought you could use a few plants," Sam said. "I've got some lilacs and hydrangeas for you." As a part-time employee of Seascapes Landscaping, Sam got stuff at a great discount.

"Oh, thanks, Sam!" I exclaimed. How touching, that he would think of me and my bare little yard. He was the sweetest guy. Digger seemed to share my esteem and attached himself vigorously to Sam's leg.

"Off. Off, boy," Sam said, prying the dog's front legs from his knee.

"The same thing happened to me at the nursing home," I laughed. "Except it wasn't a dog." Sam grinned and threw a stick for Digger, effectively ending their romance. I'd have to try that with Mr. Glover.

"Can we see the house?" Danny asked.

"Of course, of course!" I answered. I had forgotten that these guys hadn't been over since my renovations and immediately felt remiss. After all, it had been Danny's Great Gran's house.

"Why don't we just get these plants in the ground first, Dan, and give Millie a chance to, uh, shower," Sam suggested.

"Great," I said, grabbing Digger. "You want to stay for lunch?"

"Sure!" Danny replied, ever hungry.

Happily warmed by their presence, I went inside, wondering what, if any, food I had to offer them.

I showered quickly, throwing a hair band in my wet hair and pulling on jeans and a sweatshirt. In the kitchen, I watched out the kitchen window as they hauled the lilac trees and hydrangea bushes around my small yard, their voices muffled as they talked and laughed. Sam let Danny do the digging, leaning on his own shovel while his energetic son did the hard part. They looked so much alike—same hair color (aside from Sam's gray), same rangy build, same smile, same down-turning eyes, though my nephew's were Trish's chocolaty-brown. Danny was nearly as tall as Sam now, and the realization brought tears to my eyes. Danny was growing up. In just a few short months, he'd be a senior, and then go off to college somewhere. I wondered what Sam would do without him.

I snapped myself out of my musings and rummaged in the cupboards. A can of tuna, age indeterminate, was the best I could come up with. I had a tiny loaf of low-carb bread and set about making sandwiches. Mayonnaise? Not in my house! I put a little oil and vinegar onto the small slices for flavor and set the table with Gran's chicken plates and the glasses with the etched gold leaves. All I had to drink was water, so I filled a pitcher and called the boys in. They thoughtfully took off their boots before entering.

"Wow, Aunt Mil!" Danny exclaimed, turning in a slow circle in my living room. "This is great!"

"Yeah, it's fantastic," Sam said.

I beamed. "Well, thanks, guys. I'm glad you like it. Katie helped a lot, too. She's really good with decorating." It was time to insert my friend into Sam's subconscious.

"It's really great, Mil," Danny said, going down the hall into the bathroom to wash up. "Cool!" I could tell he'd seen the flamingos.

"How do you like living here?" Sam asked, washing his hands at the kitchen sink.

"Oh, it's so much fun, Sam," I answered. "You know I've never really had a place of my own. It's a blast." I smiled at him fondly.

"Good for you, kiddo," he said, putting an arm around me in brotherly fashion.

We sat down at the kitchen table, where Danny picked up a sandwich and inhaled approximately three quarters of it in one bite. "I like those little knobs," he said thickly, nodding at my cupboards.

"Oh, Katie suggested those," I said, nodding and looking at Sam. "She's great with decorating."

"So you said," Sam answered.

Danny was finished. Finished! I had yet to take one bite. "Got anything else?" he asked. "I'm starving."

"Danny," chided his father. "Don't be a savage."

"It's just Aunt Millie," was Danny's excuse.

True, true, just Aunt Millie, selfless Aunt Millie, who pushed her sandwich over to her beloved nephew.

"It's okay, Sam," I said, watching Danny devour my lunch. "I'm not really hungry. You know how it is, after a run."

Sam's mouth twitched. I gritted my teeth and decided to talk directly about Katie. It was time for Sam to move on, and time for Katie to get a decent man. "You want to go out with Katie and me sometime?" I asked, ever subtle.

"Sure! She's hot!" Danny replied, naughty boy.

"Not you, junior," I said, pinching his cheek in my auntie way. "Your aging father."

"Sure," Sam answered easily, finishing his own sandwich.

Mission accomplished! "Great. I'll call you and let you know when."

They left a little while later, laden with my profuse thanks and affection, but apparently still hungry.

"Don't worry," I heard Sam say as they got into the truck. "We'll stop at the Box Lunch for a real sandwich." I scratched my nose with my middle finger at this, and Sam grinned as he backed down my driveway. His smile made my heart swell. It had been a long time since I'd seen Sam happy, I realized, and God knew he deserved it after the pummeling Trish had given his heart.

Hanging out with Sam and Danny was so different without my sister. Though I had known Sam most of my life, he'd always been Trish's property, and she'd never been one to share. I remembered one occasion when I'd been back from college at Thanksgiving and we'd all been at my parents' house, waiting for the big meal, football on in the living room, the classic American scene. Danny was playing checkers with my dad as they watched TV, Mom and Trish were busy in the kitchen, chatting and laughing. Everyone was happy. Sam struck up a conversation with me about school, and we were talking about classes and college life when I looked up and saw Trish glaring at me from the kitchen doorway.

"Sam," she cooed, changing faces as only my sister could, "can I see you upstairs?"

About twenty minutes later, they came down, and from the happy, dopey expression on Sam's face, it was obvious my sister had just shagged him. Just to reinforce the fact that she was the important, interesting, beautiful one, lest Sam's attention, however fraternal, drift from her for a nanosecond.

But things were different now. And, thanks to Trish and her New Jerseyite, Sam was single. Katie was single. Love was in the air, although neither of them could smell it just yet.

CHAPTER SEVEN

FOR THE NEXT PART OF MY PLAN, I again turned to Curtis and Mitch.

My suffering over the past two months had paid off. By late April, I was a comfortable size eight and pretty damn pleased about it. The last time I'd been this tiny, this light, was at about age twelve. Time to see what the boys and I could do about finding me some better clothes.

In a moment of self-delusion, I had briefly entertained the idea of asking my mom and Trish to take me shopping. Last weekend, Trish had come up to visit Danny, and when I'd seen her car in my parents' driveway, I couldn't help the pretty little scene that had flashed through my head—Mom, Trish and me, laughing, shopping, going out for lunch. Of course, that was about as likely as a great white shark befriending a wounded harbor seal, but still…

My parents and Trish were seated at the kitchen table, laughing about something. Trish leaped up the moment I came in. For a second, I thought she was going to greet me, but in more characteristic fashion, it was to show me how busy she was and how unimportant I was.

"Hi, Millie. I'm just on my way back home," she said, emphasizing the last word. "Dinner in the city tonight. Nobu."

"Hi, Trish," I said flatly. I hated her constant name-

dropping. We looked at each other for a minute; she was
even taller than usual, thanks to the sleek black heels on her
feet. I wore sweats and a paint-stained turtleneck; she wore
a horribly expensive-looking red knit dress that clung to her
chiseled, perfect figure.

"Well, must run," she'd said curtly. "Bye, Mom, bye Dad.
Talk to you soon. Bye, Millie."

It was always like this. Trish never let me forget, even
though it had been almost thirty years now, that I had interrupted her starring role as Only Child. *Millie's here. Party's
over.* Message clearly received.

So Curtis and Mitch it was. They met me at my house, and
we headed out in their beautiful, buttery-yellow Mercedes.

Hyannis is the elbow on the arm of the Cape, the town that
has the airport, the ferry, the hospital, and, most importantly,
the mall. Given my tight funds, I couldn't afford the Provincetown boutiques where Curtis and Mitch did their own
shopping, so it was to the soulless but affordable mall that
we headed. As I was armed with two men whose wardrobes
were fabulous even by P-town standards, I was confident
that I would emerge well dressed.

We started with underwear. Curtis and Mitch had no
interest in me as anything but a friend, and yes, they picked
out my underwear. Gone were the days of Hanes purchased
at the supermarket, I noted as the boys chose my panties in
shades of lavender and rose and black. Matching bras! Thankfully, the boys let me try those on all by myself, and once I
found a model that was both comfortable and made the twins
look perky, the boys went to town.

Next was pants. I hated pants. Not only was I short, but I
had no waist to speak of, and pants were always a challenge.

"No pleats," Curtis stated, looking at me scientifically.

"Absolutely not," Mitch agreed. My opinion, clearly, was not required.

"Nothing flared."

"Dear heavens, no! And let's not even consider those ghastly low-risers…."

"Classic, tailored, clean lines."

"You're so right."

As the boys scoured the department store, I wandered around, fingering the sleeveless blouses, wondering if I could get away with showing my plump arms, deeply grateful to have friends who loved both me and the challenge of clothing me. I pulled a bright green top with a square neckline from a rack. "How about this?" I called to my boys.

"Put that down!" Curtis ordered sharply.

"My dear girl, how could you? Green!" Mitch murmured, in shock.

"Honey, just go sit and wait for us, okay?" Curtis said, trying to recover from the obvious horror I'd presented. "We'll call you if we need you."

I found a chair and waited, occasionally hearing Mitch or Curtis exclaim over some item of clothing, some accessory. As this was an alien world, I passed the time with my favorite hobby: daydreaming about Joe Carpenter.

The last time I had seen him was a week ago. Another wave and "Hey, Millie!" from the rooftop, like some demigod calling from the heavens. My thoughts drifted….

I am walking into the senior center, wearing tailored, classic pants with no flares and a sleeveless, non-green blouse that shows off my contoured but feminine arms. Great shoes, great purse (though I couldn't picture either). *Joe leaps off the ladder as I cross the parking lot.*

"Whoa, Millie!" he says, giving me the once-over.

"Hi, Joe!" I respond.

"You doing anything this weekend?" he asks, staring at me, his dimples just showing.

"This weekend?" I reply. "Well, I have plans for Friday, but…what did you have in mind?" (I know better than to be immediately available…it's in all the books).

"Maybe we could go out or something." He smiles.

My reveries about Joe were not that, well, imaginative. I was a realist, I liked to think. I had no illusions about Joe; I loved him for who he was, a blue-collar kind of guy with a heart of gold. And I never had silly, overly romantic dreams about him rescuing me from muggers or anything like that. Just his noticing me would be more than enough.

"Come, child." Curtis interrupted my thoughts with a wave of his manicured hand. "Time to try these on." He had a pile of clothes draped over his arm. Mitchell had a similar load. Each item was either beige, black, ivory, red or royal blue.

I took the heavy piles from them. The fabrics felt great, silky and cool over my arm. "Are thése my colors?" I asked.

"Yes, precious. You're a winter," Mitchell explained, striding into the ladies' dressing room without hesitation. Good thing there was never any help around in a department store.

The boys waited outside the stall as I tried on the clothes, instructing me through the slatted door.

"Everything is mix-and-match, Millie," Curtis informed me. "That way you don't have to worry about what goes with what."

"I know what it means, Curtis," I said. "I'm not stupid."

"Only when it comes to fashion!" Mitchell said.

I stuck my head out of the dressing stall. "Be nice!" I ordered. "Or I won't buy you lunch." But it was impossible to be mad at these two, and truthfully, I loved being Eliza to their

Henry Higginses. And, hell, they knew what they were doing. My God, I thought as I surveyed myself. I looked great!

The boys had chosen lovely, nondramatic pieces, all of which could be, in those complicated fashion terms, mixed and matched. Three shirts, two short-sleeved sweaters, four pairs of pants and a long skirt. Tailored, professional, classic. I couldn't believe how I looked. Of course, my hair would have to be worked on and I wasn't wearing any makeup, but still…I actually looked the part of confident, smart, well-dressed doctor.

"Guys," I said, coming out garbed in the long black skirt and red sweater. "Guys…" My throat closed with sappy gratitude.

"Ooh! Honey, you're so pretty!" Curtis exclaimed, darting in to adjust a shoulder pad.

"I always knew a beautiful woman was hiding in there," Mitch added, kissing my cheek. I grinned wetly back.

But they weren't finished. "The outfits are just the foundation," Mitchell pronounced, leading me to the shoe department. To save time, Curtis went to the jewelry counter. One hour and $775.39 later, we were done. I was a well-dressed woman. I weighed 134 pounds. I was a size eight. I had a decent haircut. I owned makeup.

It was time.

CHAPTER EIGHT

IT WAS ALL VERY WELL TO PLOT and stalk and plan about getting Joe, but it was another thing altogether to go out and start doing it. What exactly should I do? What was the first step? I needed input, so I called Katie. I could hear crashing and shrieks in the background as she answered the phone. "Hi, it's me," I said brightly. "Bad time?"

"No, it's fine," she answered blithely. "Hold on, I'm going in the closet."

I waited as she hid herself away from her sons. There was a sharp scream from one of them, followed by another crash.

"Do you need to go?" I asked, envisioning one of my godsons with blood streaming down his face.

"No, no, they're just playing," she answered. "What's up?"

"Well, a couple of things," I said, stretching luxuriously on my couch. There were fringe benefits to being single and childless, and talking uninterrupted on the phone was one of them. "Sam was here the other day, and I thought we really should take him out some night. He's still a little glum." Actually, Sam had seemed just fine to me, but I sensed he was only happy when he was doing stuff with Danny.

"Sure," Katie said. "Just give me a couple days' notice."

"Great. The other thing is…well, it's about Joe."

"So what's going on?"

"Well, I'm kind of ready. To make my move."

"Good for you!" Katie said cheerfully.

"So can I run the plan by you?" I asked, feeling very eighth grade.

Katie laughed. "Sure. Go for it."

"I was thinking maybe I could have him see me out running, so he could notice that I'm, uh, in shape or whatever. And he'd see Digger and then he'd realize that we're both dog lovers. And then we could talk about that when we saw each other next."

"That sounds great. Very well thought out." Katie's voice became muffled. "Michael, if you do that one more time, I'm taking that dump truck away for nineteen days!"

"I thought you were in the closet," I said.

"I am. Doesn't mean I don't know everything that goes on here."

"Nineteen days?"

"Figure of speech. He thinks it means forever," she answered, and I could hear the smile in her voice.

"So the running thing is good?" I asked, seeking validation.

"Running thing sounds great," Katie answered. I heard Mikey's lisping whine. "They found me, Mil," my friend said. "Gotta go."

"Okay. And thanks, Katie. I'll let you know about Sam."

WITH KATIE'S APPROVAL IN HAND, I set about orchestrating the casual, coincidental encounter with Joe. This is what I pictured.

I am running down Nauset Road, Digger trotting adorably by my side. I am wearing nylon running shorts and a T-shirt with an adorable, pithy statement. And what's this? Oh my goodness, it's Joe Carpenter in his truck! He slows down, ap-

preciating the feminine bouncing, then realizes it's his old classmate, Millie Barnes! "Hey, Millie!" he says, pleasantly surprised. "I didn't know you were a runner."

I stop, not horribly out of breath (because my car is hidden at the ranger's station a half mile back).

"Hello, Joe!" I answer, reaching down to pat my adorable doggy. "How are you?" Chatting ensues. Some laughter. A few appreciative glances at athletic form (his glances, my form). *We talk until a car rudely honks its horn, and Joe, regretfully, must take off. He watches me in the rearview mirror as I run effortlessly and happily until his truck rounds the bend and he can't see me anymore* (when I start walking back to my car).

Joe left for work at 6:30 every morning. This I'd learned on a stalking expedition several years ago. But timing was everything for my little running venture, and I had to be sure.

We've all done things we aren't proud of, haven't we? Things we don't want to confess to friends or parents or children. My obsession with Joe was one of those things. It was bad enough to have been secretly in love with a man for more than half of my life, but resorting to stalking at twenty-nine and a half was really embarrassing. Still, one does what one must.

Joe lived on a little dirt road on the bay side of town. It wasn't close enough to the water to be ultra-desirable, and it was close enough to Route 6 to hear the traffic in the summer. Joe had lived there all his life. When his mom moved off-Cape three years ago, Joe took the place over. It was a rambling little cottage, with two additions put on since the original house had been built. Not a ranch, not a Cape, the house actually had no particular style at all. But it had a little deck and was private, surrounded on all sides by pitch pines and bayberry. Of course, I'd never been inside, but as Joe Carpenter was indeed a carpenter, I was willing to bet it was pretty damn cute.

And so at 5:45 in the morning, a time usually reserved for crows, fishermen and infants, I battled those familiar feelings of stupidity and exhilaration, drove across town, parked at the Church of the Visitation and walked to Joe's road to begin stalking.

The birds' springtime cacophony of song echoed around me, crows screeching and red-wing blackbirds chuckling. Though it was early May, the temperature still dropped into the forties at night, and the air was cool and damp. I shivered. Digger was at home, much to his dismay, but one can't stalk properly with a licking, wagging, diarrheic dog at one's side.

Until recently, Joe's little road hadn't been officially named; it was just a dirt road off Herringbrook Road. You know, where the Carpenters live? And the Lynches? And the Snows? Not John Snow—Nick Snow. That used to be how we Cape Codders identified this bumpy, sandy little stretch. But the out-of-towners who have invaded the Cape in record numbers in recent years liked signage for their summer addresses, and Joe's road was now called Thistleberry Way.

I walked down the road, which was barely wide enough for one car. Joe's driveway was the last one off Thistleberry Way. As I got close, my heart started to pound. The thing about stalking was, obviously, I might get caught. And how mortifying that would be! There was no good excuse for me to be near Joe's house…well, no excuse other than the one I had ready. "Oh, Joe, great! I was coming home from an emergency at the hospital, and my car broke down. I was just going to see if I could use Mr. Snow's phone…"

Well-researched and with no admission of guilt. Still, being caught would be dreadful nonetheless, because I knew for a fact that I would not be the first woman seen lurking on Joe's street.

Okay. There was his driveway. I took my place across the road, about thirty feet back into the woods, well camouflaged by the squat trees and dense undergrowth. Poison ivy was rampant, but I found a sheltered patch that didn't appear to have any of the evil weed and also afforded me a fair view of Joe's driveway. Squatting down, not wanting to get my bottom damp, I began to wait.

This stalking episode seemed a bit more humiliating than the last one, less fun. Of course, the last time I'd been here, I was a first-year medical student, no pride, nothing to lose. And Katie had been with me, so it was more of a hoot. We'd snickered and whispered and tried not to wet ourselves when we laughed too hard, snorting into our arms to muffle our noise. And although my running plan hinged on Joe leaving home when I thought he did, I was nonetheless acutely aware of how ridiculous this was. *Local Doctor Caught Lurking Outside Handsome Man's Home. Charges Being Pressed.*

6:05. The birds had settled down a bit, getting to work, finding their worms and bugs and the like. The wind quieted, too, sighing gently through April's new leaves. My feet tingled from lack of proper blood supply. The tingling quickly turned to pain. I stretched out a leg from my squatting position and instantly tipped over, plopping into the cold mud, which seeped through my sweatpants, freezing my already-cold skin. My sense of idiocy grew.

6:15. I began hearing the noises of people waking up and getting ready for the day. A dog barked. *Don't find me,* I prayed. Doors opened and closed, cars started. Mr. Snow (Nick, not John) drove his blue Oldsmobile gently over the bumps and ruts as he left for work in Orleans.

6:20. I felt itchy. Could I have touched poison ivy, or was that just regular, unshowered, morning itchy? Couldn't tell. Cramp in blood-deprived legs. I stood up slowly and let the old circulatory system have a break. Not too much of a break, though. Would rather suffer agonizing pain than have Joe see me here.

6:28. Thank God! A door slammed, a dog barked, an engine started, and Joe's battered truck lurched out of his driveway. He didn't see me. I waited a few minutes to make sure he wasn't coming back, then stood up. On painfully buzzing feet, I made my way back to the road, brushing clumps of mud and oak leaves off my clothes. Luck decided to join me, and I didn't see anyone I knew as I walked quickly down the road. Once on Massasoit, I was safe. I made it to my car as Father Bruce, my pastor, opened the doors for 7:00 mass. He looked a bit startled to see me but waved as I got into my car. I ignored him and drove away.

Back home, I showered, made some coffee and got ready for work. Now that the deed was done, my feelings of stupidity faded. I had secured my information. I was armed with knowledge. Tomorrow would be the Day of the Run. Day One of Getting Joe.

THE NEXT DAY, I WOKE UP at the horrifying hour of 5:30. I had gone to bed at 9:00 the night before but hadn't been able to fall asleep for some time. The mirror was not my friend as I gazed at my puffy eyes, dark circles—and what was this? A pimple on my chin topped off my attractiveness for the day.

Never mind. I had to do this. If I didn't get started, I'd never get my man. So this was just a tiny sacrifice compared to the happiness that I would find as Joe's girlfriend/fiancée/wife.

I showered and shaved my legs, even though I would be

wearing long pants. I washed my hair and conditioned it, then spent twenty minutes applying gel, drying and spraying it into place so it looked adorably tousled and unaffected. Because I was desperate, I drank one cup of coffee as I fed Digger. Then I got dressed in shorts and a T-shirt. I had finally settled on one that said Massachusetts Department of Correction.

At 6:10, I left the house with a leaping, frenzied, joyful dog and drove to the Little Creek parking area on Doane Road. This site was used for the beach shuttle in the summer, so as not to have too many cars clogging up the area. Tourists and locals alike could park here and hop on an electric shuttle bus that would chauffeur them right to the beach. It was convenient, environmentally sound and wicked fun. It was here that I would hide my car, only about a mile and a half from my house. I could, theoretically, run from home to the Joe meeting point, but this morning was not about exercise.

Little Creek was not yet open, but I drove down the fire road and parked illegally. Even if I was caught, most of the rangers knew my Honda (thanks to my M.D. plates) and wouldn't mind, I reasoned. It was off season, after all. My watch read 6:19. In approximately thirteen minutes, I would be talking to Joe Carpenter. Time to go.

Digger and I trotted easily down Doane Road, which led to two of the world's most beautiful beaches, Coast Guard and Nauset Light. My goal was eventually to be able to run around my "block," which was roughly four miles in circumference, past these two gifts from God, past the Outer Cape Senior Center and back home. But I was still at the two-mile stage, two and a half if I was lucky.

Heart pounding healthfully away, I turned onto Nauset. I trotted along, trying to lengthen my usual trudging stride, opening up so I would look more natural and less tortured. Digger enjoyed our brisk pace, as he usually had to adjust his fast little legs to an awkward walk-trot when we weren't trying to impress a man. Now, as I glided along, he could actually canter, which no doubt looked much better to the idle observer. I looked at my watch. 6:30. Perfect. Joe would be leaving his house, perhaps already on Massasoit, headed my way. As I ran, waving occasionally at a walker or bike rider, I pictured Joe's progress across town. Now he should be at the Route 6 intersection. If the light is green, he'll be here in less than a minute. If red, maybe two minutes. Three, tops.

Mr. Demers was out in his yard, doing a little early morning gardening. He had been a friend of Gran, and I was happy to see him out and about. A tall, imposing, white-haired gentleman, he was from one of the Cape's oldest families and had that regal sense of belonging. He knew everything there was to know about local history, from native tribes to shipwrecks to Hurricane Gloria, and occasionally gave talks at the library.

"Hi, Mr. Demers!" I called, waving.

"Good mawnin', Millie Baahnes!" he bleated, his accent thick even by Massachusetts standards. He stood up from his planting. "Goin' to be a beautiful day!"

"Yes, sir!" I answered. Happy with the world, I checked my watch. Any second now.

It was at this moment that Digger decided his bowels couldn't wait. Right at the mouth of Mr. Demers's pristine oyster-shell driveway, he entered into the telltale squat.

"No, Digger!" I snapped. "Heel!"

Digger didn't heel. I was absolutely not going to have him poop on Mr. Demers's driveway, especially with the homeowner watching with a frown. I dragged my still-crouching dog along until we were off Mr. Demers's property. Then I relented, glancing anxiously down the road for a maroon truck, and let Digger have his way. When he was done, on we went.

It was now 6:36, and I was starting to breathe more heavily. That was okay. I was running, after all, I rationalized. It had been seventeen minutes, and only very athletic people can maintain this level of exercise. But I did slow down. I was a little sweaty, and I didn't want to overdo the glowing thing.

No Joe. Where was he? I kept running. The senior center was about a mile up the road, which gave me a comfortable cushion of time. I could make a mile last a good ten minutes. Twelve, even.

Oooh! I heard a truck. *Don't turn around, Millie.* I opened up my stride again, delighting my dog. Here came the truck…it had to be him. Stride, stride, stride. Truck passed. Not Joe.

Damn! Where was he? It was now 6:42. He was downright late. Maybe he'd stopped for coffee, I reasoned. That was possible, though not what my research showed. Still, it could certainly happen.

Things were getting pathetic. I was out of breath but had to keep running because this part of road was straight, and I would see a car or truck before I could hear it. Thus, I would be unable to break into a run before the driver spotted me, and hence, I would look stupid. I slowed down again. Again my dog stopped, this time to pee.

"Hurry up, Digger," I instructed. He looked at me, wagged and continued peeing. And now that he was doing that, I realized I had to pee, too. Damn that coffee!

At 6:50, we started running again. And there was the senior center! Shit! I couldn't go past it, or I'd miss Joe! I'd have to turn around and pretend to be coming from the other direction. And I'd have to do it fast, or I'd be caught. The thought came to me that Stephanie, Evil Patient Care Technician, might be getting to work about now. Didn't the shift start at 7:00? Another thing to worry about.

I passed the senior center and, looking both right and left and listening carefully, ran to the other side of the road. Done. No one saw me. I was now in Joe range again. God, I felt stupid! It was really getting late. I forced a cheerful expression on my face and reached up to wipe my sweaty forehead with my arm. Not wanting to resort to my trudge, I kept bounding along. My Achilles tendons were starting to ache. I wanted to stop and stretch them and hence prevent tendonitis, but that wouldn't do. Where was Joe? Where was Joe? It became the rhythm my feet pounded to. Where. Was. Joe. Where. Was. Joe. There. Was. Mister. Demers.

Oh, great. There he was, still gardening. He looked at me curiously.

"Everything all right, there, Millie?" he asked.

"Oh, sure," I gasped. "Just, you know, going for a run. Bye!" I trotted past him again.

My bladder reminded me of its fullness. It was 7:00. I had been running for forty minutes! This was surely a world's record! My tendons sang. A sharp pain pierced my left kneecap, and I pictured the meniscus shredding. *Keep going,* I told myself grimly. He had to be coming. My breath rasped in my ears, and I slowed down a little. Digger, the faithless cur, now walked beside me, so sluggish was my stride. But I *was* still running. I could pick up the pace when I saw Joe's truck.

By now I was back at Doane Road. Which meant I had to turn around *again*. There was nothing to do but do it, so I loped in a tight circle to change directions once more.

Is this really necessary? I asked myself. *Do we really have to keep doing this?* Alas, the answer was yes. As I approached

Mr. Demers's house, I could see the consternation on his face. My own face felt hotter as I blushed. My T-shirt was wet under my arms and sweat-darkened on the chest. Cringing inwardly, I ignored Mr. Demers. Pretended to be interested in a mockingbird instead.

Digger stopped again, crouching in the unmistakable pose of a dog pooping, and I staggered to a stop. Gasping, I looked at my watch. 7:10. I couldn't go on anymore. My legs shook, my bladder ached, my foot had a cramp in it.

As I used the hem of my now soaked T-shirt to wipe my face, exposing my shockingly white belly, and as Digger crapped in the poison ivy, Joe drove by. He didn't slow down. Perhaps he didn't recognize me (please, God). But no, Joe's golden arm popped out of the truck, and he waved as he turned into the senior center.

I limped back to my car, my Achilles tendons squealing in pain, my face, no doubt, that attractive shade of brick. At the white-shell driveway, Digger sniffed at the site of his earlier attempted defecation.

"Have a great day!" I called to Mr. Demers, who stood watching me with his arms folded in front of him.

"You too, Millie."

Not likely.

CHAPTER NINE

AS SO OFTEN HAPPENS IN LIFE, love came knocking when I least expected it.

Later that day, I was at work, staring at the anatomy poster in the small office, still smarting—no, cringing—from the earlier debacle. My ever-optimistic mind tried to put a good spin on things, but my black soul refused to forsake the throne.

"Hey, you ran farther than you ever have before!" my mind cheeped.

"Digger was crapping when he drove by," the soul replied.

"Still, you probably lost a pound," the mind continued.

"Digger was crapping when he drove by," the soul repeated. "And he saw your stomach."

"Dr. Barnes?" Nurse Jill called from the hallway, interrupting the mind/soul argument. I dragged myself into the present. When Jill called me *Dr. Barnes,* it meant a patient had come in. Otherwise, I was known as *honey* or *sweetie.*

"Yes, Mrs. Doyle?" I answered, grateful for the distraction.

"There's a patient in Room One," she said, sticking her head into the office with a file and a big grin.

I entered Room One, and there on the exam table sat an extremely good-looking man. Dark hair. Dark eyes. Swarthy skin. Heavy eyebrows, giving him an exotic, Mediterranean look. He held a gauze bandage on his right hand, and there was blood on his denim shirt.

"Hi, I'm Millie Barnes," I said, extending my hand. As he looked at it pointedly, I realized he couldn't shake at just that moment. "Sorry," I murmured with a grin.

"Lorenzo Bellefiore," he said with a smile.

I managed not to sigh. "It's nice to meet you," I said, my insides quivering. "What happened here?"

Lorenzo (*oh, Mommy!*) glanced down at his hand. "I got cut on a horseshoe crab," he answered, frowning. "I think I might need stitches."

"All right, let's have a look," I murmured, quite, quite glad that Curtis and Mitch had taken me shopping the week before.

In my best doctor mode, trying to focus on the injury and not on the intense lust that was melting my insides, I washed my hands and pulled on latex gloves. Gently peeling away the bloody gauze from the god's hand, I looked at the wound. *Focus, Millie, focus.* He was wearing a spicy cologne, and I could just barely catch a whiff of it. Again, I suppressed a lustful sigh, instead giving him a quick and reassuring (I hoped) smile. His eyelashes were sinfully long.

"Yes, indeed, you will need stitches," I pronounced cheerfully. Suture repairs were tons of fun for me. I loved suture repairs, especially on gorgeous men with delicious names.

"Promise not to hurt me," he said, cocking an eyebrow.

"I promise," I purred.

Flirting! We were flirting! With each other!

I called the charming Nurse Doyle and she, with only minimal facial contortions meant to convey her own giddy joy, got the necessary elements for a basic suture repair.

As I went to work on Lorenzo, I asked him a few questions, designed only, I assure you, to put him at ease and *not* to pry into his personal life. Well, maybe just a little.

"So, Mr. Bellefiore—"

"Call me Lorenzo," he said, watching me swab his skin with Betadine.

"Okay, Lorenzo, do you live here on the Cape?"

"No, I don't." (I already knew this. If someone this magnificent lived within a fifty-mile radius, I would have known about him.) He went on. "I was born in Brooklyn, actually, but I've been away at school so long, that doesn't seem like home anymore."

"Where did you go to school?" I asked, sneaking another look at him. Mmm.

"I finished my Ph.D. in marine biology last year," he answered, smiling gleamingly again. "In Miami. But I got a grant to do some research up here, and I just moved about a month ago."

"Marine biology. That's interesting," I said. "If you don't like needles, you should look away now." I was about to inject his hand with local anesthesia, and he did indeed look away.

"Youch!" he yelped, jumping. "That stings!"

"I know, I'm sorry. But it won't hurt in a minute. Cruel to be kind. So what are you doing up here on the Cape?"

"I'm studying the mating habits of horseshoe crabs," he answered.

"Really!" I said, squelching a giggle.

"Yes, it's fascinating," he went on, and proceeded to tell me about the sexual patterns of the strange and prehistoric horseshoe crab. I made the appropriate murmurs of interest as he went on, carefully stitching up his rather elegant hand. Before he even knew it, I was done.

"Ta-da!" I announced, cutting the last tie. "What do you think?"

He examined the stitches carefully before turning his soulful Mediterranean eyes on me.

"You did a great job, Doctor," he said, and my pulse jumped.

"All in a day's work, Doctor," I replied. I put a sterile gauze bandage over the wound and taped it into place, instructing him on keeping the cut clean and coming back for suture removal.

"Is your tetanus shot up to date?" I asked, rakishly snapping off my latex gloves and tossing them in the hazardous-waste bin.

"Just last year," he answered. He scooched off the exam table. Alas, he was kind of short, maybe only five foot seven or so, but hey! Those eyelashes made up for a lot.

"Dr. Barnes, can I ask you something?" he said.

Anything and yes yes yes. "Sure, and call me Millie," I said.

"I know we just met, but do you think you'd like to have dinner with me some night? I hardly know anyone up here, and I'd love to get to know you better."

Oh my GOD! "I think that might be possible," I answered calmly. "I'm working days all this week, so my nights are free." Whoops! Too available. "If you give me a call here, maybe we can set something up."

"That would be great." He smiled again and again, my insides clenched with heat. Lorenzo sidled past me and went to settle up with Sienna. Jill came down the hall to pump me for details, but I headed her off at the pass.

"Mrs. Doyle, that humerus fracture needs a follow-up X-ray, so if you don't mind, could you schedule that?" We had no humerus fracture. Jill jumped right in.

"Of course, Dr. Barnes. Anything else?"

"Yes. Mrs. Donahue needs a refill on her Coumadin, so if you could call that into the pharmacy, that would be great. And please make sure we're restocked on suture kits in Room One, and don't forget that we…should…should…okay, he's gone!"

Sienna came leaping back to join us the minute Lorenzo Bellefiore walked out the door. We huddled around the small window in the doctor's office that was, we had found, excellent for spying. Our newest and most favorite patient drove off, and then, like the three females we so clearly were, began with the high-pitched histrionics.

"Oh my God! Did you see his ass?" Sienna gushed.

"Oh my God, yes I did!" Jill answered with equal fervor.

"Ladies…ladies…I have an announcement to make," I said, grinning hugely. "That man just asked me out."

We were still squealing when Dr. Bala came in an hour later.

OF COURSE, I HADN'T FORGOTTEN about my humiliation and degradation of earlier that morning, but Lorenzo's Mediterranean interruption happily microscoped that event. This romantic-stranger thing never happened to me. And I could use a distraction from Joe, having been reduced in ego to the size of a deer tick. Furthermore, it would be rather fantastic for Joe to see me out with a man whose beauty nearly equaled his.

That night, I called Katie. She was tickled that I was going out on a date and, like a good friend, pumped me for every single detail of our encounter. I was happy to oblige, sighing with delight over Lorenzo's name/eyes/smile/lashes/hands/smell. And when Lorenzo called the next day to set a date, my happiness continued.

I HAD A FEW DAYS TO KILL before the big date, so I made a list. I loved lists. They comforted and protected me, minimized the margin of error and kept me focused, and I was going to need a lot of focus. I made the following list.

1. Call Curtis and Mitch for clothing suggestions.
2. Get hair trimmed by someone other than P-town psycho.
3. Clean house. (I wasn't planning on having Lorenzo either pick me up or drop me off—my brother-in-law was a cop, after all, and I had been warned many times about strange men—but cleaning my house made me feel more together.)
4. Arrange to have Joe at the restaurant where I would be going with Lorenzo.

This last item would take a little finessing. Lorenzo had asked me to choose the restaurant, and I had picked the Barnacle for several reasons. Katie worked there, so she could check him out, the food was excellent and there was indeed a strong possibility that Joe would be around. Many birds slain with just one little stone.

The day before my date, I decided to visit my parents. I had been neglecting them a bit, dropping in only briefly, and so I called dear old Mom and asked her if I could come for dinner. As most moms in the world would be, she was delighted with the chance to feed her child.

"Of course you can come, honey!" she exclaimed. "What do you want me to make?"

"Anything, Mom. Everything you make is fantastic," I replied truthfully.

"Oh, you're so sweet. How about roast chicken?"

A sudden rush of guilt washed over me. Clearly, Mom was lonely…. She and Trish had done a lot together. Both were small-boned and slender and loved to go shopping at Talbots or the outlets, having lunch, seeing a play or movie. I had done little to fill the gap Trish had left.

"Why don't you see if Sam and Danny can come, too?" I asked, knowing that the more people she had to fuss over, the happier my mother would be.

"Great idea! Okay, hon, I'll see you tomorrow night." Somehow, her happiness made me feel even guiltier.

The next night, I presented my mom with a bouquet of yellow tulips and gave her a big smooch. Danny and Sam were already there; Dad had Sam in the cellar, talking about manly things like cement and wiring, and Danny was setting up an e-mail account on my mom's computer. It felt kind of festive, especially without my sister's perpetually dissatisfied presence. Mom bustled around, half listening as Danny explained the nuances of Google, and I poured myself a glass of wine. The smell of roasted chicken and rosemary filled the kitchen, and I was suddenly starving. I hadn't had many real meals in the last few months.

"I love your outfit, Millie darling," my mom said, pausing to look at me.

"Thanks," I smiled. I was wearing black pants and a blue shirt with a little blue-and-white floral scarf tied around my neck as instructed. Gold earrings. Gold-and-blue bracelet. Black suede shoes. "Curtis and Mitch and I went shopping. They're better than Garanimals."

"What are Garanimals?" Danny asked.

My mom smiled at the memory. "They were a brand of clothes. Everything came with a tag so you could tell what would match."

"If your shirt had a gazelle tag and so did your pants, you matched," I solemnly explained. "If they had a lion tag, they wouldn't go with the gazelle tag, because lions eat gazelles. Are you following, Daniel?"

Mom and I laughed as Danny rolled his eyes. "We can only hope they bring them back," she said.

"Hi, Daddy!" I said as my father and Sam emerged from the cellar. I stood on tiptoe to kiss Dad's stubbly cheek. "How's the King of Crap?"

"Just fine, darling. How's my little girl?" He gave me a close look, frowning a bit. "Nancy, Millie looks thin. Aren't we feeding her?"

"She doesn't live with us anymore, Howard," Mom answered. "And you do look a little thin, Millie. Are you eating okay?"

My parents thought I was thin. How I loved them! I smiled sappily while Sam smiled.

"I've just been running, that's all," I said proudly. Obviously, I was not going to tell my mother what I'd been eating recently.

"Running? Oh, that's dangerous, honey. Howard, tell her it's dangerous," Mom replied.

"Millie, it's dangerous," Dad complied. "Let's eat."

We tucked into Mom's wonderful cooking. Along with the succulent rosemary chicken, we feasted on mashed potatoes (which I'd have to avoid, as Mom used half-and-half for that extra hint of cholesterol), glazed carrots and native turnips, my favorite. Apple pie for dessert. *Give me strength, Lord.*

As we ate, Danny told us about his plans for the summer. He and some other kids from his class were going to Appalachia for a week to help build houses with Habitat for Humanity. On his return, he would start a job at a local camp for inner-city kids. Sam smiled modestly at his plate, but he was just about humming with pride. With the characteristic blend of confidence and terror unique to Red Sox fans, we discussed Boston's pitching lineup (superlative), their batting (formidable) and their chances at a World Series victory (excellent). And finally, finally, Mom asked the question I'd been waiting for....

"So, Millie, how's work?"

Okay, well, that wasn't the question I'd been waiting for, but since no one would ask that question ("Are you seeing anyone, Millie?"), I would use work as a vehicle to discuss my upcoming date.

"Work's great, Mom."

"Anything interesting going on?" Sam, bless him, asked.

"Actually, I met a really nice guy a few days ago. He's a marine biologist studying horseshoe crabs, and he got cut and needed stitches."

"A marine biologist?" my dad asked suspiciously. Dad would have chosen a bricklayer or plumber for his girls—or a cop, of course. He viewed people with too much education as untrustworthy. Except his own baby girl, that is.

"Mmm hmm. We're going out tomorrow night."

This statement was met with silence. Mom put her fork down, clearly stunned. Sam looked at me from across the table, stunned. Dad scowled, stunned. The quiet was broken only by the sound of Danny's fork clattering against his plate as he shoveled mashed potatoes into his mouth in a frenzied fashion. "Where are you going?" he asked, swallowing hugely, the only one at the table who wasn't amazed by the fact that I had a date.

"We're just going to the Barnacle," I answered, plopping more potatoes on my nephew's now-empty plate. To their credit, my family had reason to be surprised. I had never had a date here on Cape Cod, so this was indeed an unprecedented event.

"Oh! That's nice!" Mom answered, aware that a response was required. "So what's this person's name?"

"Lorenzo Bellefiore," I answered.

"What kind of name is that?" Dad asked, clenching his fork and knife in his large fists.

"Italian, it sounds like. I don't really know," I said.

"Well, what *do* you know about this guy?" Dad demanded, looking quite fierce. Apparently, the only men I was allowed to love were sitting at this table.

"I know that he cut his hand and needed nine stitches," I replied sweetly, smiling at Sam, who smiled back.

"Millie, you can't just go out with some guy you don't even know," Dad barked.

Fearful that Dad might ruin my chances of matrimony (and hence, more grandchildren), Mom intervened. "Now, Howard, Millie is an adult," she explained in placating terms. "She's a doctor."

"I know she's a doctor!" Dad's voice rose several decibels. "She's my daughter! I know what she does!"

Sam strategically wiped his mouth with his napkin to hide his smile, and I kicked him under the table. This kind of exchange was par for the course in my family, and now that I didn't actually live with Mom and Dad, I thought it was cute.

"Sam," my dad said, appealing to male common sense. "Sam, could you check this guy out?"

"I'd love to, Howard, but I really can't," Sam said. "It's against the rules to use police resources for checking out your sister-in-law's boyfriends."

"It's not boyfriends!" Dad exclaimed. "It's one person! Lorenzo something or other."

"Sorry, big guy," Sam said, winking at me.

"Well, maybe we could do this," Dad said, clearly irritated

with me for complicating his life. "Why don't we all go to the Barnacle for dinner tomorrow night?"

"Dad! My God! Stop it!" I yelped. "You never did this with Trish!"

"Well, Trish had the good sense to pick Sam!" Dad thundered. Then, realizing what he'd said, he grimaced. "Sorry, son."

"That's okay," Sam said. "I know what you meant."

We were quiet for a minute, the specter of my sister's folly hanging around the table like a smelly gym towel. Sam looked very tragic and brave, very *Saving Private Ryan.* I tried not to roll my eyes.

"Who wants pie?" Mom asked.

AFTER THE DISHES WERE LOADED into the dishwasher, Sam asked me if I wanted to take a walk while Dad, Danny and Mom tuned in the often heartbreaking, always thrilling Red Sox.

The wind raked across the sky as we strolled down the street in companionable silence. The last of the evening light was seeping away, turning the sky a deep blue, and we could just barely see.

In my parents' cozy neighborhood, most of the residents were year-round Cape Codders, so lights brightened the windows and cheerful porch flags waved here and there. The road was quiet enough that Sam and I could walk down the middle of it, as there were no sidewalks.

"Sorry about the Trish thing at dinner," I said.

"Oh, that's okay," Sam replied. "Sorry about the interrogation."

"It was kind of fun, seeing Dad get all steamed up."

Sam laughed. "He's a little overprotective, that's for sure. So what's this Lorenzo guy like, anyway?"

"Well," I answered, "he's gorgeous."

"Well, that's perfect, since you're so pretty." Dear Sam! My heart warmed as he grinned at me. "Anything else other than gorgeous?" he asked.

"Oh, he's smart, and he smells wonderful."

"I guess that's a good start," Sam said.

I linked my arm through his as we turned onto another little street.

It had always bothered me that Sam had gone to someone like Trish. Granted, he'd been a teenager when they'd gotten together, but it always seemed like the best men went to those too-beautiful, ungrateful women who felt they were owed everything and were grateful for nothing. And Sam *was* everything a woman could want in a man, quiet and funny and just so decent and reliable. Trish never seemed to appreciate those qualities. Sam deserved someone who really loved him. And so...

"Are you still going out with Katie and me on Saturday?" I asked.

"Sure. It'll be fun."

"Great." I left it at that. "Boy, your son can sure pack it away," I observed, kicking a stone.

Sam laughed again. "Growth spurt," he said. "Did he tell you he's going down to New Jersey next weekend?"

"No, he didn't mention it. How do you feel about that?"

"It's still pretty weird. But still, she's his mother, and he misses her, even though he doesn't say it much. She calls him every night."

"How nice." A car passed us, the driver waving. We waved back.

"So, Sam," I ventured, "how are you doing with being alone and all?"

He shrugged, but I could feel the muscles in his arm tighten. "Not bad, I guess." He was quiet for a moment. "Aside from doing stuff with Danny, or going to his games, things are pretty quiet. Before, Trish pretty much planned all the stuff we did."

"Do you miss her?" I asked curiously.

"I miss being married," he answered honestly. "I don't know if I miss *her*...I mean, she cheated on me, and I'm still getting over that little fact. But yeah, I'm sure I will miss her, once I stop..."

"Hating her?"

Sam laughed. "No. I don't hate her. I hate what she did, but I loved her."

"Why?" I blurted, unable to keep the bitterness from my voice. Trish had been like a drill sergeant with Sam, always barking orders, never even noticing how steadfast he was.

"You were always too hard on Trish," Sam said, clearing a small branch from the road and throwing it into the woods. I snorted.

"You were," he insisted. "I never understood how the two of you could be so mean to each other. I would've loved a brother or sister."

"I wasn't mean to her! She was mean to me!" I sounded like an eight-year-old, but I couldn't help it.

"Well, she was jealous of you."

"What?" I yelped. "You've got it backwards, Sam my man."

"No, I don't," he replied matter-of-factly. "You went to college, you went away to Scotland, lived in a big city. Come on, Mil, you became a doctor. Trish never had anything like that."

"Well, she could have! Instead, she—" I broke off.

"She got knocked up by me?"

We had stopped walking. Sam and I had never talked like this before, and the conversation was quickly heading out to stormy seas.

Yes, Trish had gotten knocked up, but I couldn't let Sam take the blame on that one.

"Sam, I have to tell you something." I took a fortifying breath, glad that it was dark enough so I wouldn't have to see the shock on his face. "Maybe I shouldn't, but I think it's time you knew."

"Knew what? That she got pregnant on purpose?"

"You knew?" I gasped.

"Sure, Millie. Didn't take a rocket scientist to figure that one out. Give me a little credit, kiddo."

I remembered the fateful weekend as if it were yesterday. Sam had been off at his sophomore year at Notre Dame. It was a Saturday afternoon in the late fall, and we were all sitting in front of the TV, hoping for a glimpse of Sam in the masses of second- and third-string football players. And then, like magic, a time-out was called in the fourth quarter, a Fighting Irishman limped off the field, and then, those golden words… "Now playing for Notre Dame, number twelve, Sam Nickerson!" And Sam's picture filled the screen, and there were screams and hugs and tears and all sorts of delirium in our living room. Sam took the field. Two plays later, he caught a twenty-eight-yard pass, dodged three guards and ran it in for a touchdown. Irish 21, Trojans 17. It was glorious.

Three hours after the game ended, a glass pressed to the wall that separated our bedrooms, I listened to Trish utter those fateful words to her best friend, Beth.

"I am throwing out my birth-control pills this minute."

Why had she done it? Because Sam had seemed destined for greatness, for riches, for an NFL contract, maybe even for TV commercials, and Trish had wanted a piece of it.

Silly me. I thought it was a huge secret from which Sam—and certainly Danny—needed protection.

"You coming?" Sam's voice snapped me out of my stupor, and I trotted to catch up to him.

"Sam, how did you know? When did you find out?"

He sighed. "I don't remember, Millie. But it doesn't matter, does it? I mean, I got Danny."

There it was in a nutshell. Danny was everything to Sam, and that was it.

It wasn't that simple for me. "But didn't it drive you crazy? I mean, Trish pinned the rest of her life on you because she thought you were going to be a famous jock. And then…then she blamed you for not being one."

In the third game of Sam's senior season, in another unforgettable scene that we'd all witnessed on TV, an evil Michigan State defenseman had slammed into Sam after the whistle had blown. Sam's right shoulder had shattered like a teacup, and it was all the doctors could do to pin it back together into some semblance of normalcy. The NFL scouts who had been wooing him fled. Sam's pigskin dreams (and Trish's dreams of wealth) had ended, and they'd come back to the Cape. Sam had gone to work cleaning septic tanks for my dad until he'd become a cop.

Sam sighed. "Well, what can you do? We were already married when I broke my shoulder, already had Danny."

"And you still loved her?" I asked incredulously.

"Sure."

"Does Danny know?"

"Of course not. Why would I tell him?"

I shook my head. "You're too good, Sam."

"Not really." He put his arm around my shoulders. "You cold? Want my coat?"

"No, thanks." I trudged along, digesting the information. Trish had told him, or he'd figured it out. And he didn't care. Further evidence that he was, plain and simple, a great guy.

"I told your dad I'd stop by the Barnacle tomorrow night," Sam said, snapping me back to the present. I could hear the laughter in his voice, though it was now fully dark.

"Be subtle, okay?"

"You bet, kiddo."

CHAPTER TEN

ON THURSDAY NIGHT I was all ready to go. As usual, I had left the clinic around four o'clock and headed straight home. I took Digger for a quick walk (he was getting better about not pooping in the house, and if he did, he very considerately went on the linoleum). I snacked on some carrots to avoid unpleasant stomach rumblings later and fed my dog. Then began the preparations for my date with Lorenzo. Shower. Hair. Clothes. Makeup. Jewelry. I took a long look at myself in the full-length mirror on the back of my bedroom door and was quite pleased with what I saw.

Curtis, Mitch and I had chosen the long black skirt and black ankle boots. For a top, we'd gone for the red sweater, which had a graceful, wide neckline. The sweater stopped right at the curve of my tummy, just camouflaging the little roll of fat that clung stubbornly to my abs. After a half an hour with the hair dryer and a few ounces of mousse and gel, my hair was gleaming and symmetrically fluffy all around, just brushing my earlobes. Red-and-black earrings discreetly echoed tonight's color choices, as well as an antique-looking black beaded bracelet. *Millie Barnes,* I assured myself, *you have never looked better.*

The problem was, I had an hour and half to kill. Digger, sensing my impending departure, decided he wanted love.

"No, Digger. Sorry, baby. Lie down." He whined but obeyed, looking reproachfully over his shoulder as he made his way to his corner. To make up for my neglect, I gave him a rawhide bone.

I called Katie, forgetting that she was already at work and that I would see her the moment I walked into the restaurant. I chatted with her mom for a minute, but I could hear the sounds of supper in the background and signed off quickly. Next I called Mitch and Curtis, but they were busy with guests. I debated calling my mom but decided against it, in case my dad changed his mind and came to the Barnacle after all. I checked my e-mail and answered a chatty note from Janette, my best friend from residency, and signed off. Skimming a *New England Journal of Medicine,* I found that I couldn't concentrate. I clicked on the TV, but as I had eschewed cable, only the local news was on. I switched off the TV, leaned back in my chair and sighed.

Of course, having gone to so much effort, and having also announced the fact of this date to my family, I was filled with the fear that I would be stood up. But Lorenzo had called me the very day after we'd met, and he had called again to ask for directions to the Barnacle, which was certainly a good sign. On the phone, he had sounded very upbeat and sincere. I could only hope he was.

I imagined seeing Joe tonight. How great that would be! Just the same, make no mistake, I was excited about seeing Lorenzo. It's not every day a woman gets to gaze at someone as drop-dead delicious as he was.

Finally, it was time. I had planned on leaving the house at five of seven, which would get me to the restaurant at 7:08. This, I thought, was just right; just a teensy bit late so as not to seem overeager, but close enough to the mark so as not to be rude.

I got to the Barnacle without an accident or even incident. I walked in without falling in a puddle. Despite its being only a Thursday in early May, the restaurant was filling up with regulars. I immediately sensed that Lorenzo wasn't there.

Katie came up to me instantly. "Not here," she confirmed. "You look incredible, Mil! And don't worry. He'll come. And in the meantime…dadada-dum!"

She stepped back a little, and who should be sitting at the bar but Joe Carpenter.

Oh, thank you, Powers That Be, thank you.

As I was a regular, sort of, at the Barnacle, I had hoisted a beer many times on my own. But tonight was different. Tonight, when I waved to Chris, the bartender, he smiled and raised an eyebrow and said something to Joe, who turned around and smiled, too. And I, the well-dressed, well-groomed, sweet-smelling woman that I now was, had no problem claiming the stool right next to the man I had loved for so long.

"Hey, Millie," Joe said.

"Hey, Joe," I smiled.

"What can I get you, Millie?" Chris asked.

"Oh, I don't know." What should I drink? What went with my image tonight? "How about a vodka and tonic?" That seemed very sophisticated.

"What kind of vodka?" Chris inquired.

"Oh…uh…Absolut?" I suggested, not that I could have thought of another brand with a gun to my head. I was really more of a beer person, occasionally a glass of wine. I turned to Joe. God, I was sitting next to Joe! He dimpled at me, and I tried not to grip the bar for strength.

"Good choice," Chris said. "Regular? Citron? Vanilla? Raspberry? Pepper?"

I turned back to Chris. "The first one," I answered firmly. "Lemon? Lime?"

"Lime, Chris." *Just get me the damn drink,* I thought, looking at Joe. He looked like an angel in the soft golden light of the bar. "So, Joe, what's new?"

"Not much, Millie, not much. Hey, was that you I saw running the other day?"

"Might have been," I answered, feeling my face flush. I gratefully took the drink from Chris and took a huge slurp, hoping Joe would drop the subject.

"On Nauset?" He didn't *seem* as if he was trying to bust my chops with those big green eyes of his looking at me so innocently, his golden lashes catching the light.

"I live on Cable," I said, artfully dodging the question. "I run on Nauset every once in a while."

"Oh, yeah? I thought you lived on Oak Street."

"My parents live on Oak." I took another large swig of my drink. It wasn't bad. Not good, either, but not bad. "I live not too far from the lighthouse." Great! Now he knew where I lived.

Someone tapped me on the shoulder, and I turned around. It was Lorenzo.

"Oh! Hi, Lorenzo!" I said.

"Sorry I'm a little late," he said with a frown, glancing at Joe.

"Oh, that's okay. Lorenzo, this is Joe Carpenter," I replied. "Joe, Lorenzo Bellefiore."

"Good to meet you," Joe said, extending a hand to Lorenzo. They shook. My boyfriends shook hands. I fought the bubble of laughter that wanted to burst out of me.

"Lorenzo's new to the Cape," I told Joe. "He's a marine biologist."

"Oh, yeah?" the golden one replied affably. "Great."

"What do you do, Joe?" the dark god asked. Was it my

imagination, or did Lorenzo sound a little…impatient? Impatient to be with me?

"I'm a carpenter," Joe answered.

"Oh. I thought that was your name," Lorenzo said, looking perplexed.

"It is. Joe Carpenter the Carpenter. It's my slogan." Joe smiled at me again, and my heart stopped beating for a second.

"Gotcha."

I could have watched them all night, my head swiveling back and forth like a frenetic windshield wiper, but thankfully, Katie interrupted. "Your table is all set," she said in professional-waitress mode.

"Nice talking to you, Joe," I said, sliding out of my seat to follow Katie.

"Don't forget your drink," he replied, handing me my glass with a half grin.

"Thanks." Oh, he was so sweet!

Lorenzo and I sat down at an intimate little corner table (thank you, best friend). Katie handed us our menus and gave the wine list to Lorenzo. When she was safely out of his field of vision, she gave me the thumbs-up.

"So," I said to Lorenzo, "how's your hand?"

He frowned. "It's all right. It still hurts. Do you think it's infected?"

I took his hand and studied the cut. The stitches were holding fast, and the cut was healing perfectly, no inflammation, no redness. "It's not infected."

He raised his eyebrows as if dubious.

"Well. So, Lorenzo, what do you think of the Barnacle?"

He looked around, taking in the mishmash of nautical decorations and eclectic tablecloths. "Very cute. Have you eaten here before?"

"Oh, absolutely. Lots of times. The lobster bisque is out of this world."

For what seemed like forever, Lorenzo studied the menu. After all, he was a scientist and clearly needed all the facts before making a decision. I sipped my drink and looked around casually, wondering who, other than Joe, Chris the bartender and Katie, would see me tonight with this divine creature.

"I guess I'll try the bisque," Lorenzo said, giving me a smile that was very nearly as beautiful as Joe's. "And the grilled swordfish."

Katie came back with a refill on my drink and took our orders. I was already starting to feel a little warm, so I asked Lorenzo a few questions designed to get him to talk until my bloodstream adjusted to the vodka I was pouring into it.

"Do you like it here so far, Lorenzo? Spring on the Cape is gorgeous."

He leaned back in his chair and regarded me with his bottomless brown eyes. "It's fine," he answered. "Very pretty in parts. But the thing that's driving me a little crazy is the lack of decent conversation. It's great talking to you."

Hmm. Was that a compliment? Hard to say.

"The people…I don't know," he went on.

Alarm bells went off in my head. I sat up a little straighter. "What about the people?"

"Well…no one is exactly welcoming. I mean, I've been here a month, and you're the first person I can actually talk to."

"I think that's just the way it is in an area that relies on a tourist economy," I said reassuringly. "The locals are generally a little reserved. They need the tourism dollars but feel a lack of respect from the out-of-towners." Nicely said, I thought, despite (or perhaps because of) my buzz.

"I suppose that's true," Lorenzo agreed. I smiled at him to show there were no hard feelings.

Katie arrived with our soup. "Enjoy," she murmured, deliberately stepping on my foot as she set the bowl in front of me. Lorenzo took a slurp.

"Oh, that *is* good," he said. The bisque was, as always, rich and piping hot, with huge chunks of lobster swimming in the creamy liquid. I managed not to dribble any on my bosom and forced myself not to tip the bowl up and drink from it.

"How about the accent up here?" Lorenzo said, just as I put another spoonful into my mouth. A spoonful with a big lobster piece in it, which would require significant chewing.

"Did you hear that guy at the bar?" Lorenzo went on, oblivious to my accelerated mastication. "'Joe Cahpenteh the Cahpenteh.' Is that still considered English?"

I put my spoon down and swallowed. "Actually, as *you're* visiting *here*," I said as if addressing a child, "*you* are the one with the accent, not the Cape Codders." And should a Brooklyn native be making fun of anyone's accent?

"I know, I know," Lorenzo said, grinning sheepishly. "But come on."

"And Joe Carpenter happens to be a very nice guy."

This got his attention. "Do you know him?" he asked.

"I was talking to him, wasn't I? We went to high school together."

"Oh, shit! You're from here?" His dismay, whether at putting his foot in his mouth or at my point of origin, was almost funny to see. Almost.

"Yes, I was born and raised here," I said sternly.

"But you don't sound like those…those people, uh, the natives," he backpedaled.

"Well, I haven't really lived here since I was eighteen. And my mom's from Connecticut, so I suppose I sound more like her."

Lorenzo wisely refrained from further comment, and we turned back to our bisque.

My mind was whirling. Lorenzo, his dark god looks aside, had yet to say something to make me like him. However, he did have the aforementioned dark god looks, and furthermore, Joe Carpenter was sitting twenty feet away, well aware that I was on a date with a very handsome man.

"Why don't we talk about something else?" I said, offering the olive branch.

"Good idea," Lorenzo replied.

"Tell me about your graduate work," I said.

Oh, how I regretted those words twenty minutes later! Lorenzo was off and running with the subject, clearly very full of himself and his subject. When Katie brought our dinners, I toyed with my earring, our teenage sign language for *Help me*.

"Can I get you anything else right now?" she asked with a pleasant smile. Apparently she didn't remember. I tugged on the earring.

"No," Lorenzo answered, not politely. Katie cocked an eyebrow at me and made her escape.

"So, anyway, as I was saying, this professor just didn't grasp my theory about the species' mating habits, even though I knew, and everyone else knew, that I was really onto something. I mean, with tidal patterns that consistent, you'd expect that the head of the migratory crustacean department would have given even a little thought to the fact that…"

His voice droned on. And on. And on. The next time I suffered a bout of insomnia, I would recall this conversation word for word, and I'd be out in seconds flat. Taking a few sips of my drink, I could clearly understand why my fellow

Cape Codders had passed this guy over. I glanced at the bar, where Joe was tucking into a burger. He waved a little, and I smiled back. Now *there* was a man. A good, unassuming, hardworking, honest man who must be tricked into thinking I was having a wonderful time with this idiot in front of me.

Pretending Lorenzo had said something funny, I burst out laughing, shaking my head as if I couldn't believe what he'd just said. Lorenzo stopped talking, confused.

"That's too much," I exclaimed.

"What?"

"That they, uh, didn't get your theory?" I guessed.

"Right. Actually, I was telling you about my third-year in the doctorate program."

"Oh, I know," I said, grasping. "It's just that, before, you know. They didn't understand."

"Uh-huh."

Again, Katie came to the rescue. "How is everything tonight?" she asked. A loaded question. Speaking of loaded, I took another slug of my vodka drink, which was becoming more and more delicious as my tongue grew more and more anesthetized.

"Everything is wonderful," I answered, opening my eyes a fraction too wide. She smiled in understanding. Hopefully, she'd been eavesdropping as she'd served the tables around us. I'd have been disappointed if she wasn't.

"Actually, my swordfish was a little tough," Lorenzo stated. "Are you sure it was really swordfish? Because I've eaten at places that try to pass off shark as swordfish."

Katie's expression became granite. This was taboo. Visitors to the Cape should never disparage our fish. Fishing is the heart and soul of the Cape, and out-of-towners were not allowed to question our fish's authenticity. I took another gulp of my drink.

"I'm quite sure it's swordfish," Katie said in a voice as cold as the Atlantic in February. "Would you like to speak with our chef?"

Them was fighting words. Uh-oh. If the chef came out here, then everyone in the entire restaurant would know what I knew: Lorenzo Bellefiore, Ph.D., was an idiot.

"Oh, no, no, no, no," I interjected hastily. "No. Lorenzo, the cheesecake here is wonderful. Want to try a piece?"

"Fine," Lorenzo muttered, still staring sullenly at Katie. "And coffee. But if you don't have real cream, forget it. I hate when restaurants charge you two dollars for a cup of coffee and then give you skim milk to put in it."

"It's cream," Katie gritted out, slapping our plates onto a tray with a clatter. "Would you like to inspect the cow?" She stomped off. God, I was so sorry I had to put her through this. Hopefully, we could have a laugh later on. Maybe she would forgive me. Maybe if I took Mike and Corey for an overnight...or a month.

Lorenzo and I were alone again. Although I now knew that I never wanted to see Lorenzo of the Crabs again, I also sensed that we were being watched. By Joe. With a sigh, I leaned forward and fake smiled. "So, Lorenzo, do you have brothers or sisters?" I asked.

"Yes," he answered, still looking pissy. "Two brothers and two sisters."

"Oh, that's nice," I said, though, based on his expression, it was not. Toying with my fork, I laughed again, hoping it looked as if we were having fun. "I have a sister."

"Really."

And speaking of my sister, in came her ex-husband! In his uniform, no less! How handsome he looked, how alpha and official! Oh, yes—I remembered now. Sam had to check on me. I took another slug of vodka and tonic, watching Katie greet Sam and gesture my way. Sam came over to the table.

"Hello, Officer," I said, turning my head to look up at him. Whee! The room spun and my vision blurred.

"Hello," Sam answered. He looked at Lorenzo in his cop way, assessing, judging, intimidating. "Is that car with the Florida plates yours?" he demanded, very bad-cop. Unfortunately, his question epitomized the Cape Cod accent that Lorenzo found so amusing, coming out as *Is that cah with the Flarrider plates yaws?* And Lorenzo, the asshole, smirked.

Sam flicked his glance to me. "You left your lights on, buddy. Battery's dying." With that, Sam left the table.

"Whoops," I said, pleased beyond belief. "I'll give you a jump. Well, your battery, anyway."

Katie came over with our cheesecake and coffee. She tossed down the little bowl of creamers—light cream—and quickly left. Lorenzo picked up his fork and watched her go.

"Boy," he said. "That waitress is a real bi—"

"Okay, hotshot," I interrupted, smacking my hands down on the table and standing up. "Get out."

"Excuse me?" Lorenzo said snottily. "Are you crazy? I'm not going anywhere."

"That bitchy waitress," I ground out, "happens to be my best friend. You've been sitting here all night, insulting everyone around you, complaining and whining about how nobody likes you, and I'll tell you why. Because you're an ass. Now go. I'll pay for dinner. It will be worth it just to get rid of you."

The restaurant had fallen absolutely silent.

"Well, too bad," Lorenzo said, glancing around at the frozen patrons and leaning back arrogantly in his chair. "I'm not going anywhere."

What to do but pull out the trump card?

"Officer!" I called. "This man is disturbing my peace."

That was enough for my brother-in-law. He came over instantly.

"Let's go, pal," Sam said, taking Lorenzo's arm.

"But she—I didn't—this has to be against the law," Lorenzo stammered. I enjoyed a thrill of appreciation as Sam, my hero, hauled Crab-Man out of his chair and guided him to the door, which was held open by a smiling Katie. As they left, the customers began applauding.

I looked around, adrenaline zinging through my elbows and knees. My face began to burn. Had I really just... Was everyone really...? There was Joe, clapping along with the rest of them, laughing and nodding.

"Thank you," I said, wobbling drunkenly. "I'll be here all week."

And then I plopped back into my chair, covering my mouth with my hands, laughing as the applause died down. Katie came over, swiping a clean fork from an empty table. She sat down. "Thanks for defending my honor," she said dryly. "Christ, what a jerk."

I smiled at her, my throat closing with drunken love. She took a bite of my cheesecake.

"Dinner's on the house, Millie!" called Chris. More clapping. I waved my thanks. When Sam came back in, there was yet another round of applause. He came over, pulled up a chair and helped himself to Lorenzo's untouched cheesecake.

"I think I deserve this," he said, grinning.

"Taste better than donuts?" I asked. "And thank you for saving me, Officer Sam."

"Got yourself a spine, there, Millie," he answered. "And you're welcome."

And then, yup, you guessed it, Joe Carpenter came over.

"Wow, Millie," he said, also pulling up a chair. "What did he do?"

"Joe," I said, pretending to be casual though my heart was soaring, "some guys just need an ass-whipping. Are you one of them?" My toes curled in my shoes as I smiled.

He laughed. "Not me, Millie, not me. Way to go, though. Right, Sam?"

Sam just nodded.

"Joe, I saw your truck at Mrs. Bianco's house the other day," I said casually, carefully enunciating. "Are you doing some work for her?" Mrs. Bianco, an ancient little old lady who used two canes to get around, lived around the block from my parents.

"Well," Joe replied, ducking his head bashfully, "not really. I was just fixing her back stairs. They looked a little wobbly."

Oh, he was sweet! Fixing a little old crippled lady's back steps! The warmth in my chest bordered on painful. How I loved Joe Carpenter!

"Okay, see you guys later," Joe said, rising from our table and glancing back at the bar.

"Good night," we called after him.

Sam drove me home, as I was in no shape to operate a vehicle more sophisticated than a tricycle. My mom or dad, both early risers, would no doubt take me back to get my car in the morning.

As I unbuckled my seat belt, Sam leaned over and kissed my cheek. "You did good tonight, kiddo," he said.

"Thanks, Sam." I squeezed his arm fondly. "Thanks for the bad-cop thing. You're such a natural."

Sam laughed. "Sorry he was such a jerk."

"What are you gonna do?" I climbed out of the cruiser and tripped inside.

CHAPTER ELEVEN

A WEEK LATER, MY THRILL at putting Lorenzo of the Crabs in his place had significantly faded. Sure, it had been a moment, and Joe had seen me in that moment. Beside that, I had stuck up for Katie and my other fellow Cape Codders. But I was still alone. No interim boyfriend. No Joe. No closer to getting Joe.

I had lost count of how long it had been since I'd been properly kissed. A long time. More than…I hated even to think it…more than a year. It had been in Boston. A first date with a nice radiology tech. We'd had a really great time, dinner and a stroll down Newbury Street. He kissed me good night at my apartment door. Kissed me very well, as a matter of fact. The next week, I'd seen him smooching a nurse in the ultrasound room, and that was that.

With Memorial Day, tourism season hit full swing, and I saw happy families everywhere. Thousands of couples. Lots of hand-holding. Lots of laughter. Sure, they were on vacation, so what wasn't there to smile about? And every time I saw such a couple, whether they were sixty-five or twenty-five, with kids or without, I felt a familiar hollowness echoing in me. My heart had a lot of room. I had a lot to offer. Friendship. Love. Loyalty. Humor. Free medical care. Whatever. When, I wondered late at night, was I going to be able to give it away? When would I have a guy laugh at my jokes? When would someone bring me a cup of coffee, fixed just how I liked it? When would I have a little sticky hand in mine as a child looked trustingly up at me?

A few times, Joe and I ran into each other...the post office (he usually went around 4:30); Fleming's Donut Shack (10:30—he always got a coffee roll and a light coffee with three sugars); the grocery store (this one was a genuine co-incidence, since I had been unable to stalk this out). When I was checking patients at the senior center, I'd linger in the parking lot, watching for Joe, hoping our paths would cross.

Each time I saw my golden boy, he was friendly, sweet—and brief. Each time I would get a "Hey, Millie, how are you?" Each time I would will him to notice my more attractive state, certain that if he just paid attention, he'd fall crazy in love with me. But Joe was the same, pleasant and cheerful, always on his way somewhere, and if he noticed me in a special way, he hid it well. I was at a loss. Short of molesting him in the parking lot, I didn't know what my next step should be.

As for my other little project, Katie and Sam, that was going nowhere as well. Twice we'd planned a night out, and twice our plans had fallen through, once because Corey had a cold and once because Sam had to cover a shift unexpect-edly. We'd been unable to reschedule yet. Granted, Katie was busy. Actually, *busy* wasn't the right word. *Busy* sounds like she had a bunch of errands to do, when in fact she was raising two children, which is a bit more than that. *Busy* is when you need to do your grocery shopping, clean the bathroom and go to work all on the same day. Raising two children, espe-cially without a husband, was a holy mission.

This was all the more reason that I wanted my friend to be with Sam. I could just see them together, Sam with another chance to be a father, Katie finally with someone to take care of her. Not that her parents didn't help…they did. But Sam…he was such a wonderful father. I'd seen him with many kids over the years, giving a talk to Danny's Boy Scout troop or lecturing on bike safety at the Visitors Center. What woman wouldn't want to be married to a guy like that?

But there he sat, spinning his wheels while Katie blanched at the slightest thought of a relationship with anyone. And yet they'd be perfect together. They were both on the serious side. They were both parents of boys, both attractive, quite so. They both had hearts of gold, if not platinum. And, of course, they both liked me, so they had that in common.

I had the chance to bring up this subject more bluntly, since it was apparent that bluntness was called for. As I grimly huffed up the hill between Coast Guard and Nauset Light beaches one sunny day, I glimpsed a fellow runner behind me, taking the hill without apparent effort and gaining fast. Digger began leaping with glee. I looked again. It was Sam.

"Looking good, Millie!" he called, grinning. How people could smile—or speak—while running was beyond me.

"Hey…Sam," I wheezed. I lurched to a stop—this was my third mile after all—but Sam loped to my side.

"Don't stop, Mil," he said, smacking me on the shoulder (the pain meant to distract me from my respiratory distress, perhaps?). "You're doing great! How far have you gone?" He now turned around, running backward, quite easily keeping pace with me.

"Keep going," I panted. "Nothing…to see. Move along."

"Why, kiddo? I'll run with you. It'll be fun."

I glared at him evilly, sweat running into my eyes. "Sam, if I could catch you…I'd strangle you. I hate you."

"Really, Mil, you're doing great. Don't worry about how fast you're going. Just relax and loosen up."

I willed him away, as I was incapable of speech. Loosen up. Right. As soon as my muscles unseized, I would definitely loosen up.

"Here," he said, still running backward. "Do what I do." He shook out his arms and rolled his head around, somehow not looking like an ass as he did so. I reluctantly copied him, if only to distract myself briefly from the sharp pain in my calves.

"You have to make sure you drink enough beforehand," he advised, coach-like. "Otherwise, your muscles will ache."

"Okay, Notre Dame," I puffed.

"Do you stretch out after?" he asked, finally, mercifully turning to run frontward. This made me look less pathetic, I hoped. We started down the hill, and my breathing became less labored.

"No," I confessed. "I don't really know what I'm doing. I just put on my sneakers and go."

"I'll run you home," Sam volunteered. "I can show you some stuff. It makes a big difference."

"How far do you…usually run?" I asked between gasps.

"Oh, I don't know. Six or seven miles. Ten sometimes. Depends on my schedule."

"Wow! Ten miles! I'll never…get that far." Today, in fact, was the farthest I'd ever run, it being past three miles now. I usually walked the last mile of my outing, but with Sam at my side, I didn't want to stop. Ten miles. Damn him. I sneaked a glance at him. He looked calm and unsweaty…effortless. He was even smiling. How irritating! We rounded the turn onto my road. Only half a mile to go! My legs seemed to have sandbags tied to them, but I didn't want Sam thinking I was a whiner.

"Sam, you should…ask Katie out," I said, unable to let nature take its course on this one. Sometimes nature needed a shove.

"Katie?" He looked at me sharply, obviously surprised.

"Yes, Katie," I answered, trying to control my breathing so I wouldn't hyperventilate in front of FloJo here. He didn't say anything.

"Don't you think it's time?" I panted. "Katie's nice. You know that. She'd be a good way to, you know, break the Trish curse."

Sam laughed. "Trish curse? What exactly is that?"

I smiled at him…and at my neighbor's mailbox, the sign that the torture was about to end. "You know…making you feel that you're…that you're…"

"A loser?"

"Jeez, Sam! I was trying to be diplomatic!" I darted a quick look at his face, and he seemed okay. "I too suffer from…the Trish curse, after all… We're home! Thank you, dear, dear Jesus."

I stumbled to an abrupt halt in my rutted driveway, bracing myself against a sticky pitch pine and gasping. My dog whined to be let off the leash, and I obliged, amazed as always that he could circle madly around the yard or chase chipmunks in the woods after our ordeal.

"No, no, you don't," Sam the know-it-all instructed, grabbing my arm and towing me toward the house. "You walk until you're cooled off. Then you stretch. Come on."

"I really do hate you, Sam," I said. He smiled but otherwise ignored me, leading me up the driveway, which was a good fifty feet long. Then he proceeded to force me into myriad stretches designed to relieve the strain my poor body had been under. But it was good, because where was I going to learn this stuff otherwise? Even though I felt kind of like a jerk, I paid attention as he showed me what to do. And by the time we were done, a mere ten minutes after arriving home, I wasn't sweating anymore and my legs weren't trembling; I didn't feel like throwing up, and I could breathe normally again. So it worked, I guess.

"Thanks, Sam," I said, letting Digger inside. "Come on in, I'll give you a drink of water for all your hard work."

As we leaned against my counter, I brought Katie up again.

"So, Sam…what about Katie?" I asked. "What do you think?"

Sam petted Digger's silky head. "Uh, I don't know, Mil," he said awkwardly, avoiding my eyes and concentrating on the dog.

"I think she'd say yes, you know," I encouraged.

"Have you guys talked about this?" he asked suspiciously.

"No! Come on, Sam. This is not eighth grade, though it probably would have been easier back then."

"I don't think I want to date anybody just yet," he said, scratching Digger's ears vigorously, not looking at me. Digger began to moan with joy, a sign that he was becoming aroused. Soon he would be humping Sam's leg, but Sam didn't need to know that.

"Sam, it's been, what, six, seven months since Trish left you? Don't you want some female companionship? It's only Katie! She's not going to expect a ring and a marriage proposal, for God's sake."

Sam slid onto the floor to better scratch my dog's proffered tummy.

"I've got you and your mom for female companionship. And Ethel." Ethel was Sam's partner on the Eastham P.D. She was about sixty years old, with a leathery face, nicotine-stained teeth and the ability to curse so obscenely that she could put a Portuguese sailor to shame.

"Ethel is not a woman," I said. I sat down on the floor with him, and Digger wriggled over to me, his tail thumping loudly on the fridge as he enjoyed the simultaneous tummy scratch.

"Well, Mil, I don't know if Katie's really my type," Sam murmured.

"Not your type? She's gorgeous! And she's nice, mostly. Plus, you already know her."

"Sure, I like her. She's great. I just…I don't know. I don't really think it's a good idea."

"Why not? Just say, 'Hey, Katie, want to grab a bite sometime?' How bad is that? Is that so hard, Sam, dear? Is it?"

He laughed. "Okay, okay, lay off. I'll ask her out. But you know, nothing romantic. Just two old pals."

"Perfect!" I exclaimed. "God, you are so stubborn."

"Me? No, Millie, kiddo, I'm not the stubborn one on this floor," he replied with a grin.

"Then you must be referring to Digger," I said, smiling back.

"Digger's a good boy," Sam crooned at my puppy, who then mounted Sam's leg. I giggled as Sam, horrified, pried him off. *Aha!* I was thinking. Love, and not just from Digger, was just around the corner.

A FEW NIGHTS LATER, Katie, Sam and I were seated around a table at the Barnacle. Katie had said she didn't mind going there, though I suspected this was to give me a chance to see Joe. Whatever her reasons, I appreciated it.

If Katie suspected that I was trying to fix her up with Sam, she hadn't said anything, and I took this as a positive sign. Many times in the past three years, she had told me that she just needed to concentrate on her sons, that a boyfriend was the last thing she wanted and the thought of being married again gave her the cold sweats.

But of course, she was thinking of being with someone like her horrible ex-husband. Not someone like Sam. Never before had Sam been free for speculation, and believe me, there was speculation. Every single woman in Eastham under the age of seventy was hankering for a shot with him. I didn't want Katie to miss the boat.

We had to raise our voices to be heard over the din of the packed restaurant. From the bar, a crowd cheered as the Sox scored. Servers and busboys hustled about, rattling plates and silverware, keeping the customers content. Tonight was the night. I smiled at my friends across the brightly colored tablecloth, imagining the nice couple they'd make. Sam, clad in khakis and a white polo shirt, shifted in his chair, glanced at me and began peeling the label off his beer bottle. Katie gazed out at the crowd, no doubt assessing the flow of the service and the contentment of the patrons. I sighed. They needed help, these two.

"So, Sam, how's Danny?" I asked, hitting on Sam's favorite subject.

"He's great," Sam answered. Katie turned to look at him and smiled, too.

"Is he playing baseball this summer?" she asked.

"Yup. He'll be shortstop for Bluebeard's Bait and Tackle." Sam returned his attention to the label.

"Two of my brothers are playing, too," Katie said. "I think Trev is playing for Bluebeard's. And you're playing for Sleet's Hardware, right, Sam?"

"Yes. First base."

Summer softball was regarded as almost a sacred ritual here. There was a league for women, which even I had played in many years ago, and another for men. Katie's brothers played, Joe played, Sam played, even my dad had played, although he had retired from the sport in a ceremony rivaling anything at Fenway. When Danny had turned seventeen this past winter, he had qualified, and the fact that he was varsity baseball hadn't hurt. Now with my nephew and the object of my desire playing, I would be going to my fair share of games.

I gritted my teeth as the silence continued. *Speak to her, idiot,* I silently commanded Sam. He didn't obey.

"I haven't seen a game in a long time," I announced. "Katie, we'll have to go. When do you play, Sam?"

"Well, um, we start in a few weeks," he mumbled, picking away.

"Great!" I barked, hoping to snap him out of his fog. The urge to kick him in the shins was strong. I psychically threatened him to look sharp, and this time he seemed to hear me.

"So, Katie, how are your boys?" he asked, putting the beer bottle at a safe distance.

"They're good. Fine. Thanks."

I ground my teeth and gave her a look.

"What?" Katie asked.

"What are the boys doing? Give Sam some details. He doesn't talk to you every day, like I do."

"Um, okay, let's see. Well, Millie had them for a sleepover a few days ago, and they loved that. They really love her dog, and now of course they want one, too. And, um, they're in the library reading program, well, Corey is."

"Oh, really? What's he reading these days?" Sam straightened up and leaned toward Katie. *See?* I wanted to tell her. *See how interested he is? See what a good daddy he would be?*

"He likes the *Magic Tree House* series. And I'm reading

Harry Potter to him, and he loves that. And Mike likes just about everything, especially stories about animals."

"That's great. The *Magic Tree House* is great for a six-year-old," Sam said. "I miss those days…. Trish used to come back from the library with a huge bag of books, and we'd read to Danny every night…." Sam's martyred look crept onto his face, and this time I didn't resist the shin-kicking urge. He jumped and looked at me, his baffled expression a significant improvement from the tragic one he'd perfected.

"Well! It's great when kids like to read!" I blurted idiotically.

"Sam, remember when we saw you at the market last week?" Katie asked, finally initiating some conversation. "Well, Mikey wanted to know if they could take a ride with you in the cruiser. I told them it was probably against the rules and stuff, but that I'd ask."

Sam grinned, his eyes crinkling in the corners most attractively. "Well, for your boys, I think we could sneak a ride in around the block."

I smiled, relieved that the ball was rolling. Soon I would be picking out my maid (or perhaps matron?) of honor dress for their wedding, planning Katie's shower…

We ordered dinner and while we waited, I entertained Katie and Sam with stories from the clinic. "I saw eleven poison-ivy cases in two days," I said. "Eleven! I had to put five of them on steroids, the hives were so bad. I think we should hang giant signs from the bridges. A big picture of poison ivy and the words *Don't Touch* in ten-foot letters. Jeez. Is it really that hard to recognize? And why do people feel the need to bathe in it?"

My audience laughed. Sue brought us our dinners and we dug in. Sam had ordered what Katie referred to as "man food," stuff that most females wouldn't touch: a huge bowl of mussels and clams and scallops, complete with shells, atop a mountain of linguine and drenched in garlic and olive oil. Katie and I ordered the Barnacle's famous gourmet pizzas. Mine had shrimp, mustard and pinoli nuts on it; Katie's had clams, bacon and basil.

"What's new on the Eastham P.D., Sam?" I asked as we ate.

"Oh, not much," Sam answered. "Neighbors complaining, dogs barking, kids speeding, the usual stuff."

At that moment, Joe Carpenter entered the building, wearing faded black jeans and a soft-looking T-shirt. He glanced around and saw us, waved and walked over.

"Hey guys," he said amiably. "We meet again."

"Hi, Joe," I said, trying not to sigh.

"Great season for Notre Dame, hey, Sam?" Joe said.

"Sure was," Sam answered.

"Go Irish," Joe said, grinning.

"You got it. Want to sit down?" Sam offered.

A great idea leaped into my head. "Joe! You know what? My dad wanted to ask you something…um, listen, I can barely hear myself think. Are you going to eat at the bar? Let's go over there." I stood up and took Joe's arm and steered him away from the table. Looking back at Sam, I widened my eyes and scowled, my personal sign language for *Ask her out, stupid!*

"What's up, Millie?" Joe asked. He leaned against the bar and looked at me.

"Well, nothing, really," I said. "I just wanted to give Sam a minute with Katie. Alone." I smiled conspiratorially, supremely pleased with my quick thinking.

"So, are they going out or something?" Joe asked.

"No, Joe. Not yet. I'm hoping that will change any minute,

though." I laughed, and Joe smiled back at me, causing my knees to soften.

"Millie the matchmaker," he said teasingly.

"That's me. Now let's watch."

Sam was fidgeting like a kid in church. He toyed with his silverware, then glanced up at Katie. He said something, managing to make eye contact, though with great effort, it seemed.

"Here we go," Joe commented. After all, he was quite an expert in courtship rituals of the Barnacle.

Uh-oh. Katie's face had turned to granite in her classic "Don't mess with me, boy" look. Sam was talking to the tablecloth, glancing up guiltily.

"Doesn't look good, Mil," Joe said with a laugh. "Sam is going down."

"Don't be mean, Joe!" I pretended to scowl at him. "How could she shoot him down? He's such a great guy." Honestly! Didn't Katie want him coming through the door every night, catching the boys in his arms, giving her a kiss? Didn't she want the stability and kindness he offered? And he was tall and lean and had those nice lines around his eyes that were so... And let's not forget his union benefits! What the hell was wrong with her? She was leaning closer to him, but definitely not in a good way. In a "Go to your room" way.

"Glad I'm not Sam right now," Joe said. "Hey, Chris, can I get a beer?"

Chris obliged. "What are you guys watching?" he asked.

"Nothing!" I said, squeezing Joe's warm, hard bicep. Oh, boy. I drew a quick breath. "Nothing, right Joe?"

Again he smiled at me. "Right, Millie."

With difficulty, I turned my attention back to Sam and Katie. Hey, this was good. Katie and Sam were laughing! She patted his arm. Oh, hooray! And Sam looked infinitely more relaxed.

"Okay, I think I can go back," I said. "Have a good night, Joe. Bye, Chris."

"Nice to see you, Millie," Joe said before turning to the bar.

Yes! I had spoken with Joe, we had shared a mildly intimate moment, and oh, Lord, I had squeezed his arm! And what a lovely arm it was! And Sam and Katie chatting away! Making my way back to the table, my heart was full of joy.

"So what's up?" I asked innocently, taking my seat.

"We're getting married," Katie answered, and she and Sam burst into laughter.

My heart stopped singing. "You're both idiots," I mumbled.

"No bridesmaid dress for you," Sam said. I gave him the finger, which just made him laugh harder.

The amusement ended as Katie and I drove home.

"Millie, I can't believe you forced Sam to ask me out," she said through gritted teeth.

"Forced, nothing! Come on, Katie. Don't you know how pretty you are? How great? I mean, all that stuff about wanting to concentrate on the boys is noble and all, but don't you want someone in your life? Honestly?"

"No, Millie, I don't!"

"Well, I don't understand," I said, looking out the window.

"I know you don't," she answered sharply. "No offense, Millie, but you don't know what's best for my boys. I do. It isn't a stepfather."

"Not even Sam? Sam is so wonderful! How can you not want Sam?"

She shot me a veiled look. "Sam is great, yes, and no, not even Sam."

"But why? What about you? What about your—"

"Millie, back off!" she barked. She turned suddenly into the Visitors Center parking lot, tires squealing, and jerked to a stop. She took a deep breath and turned to me, her voice tight and quiet. "Listen, you're my best friend, okay? You've done so many nice things for me… I— Look. I love you and you're great. But for crying out loud, stop trying to fix my life! It's not broken, Millie!"

"I'm not saying it is," I began.

"Yes, you are!" She gripped the steering wheel tightly. "Millie, I know you mean well. But the thing is, you're pretty goddamn condescending when it comes to me."

"What?" I gasped.

"You think that if I just hook up with Sam, then everything in my sad little life will be fine. I've got news for you, Millie. I'm fine. My boys are fine. My being alone is not sad. Our life is not sad, it's wonderful! I wish you'd get that through your head and just…just…just be friends with me. Stop treating me like I'm your charity case, okay?"

Tears pricked my eyes. "Katie, I don't think of you as a charity case. God," I sniffled.

She stared ahead at the locust trees illuminated in the parking-lot lights. "Look. When Elliott first left me, you were a rock. I'm really, really grateful for all that you did. I am. All those trips up from Boston, all those Chinese-food dinners you'd bring me…" Her voice softened. "You were the best. But now things are better with me. I'm making decent money. The truth is, I probably make more than you, Millie. Chris made me a manager, I make a couple hundred a week in tips alone, and now I'm getting benefits. I'm even saving up for a house. Corey and Mike are doing great. I don't need you to prop me up, Millie. And I really, really don't need—or want—a husband. Okay?"

I rummaged around in my purse for a tissue. "Okay," I whispered. "I never meant to make you feel like that, Katie."

"I know. And I know you can't imagine wanting to be single. But you're going to have to accept that I *do* want it."

"Okay," I said.

She continued looking at me with her lovely blue eyes. "I love you, Millie," she said solemnly. "I love hanging out with you, I love the way your crazy mind thinks, I never laugh so hard with anybody the way I do with you. I want us to be friends forever, but you have to start thinking of me as an equal. Okay?"

"You're not my equal. You're my hero." I leaned over and hugged her. "I'm really sorry."

She hesitated, then chuckled and patted my shoulder. "Let's go out sometime, just the two of us, okay? Maybe we can do an overnight or something. No matchmaking, no Joe Carpenter, just you and me."

"That sounds fantastic," I said. And I meant it.

IT'S VERY HUMBLING TO REALIZE you've been an idiot, especially to someone you care about. With that in mind, I headed for Sam's the next day. He and Danny were working in the yard, hefting bags of mulch and looking very sweaty and manly. Both of them were shirtless, and I noticed for the first time that my baby nephew had washboard abs. So did his daddy. Had Sam always been so...built? *Very* nice.

"Oh, such masculine pulchritude!" I called out, hoping Sam wasn't as mad as Katie had been. "Clothe yourselves, boys! There's a woman on your property."

"Get my gun, Dan," Sam answered. They stopped their machismo activity and came to greet me, Danny giving me a sweaty smooch.

"Hey, Aunt Mil," he said. "Dad told me how you tried to fix him and Katie up."

"And wasn't it a great idea?" I asked.

"I thought it was," he replied agreeably.

"Thanks, young man," I said. "Sorry to say, we're a minority."

Sam pulled on an old T-shirt. Without looking at me, he said, "Dan, could you get us something to drink?"

"He just wants me out of the way while he chews you out, Aunt Mil," my nephew whispered loudly. He grinned cheekily and bounded off to the house.

"He's right," Sam confirmed, folding his arms. He gave me the old "I'm disappointed in you" stare. The kind that really works.

"Before you lecture me," I said, "I want to apologize. I'm really sorry. I just thought…I don't know, you guys would be so…I'm sorry." I kicked at his shell driveway, trying to look genuine. I peeked. He wasn't fooled.

"Uh-huh," he said. A grin tugged at his mouth, but he tried to look stern.

"Katie reamed me another orifice last night," I said. "And I've sworn off matchmaking, so even though you two would be perfect together, I'll just leave it alone and let you walk away from what could be the greatest love of your life."

"Well, you know, in one sense, it was nice of you to think of us. But in the other, you're a real pain in the ass," he said, far too seriously for my taste.

"Sam!" I cried. "Come on! I just wanted to help. You're just too pathetic, sitting around here, mooning over Trish. It's time you—"

"I think you should shut up now, Millie," Sam said quietly. Any amusement he'd felt was gone. A warning prickle went through me.

"Sam, it's just hard to see you—"

"Millie. Stop talking. You're a great person, and I appreciate your concern over me, but the thing is, you don't know squat about marriage, or divorce. Or, obviously, how I'm feeling these days. Not to mention how Katie feels about dating. So the best thing you can do is go back to the 'I'm sorry' part of your little speech and leave it at that before I get really mad. Okay?"

I swallowed at the idea of Sam not liking me. Bending to pull up a weed, I said—sincerely, this time—"Okay, Sam. I really am sorry. I think you're the best guy in the world, you know that. I just want you to be happy."

His hard expression softened, his sad, downturning eyes crinkling with a smile. "I know, kiddo. You're off the hook, as long as you've learned your lesson. Now stop killing my flowers and come have some lemonade." He took the plant out of my hands and replaced it gently in the flower bed.

Inside the house, Sam went to shower. Relieved that I was forgiven, I made Danny lunch, because the poor boy was weak with hunger, having only eaten, from his recounting anyway, eight pancakes for breakfast an hour and a half before. As I slathered mayonnaise on four slices of bread, he leaned on the counter, nearly drooling.

"Mom wants me to come and visit her for a couple of weeks this summer," he said.

I hadn't seen my sister since our brief encounter at our parents' house. Aside from a couple of perfunctory phone calls and two e-mails telling me about the fabulous parties she'd been to with Mr. New Jersey, we hadn't really talked. Sometimes I felt that my role of younger sister was just to admire and agree with Trish.

"Are you going to go?" I asked.

"Well, actually, I don't think I can, what with Appalachia and my job and the baseball team and stuff. But I might go for a long weekend before school lets out."

"How is it for you when you're down there?" I asked, layering cheese and turkey and thick slices of tomato on the bread.

"Well, it's not too bad. A little uncomfortable, a little weird, but mostly okay. She came up to see me a couple days ago, did Dad tell you? We had dinner, just her and me. It was nice."

"No, your dad didn't mention it. How is she?"

Danny grabbed one of the sandwiches and stuffed a third of it into his mouth. "She's good, I guess. Seems happy." He paused to swallow, Adam's apple bobbing wildly. "She looks great."

"She always does," Sam said, laying a hand on my shoulder as he leaned in to claim a sandwich. The smell of shampoo and soap wafted toward me. I started making two more sandwiches, knowing how these boys ate.

"And how was it for you, seeing her?" I asked Sam, curious.

He ran a hand through his damp hair, making it spike up. "Oh, it was okay. Strange, but not bad. She was just here for a little while to pick Danny up and then drop him off again. It was…fine." Whatever mysterious emotions Sam had running through him, he seemed to mean what he said. I reminded myself not to assume I knew everything about the people I loved and opened a bag of chips.

Danny inhaled the second sandwich, gulped down some milk and wiped his mouth. "Gotta go!" he announced cheerfully. "I'm helping Sarah's dad clean the cellar." He thundered upstairs, thumped around in his room for a minute and clattered back down.

"Bye, Aunt Mil," he said, kissing my cheek. He one-arm

hugged Sam and then banged out the back door. A second later, we heard the car start, and he was gone.

"Noisy little fella," I said, smiling at Sam. He smiled back, and we shared a moment of silent Danny adoration.

"You want a sandwich?" Sam asked, pointing to the last one.

"No, thanks," I answered. There was far too much cheese and mayonnaise on that sucker for me. But I poured myself a glass of lemonade and sat at the counter next to him. There were a few catalogs, and I opened one for flowers, idly flipping through the pages, wondering aloud what might look nice in window boxes for my little house. Sam made a few suggestions, and I scribbled down names in the margins.

"What are you doing on the house these days?" Sam asked, ripping open a package of Oreos. I steeled myself against the temptation, forcing a mental image of myself in a bathing suit into my head. Could I actually do it? Appear in public in a bathing suit? It would be the first time in my adult life. It would take a great deal of courage....

"Millie? The house?"

"Oh. Sorry." I gratefully extracted myself from thoughts of cellulite and pasty skin. "The house is great. Very cute. I'm almost done painting the other bedroom. You should come see it."

"I'd love to," Sam answered. He popped an Oreo into his mouth, whole, like a giant black communion wafer, grinning at me as he chewed. "How's work going?"

"Oh, it's great," I said. "I love it. I just hope..."

"Just hope what?"

I drew my initials in the condensation on my glass. "Well, I hope Dr. Whitaker will take me on in the fall. The clinic is only open till October, and if he doesn't want to hire me, then I don't know what I'm going to do. I mean,

I *think* he'll take me on, he hasn't said anything negative. But if he doesn't, I'll have to think about something else. I just got an offer from a doctor in Wellesley, but I don't want to live off-Cape."

The offer had come as a surprise to me. Alan Bernstein was one of the nicer supervising doctors I'd met when I'd been a resident, and he had a growing practice with two other doctors. They wanted to expand, and Alan had called me last week. Wellesley was a lovely, affluent suburb of Boston, and if I hadn't been so determined to stay on Cape, it would have been perfect.

"You could move, couldn't you? Come up here on the weekends and stuff?" Sam asked.

"I could. But I just got back here," I answered. "And I don't want to live anywhere else. I mean, how could I? You didn't want to stay out in Indiana, did you?"

"Landlocked? You kidding? I couldn't wait to get back," Sam smiled. "Curse of the Cape."

It was true. Once you've lived on the Cape, you'd be hard pressed to move. The natural beauty of the place, the loveliness of so many neighborhoods, the smell of the air, the sound of the ocean…it was unsurpassable. Even when I'd lived in Boston, just a couple of hours away, I'd yearned for Eastham. It was my dream since childhood to be a doctor in my hometown, and I was determined to make that work.

And of course, there was Joe. Even though my plans were going nowhere at the moment, I couldn't quit now. I had been putting this plan into effect for quite some time, dreamed about it for years. Surely, something would have to give, and he would finally, finally notice me, fall in love with me and marry me. Hopefully before my fiftieth birthday.

CHAPTER TWELVE

BY THE MIDDLE OF JUNE, cars crowded Route 6, people waited at least a half hour at any restaurant, and the T-shirt and gift shops were hopping. Our clinic was quite busy, and though the cases I saw weren't that challenging, it was great to be bustling around, writing out prednisone prescriptions for the never-ending stream of poison-ivy victims, stitching up boo-boos, and shipping patients down to Cape Cod Hospital. We had a nice rhythm going, Jill and Sienna and I. The mysterious Dr. Bala was quite cordial, having gotten over his initial formality. Now that it was busy, we really clicked along, and I was more than holding my own.

I loved working at the OCSC, too. Mr. Glover and I had had a little chat, and he'd been quite well-behaved since our initial visit. There, the cases were often more complicated, and with that came the deep satisfaction of really getting to know the patients and their families. Even though I was just covering for Dr. Whitaker, it was an honor to be taken into their confidence, to be trusted with making them feel better, to be a part of their lives.

I was even becoming a better cook. I invited my parents over for dinner and made a vegetable lasagna that did not nauseate any of us. I brought a chicken casserole over to Sam and Danny one night and stayed to eat it with them. But it was no fun cooking for one person. Most recipes served at least four people, and more often than not, I'd end up throwing the leftovers away. I ended up making salads or omelets or quick, one-person vegetable dishes and eating them while I read.

I continued to run; Sam's athletic advice had come in handy, and I wasn't suffering quite so much anymore, regularly covering four miles with my sweet black-and-white doggy. And I worked on my house, filling window boxes and putting out little pots of flowers. The lilac trees Sam had planted bloomed, and all in all, it was a lovely time. Except for Joe. Aside from our little moment at the Barnacle, I had hardly seen him.

One Friday night, I planned to hang out at the Barnacle while Katie worked, something I did from time to time. The restaurant was noisy and crowded, and when I walked in, my energy suddenly flagged. In a few weeks, I would turn thirty, and I was tired of hanging around bars. Suddenly, all the single women in the restaurant looked much younger than I was. The women in my age group all seemed to have adorable children with them, or were radiant in pregnancy, or held hands with their husbands. Nearly thirty years old, and I was still stalking Joe, just as I had been at twenty-two…and nineteen…and fifteen….

Speaking of Joe, there he was. Tonight, the sight of his beauty made me feel…tired. Exhausted. Would my love for him ever be reciprocated? Would he ever discover that he could be very happy with me, and not the willowy, red-haired out-of-towner he was currently flirting with?

Katie came up to me. "Hi," she said, glancing Joe's way. Her expression was sympathetic. "Sorry. Squeeze of the week."

"Yeah, except he was with her last week, too," I said,

feeling my heart grow leaden. I looked around the restaurant. "Katie, I think I'm gonna go," I said. "I'm not up for this."

"Okay," she said, giving my shoulder a squeeze as a customer waved impatiently. "I'll call you tomorrow."

I stopped at the market on my way home and bought a jumbo bag of Cheetos, the ultimate self-pity food. Changing into my pajamas, I turned on the TV and tore into the bag. What was the point? I thought, sucking orange powder off my fingers. I had no one to impress. There was nothing on the three channels that my antenna picked up. Maybe I should invest in a satellite dish, since I obviously wasn't going to have a boyfriend.

I tossed Digger a Cheeto, which he caught midair and swallowed without apparent chewing. Digger and I could have lots of fun together, eating Ben & Jerry's and cheese curls and Hershey's bars. I could become fat again. I would just eat and eat, all sorts of grossly delicious things, like an entire Pepperidge Farm coconut cake, and six scrambled eggs with cheese, and a dozen Krispy Kreme doughnuts, and so what? Who would care? It wasn't as if all this work had paid off one tiny iota. Joe paid just as much attention to me now as he had when I'd been fat and worn braces.

Digger stood up and put his head in my lap. I stroked his silky ears and gave him another Cheeto. Who needed stupid Joe Carpenter? I had a dog. I didn't need anybody. Even as I thought it, I felt the ultimate humiliation: tears pricked my eyes. Oh, fantastic. Here I was, 8:30 on a Friday night, relentlessly stuffing my face, while the love of my life, the man I knew better than anyone, was probably making out with his girlfriend at my favorite restaurant. It just sucked. I started to cry in earnest, choking a little on the soggy orange mass in my throat. A good cry would make me feel better, wouldn't it? But I felt stupid, crying by myself, and besides, Digger kept trying to climb up on my lap and lick the delicious combination of salty tears and Cheetos dust off my face. I pushed him down and blew my nose.

I wanted to call someone. Katie was working. My mother would be horrified that I was crying and would no doubt rush right over, which I didn't want. I just wanted someone to feel sorry for me, to share my misery. Trish? We'd never had that kind of a relationship. Sam? He didn't know about my love for J.C., and I felt embarrassed at the thought of telling him. Mitch or Curtis? No, they would be busy on a Friday night, holding hands and exchanging pithy witticisms with their P-town friends. There was nobody. Nobody would understand. Boo hoo hoo.

Pulling the afghan over me, I fumbled for the remote and clicked on the TV, unaware that the next day, everything would change.

I WOKE UP LATE, STIFF and crusty-faced, cramped from spending the whole night on the couch. Digger was draped over my lower half, having cut off my circulation for God knew how long. I staggered into the bathroom, wincing at my puffy eyes ringed with smudged mascara. A smear of orange ran across one cheek.

Heaving a great sigh, I washed my face and made some coffee. Forcefully deciding to think of something other than Joe, I read the paper instead. I was off for the weekend. I had no plans. Maybe Mitch and Curtis had a room open, and I could visit them. Their place was so charming, and P-town so festive and cheerful that I would surely feel better if I got out of town for a night. I hadn't seen the boys for a few weeks, and it might be fun to get all dolled up and show them the fruits of their labor.

But first, a run. After consuming about eight thousand grease-saturated calories in one sitting the night before, I felt rather ill. I had to exorcise all of that hideous, orange fat from my body and get my brain into gear. Plus, Digger was staring pointedly as his leash and wagging his tail.

I tidied up the living room, cringing as I balled up the empty Cheetos bag and stuffed it deep into the trash. Changing into running shorts and T-shirt (*Al's Slaughterhouse, Des Moines, Iowa*), I decided to drive to Coast Guard Beach and run along the water with my pup. It would be harder than running on the road, and I needed the extra work. Besides, it was impossible to be sad if one ran near the ocean in June.

Digger was doubly joyful to be going in the car, and he thrust his head out the window, snuffling happily as we zipped down Ocean View Road to the beach. The air was clear and cool, and seagulls soared on the breeze. Because school had not let out yet, there was still parking at the beach available, and I pulled into a spot and got out of the car, Digger leaping excitedly next to me. Maybe today would be a good day, I thought. Couldn't be worse than yesterday.

As I got out of the car, my heart sank. Joe's truck sat in the parking lot. Damn it. I stared at the truck, wondering if I wanted to go down to the beach. Nope, I decided. I'd just run down the road instead. A Joe encounter would be too disheartening, and my heart was low enough.

So lost in thought was I that I didn't notice Sam's cruiser pulling in next to me.

"Hey, Millie," he said. I jumped.

"Oh, hi, Sam. Hi, Ethel." Sam's partner glared balefully at me and nodded her gray head in greeting.

"Going for a run?" Sam asked.

"I guess," I answered.

Suddenly, the cruiser's radio crackled. We all listened obediently.

"Attention Eastham Fire and EMS. Signal forty-two. Report of woman in active labor. Coast Guard Beach. South of boardwalk, near lifeguard stand number four. Father will be waving a yellow towel."

"Fuck me!" Ethel cursed, snatching up the radio to respond. Sam leaped out of the car.

"Help us out, here, Mil!" he called over his shoulder, running for the boardwalk.

"Here!" I said, thrusting Digger's leash into Ethel's hand. I sprinted to my car, grabbed my doctor's bag out of the trunk and raced down the boardwalk, sliding on the sandy planks, and headed south down the beach. There was the dad about a hundred yards down, waving the yellow towel. I dimly registered the sand in my sneakers, the bright colors of the beach, the hiss and boom of the waves. A crowd clustered around the woman. Sam was a few yards ahead of me, and I raced up to him. Ethel trailed us with my dog, her decades of smoking not allowing her to run.

The woman was lying on her beach blanket. There was a dark stain of fluid underneath her, but it was not blood.

"Okay, folks, let's give her some room," Sam called out, gesturing the crowd back.

"Hi, I'm Millie," I panted, kneeling by the woman's side and squeezing her shoulder gently. "I'm a doctor. How are you doing?"

"I think I'm having the baby," she gasped, her eyes wide, her hands clutching fistfuls of sand.

"Your first?" I asked, opening my bag and pulling on latex gloves.

"It's my second," the woman answered. I glanced up. There was a little boy about two years old holding on to the towel-waver's leg.

Sam knelt next to me. "What can I do?"

"Keep those people back, okay?" I murmured. "I'll need you in a second."

As in so many emergency situations, there were about twelve things going on at once. Sam pushed back the quickly swelling crowd. I heard him talking on the radio to the ambulance. Music was playing nearby. The woman gave a low moan, and her husband came up and clutched her hand. I felt her abdomen. It was rigid with the strength of her contraction.

"What's your name?" I asked.

"Heidi," she panted.

"The ambulance is on the way, Heidi," I said. "I'm going to check you and see where we are, okay? Do you have a clean towel?" I asked the dad. He grabbed one out of their beach bag and thrust it at me, and I slid it beneath her bottom.

"Will she be okay? Is the baby coming?" he asked.

Using the bandage scissors from my bag, I cut through the woman's bathing suit.

The top of the baby's head was clearly visible. "Your baby wants to see the ocean," I said, smiling at Heidi. Her brown eyes grew even wider and she looked at her husband.

"Is your son okay?" I asked. The little boy looked terrified, eyes popping, chin trembling.

"Mark, watch him," panted the mom, extricating her hand from her husband's grip. "Can I push? I want to push. I think I need to push."

"That's fine, Heidi. Wait for the next contraction. Sam!" I called. "Give me a hand!" The crowd murmured collectively, and Sam was at my side in a flash. He took Heidi's hand and slipped his arm under her shoulders to prop her up a little.

"I'm Sam," he said kindly. "Looks like you're a pro at this."

"The baby's not due for three more weeks!" she cried.

"Don't worry, Heidi," I said, giving her a quick smile. "Your body knows what to do."

"It's not a show, people!" Ethel barked in her rusty, crackling voice. "Back up!"

"Okay," I said, feeling her abdomen begin to tighten again. "Here comes the next contraction, so give us a big push. One, two, three..."

She pushed, her face scrunching with effort. The baby's head emerged a few centimeters more. Heidi gave a high, keening cry, and the crowd gasped.

"You're doing great," I said, easing a finger next to the baby's wet, dark head. An ambulance siren wailed. "We're almost there." Her abdomen tightened again. "The head is the hard part, remember? Okay, here's another contraction. Push, Heidi, a really big push now..."

She pushed again, and the baby's head slid out, covered in blood and vernix and black hair. "Got a brunette here, just like you," I said. "Now don't push, okay? Hold on one second and just pant."

I slipped my gloved finger into the baby's mouth and slicked out a wad of mucus. Gently turning the head skyward, I could see that the baby's face was blue.

"Oh, God," said the father, dropping to one knee and clutching his son against him. "Oh, Jesus, please."

"What's wrong?" Heidi sobbed.

"Got a tight nuchal here," I muttered. Sam nodded. The umbilical cord was wrapped once around the baby's neck.

"Hang on, Heidi," he said. "You're doing great. Just give Millie a minute, okay?"

I worked my finger under the cord and carefully, carefully eased it up over the baby's head.

"Please, God," the husband choked.

"Is everything okay?" Heidi asked breathlessly.

"Everything is fine. One more second...okay. One more push, Heidi. Nice and easy."

She pushed and the baby slid into my hands. I scooped out the baby's mouth again. The infant gagged and another wad of mucus and liquid came up, and then, that most wonderful of all sounds, the first cries of a new life. "It's a girl!" I announced, and the crowd gave a mighty cheer and began to applaud. Even as I rubbed the infant with a clean Scooby-Doo beach towel, her face began to turn pink. Leaving the umbilical cord for the paramedics to deal with, I placed the baby on her mother's chest. The crowd cheered again as Heidi sobbed happily.

"Trevor! Come see your sister!" she wept. The father and little boy knelt by her side, and Sam eased away.

"Need me to do anything, Millie?" he asked as I placed another towel over the mother's belly.

"I think I'm all set," I said, smiling up at him. At that moment, the paramedics arrived with a stretcher. One of them came up to Sam.

"Taking over my job?" he asked amiably as his co-workers loaded Heidi and the baby onto the stretcher.

"Hey, Dave. Better talk to Dr. Barnes," Sam answered.

"Thirty-seven weeks, para two, nuchal times one, spontaneous cry. No placenta. I saved that for you." I grinned at the paramedic.

"Nice work," he said. "Lucky you were here."

As Heidi was bundled off, her husband and son in tow, the crowd once again began to applaud. I grinned, suddenly euphoric, my heart filled with joy. I turned to Sam for a hug.

"Well done, Officer," I said into his shoulder, my throat tight with emotion.

"You're the one who did everything, Mil," he answered. "Great job." We looked at each other for a moment, grinning. Sam's eyes were warm...and a little wet. My heart squeezed. Could there be any better man to have at your side during an emergency than Sam Nickerson? I thought not.

Ethel came up and handed me Digger's leash. "Thank the Christ I didn't have to do that," she grated. "Goddamn gross, if you ask me."

"I thought it was beautiful," said a familiar voice. I turned around.

Joe Carpenter, his blond hair glowing in the sun, wearing some old cut-off jeans, smiled at me. "Wow, Millie. You were amazing."

"Thanks, Joe," I said, smiling back. "Can't take any credit, though. The mom did all the work."

A baby! I had delivered a baby on Coast Guard Beach! Even Joe Carpenter's golden beauty couldn't touch that one.

The crowd was beginning to break up. A few people came up to Sam and me, congratulating us or making jokes.

As I bent down to pack up my medical bag, I noticed I was rather messy, my T-shirt smeared by the fresh-from-God baby. Oh, well, who cared? Badge of honor. I patted Digger and let him lick my face before standing up. My heart was so full that it actually caused a pleasant ache in my chest.

I stood up. Joe was still there.

"So, Millie...you doing anything tonight? Want to get a beer or something?"

For a minute, I just soaked it in, the cries of the seagulls and the roar of the waves and the voices of the people blending into a beautiful summer melody. The sun was warm and the breeze gentle, and this was clearly the best day of my life. I smiled again. "Sure, Joe."

He smiled back, dimples appearing. "How about if we meet at the Barnacle around eight?" he suggested.

"Sounds great," I answered, strangely calm.

"See you later, then," he said and walked off.

Still beaming, I turned to go. Sam approached me.

"Amazing, huh, Millie?" he asked, running his hand through his short-cropped hair.

"You don't get to deliver a baby every day, do you?" I laughed.

"Hey, you want to grab dinner later?"

I remembered belatedly that Danny was with Trish this weekend. "I can't, Sam, I have plans. Sorry, bud." I *was* sorry. It would have been nice to relive this glorious morning with him.

"No problem. Maybe I'll see you later." Sam grinned and went off to make his report.

As I walked off the beach, I was congratulated and complimented eleven times. Finally reaching my car, I drove home, filled with gratitude that life could be so sweet.

THE REST OF THE DAY PASSED in a dream. I called Katie and my parents and Mitch and Curtis and Janette in Boston and Dr. Bala and even Trish. After telling the story six times, it was starting to feel real. I sat outside on my tiny deck and went over every detail again and again. How lucky I felt to have been part of that baby's birth! How proud I was of that mother, who'd managed to deliver a healthy baby on a beach in front of a crowd! How proud I was that I'd done everything right! How proud I was of Sam, so gentle and caring and calm! And of Digger, who'd been so well-behaved during the whole event! And then, after despairing last night, after eating all those Cheetos, after crying pathetically and being a loser, Joe Carpenter had asked me out! When I was unshowered and when my hair stuck up in odd places and when I was covered in blood and vernix and amniotic fluid, Joe Carpenter had asked me out.

I got a few calls from people telling me I did a great job and asking how the baby was. I called Heidi at Cape Cod Hospital to check on her, and she tearfully thanked me and "that wonderful officer." Then I just floated around my house and yard, grinning and laughing and thrilled.

The baby had made me feel like a winner. Joe's asking me out merely confirmed that feeling. Yesterday, I would have been deeply grateful to be noticed by J.C. the C.; today, it was merely what happened to competent, friendly, quick-thinking doctors who cleverly delivered babies on the beach.

Joe Carpenter was what I deserved.

CHAPTER THIRTEEN

IF I DIED AT THIS MOMENT, that would be A-okay, I thought to myself.

Joe had greeted me at the Barnacle with a kiss on the cheek, leading me to a table for two in the corner. Katie was working, and Sam had dropped in, too. We heard from the Eastham Police Department that mother and baby were just fine, happily sharing their story with reporters at Cape Cod Hospital. And though I'm sure Joe and I must have talked about something, I couldn't remember exactly what it might have been, so happy was I on this most perfect day.

And now, Joe led me from the Barnacle. Outside, in the clear, cool night, with stars shining and wind whispering, I felt that the world was my own movie set. Everything was so perfect. Our feet crunched on the gravel driveway, and a pleasant nervousness suddenly flooded through my limbs, the shot of adrenaline tingling in my knees. It was the first feeling that managed to break the surreal quality of the day.

"This is your car, right?" Joe asked, pointing to my Honda.

"Yup, that's mine," I said. My mind went blank as I searched for something to say. Joe walked me over to the driver's side and leaned against my door.

"So, Millie," he said, grinning slowly.

"So, Joe," I answered, my mouth going dry. The pinkish

lights of the lamppost cast a romantic glow. Joe took both of my hands in his. His were rough and callused, and just that touch made my nether regions melt.

"Can I see you again?" he asked softly.

Yes! My God! It was happening! A hysterical laugh wriggled around in my stomach. "Sure," I said, trying to react normally and not as if I had just won the Powerball lotto.

"Great," Joe smiled. He pulled me closer and slid his hands up my bare arms. *Take me now!* my mind cried, and I bit my lip to still the laughter.

"What?" Joe asked, not offended.

"Oh, it's noth—"

Joe's kiss stopped whatever I was going to babble. His lips were smooth and firm and warm and oh, God, I was going to dissolve into a puddle of lust with just one kiss. It took me a minute to notice he'd stopped kissing me. I opened my eyes and looked at him.

"Want to catch a movie tomorrow?" he whispered. His hands slid back down my arms and caught my hands again.

"Um…I, uh, I have to work tomorrow night," I stammered, my toes curled tight in my sandals.

"How about Monday, then?" he suggested, his eyes twinkling.

"Oh, Monday. I, um, yes, that would be okay. Sure."

"Great," he said with another endorphin-inducing grin. "See you, Millie." He straightened up from his pose against my car and kissed my hand. "I'll call you Monday, okay?"

"Okay," I answered. "Good night."

I got into my car, ordering myself not to laugh hysterically or even smile too maniacally. *Key in ignition, roger that. Seat belt, check. Turn key. Car has been activated. Put car in gear. Try not to hit Joe backing out. Put car in first. Depress gas pedal. Proceed slowly out of restaurant lot. Turn…what is it? Right? No, left! Turn left. Proceed home.*

Once I was safely on Route 6, the laughter burst forth. Shrieking and cackling like a demented hyena, I pounded on the steering wheel. *I did it! I did it! Joe Carpenter kissed me!*

As I pulled in my driveway, I contemplated racing around the house in a victory lap, the way Digger did after our runs. Instead, I went in and rolled around on the floor with my doggy. "I had a date with Joe, puppy! He asked me out! He kissed me!" Digger, hearing *kiss,* one of the few words he recognized, began licking my face exuberantly. "Yes, I know! I know it!"

Finally, I got off the floor and went into the bathroom to look at the woman Joe Carpenter had finally discovered. The woman he had kissed. Whose *hand* he had kissed. My reflection smiled back at me. There she was. Millie Barnes, M.D.— also known as Joseph Stephen Carpenter's girlfriend.

For the next two days, I grinned endlessly, sighed rapturously, floated around the clinic, treating the right patients, hopefully, for the right ailments. Jill and Sienna had heard about the baby and they thought that was the reason for my euphoria. I didn't tell them about Joe. It was too wonderful to share with anyone just yet. I wanted to keep the memory of Saturday night like a secret jewel in a velvet box. Every time I remembered something, whether it was our knees bumping under the table or his pulling me in for The Big Kiss, a warm rush of happiness and lust would flow through me. Oh, I loved Joe! And soon he would love me back.

On Monday afternoon, I got home and immediately checked the answering machine. There was my light, flashing happily away.

"Hi, honey, it's Mom."

Shit. My heart sank. Not at my mom's voice, of course…

you understand. Why hadn't he called? He'd said he'd call! It was four o'clock! We were supposed to go to a movie! I half heard my mom invite me over for dinner one night this week, but I wasn't really paying attention. *Calm down, Millie,* I told myself. *Joe is probably not even home from work yet. Settle down. He kissed you on Saturday and wanted to see you on Sunday and made a date for Monday. He will call. He. Will. Call.*

Making sure the phone was properly charged, I took it out onto the deck and watched Digger poop three times. I'd have to ask the vet about those overactive bowels. On our first visit, the vet had told me Digger was just excited, and once he settled down, he'd stop going so often, but maybe it was something else. The dog seemed so sleek and healthy that I wasn't really worried, but it should be checked.

Okay, that was good! I'd had a non-Joe thought. *Well done, Doctor,* I told myself. *That's the way to do it. After all, you are the deliverer of the lovely little beach baby. You and Sam.*

At that memory, I thought of Sam. I wondered how Danny's visit to New Jersey had gone…and how Sam had done without him. Had he spent the whole weekend alone? Instinctively, I reached for the phone, then mentally slapped my hand. What if Joe was trying to call? Wouldn't want him to get a busy signal, would we?

I went back inside and got myself a glass of seltzer water, then returned to the deck and weeded my little railing boxes. Maybe I'd see if the budget could support some nice pieces of deck furniture. Right now all I had was a set of two plastic chairs and a matching table. Wicker tended to get moldy in the damp Cape air, so that was out. A little wrought iron, maybe.

The breeze rustled in the pitch pines and scrubby oaks of my property, and the waves roared rhythmically in the distance. I guessed it to be pretty close to high tide. I was getting good at that sort of thing. I sat down and watched a bluebird disappear into the little bird house Danny had helped me put up earlier this spring. Its deep blue flashed against the white of the house as it flew out.

The phone trilled, and I jumped up, sloshing seltzer down my front. Thank God I was alone, I thought, surveying my damp bosom as I picked up the phone.

"Hey, Millie, it's Joe," said the voice I loved.

"Hi, Joe." *Thank you, God.*

"What are you doing?" he asked.

"Oh, just sitting on my porch, watching the birds," I answered, unable to think of any answer except the truth.

"Millie, you're so funny," he said. "So, we still on for tonight? In the mood for a movie?"

"Sure," I said, feeling that swell of laughter and euphoria rise again. He named a movie, which I agreed to, and told me he'd swing by around 7:00 for the 7:15 show.

"Sounds great," I said. "See you then." I clicked off, set the phone down and began hopping up and down. "I'm going out with Joe-oh, I'm going out with Joe-oh!" I sang merrily. Luckily, my neighbors didn't live too close. Seeing my manic leaping, Digger leaped onto the deck to join in the celebratory dance.

At seven o'clock sharp, Joe's truck trundled up the driveway, setting off Digger's frenzied barking. "Quiet!" I ordered, grabbing his collar. "No, Digger!" He began clawing at the front door, barking so loudly that my teeth vibrated. The doorbell rang.

"Just a minute!" I called over the din. I dragged Digger to the cellar, gave him a chew stick and blew him a kiss. Nervousness and anticipation flooded through me. Straightening my shirt, I glanced in the mirror, hoping my hair would behave, hoping Joe didn't see me as I stubbed my toe on the footstool, hoping Digger didn't claw down the cellar door and maul my gentleman caller. Or worse yet, hump his leg.

"Hi," I said, smiling as I answered the door. There he was, Joe Carpenter, leaning in my doorway, smiling at me, his dirty-blond hair damp and rumpled, hands in his worn jeans pockets, green T-shirt with smear of white paint over the heart.

"Ready?" he said. We walked out to his truck. He got in and started clearing stuff out of the way to make room for me. I opened the passenger door and climbed in, something of a feat when you're five foot three.

"Okay," Joe said. We backed out of my driveway and went off. *Say something, Millie.* My mind instantly emptied. What to say, what to say…I looked around the truck cab for inspiration. It was pretty grubby, a stark contrast to the last pickup truck I'd sat in—Sam's, which was immaculate enough for surgery. Two old plastic cups careened around on the floor, rolling into my shoes. Wads of paper, an unwrapped cough drop furred with hair and lint. A hammer. A wrench. An old coat lay between us on the seat. There was that pleasant masculine smell…oil and coffee and cut wood. Tucked under the sun visor was a sheaf of papers. I could see the edge of a fishing license. Aha!

"Have you been fishing much this summer, Joe?"

"No, not really," he answered, slowing to a stop at the light on Route 6. "I've been pretty busy."

"Oh." Great. End of conversation.

But there was the theater, so it was okay. "You haven't seen this one, have you?" Joe asked as we waited in line.

"No, not yet. It's supposed to be good, though."

He smiled. I melted.

"Can I help you?" said the teenager at the window.

"One for James Bond," Joe replied. The teenager took his money and handed Joe a ticket. It was my turn.

"Oh, uh, yeah, one for James Bond."

He wasn't buying my ticket! I had cash, thank God. I fumbled in my pocketbook and handed over a ten. "Thanks," I told the kid. Joe had gone over the to the concession stand.

He hadn't bought my ticket! Wasn't this a date? But, I quickly rationalized, why should he? There was no reason I couldn't buy my own ticket. Right?

"Want anything?" he asked me as the concession-stand person filled up a box with popcorn.

"Oh, no, I don't think so," I answered, relief washing over me. He'd offered to buy me something. It was still a date.

We found seats in the theater. Again, I wracked my brain for a way to start a conversation. Joe waved to someone and began to shovel popcorn into his mouth. God, the way men ate. "If you choke, I'll Heimlich you," I said, pleased with my cleverness.

"You're a good person to have around, Millie," he answered, checking me out just a wee bit. He put his arm around the back of my chair and balanced the popcorn on his lap. "Very good."

Even with a fistful of popcorn in his mouth, Joe Carpenter was gorgeous. *Oh, Joe,* I thought. *You won't be sorry you picked me.*

The previews started, and for the next two hours, I was in heaven. We held hands. In the movie theater. How romantic was that? His work-roughened fingers twined with mine, his thumb occasionally rasping gently over my skin, and nothing had ever felt so good in my life. He smelled wonderful. Soap (Ivory), wood, popcorn, *butter.* I was in a perpetual state of horniness. James Bond, nothing. Joe was all I needed.

We drove home, chatting about the movie. I wondered if I should invite him in. Hmm. Probably not. No, definitely not! I wanted to be different from those easy types, after all. Show Joe that I had some moral fortitude. Make him work for me a little. Make him wait.

We pulled up to my house. I could hear Digger's insane barking.

"Great watchdog you've got there," Joe said, turning to me. He looked in my eyes, then down at my…mouth. Back to my eyes.

"He is great, actually," I answered. "And so is Tripod. What kind of dog is he?" (Three-legged, eight-year-old Golden Retriever/German shepherd mix.)

"He's some kind of mutt. Good dog, though." Joe smiled slowly at me. "So, Millie, are you gonna ask me to come in?" His white teeth gleamed in the dimness of the truck. He reached over and tucked some hair behind my ear.

I was on him faster than a seagull on a potato chip, kissing him with all the pent-up desire of the last half of my life. We kissed like there was no tomorrow, like we'd been separated by war, like we were the only two people left on earth and had to repopulate the world. His hands were warm on my back, and I clutched his shirt with both fists. I could dimly hear those little humming noises that kissing people make, shifting, pulling closer, sliding our hands around each other, into each other's hair, down arms, under shirts.

The sound of the truck horn blasted us apart like guilty teenagers. I was half sitting on Joe's lap, and apparently I'd hit the steering wheel the wrong way as I squirmed to get closer. It was just what I needed.

"Sorry!" I said, laughing a little and scootching off his lap. He smiled back.

"Can I come in?" he asked.

Yes. Come in. Come in and stay and kiss me and touch me and bang me silly. Oh, God, that was exactly what I wanted.

But I couldn't. Not yet. My years of stalking Joe had shown that this was what happened with everyone. Who could resist this man, after all? Why make the most beautiful of God's creations wait? It was a joy just to be near him, let alone have his hands on you, his mouth on yours.

But I was determined to be better than the rest of them. I had to stick with what I knew would work and make something better than one or two glorious nights of sex with the golden boy.

"Millie?" Joe asked. He leaned forward and kissed me again, softly. "Can I come in?"

"Um, no, Joe," I managed to say. "Sorry. I, uh, I can't have you come in."

He looked surprised. "Oh. Why not?"

"Well, you know. Not that kind of girl." *Oh, please,* I begged silently. *Let this work.*

He looked at me for a long minute, then tilted his head a little. "Not that kind of a girl, huh?" He smiled. "Well, Millie…" He ran his hand up my leg. "When do you think you *will* be that kind of a girl?"

I smiled and bit my lip. "I don't know, Joe. But definitely not on the first date," I answered, stopping the slide of his hand.

"This is our second date," he replied in a whisper. Oh, *God.* My insides leaped, then knotted in a warm tug.

"Is it?" I answered, as if I didn't know. "Well, not on the second date, either."

He laughed. "Okay, Millie. I get the message." He straightened up and opened his door. "I'll walk you in, then."

I scrambled across the truck seat and climbed down. We walked to the door, Digger's barking becoming more hysterical by the second.

"It's me, Digger," I called. The barking stopped. I turned and faced Joe. "I guess I'll see you," I said, suddenly nervous. After all, this was taking a big chance, playing hard to get.

"Okay," he answered. He leaned in and kissed me again, sweet, warm, slow. God, the man could kiss! I tried not to sag against the door when it was done, but it was hard.

"You busy tomorrow?" he asked.

Ha! It was working! "Um, tomorrow, well, I have to work tomorrow night…" Again, I pretended to think about when I might be free to see him again. "Maybe I could call you on Wednesday or something?"

He straightened up. "Millie, if you don't want to see me again, just tell me, okay?"

"Oh! No, I mean, no, I don't *not* want to see you—" *Calm, calm, Millie.* "I'd love to see you again, Joe. My schedule is just a little tricky. But I'll call you on Wednesday and, um, see when we can get together. Is that okay?"

He smiled. "That would be great, Millie." He kissed me quickly once more and headed off down the walk. "You got my number?" he called.

508 555 9914. "No…are you in the book?" I answered.

"Yeah. Carpenter on Thistleberry Way."

He opened the door to his truck. "Night, Millie."

"Good night, Joe."

Closing the door behind me, I finally allowed my weakened knees to give out, sliding down to the floor in a happy lump of lust and triumph, hugging myself and squeaking with glee. After a few minutes, I was roused by Digger's pathetic cries. I let him out of the cellar, assured him that I still loved him best and gave him a piece of salami as proof. Then I floated over to the phone. Katie wasn't working tonight, and she'd told me to call her when I got home.

"Hello?" Katie answered.

"It's working," I sang.

CHAPTER FOURTEEN

EVEN THE WEATHER SEEMED HAPPY that I was with Joe. For the next few days, the tourists got their money's worth. The sun shone warm and the sky shimmered with pure, clear blue. The wind sang gently through the pines and the birds answered cheerfully, red-winged blackbirds chuckling and mourning doves cooing. On Tuesday, I had to work the later shift, so I had the whole morning to myself. I liked these days, since I had time to grocery shop, clean, drop by the senior center and visit my patients, whatever. Sometimes I'd pop in on my mom or bring doughnuts and coffee to Katie and my godsons, but today I chose to stay home.

Digger and I had gone for a run, and my dog was now panting contentedly on the deck. I was cooling down a little before showering, watering the flower boxes that I had planted on the recommendation of Sam, my part-time landscaper. He'd advised me well, and the plants were in full flower, trailing purple petunias tumbling out amid dark green ivy and brilliant pink dianthus. Good old Sam. Always knew what he was doing.

Digger leaped up from his slumber, growling, as a sleek convertible pulled into my driveway. I gaped, water dribbling from my watering can onto my sneakers, as my sister got out of the car.

Trish! I hadn't seen her since April. As was her custom, she looked…rich. Wearing a calf-length, silky white skirt and matching sleeveless top that showed her well-toned arms and a discreet stripe of her lean, tanned tummy, she stood for a moment, looking around as if she had just arrived on an alien planet.

"Millie?" she called, sliding her expensive-looking, narrow sunglasses onto her head.

"Hi, Trish!" I called, grabbing Digger's collar. "It's okay, buddy," I soothed. Taking another look at Trish's outfit, which probably cost about a week's worth of my salary, I pictured it covered with dog hair and saliva. "Come on in," I said. "I'll just put Digger in the bedroom."

Hurriedly and apologetically, I imprisoned Digger, though I thought perhaps I should have kept him around for moral support. Glancing around my kitchen, I saw that it was, well, immaculate, thanks to my morning bout of scouring. A coffee cup in the sink. Not bad at all. "Come on in, Trish."

She deigned to enter, unspeaking, posture perfect, hair falling in rich waves to her shoulders.

"How have you been?" I asked, self-consciously running a hand through my own sweat-stiffened hair.

"Great," she replied absently. Her gaze flicked up and down my frame, quickly assessing my appearance and then apparently moving onto other, more pleasant things. "It's really…different in here."

"Do you like it?" I asked, then practically bit off my tongue. I knew better than to fish for compliments from this one.

"Well…" my sister answered stoically. "It's very…cute."

"Have a look around," I said resignedly. She was already in the living room, surveying the family photos I had placed on the wall.

"Who are these kids?" she asked, pointing to a picture.

"They're Katie's boys! My godsons?"

"Right."

No praise issued from Trish's perfectly glossed lips as she walked through my small domicile. But she wasn't really *hostile* either, so that was a plus. Part of me wanted to show off to Trish, because even if she wouldn't say it, I thought she might be impressed. I watched her as her size-four frame walked from room to room. Digger's tail thumped hopefully against the bedroom door, and I silently promised him a long tummy scratch after Trish had left.

"Want some tea?" I offered, more for something to say than anything else.

"Sure," she called. I almost had to grab the counter to keep from falling down in shock. This was a first. Me, playing hostess to Trish. Very weird.

"Well," she said, coming back into the kitchen, "It's better than what Gran had, I guess."

"Gosh, thanks," I replied, putting the kettle on to boil.

"You're welcome," Trish said, brushing off the seat before sitting.

Trying not to grind my teeth, I got the last two cups left from Gran's wedding china, set them on their translucent saucers and dropped in a couple of tea bags. Not to impress, Trish, of course, because that was impossible. No, just to show her that we Cape Codders had a little class. I got out the sugar bowl. Of course, Trish didn't take sugar—empty calories!—but I did, and I defiantly shoveled a healthy teaspoon of it into my cup.

"You could do a lot with this place," she commented, tapping a perfectly manicured nail on the table.

"I already have," I said sharply, taking a seat across from her. Trish looked startled.

"Oh, sure," she placated. "Um…did you do it all yourself?"

"Well, Katie helped a bit, and Curtis and Mitch gave me some suggestions. But mostly, I guess I did. I sanded the floors and painted and all that stuff."

"Mmm hmm," Trish commented. "Well, I hope you know how much it's worth."

"Yes, Trish, I know," I sighed.

"We wouldn't have to worry about Danny's college tuition if Gran had divided her house between us," Trish said, adjusting a gold bracelet on her slender wrist.

Ah, the trump card. Danny. There was nothing for me to say. Yes, I felt a bit guilty that I had inherited this house and Trish had gotten only a few thousand dollars, but I wasn't the one who'd made that decision. Gran had given me her sweet little home, and I loved and cared for it as she knew I would. At the time our grandmother had made the will, Trish had had her own home. I'm sure Gran had assumed that my sister and Sam had done just fine. Of course, it would never cross Trish's mind to actually get a job to help pay for Danny's tuition…. I took a deep breath and tried to quell my irritation.

We sat awkwardly for a minute. Digger whined from the bedroom. *I'd rather be with you, puppy.*

"How's New Jersey?" I asked.

"Wonderful," she answered immediately. "Avery is fantastic, and there's so much to do in the city. And his place down there…well, there's nothing like it on the Cape."

It was my turn to murmur "Mmm hmm." Avery. What a dopey name.

"Does your, uh, does Avery get along with Danny?"

"Of course!" She looked annoyed that I'd even ask. "He loves him like a son."

Well, then maybe he could kick in a little tuition money, I thought. Avery was richer than God, wasn't he? "How nice," I managed to say. Fortunately, the kettle was boiling so I could get up and make a face behind Trish's back. Pouring the water into our cups, I set our tea on the table.

"So, Trish, tell me. What exactly do you *do* all day?" I asked. "I mean, Avery must put in long hours on Wall Street…what do you do when he's gone?"

Trish daintily bobbed her tea bag up and down in her cup. Satisfied that her brew was the right strength, she dangled the dripping tea bag over the cup and raised her eyebrows questioningly at me. Rats. I'd forgotten spoons. Irritated, I snatched the hot tea bag in my bare hand and tossed it into the sink, not getting up from my seat.

"Well," said Trish coolly, "we do so much entertaining. There's always a million things to do, make reservations, research the latest restaurants, make sure we have tickets to whatever's on Broadway in case Avery needs to impress some clients. Plus I work out every day at our club. And I have to supervise things like the housekeeping."

"Wow. You must be so busy."

"I am, Millie," she retorted. "You have no idea what that sort of lifestyle demands. And I like it. I like not being a cop's wife and vacuuming sand out of my car every week. I like going to the city and visiting museums and seeing plays. There's more to the world than Cape Cod, you know."

"Oh, I do know. It's just that there's nothing *better* in the world than Cape Cod. And no one better than Sam! How can you not miss him? Don't you ever wish for your old life, Trish?"

"Not really. I mean, of course I miss Danny, and Mom and Dad. But wait till you've lived here another decade, Millie," she said, a trace of bitterness in her voice. "We'll see what you think then."

"Well, if the Cape is so hick, then why does Avery have a house in Wellfleet?"

Avery owned one of those monstrosities overlooking Wellfleet Harbor, a massive, glaringly modern house of glass and chrome. In fact, that was how my sister had met Mr. New Jersey; Trish had been organizing a tour of homes last spring, and apparently she'd found Avery's bedroom particularly interesting.

"Oh, that," she said dismissively, sipping her tea. "We sold that."

Digger began to whine pathetically.

"I can't believe you got a dog," Trish stated, her expression sour.

"Trish, why are you here?" I asked rather rudely.

"What?"

"Why did you drop by here? Just for a sisterly chat?"

"Oh," she replied. "No, not really. I'm here to pick up Danny for a visit, and he and Sam are out somewhere, apparently. Mom wasn't home, so I drove over here to kill some time."

Digger's whines took on a deeper note, becoming more of moan. I felt like joining in.

"Trish..." I began. The ring of the phone interrupted me. Grateful for the distraction, I got up to answer it. Digger began to claw maniacally at the door at the sound of my footsteps. "Down, killer," I said before picking up the phone. "Hello?"

"Hi, Millie."

Joe! Hooray! It was Joe!

"Hi, Joe," I said, stepping into the living room so Trish wouldn't see the goofy smile that spread across my face.

"How you doing?" Joe asked.

"Great," I lied. "What's up?"

"Oh, I had a few minutes, thought I'd give you a call."

Aw! Loved him! "How are you?" I asked, blushing with the newfound pleasure of just chatting.

"Well, I'm good now," he said.

"Aw," I couldn't help saying. In the kitchen, Trish rattled her cup on the saucer, lest thirty seconds pass without her being the center of attention. "Listen, Joe, I'm sorry, but this isn't the greatest time…. My sister is here, so I shouldn't really be talking on the phone. I'll call you, um, tomorrow, all right?"

"Okay," Joe said agreeably. "You have a good day. Catch you later."

"Bye." I grinned and hung up gently. I stood for a minute, savoring the sound of his voice and the warmth it brought.

"Who was that?" Trish asked as I came back into the kitchen.

I took a breath. "Oh, that was just, um, a friend." I stood up a little straighter. "Joe Carpenter."

Trish's mouth dropped open. Even my gorgeous, snobby sister was not immune to Joe's glorious beauty.

"Why would Joe Carpenter be calling *you?*"

I couldn't help myself. I stamped my Nike-clad foot. "Trish, for God's sake! You've been here for half an hour and you haven't even noticed that I've dropped twenty pounds since Christmas. My hair is eight inches shorter and three shades lighter. I'm not your ugly-duckling little sister anymore! Maybe Joe's calling me because he's my boyfriend!"

"Joe Carpenter is your boyfriend?" she asked, ignoring everything else I'd said.

"Sort of," I muttered, gathering our cups up and putting them in the sink.

"Well. That's…that's great," she said. "And you do look much better." She offered me a little smile, and I felt my anger drain away, well-trained little sister that I was.

"Thanks," I said.

"Just about, what, ten pounds to go?"

I walked over to the bedroom door and released the hound. In a blur of black and white, paws scrabbling, he went straight for Trish's crotch.

Good dog.

CHAPTER FIFTEEN

ON WEDNESDAY AT 5:37 P.M., after a day spent counting the agonizingly slow passage of minutes, I called Joe. I knew that he usually got home around 4:30 or 5:00 and then, if he were going out, would usually leave around 7:00 or 7:30, depending on where he was going to eat—the Barnacle, the Crow's Nest or the Humpback. Perhaps, I thought as his phone rang, he was just now changing into clean clothes after a shower, tugging on some faded jeans. Perhaps he was carelessly running his hands through his water-darkened golden hair, idly reminding himself to get it cut one of these days. Perhaps his long eyelashes were spiked from the water, his T-shirt clinging to his still damp...

"Hello?"

I jumped. "Joe! Hi. How are you?"

"I'm good. How are you?" he answered pleasantly.

"Great. Been busy?" I asked.

"Oh, sure." I heard a familiar sound as he spoke, the sound of dry dog food clattering into a pan.

"How's Tripod?" I smiled, picturing Joe's cute, three-legged friend hopping eagerly around the kitchen as his master got dinner ready.

"He's great," Joe answered. I heard him set the pan down, heard the jingling of dog tags as Tripod dug in. "Can I ask you something?" Joe said.

"Sure, anything," I answered warmly.

"Who is this?"

Shit! Had I forgotten to say? "Oh, sorry. It's Millie." My cheeks burned. He didn't know who I was, even though we had just spoken yesterday! Well, it was still early in the relationship, right?

"Millie! I thought you were blowing me off. You got off the phone pretty quick yesterday." He sounded like he was smiling. He was probably teasing.

"You were wrong, young man," I said. "I told you I would call you today, and here I am."

"Uh-huh. So what's up?" he asked.

I looked around my tidy kitchen, hoping for inspiration and finding none. "Oh, not too much. What are you doing?"

"Not much, either. You wanna see me again?" He *was* teasing, I could definitely tell that now.

"Well, I guess I do. Sure. What did you have in mind?" Nicely done, Millie. Ball back in his court.

"What did *you* have in mind?" He chuckled, low and sexy, and lust tightened my loins. I clutched the phone in my suddenly sweaty hand. *Play it cool, Millie,* I advised myself.

"Hmm. Well, how about if you come over for dinner?"

"Tonight?"

"No!" God, no! I was not the type of person to whip up a dinner to impress. "Sorry, I have, um, some plans tonight. How about Friday?" That should give me enough time.

"Friday? Sure." Oh, Joe. So amiable and sweet. Such a good kisser.

"Maybe around 7:00?" I asked.

"That would be great," he answered.

"Good," I said. We were quiet for a minute.

"Millie?"

"Yes?"

"I can't wait."

My chest ached with joy. "You're sweet, Joe," I answered softly.

"You're the sweet one," he replied, uh, sweetly.

"Well. Have a good night," I said.

"See you Friday." He hung up the phone.

Very gently, I replaced my phone back on its charger and stared at it. Digger came over and wagged happily at me. From the kitchen, I could smell his defecation, the only real note about my surreal evening.

Sweet. Joe Carpenter thought I was sweet and couldn't wait to be with me on Friday. "I knew it would work, Digger," I said to my dog. "I knew he'd fall for me, I knew it, I knew it, I knew it." Joe Carpenter was coming here, to my clean, adorable, cozy house to eat a fabulous meal with attractive, sweet me, to meet my wonderful doggy, to…maybe…was it too early to…? For fifteen happy, dazed minutes, I sighed and cooed before snapping myself out of my lustful fog. I had work to do.

In order to get through medical school, you had to be pretty organized (*anal retentive* is another term). You have to love lists. And I did.

Wednesday p.m. (that was tonight)
1. Clean fridge. Throw out yeast.
2. Clean oven.
3. Wash bathroom with bleach so smell dissipates by Friday.
4. Dust.
5. Make shopping list for dinner.

Thursday
1. Buy groceries, beer, wine.
2. Wash floors on Thursday p.m., Friday noon if raining.
3. Clean sheets just in case.
4. Rent movie in case #3 doesn't happen.
5. Call Curtis/Mitch for wardrobe suggestions.

Friday
1. Wash Digger and make sure he doesn't roll in dead
things afterward.
2. Cook.
3. Sponge mop kitchen floor if needed.
4. Set table.
5. Shower/hair/makeup/clothes.

Now, what to cook, what to cook? The ever-important first
meal I would cook for my *boyfriend*. Because, after Friday
night, I think I could definitely consider myself Joe's Girlfriend.

Having learned many painful lessons about ingredient
substitutions, I knew that I would have to follow directions
meticulously. I wanted to find something delicious, not so
hard as to cause mayhem and despair, but difficult enough to
impress subtly. Not too garlicky, I thought, rejecting all things
Italian. Perhaps something that could stay in the oven
warming, like a casserole. But not a casserole. Too mom-ish.
Hmm. Hmm. Nothing too cliché, too old ladyish, too spicy,
too bland or too messy.

After poring over my three cookbooks for a couple hours,
I finally decided on the following meal to win Joe's heart via
the gastric route: mixed green salad with raspberry vinai-
grette, shrimp étouffée over rice, broiled summer squash and
zucchini with parmesan, finished off with blueberry pie.

Joe loved shrimp, as I had witnessed many times at restaurants over the years. The summer squash-zucchini thing would be nice, since it was seasonal and colorful and the pie…well, what man doesn't love blueberry pie? All in all, I didn't think those dishes would be too hard. After I read and reread the recipes, I decided the only thing I might have trouble with was the pie crust.

But never fear! My mom was a master baker, and I imagined she'd love helping me put a pie together. I gave her a call, and sure enough, she was delighted to be needed.

Though it was now after eight o'clock, I popped a Tom Petty CD into the stereo and set to work, cleaning, scouring, chiseling the mysterious charred remains of some long-ago dinner from the bottom of the oven. I threw the curtains in to wash and assessed my napkin and place-mat options. Clearly I would have to buy more…would I have time for a quick trip to Sleet's Hardware, where all the really nice kitchen stuff was sold?

It was after midnight when I finally went to bed, but I was pleased that everything was going according to plan. Just as I started to doze off, I jolted awake with an unpleasant thought…work! Shit! I would have to take off work, because clearly I wouldn't be able to get everything done otherwise. A guilty wave cramped my stomach. I was a doctor, after all, and calling out so I could prepare for a date was just awful. Stupid. Moronic.

However…it was just once. The means to an end. I deserved to have a life, right? I had vacation time. And it wasn't like patients were asking for me in particular. Granted, I wasn't giving a lot of notice, but Cape Cod Hospital would send another doctor up to cover for me. Juanita had said so at the orientation.

Telling my conscience to take the night off, I focused on Joe. Once we were an established couple, I wouldn't have to go to these lengths anymore. It was just this once. I stuffed the guilt into the dirty-laundry area of my soul and moved on.

I would have to call Juanita. I got up, fumbled in my desk and located her card, then taped it to my phone so I'd remember to call her first thing. Luckily, Dr. Bala was scheduled for the second shift tomorrow. I'd try to leave early, and definitely would have to take Friday and Saturday off.... Saturday, because I might be dressed in only a sheet with the object of my love in bed next to me, and obviously I wouldn't want to be dashing off to work. As I got back into bed, I went over my conversation with Juanita in my head.

"Hi, Juanita, it's Dr. Barnes from the clinic...I'm making dinner for my boyfriend and need a few days off."

Hmm. Though it was the truth, it lacked a certain something. Maturity, perhaps?

"Hi, Juanita, it's Dr. Barnes. I have a slight emergency here and can't come in to work for a couple of days."

No. Growing up Catholic, I was taught not to say such things, because God would be irritated with my lie and make it true. Now, as an almost thirty-year-old adult, I could intellectually dismiss this argument—God wasn't hanging around waiting for me to tell a lie so He could strike me down—but just in case God was having a slow day, I figured I should work on something else.

"Hi, Juanita, Millie Barnes. I've had something unexpected come up here and need to take Friday and Saturday off."

That was more like it. Not a lie, not full disclosure. Inspiration struck: I would call her now and leave a message on her voice mail! That way (A) it would seem urgent, as it was now one in the morning, and (B) I wouldn't have to talk to her. Brilliant. I got up yet again, made the call, and finally padded back to bed.

The next day I set about accomplishing the items on my agenda. After work, I bought groceries, stopping at no fewer than four markets in all (basic food, liquor, seafood, farmers). Once back home, I stashed the food and decided I had time for a quick run. I pulled on an old T-shirt (*Guinness for Health*) and began stretching the way Sam had taught me. At the thought of my brother-in-law, I sighed.

It was hard to accept that he and Katie wouldn't be a couple, and yet, a small, selfish pleasure glowed in the knowledge that he remained unattached. Sam had a way of making people feel so enjoyed somehow—myself most definitely included. All through those long, miserable adolescent years, I'd always felt good around Sam, never awkward, never unattractive, just welcomed and funny and smart.

Would I ever be able to feel that way with Joe? As thrilling as it was to be near the Golden One, dancing through my self-created hoops was a little difficult. Still, my Joe strategies were working—this would be my third date with him in a week. The power of research, I commended myself. The naturalness would doubtlessly come with time.

Later that evening, my mom came over with some Chinese food. We sat companionably in the kitchen, eating out of the cartons and chatting about pie-crust techniques.

"I know it's bad for you, but I use lard instead of Crisco. Lard really makes the best crust. And everything has to be as cold as you can keep it, hon," Mom preached, her eyes taking on a religious shine. "You have to work fast if you want it to be flaky. Otherwise, the glutens…well, it isn't pretty."

"Cold and fast. Gotcha." Actually, I was pretty much hoping that Mom would do everything and I could just watch and later take credit for her hard work.

"So…why the sudden interest in pies?" Mom asked slyly, delicately biting a little ear of corn.

"Oh, I'm making dinner for, um, a friend, and since it's summer, I thought a pie would be nice. Seasonal." Actually, blueberries were not yet in season, and I'd had to pay almost ten bucks for enough berries, but it would be a small price to pay for Joe's delight.

"A friend? That's nice," Mom said, smiling. I blushed. She didn't ask any more, and I grinned. Good old Mom. She still knew everything.

As I had hoped, my cute little mom took over, telling me just to watch the first time. Her capable hands whipped the crust out, and she deftly mixed the berries and sugar, instructing as I sat on the counter next to her and sipped my Corona.

"I love you, Mom," I interrupted as she lectured about egg versus milk glazes. She looked up abruptly, and her eyes filled with tears.

"Oh, Millie, sweetie, I love you, too!" she said, giving me a floury hug. "And I'm so happy to have you around, honey." She paused to put the pie in the oven. "With Trish gone…" Her voice tapered off.

With Trish gone, my mom was lonely, and I'd been too busy stalking Joe to notice. I had only called her because I needed something from her, and I suddenly felt ashamed. For all her flaws, Trish had been a great daughter, to our mom at least.

"Let's do something next week," I said. "Just us. Let's go shopping in Providence."

"Oh, honey, that would be so much fun! We could have lunch, too."

"I'll even let you pick out an outfit for me, now that I'm not so chubby," I offered. It had long been a bitter pill for Mom to swallow, that she, the reigning queen of Talbots Petite, had spawned an overweight daughter who'd worn almost solely scrubs for eight years.

"I can't wait," Mom said. "Well, I have to go home and watch the Red Sox. Daddy and I watched them yesterday, and they won. Now he's afraid they'll lose if I'm not there to cheer them on." She rolled her eyes and we laughed, knowing my dad was dead serious. "Keep the temperature at four hundred for fifteen more minutes, then turn the oven down to three-twenty-five and bake it for another forty. Call me if you have any questions." Mom washed her hands and gave me another hug. "And Millie…I hope he appreciates you."

"Thanks, Mom," I said, my throat tightening in a rush of gratitude.

After Mom left, I called those fabulous P-town boys for their wardrobe recommendations. I hadn't seen them for a while, since they were busy with the Peacock, and we set up a night out.

"Bring the boy," Curtis commanded. "We want to meet him."

"We'll see how it goes," I answered, grinning. What fun that would be, introducing Joe to my friends, like a real girl-friend! Eventually, I'd even take him home for the official meeting of my parents. My dad would be pleased to have me with a laborer, and everyone was charmed by Joe. Soon, soon, he would be a real part of my life, not just the fantasy that had been playing in my mind for the past fifteen years.

CHAPTER SIXTEEN

FRIDAY MORNING WAS FOGGY and a little cool for the end of June. The forecast was for steady rain toward evening. Great, I thought. Cozy, romantic, good for cooking, good for cuddling. So he would smell pleasingly of rosemary and lavender, I washed my puppy, ignoring his mournful eyes as I lathered, rinsed and repeated. At ten o'clock, I began chopping, mincing, sautéing. I shelled and deveined the shrimp. You'd think that a person who has dissected a cadaver would not be dry-heaving over a little seafood preparation, but such was not the case. Still, I managed to keep down my meager bowl of Special K as I ran my thumb up each gray, cold crustacean.

I boiled, reduced and strained. I stirred, blended and drained. As the steamy, spicy smell of étouffée filled my kitchen, it began to dawn on me why people liked to cook. I washed the lettuce for the salad, chopped in some red and yellow peppers, threw in a few grape tomatoes, then cut up the green and yellow squash.

Mom's pie looked fabulous, its golden-brown crust scattered with sprinkles of sugar. I vowed to learn to bake for real once Joe and I were together. I had plenty of Cape Cod coffee, my favorite brand, and light cream. My curtains went back up, clean and freshly ironed. After arranging the flowers I had bought at the farmer's market yesterday in a mason jar, I set the table. The wine and beer were chilling.

After Joe had arrived, I planned to finish cooking the étouffée, for that nice, cozy domestic atmosphere. The rice would be put on just before he came. I'd stick it in a bowl and warm it in the oven in order to get the nasty cleanup of the rice pot done before Joe's arrival. Planning, planning, it was all in the planning. It seemed I had just about every angle covered.

Finally, I stepped back to survey my work. My house gleamed and sparkled. My dog also gleamed and sparkled. Now it was my turn. I showered, using the expensive, fabulous-smelling bath products Curtis and Mitch had given me for Christmas. Carefully, oh so carefully, I shaved my legs. I blew my hair dry—the humidity made it a little tricky, but I managed to come out with fairly well-behaved hair. Next, the precise application of makeup. Too much and I'd look slutty; not enough, adolescent. On to the clothes. Cute cotton pedal pushers in black and cream, sleeveless cream-colored top, short-sleeved little black sweater. Black leather mules on the feet.

I took a long hard look in the mirror. I'd never be Trish, but still…I looked about as good as I would get. Stylish. Attractive. Not beautiful, but pretty damn cute.

It was now 6:30. I went to my stereo and picked out a few CDs for mood music. Elvis Costello. Sting. Norah Jones. Dave Matthews. Again, all calculated to set a mood of romantic, slightly funky, low-key homeyness.

I took Digger out again on the leash, warning him not to poop in the house on this night of nights. He waggingly agreed (or so I hoped), and flopped down in front of my chair to dream his doggy dreams.

I put the rice on and fussed around the kitchen. There

wasn't really much to do, since I had planned so very well. We would eat in the dining room, which had been used once when my parents had come over. It was a small room that I'd painted last month in a deep shade of rose. The little table was a mellow-stained maple, and I'd just set it with place mats instead of a table cloth. Didn't want to look like I was trying too hard, although frankly, planning this evening had been harder than my surgical rotation.

I poured myself a glass of wine and took a healthy slug. It wouldn't hurt to be a little relaxed when Joe came over. In ten more minutes, it would be seven, when, no doubt, I would start peering out the window for his truck. But hey, why wait? I peered out now. No Joe, just the promised steady rain pattering in the gutters. I turned on the porch light.

I decided I had time to call Curtis and Mitch for a check-in. Katie was working, and besides, she and I had had a nice chat earlier. I sat carefully in my wing chair so as not to wrinkle and called P-town.

"Good evening, the Pink Peacock!" Mitchell purred into the phone.

"Hi, Mitch! It's Millie," I said.

"Hallo, my darling! Is all in readiness?"

I giggled at the quaint phrase. "Yes, all is in readiness, including myself."

"Which earrings did we choose?" he asked

"Little gold swingy thingies," I answered. I heard Curtis ask if it was me. Mitch didn't answer.

"Is that Millie, I said?" Curtis demanded in the background.

"Yes, it's Millie!" Mitch huffed. "Am I allowed to talk to her without you?"

Uh-oh. The Golden Couple rarely fought. "Bad time, Mitch?"

He paused, then laughed. "We had a fight. I had the audacity to change the flower order—he wanted tulips, but they were twice as much as the roses—and now he's ready to take my head off."

I giggled. "Can this marriage be saved?"

"Let's hope, shall we? Very well, my dear. Have a smashing night. Here's Curtis. Hang on, can you?" I heard Mitch talking in the background, then the unmistakable sound of a kiss. Aw.

"Hi, Millie," Curtis said, and I could hear the smile in his voice.

"Is everything okay, Curtis?" I asked.

"Yes, now that he's groveled. How are you, princess?"

"Oh, I'm fine. Just waiting for Joe."

"That's right! 'Tonight's the night,'" he sang. "Are you nervous?"

"Yes, of course. That's why I'm calling you."

"Well, don't worry, sweetie. It will be wonderful. I want every detail tomorrow, okay?"

"Okay," I smiled. "Thanks, Curtis. You're the best."

"I know. Love you."

A truck rumbled up my street. I hurled the phone back into the charger and leaped up. Here! He was here! Digger continued to lie rug-like in front of my chair. Going into the kitchen, I peeked out the back-door window...no truck. No Joe. Not here.

Hmm. Well, it was only seven after. Not really late.

However, twenty-three minutes later, he *was* really late. It was 7:30. A half hour late was pretty late, right? But still acceptable, if he came right this instant. I covered the rice so it wouldn't dry out and turned off the heat from under the étouffée, which still awaited the shrimp. Checking my reflection in the bathroom mirror, I saw that I looked worried.

Joe wouldn't blow me off, would he? I finished my glass of wine, the alcohol lightening my head a bit. No, Joe wouldn't do that. He had said he couldn't wait, I reminded myself. And that I was the sweet one. And God, the way we'd kissed! No, I didn't think he would stand me up. Maybe his truck had broken down? It wasn't the newest truck, but it seemed to run well enough.

The phone rang, and I jumped. "Don't sound worried," I advised myself. Or pissy.

"Hello?"

"Hi, sweetness, it's Curtis. Sorry, I couldn't resist. How's it going?"

My heart sank. "Curtis, he's not here."

"Oh." There was a pause. "Well, how late is he?"

"Thirty-four minutes."

"Ooh. That's not good. Well, he's a bit absentminded, isn't he?"

"Should I call him?"

"No!" Curtis shouted. "No," he continued more calmly. "That's for desperate women, and you're not desperate."

"Right," I said, feeling actually quite desperate. "So what should I do?"

"Have a glass of wine," he advised.

"Already did that."

"Have another one, honey. Don't just sit there waiting for him. When he does come—and he will, sweetie—we want you to be happy and fun. Right?"

"Okay," I said. "Happy, fun, but not drunk."

"Exactly. I'll call you in a little while and check in."

"Thanks," I said, grateful to have a pal like Curtis. Someone with whom one could discuss these stupid situations. What to wear, how to set the table, stuff like that. Most people had done this in high school or college or in their early twenties, but I was a late bloomer.

I walked around my house, nibbling a cuticle. Digger leaped up for some lovin', tail thumping against my freshly vacuumed ottoman.

"No, Digger!" I ordered tersely. Then, filled with shame at taking my frustrations out on my dog, I sat down and called him over.

"I'm just a little worried," I told him, stroking his sleek head. He wagged understandingly.

The clock read 7:45.

An all-too-familiar emotion surged through me, that enchanting blend of dread, certainty and disgust. All this work. Two days off from work, ninety-seven dollars worth of food and beverage, God knows how many hours, a new outfit, new place mats...for what? For this. For being stood up. Stupid, stupid, stupid. Clearly, finishing medical school in the top tenth of my class didn't translate into romantic intelligence. Hot tears burned the back of my throat, and I swallowed hard. *No crying,* I ordered myself. Damn it! Damn Joe Carpenter! How could he be so thoughtless?

Digger, his appetite for affection sated, flopped down at my feet. I slumped back in the chair, not caring now if I wrinkled my pants. A headache began to bore into my skull right between the eyes, and I rubbed my forehead hard.

I should have called him yesterday with a question, like was he allergic to shellfish or something, though I knew damn well he wasn't. But it would have reminded him of our date. As Curtis had said, Joe could be a bit forgetful. Or was this deliberate? Did he forget or was he not interested in me? What about that redhead I'd seen him with last week? Was he with her?

The phone rang again, and I leaped from my chair, heart pounding. *This has got to be him,* I thought. I took a deep, fortifying breath and reached for the phone. I noticed my hands were shaking.

"Hello?" I said.

"It's Curtis," my friend said. My throat closed up.

"Oh, I'm sorry, honey," Curtis went on, gleaning the situation from my silence. The kindness in his voice made me feel worse.

"I feel like such an ass," I whispered.

"Oh, no, honey. Joe's the ass. Truly. If he can't see how wonderful you are, he's just a really gorgeous jerk."

"But when we saw each other the other day…Curtis, it was so amazing! And he seemed so…I just don't understand," I said miserably.

"Men are such assholes," he commiserated.

I gave a halfhearted laugh. "Except you. And Mitch."

At that moment, my dog leaped to his feet, barking wildly. "Oh my God," I said as the adrenaline rushed into my extremities with a tingling surge. "He's here!"

"Stay on the phone!" Curtis ordered. "Keep talking! Answer the door with the phone in your hand."

I could barely hear him over Digger's frenzy. "Quiet, Digger!" I commanded. Surprisingly, he obeyed and stood by the kitchen door, wagging his tail so hard it looked as if he would break his spine.

"Smile," Curtis instructed as I quickly checked myself out in the reflection of a framed print that hung over my couch. There was a knock, and Digger whined excitedly.

"Grab your wineglass," the drill sergeant continued. "Laugh. Pretend I said something funny. Vagina. That's funny."

I laughed a bit hysterically as I grabbed my half-filled

wineglass and went to the back door. I stopped suddenly. It wasn't Joe. It was Sam.

"It's Sam," I told Curtis.

"Sam? Your brother-in-law? What's he doing here?" Curtis asked.

I opened the door. Digger jumped onto Sam's leg and began moaning. The rain gushed off the roof onto the deck as the wind blew in gusts.

"Hi, Millie," Sam said. He disentangled Digger and ran a hand through his damp hair. "Got a minute?"

"Uh…come on in, Sam," I said, opening the door. "Can you hang on one second?"

"What's going on?" Curtis demanded. "Are you talking to me?"

"Take off your coat," I said as Sam stood dripping in my kitchen. He looked around, noticing the dining-room table and food simmering on the stove.

"I didn't mean to interrupt your plans," he said. "I can go."

"No, no. Make yourself at home, buddy. Just give me a second," I said, giving him a pat on his wet shoulder. I scurried down the hall to my bedroom and closed the door.

"What should I do?" I asked Curtis. "He looks upset."

"Hmm. Okay. Here's what we're going to do. It's five after eight. Joe is unacceptably late. Feed the cop. If Joe does eventually come, he'll see that you're not just sitting around waiting for him. If he doesn't, then at least your dinner won't go to waste."

"What should I tell Sam? That my un-boyfriend blew me off?"

Curtis sighed dramatically. "No, Millie. Don't tell him that. Just say you made dinner for a friend who had to cancel at the last minute and you're glad he came."

"Okay. That sounds good. Can you say it again so I get it right?"

"Millie, you're such a sweet dope sometimes. I have to go. Love you! Kisses!"

I heaved a sigh. Curtis was right. I was a dope.

"Millie," Sam said as I reentered the kitchen, "I'm really sorry. I can see that you have plans and—"

"Actually, Sam, my friend just canceled, so it's great that you're here. Otherwise, all this food would go to waste. Sit down." I gave him a smile and pulled out a chair.

He hesitated, then took off his jacket and hung it on one of the hooks near the back door. "Thanks," he said, sitting at my kitchen table.

"Are you hungry?" I asked.

"Sure."

I poured him a glass of fumé blanc (eighteen bucks a bottle, thanks a lot, Joe Carpenter) and handed it to him.

"Thanks," he said. Once again, he ran his hand through his military-short hair, a sure sign of distress. The lines around his eyes were more pronounced, and he stared distractedly at the floor.

"So what's going on?" I asked, sitting with him.

He looked up and sighed. "It's Trish."

"Oh." Of course it was Trish. I felt the decades-old irritation with my sister, ever the center of attention. Even from New Jersey, she was making waves. Tropical Storm Trish. I refilled my own wineglass and took a sip. "What's going on?" I asked.

Sam looked out the window. "She wants Danny to do his senior year in New Jersey," he said.

"What?" I yelped. "Why on earth would she want him to do that?"

Sam sighed again and swallowed some wine. "She says that Avery can get Danny into some swanky prep school down there that he went to, and it would be better for Danny to graduate from there instead of Nauset." He met my eyes, and I saw the worry there.

"Well, I think it's a crappy idea," I said, reaching out and patting his hand. "I have to put the shrimp on…want to help?"

"Sure," he replied, standing up. I went to the stove, turned on the étouffée mixture and got the shrimp out from the fridge. Sam leaned helpfully against the counter, watching me closely.

"Can't say I ever saw you cook before, Millie," he said, a ghost of a smile flitting across his face. "Who was this friend who canceled?"

"Well, Sam, I think I'd rather not say, if you don't mind." I dumped the shrimp into the pan, where it hissed in a most satisfying way. I didn't want to think about J.C. right now, and the wine buzz and Sam were doing a great job distracting me. "So what does Danny think about all this?"

Sam took the spatula out of my hand, nudging the quickly pinkening shrimp. "We haven't talked to him about it yet. But Trish says if I put it to him in positive terms, he'll see what an opportunity it is. Or something."

"I think it's a stretch to think that Danny would want to transfer," I said. "He's doing so well here, and he's got so many friends, so much going on."

"That's what I said. There are a lot of good reasons for him to stay. He's varsity baseball up here, he knows the teachers, straight As…I don't think he needs Rich Guy Prep to get into a good school. But Trish says it's a golden opportunity."

"I'm with you, buddy," I said. "Screw Rich Guy Prep! Now get out of the way so I can get this stuff on the table."

With Sam's help, I brought our meal into the little dining

room. I lit the candles and we sat down, filling our plates with the rather beautiful dish that I had spent days planning.

"Whoever it was who canceled, Mil…he's missing out." Sam smiled at me across the table. "But it was kind of good luck for me."

I smiled back, suddenly very glad that I was here for him in his hour of need. Sam deserved at least that from me. "Cheers." We clinked wineglasses and started eating.

And guess what? It was fantastic! Definitely the best meal I'd ever made. We ate pretty much in silence, but it was comfortable. Peaceful, even, with the rain strumming on the roof, the music playing softly over the stereo.

"Great food, Millie," Sam complimented, helping himself to more étouffée. "You really did all this yourself?"

"Except for dessert," I confessed. "I wouldn't be able to fool you on that one."

I sat back and admired my work for a minute. I had really outdone myself. Granted, the wrong man was sitting across from me—I squelched the stir of dismay the thought caused—but I had pulled off a really nice dinner. The flowers on the table looked great, my new place mats and napkins matched the plates, the food was excellent, the wine was rapidly disappearing…. It felt good. And it was so cozy to have Sam here, good old Sam, so comfortable and solid and real. Irritation with my sister—she was still tormenting him—turned my smile into a frown.

"Sam, do you think there's something else going on with Trish? Some other reason that she's asking Danny to come down to New Jersey?"

Sam wiped his mouth with a napkin. "Other than just missing him, you mean?"

"Other than that. I mean, sure, she misses him, he's the

greatest kid in the world. But I wonder if she really thinks that transferring out of Nauset senior year is what's best for Danny. I think she's up to something."

Sam sighed, giving me a rather sad smile. "You two...I don't understand how two sisters could be so different." He thought for a moment. "I don't know, Millie. To tell you the truth, I never could tell what Trish wanted, and I sure as hell don't know now."

"Would you want her back, Sam?" The question rose unplanned from the depths of wine I had consumed. I had never really entertained such a thought before, wrapped up as I was in the old Get Joe plan. But now that I had asked, it was suddenly very important that he say no. Sam and I stared at each other across the table. He shrugged.

"Do I want her back? No, I guess I don't." He tried to refill his wineglass, but the bottle was empty. "Got any more of this?" he asked.

"In the fridge." I sat back in my chair and listened as Sam uncorked another bottle. Ever the gentleman, he came back in and filled up my glass before pouring himself some more, then sat back down and slumped comfortably in his chair.

"No. I don't want to be married to Trish again," he mused, taking a sip of wine. "I wasn't thinking about divorce, but the truth is we weren't happy for a long time. I didn't really want to admit that, but there it is. We had Danny in common, and that was about it. I don't think she ever got over not having the life she thought we were going to have."

"What about you, Sam? Were you disappointed, not becoming a football player?"

He laughed. "Not really, to be honest. I would have done it, if I'd been recruited, but it's not what I wanted to do with my life."

"And what did you want to do?"

He paused. "Well, pretty much what I'm doing now. I love being a father, love my job. I would have liked to have had more kids, maybe…I don't know. Trish wanted something different. I think she always felt a little trapped. But I never did. Never felt like we missed out on anything too important."

"So are you over her?" I asked.

"Well, I don't know about that. I mean, I'll always love her in a way, because she's the mother of my son. Hell, she was the first girl I ever kissed. But I'm not in love with her anymore. Haven't been in a long time, I guess. And yeah, things don't feel so raw anymore."

Looking at his soft, gentle eyes, I felt a strange, warm ache in my chest. "I know I've said this a million times, Sam," I said, "but I always thought you were too good for her."

He didn't answer for a moment, just looked at me, then smiled. "Well. Thank you, Millie." He took a deep breath and shifted in his chair. "This was an outstanding dinner."

"I rented a movie," I offered. "One of those spy-guy things…Robert Ludlum or Tom Clancy or somebody. Want to stay and watch it?"

"Sure. That would be great. And was that a pie I saw in your cupboard? A Nancy Barnes pie?"

"Good eye, Officer, good eye. Help me clean up, and we can make some coffee, too."

We tidied up the kitchen, chatting about work and the summer season, then popped in the movie and drank coffee. I allowed myself a tiny slice of my mother's incredible pie. Sam ate, no exaggeration, a third of it. *Men,* I thought, smiling fondly at him as Massachusetts hero Matt Damon defeated the bad guys onscreen. At the end of the movie, Sam rose to leave.

"This was really great, Millie," he said, shrugging into his coat and bending to pet Digger.

"I'm glad you came," I said truthfully. He stood up and gave me a hug, his chin resting on the top of my head for a beat.

"Thanks again," he said. He opened the door, started to leave and then turned back.

"Millie?" he said.

"Yes?"

"You look beautiful, by the way." With a half grin, he bounded off the deck. Digger and I watched him go, the fresh, damp air blowing into the kitchen.

I put the dessert dishes into the sink, shut off the lights and said good-night to my doggy. As I got into bed, my thoughts bounced between Sam and Joe. As always, I was completely dumbfounded that my sister could have left Sam Nickerson. He was so…whatever. He was, and she blew it, and someday she would be sorry.

In the meantime, I had my own problems. What had happened with Joe? What about my plan? What possible reason could there be for him not showing up? I hugged my pillow, swallowed and ordered myself to sleep. I'd think about it tomorrow. Me and Scarlett O'Hara.

CHAPTER SEVENTEEN

I CALLED DR. BALA EARLY the next day and offered to take the daytime shift. He accepted, warned me that the EKG machine had a malfunctioning lead and hung up.

The clinic was hopping. Sunburn with blistering on a middle-aged man's bald head; jellyfish sting on a ten-year-old boy; the old favorite, poison ivy, resulting from a boisterous bachelor party; and a mom who had slammed her finger in a car door. It was good to be busy. I x-rayed the lady's finger, splinted it, admired her well-behaved seven-year-old daughter. The jellyfish sting was no problem, just a little itchy, so I gave the kid's mom some cortisone cream. A prednisone prescription for the hungover bachelor, and some lidocaine cream for the sunburned baldy, with advice on wearing a hat.

Things slowed down in the afternoon, and I called a few patients to check on them, filled out some paperwork, dictated my cases and closed up. On Saturdays, the clinic closed at five. It was a beautiful day, clear and dry after last night's rain, and Route 6 was packed with tourists. I got home and changed into my running clothes, Digger staring fixedly at my sneakers and wagging maniacally. He knew what sneakers meant. I pulled a T-shirt over my head (*Free Your Inner Lance*) and headed out for a leisurely run.

I was now a proficient runner in that I didn't have to stop every thirty yards to vomit, wheeze or collapse. Granted, I would never be a natural athlete, and my stride was short and slow, but I had actually come to enjoy running, the fresh, salty air, the time with my dog, and, best of all, the smugness I felt when I was done. Today, the breeze rushed overhead, the sun beat down in bright, cheerful beams. I could hear the song of the beach as I ran down Ocean View, the cries of the gulls and shrieks of children mixing with the roar of the waves, waxing and waning with the breeze.

Now that I had no distractions, my thoughts of Joe, kept energetically at bay for the past twelve hours, returned with a sodden thump. Now what was I going to do the next time we saw each other? Pretend nothing had happened? That would be tough. I loved him, for God's sake. I had sunk a lot of time, money and effort into getting him to notice me. And he had! So what the hell had gone wrong?

I finished my run and went inside, sweaty and irritable. I sat grumpily in my living room, not even feeling motivated to shower. Katie would be working. Curtis had put up with me enough last night. Maybe I would drop in on my parents…but then my mom would want to know how dinner had gone, and I'd have to tell her that I'd been stood up. Perhaps a drive into Boston to see Janette? Nah. Traffic was too heavy, and I lacked the energy. Clearly, I needed more friends. Maybe Sam would want to catch a movie.

Digger leaped up as if shot, barking maniacally as he jumped against the back door. I heaved myself out of my chair, running a hand through my sweaty hair. It was probably my dad, dropping by to see if I needed any man-things done around the house.

Joe Carpenter stood on my back porch.

All coherent thought drained from my head. I opened the door mechanically, and Digger launched himself at Joe, still barking. Joe bent and patted his head, grinning at me, and Digger quieted.

"Hi, Millie," he said with a chuckle.

"Joe," I breathed.

"You forgot, didn't you? Wow, I can't believe it." He straightened up and shook his head. "Millie, Millie, Millie. You invited me for dinner, remember?" He wagged a finger at me. "Bad girl."

"But...but..." I stammered. My brain refused to accept the horror that was dawning: Joe here. Me, sweaty and flushed. Joe here. Wrong day. Of course, *he* had gotten the day wrong...but he was here. And oh, God, I looked...

"Can I come in?" Joe asked, his dimples flashing again.

"Oh! Of course, sure." I backed up and let him in. Digger followed, his nose glued to Joe's work boots, sniffing with religious fervor.

"Joe, it was—you actually—" I said. A light flared in my brain. "God, I *did* forget. I'm so sorry."

"That's okay," he replied amiably. "Can I stay?"

"Yes! Sure! Uh, just let me, you know, I just got back from a run..." I cringed mentally, knowing how I looked—and smelled.

"Sure. Take your time." He looked around the kitchen. "So nothing's cooking, huh?"

"Um, no. But I can whip us up something after I jump in the shower." Again I winced, knowing that the most elaborate thing I'd ever whipped up was toast. Thanks to Sam last night, there were no leftovers, either.

"Sure, whatever. Got any beer?" I nodded and Joe opened the fridge and helped himself to a Corona.

"Make yourself at home. I'll be quick," I said, trying to back out of the kitchen in a dignified manner. I bumped into the door frame, then turned and fled to the bathroom.

In a frenzied manner, I peeled off my T-shirt, sports bra, shorts, shoes and socks. I avoided the mirror. Shit! But thank God! He hadn't blown me off; he'd just had the wrong night. All that money and time, down the drain—or, more accurately, down Sam's esophagus. *Don't worry about it, Millie. He's here.*

I leaped into the shower without waiting for the water to heat up and doused my damp head. Furiously lathering shampoo into my hair, I mentally went over what to wear, what to do with my hair, how much makeup I could put on without taking forever. Joe had turned on the stereo and had one of the Cape's classic rock stations tuned in—Black Sabbath blared over the speakers, a far cry from last night's carefully chosen CDs. Frantically, I toweled off my hair. Blowing it dry would not work…didn't want to give Joe the impression that I was a high-maintenance kind of woman.

I slapped on some moisturizer, mascara and lipstick, yanked on my robe and leaped across the hall to my bedroom. From the closet, I pulled on some cropped jeans and a sleeveless button-down shirt, brushed my hair out and slapped on a hair band. Thank God for hair bands. Was I ready? No. Shoes. I grabbed some sandals and stuffed my feet into them. Looking in the mirror on the back of my door, I took a few fortifying breaths.

Your man is here, Millie, I told myself. *Nothing has changed. Calm down. This is a big night. Not what you had planned, but still. Joe Carpenter is out there waiting for you.*

At least my house was clean. And there were still flowers on the table, making it seem like I always had flowers on the table. Joe smiled as I came into the kitchen. He was standing at the stove, stirring. His jeans looked soft with age, slightly torn at each knee, and he wore a blue T-shirt. I had never seen a more beautiful male in my entire life.

"Better?" he asked.

"Yup," I said, getting a beer out of the fridge.

"I found this in the cupboard. I love this stuff," Joe said. He was stirring a pot of macaroni and cheese, the really orange kind that comes in a box, which I kept on hand for Katie's boys.

"Oh," I said, the grocery bill from last night flashing through my mind. "That's great." Fattening, salty, pasty... pretty much Cheetos in a less crunchy form. Joe stopped stirring. Taking me by the shoulders, he gave me a quick, soft kiss. My stomach flip-flopped most pleasantly.

"I missed you," he said with a little smile.

Oooh. "I—I'm just so sorry I forgot about this," I stammered.

He looked at me sideways. "It *is* kind of a first," he acknowledged, just sheepishly enough to be adorable. "I'm usually the forgetful one."

Score another point for Dr. Barnes, ladies and gentlemen!

Dinner with a shelf life of three years wasn't exactly the romantic meal I'd planned, but nevertheless, Joe Carpenter and I were together.

"How's work going?" I asked as Joe shoveled in heaping spoonfuls of the glow-in-the-dark food.

"Great," he answered. "Almost done on the new wing at the senior center."

"That's wonderful," I answered, taking a swig of beer.

"How's your work?" he asked.

"It's good, too. Pretty busy these days."

"What is it again that you do?"

I blinked. How could he not know that? Not to toot my own horn or anything, but a small-town girl who becomes a doctor and returns to her place of birth…Everyone knew me. "I'm a doctor, Joe."

"Oh, that's right. Hey, you want some more mac 'n' cheese?" He smiled so winningly at me that I forgave him his lapse, though my befuddlement remained.

We took our beers out onto the deck. It was getting dark. God had obligingly sent us a beautiful sunset; fuchsia and lavender suffused the entire western half of the sky, and the stars were beginning to wink in the deepening blue of the east. I lit the citronella candles that dotted the railing and put one on the table between us.

"This is a really nice house," Joe said, gazing skyward.

"Watch this." In another minute, Nauset Light's beam flashed across the tops of the trees.

"Wicked cool," Joe said. He reached over and took my hand, moving a candle so our flesh wouldn't singe.

Was there ever a more perfect moment? Joe and Millie. Millie and Joe. *Mr. and Mrs. Howard Barnes request the pleasure of your company at the wedding of their daughter, Millicent Evelyn Barnes, M.D., to Joseph Stephen Carpenter the Carpenter*…I squelched a giggle.

"What's your house like, Joe?" I asked to distract myself from my silliness.

"Oh, it's kind of a work in progress," he answered, turning to look at me. "I'll show you sometime."

"That would be nice."

"Have you watched that movie yet? The one you rented?" Joe asked. "That looked good."

"No, I haven't watched it yet," I lied. "Want to put it on?"

"Sure. And can I have some pie? I saw it in the cupboard."

Ten minutes later I was watching *The Bourne Identity* for the second time in twenty-four hours. But this time, Joe Carpenter was sitting next to me, his big work boots on my glass coffee table, his strong, tanned arm around me. My heart pumped furiously, sending the blood flow straight to my nether regions. His hand brushed the back of my neck, his fingers played in my hair. I turned my head away from the TV and looked at Joe. He looked back. We looked and looked, and this time I couldn't squelch the giggle that rose up.

"Millie Barnes," Joe murmured, a slow smile lighting his perfect face. "Why didn't I ever notice you before?"

And then he was kissing me, warm and soft and just right, nice and slow. My hand went to his neck, and I could feel his pulse thumping against my palm. Slowly, smoothly, he eased me back so I was half lying on the couch, Joe on top of me. Matt Damon screeched out of Paris. Joe slid his hand under my shirt, along my ribs and I sighed against his mouth. His hair was so soft, like a baby's, and I ran my fingers through it. Then his hand cupped my breast, his thumb scraping over the lace of my bra, and my hands clenched into fists.

"Is this okay?" Joe whispered.

It was hard to think with him lying on top of me, his hand where it was, the clean, sunshiny smell of him.

"Millie, I really, really want to go to bed with you," he whispered, kissing my neck.

"Okay," I croaked.

SEVENTY-FOUR MINUTES LATER, Joe Carpenter was sleeping next to me in my bed. And guess what? We were naked, that's what! We lay spooned against each other, Joe's breath tickling my neck, his arm around my ribs. He was sound asleep.

I, on the other hand…I wanted to jump up and create a Web site that told the world I had just shagged Joe Carpenter. Joe Carpenter and I had had sexual relations. We had known each other biblically. We had *done* it. I had done it, too—I got my man, just as I had dreamed.

On the other hand…oh, damn. There was no getting around it. It hadn't been perfect.

Of course, the first time can be awkward. I *had* felt pretty self-conscious…being naked with someone as magnificent as Joe made me feel rather imperfect myself. At least the lights had been off and we could barely see. Not that I didn't want to see him, of course.

That wasn't the only thing, though. I mean, the kissing on the couch had been glorious. But as soon as I had flashed the green light, my body had tensed up. We'd gone into the bedroom, and everything had been fine, but I couldn't seem to get out of my head and enjoy what Joe was doing to my body and what I was doing to his. I had been just too nervous to really be present. Instead, my brain had narrated the whole thing. "Joe is taking off his shirt. Joe's neck is very smooth. Joe is a boxers man."

Well, it was only the first time. If I had just sort of gone through the motions, that was to be expected, perhaps. And Joe hadn't seemed to notice.

I turned so I could see Joe's face. Awake, he was the most beautiful man on earth. Asleep, he was an angel. The moon had risen and now cast a white light that turned his skin marble. His eyelashes were so long, his lips full and generous, his cheekbones…everything about him was beautiful. His hair fell across his forehead, and I smoothed it away.

Yes, I reassured myself, things would be perfect between us. This first-time awkwardness would surely pass.

I HAD TO WORK IN THE MORNING, so I crept out of bed, grabbed some clothes and tiptoed to the bathroom. After I showered, I took Digger out, made coffee and peeked in on Joe. He lay on his back, half-covered by the white sheet, looking like an ad for Calvin Klein cologne.

I sat on the edge of the bed and put my hand on his warm chest. He didn't stir. "Joe?" I said softly. He opened his eyes.

"Oh, hey," he said huskily, pulling me in for a kiss, making me glad I had just brushed.

"I have to go to work," I said regretfully, running my hand over his smooth shoulder.

"Okay," he murmured, closing his eyes again.

Okay? Was that it? As if reading my mind, Joe opened his eyes again,

"See you later?"

"Sure," I answered. "There's coffee if you want it." I kissed him on the cheek and left.

Things were going great, I thought as I drove to work. I hadn't been overeager, hadn't tried to pin him down for our next date. The mix-up in nights had actually worked out well, since it seemed as if I wasn't fixated on Joe, when of course we all knew the truth. But it had fooled him, and I had actually come off looking pretty good.

I think I could now safely say that Joe Carpenter was my boyfriend.

THE CLINIC WAS ALWAYS SLOW on Sundays, and we had only a few patients that day. Jeff, our college-boy temp, greeted me sweetly and then immersed himself in his books, leaving me free to talk on the phone, starting with Curtis, who definitely deserved the first call. After filling him in on the mix-up and subsequent nooky, we giggled happily together like ninth graders.

"So when can we officially meet your new boy toy, princess?"

"I'll let you know," I said. "Soon, I hope. Maybe we can have drinks down here."

"Oooh. Venture into Hetero-Land? Well, now, that could be fun. And we could see your house. What have you done on that lately?"

We chatted a while longer in the comfortable way of old friends, talking about trivial things like the new lantern that Curtis had found at the marine surplus store or the teak desk organizer that I had ordered from Target. Once again, I thanked him profusely for his moral support, undying friendship and wardrobe advice, all of which were of equal import, reminded him that he was due for a tetanus booster and blew kisses into the phone.

After hanging up with Curtis, I wandered into the reception area and chatted up Jeff for a few minutes. He handed me some insurance forms, and I went back to my office to fill them out. That took ten whole minutes. I picked up the phone and called Katie.

"Hello?"

"Hi, Katie, it's—"

"Michael, get out of that cupboard right now! And don't whine at me! I am on the phone! Hello?" she demanded in that schizophrenic way mothers of young children have.

"Having a bad day?" I asked.

"Oh, hi, Millie," she said.

"Want me to call back?" I asked.

"You know, lately they just hate me talking on the phone," she answered. I could hear the sound of a toy siren in the background, followed by a crash and then a wail. "I don't want to hear it!" Katie tersely informed...me? No, the boys. "Okay, they're locked out. How's it going?"

"Oh, fine," I said, smiling.

"Do I hear the purr of a satisfied woman?" Katie laughed. Her voice changed. "Stop banging!"

"I hope you're not talking to me," I giggled.

"No, *you* can bang all you like," she answered. "Listen, you can hear that this really isn't the best time. Do you want to have that overnight we talked about? I have a couple of days off this week."

"Sure!" I said. "I'll tell you all about some recent developments." We consulted our calendars and made a date.

"Mil, I have to run," Katie said. "But I can't wait for our night out. Corey, do not hit the door with that thing! You're making dents! I'll call you tomorrow, Millie. Put that down! Bye!"

Joe was gone when I came home, his coffee cup in the sink next to mine. I gave Digger a long tummy rub, cleaned up his mess on the kitchen floor (hoping he hadn't pooped while Joe was still in the house) and wandered around. Peeking in the bedroom, there was absolute proof that I had indeed accomplished my mission...rumpled sheets and a condom wrapper in the wastebasket. And oh, hooray! There was a note on the pillow!

Millie—See you soon.
—Joe☺

A man of few words. The smiley face was cute. A little dopey, but cute. I gave the note a kiss, then lay back on the bed, grinning like an idiot. Complete and total satisfaction radiated from me. Joe had spent the night. I grabbed the pillow on which his perfect head had rested and inhaled. After a few minutes of reverie and self-congratulations, I rose, poured myself a glass of water and went out on the deck. The phone rang the instant my bottom touched the seat.

"Hi, Aunt Mil! It's Danny!" my nephew barked into the phone like the Irish setter that I suspected he was.

"Hello, Danny," I grinned.

"Wanna go to the movies with my dad and me?" he asked. Now granted, most seventeen-year-old boys would not be caught dead going out with their dads and, God forbid, their aunts. But Danny was exceptional. He would probably start a new teenage trend in airing out aging relatives.

"Sure," I answered, feeling a sudden bittersweet rush of emotion. A year from now, Danny would be getting ready for college, and an evening like this one would be a thing of the past. I could hear Sam's voice low in the background

"Dad wants to know if you'd rather see *Sisters Forever*…the new Jackie Chan flick…*Star Fighters* or…what was that last one, Dad? *Guerilla Politics*, 'an important documentary from one of America's finest filmmakers.'"

"Jackie Chan," I answered immediately.

"Whoo-hoo! Jackie Chan it is, Dad! We'll pick you up in half an hour, okay?"

They arrived shortly, and I squeezed into the pickup's front seat between them like a giant toddler. Once at the theater, Danny bounded to the concession stand while Sam paid for all three tickets.

"You don't have to buy my ticket anymore, Sam," I protested.

"Years of habit, Millie." He smiled down at me as Danny

returned, carrying a bucket of popcorn the size of a silo and a vat of soda that contained enough fluid to hydrate a human for a week. We found our seats, me again in the middle.

"So what made you boys think of old, decrepit Aunt Millicent tonight?" I asked as Danny waved to three girls a few rows in front of us. They giggled in response and began whispering furiously, casting playful glances back at Danny as he devoured the popcorn with shocking speed.

"Oh, well," Sam said, looking a little bit embarrassed. "I just thought maybe you felt a little, uh, down after Friday night." At my blank stare, he said, "You know, your friend canceling on you and all."

"Oh!" I said. "Actually, we saw each other last night." At the words, a blush warmed the tips of my ears as I remembered making out on the couch with the lovely and delicious Joe Carpenter.

"Millie's got a boyfriend, Millie's got a boyfriend," my nephew chanted, tossing some popcorn at the girls, who shrieked obligingly.

"Children should be seen and not heard, Daniel," I said, smiling as I said it.

"Really?" blurted Sam. "You're seeing someone?"

"Try to conceal your surprise, Officer," I said sharply.

"No, I just…you didn't say anything, that's all. So who is he?"

"Never you mind, Sam-I-Am," I replied, enjoying my moment of mystery.

"I'm gonna say hi to those girls," Danny announced as he unfolded his lanky frame from the seat. As soon as he was out of earshot, I turned to Sam.

"Did you talk to him about Rich Guy Prep?"

"Yup. He doesn't want to go," Sam answered, the relief

clear in his eyes. "Doesn't see any point in it. I did try to put it in terms of being an opportunity and all that crap."

"Which he saw right through," I surmised.

"Yup. Trish wasn't happy, but I sure as hell was. I can't imagine why she thought he'd want to leave his senior year, but he talked to her."

"I'm glad," I said, patting Sam's arm. "We can't have you rattling around in that house alone."

"Well, it would have been okay, if Danny had a real reason for going, not just some new idea of Trish's." Sam smiled. "But, yeah, I was glad."

"Good thing Danny's so sensible."

"Yup. Always been a smart one," Sam agreed, nodding.

"And handsome," I added.

"Just like his old man," Sam said. I laughed. Danny returned to his seat and the previews started.

About halfway through the movie, which, I must confess, I was thoroughly enjoying, Sam got up and climbed over Danny and me, presumable to hit the loo. Danny leaned over to me.

"Can you keep a secret?" he whispered.

"I hope so," I whispered back.

"It's important."

"Okay. What is it, big guy?"

"I need help on a college application," he whispered, taking a quick look around.

"Sure," I said. "Why is it a secret?"

"It's for Notre Dame. Early decision," Danny concluded. "I don't want my dad to know in case I don't get in."

My eyes grew wet as I imagined Sam's joy if Danny went to his alma mater. "If you don't get in, there's no justice in the world," I said. "Of course I'll help you."

"Great. You're the best, Aunt Mil."

How was it that a compliment from a child, albeit a rather old, very tall child, could make me feel so humble? I squeezed Danny's arm as Sam clambered back to his seat. He handed me a box.

"Milk Duds," he whispered, opening his own. "It's just not a movie without Milk Duds."

CHAPTER EIGHTEEN

A FEW DAYS LATER, after several dozen kisses for her boys and myriad instructions for her parents, Katie climbed into my car for our sleepover.

It was the end of June, a perfect, clear summer afternoon, the temperature about seventy, the breeze just stirring the leaves. Katie and I hadn't had any real time together for a while, and I felt a rush of love for her as we drove to my house. Each time I thought about my idea that she needed a husband, I felt slightly ashamed. She did seem happy, the boys were wonderful and her apartment clean and cheerfully cluttered. Who was I to say she needed more?

Once home, I showed her the newest changes and additions, pointing out the recent picture of Corey and Michael that I'd had matted and framed. She blushed with pleasure at seeing their photo hung so prominently in my living room and accepted the beer I handed her.

"Is it too early for alcohol?" she asked.

"Oh, no," I answered. "It's thirteen minutes after four. Perfectly acceptable."

"Don't even think about it, dog," she said to Digger, who was gently preparing to mount her leg. He slunk away, dejected, and I slipped him a chew stick as a consolation prize.

"Look what I brought, Millie. Just like old times." From out of her overnight bag, Katie pulled an array of containers…mud masks, moisturizers, nail polish.

We spent a happy hour (so to speak) applying various products to our faces and lounging around, looking at the *InStyle* and *People* magazines I had bought for the occasion.

"So things are good, Katie?" I asked, somewhat hesitantly.

She smiled. "Yeah, things are really good. The boys aren't so demanding, although they tend to bicker a lot these days. And I talked to the bank about a house. My parents will help, but I want to do most of it alone. They've already helped me so much." She leaned her head against the arm of the sofa and looked at her fingernails, now polished a deep red. Her blond hair fell in a smooth curtain, almost touching the floor.

I was struck, as I often was, by her effortless beauty, and even more by the fact that she was completely unaffected by it. Knowing Katie's merciless four older brothers, I imagined whatever vanity Katie might have once had had long been erased.

She smiled at me. "So, Millie, I've been dying to hear. How's Operation Joe?"

I sat up straighter in the chair I was lounging in. "Well, Katherine, funny you should ask." I told her about last weekend's big dinner, Joe's screwup in nights, the macaroni and cheese, all of it.

"And tell, me, Millie," my friend asked, "did you…*do* it?"

I paused for effect. "Yes. We did it."

"Oh, my God!" she shrieked. "Oh, Millie!" We burst into a fit of adolescent giggling, clutching hands and snorting. "Fifteen years in the making! I can't believe it!"

"It was sixteen years, thank you very much, and you have to believe it, because it's true. I videotaped it."

"Oh, my God, did you really?" Katie sat up abruptly.

"No, no, for God's sake…well, not yet, anyway." We laughed some more.

"So." Katie took another swig of her beer. "How was it?"

My face grew warm. "Well…um, well, it was actually…you know…it—it wasn't great."

"Wasn't great? Not great? Oh, my God! How could it not be great? You've been dreaming about this since we were teenagers! What happened?"

"Nothing, nothing." Needing to look away, I gathered our beer bottles and straightened up the magazines. "It was fine. He was fine. It's just—I don't know, I was nervous or self-conscious or something. All the parts went into the right places, you know, but…it just wasn't…shut up, Katie."

My oldest friend in the world was shaking with laughter, tears streaming down her face. I glared for a moment, then gave in and laughed with her.

A FEW HOURS LATER, WE WERE at the Orleans Prison, a cute and reliable restaurant that used to be, obviously, a prison. Thick stone walls and barred windows made up the bar, and the restaurant spread out in a new wing behind us. We were deep into a discussion of reality dating shows.

"I'd like to see one that's really real," Katie said. "Like, I could tell a guy how my life really is, and then see if he'd want to share his trust fund with me."

"What would you ask?" I took a slug of my wine.

"Oh, like, 'Bachelor Number One…my son has diarrhea and missed the toilet. Do you wipe his crusty little bottom first or clean up the floor?'"

I laughed. "Or 'Bachelor Number Two…I haven't had

time to shave my legs or underarms in six weeks. Do you feel this makes me less attractive?'"

"How about, 'I have dry, itchy winter skin, Evan. How do you feel about scratching my shins?'"

Heads turned at our laughter, but we didn't care. We ordered some Frangelico for after-dinner drinks, feeling very sophisticated, despite all evidence to the contrary.

"Guess what Mikey told my parents the other day?" Katie asked, smiling.

"What?" I had a definite soft spot for my younger godson.

"He wants a vagina."

I choked on my drink and then exploded into giggles. "Oh, no! What did they say?"

"They told him to ask Santa." Katie wheezed with laughter.

"I'm sorry. I should never have given them that anatomy book," I said, wiping my eyes.

"Yes. 'Winky' and 'down there' sound so much better," she answered. "Speaking of vaginas and winkies, tell me more about Joe."

I grinned, happy for a chance to discuss J.C. "Hmm. Well, he's very sweet," I said.

"What does he do that's sweet?" She took another sip of Frangelico, only to find her glass was empty.

"Oh, he stopped by yesterday on his way home," I said. This was a mere four days after our first time, and I'd been absolutely thrilled that Joe was seeking me out.

"Stopped by for not-great sex?" Katie asked, smiling wickedly.

I blushed. "It's not him, I'm sure. And yes."

We heard a murmur go up from the bar, and there he was, my very own Joe Carpenter. He called a hello to the bartender and looked around, waving when he saw us.

"He really is gorgeous," Katie murmured appreciatively.

I sighed with lust. "I know." Wearing only blue jeans and a worn T-shirt, Joe was nonetheless breathtaking. Every single woman at the bar, regardless of age, checked him out, and so did some of the men. He extricated himself from the crowd and came over. "I told him we were coming here," I explained to Katie.

"Mmm hmm."

"Hey," Joe said, smiling down at us. "How was dinner?"

"It was…you know…not great," Katie answered with a wicked smile, and I choked a little.

Joe straddled a chair and leaned in to kiss my hot, no doubt scarlet-colored cheek.

"Don't make yourself too comfortable, Joe," I said, patting him on the leg with feigned casualness. His leg was warm and firm under his age-softened jeans. I caught a whiff of Ivory soap and wood and nearly swooned. "As I believe you were told, this is girls night out. No boys allowed."

"Oh, you don't have to—" Katie began.

"No, no," I insisted. "We don't get too many nights out together, after all."

Joe smiled. "I didn't mean to interrupt, girls. Just wanted to say hello. But I'll see you tomorrow, right, Millie?"

"Um, yes. You bet." It was hard to speak normally—Joe referring to our togetherness was quite overwhelming, and the alcohol in my system wasn't helping. Still, I managed to smile at him.

"Great. Have a good time," he said and ambled back to the bar. Katie and I watched as he was immediately approached by two women.

"Thanks for sending him away," Katie smiled.

"Oh, sure," I said, still gazing at Joe.

"You're purring," she commented.

"He's so...I just..."

Thankfully, the waitress interrupted my drooling idiocy by placing two glasses of wine in front of us. "Courtesy of Brad Pitt over there," she said with an appreciative nod at Joe, who waved cheerfully.

We talked about normal things like work and family and were reluctant to leave. My brain was blurry from the wine, despite the fact that I had stopped drinking a while ago. "You know, Katie," I said, "I think we need to call someone for a ride. I don't usually have more than a beer or two, and I definitely shouldn't be driving."

"Okay," she said. "Joe would give us a ride, I'm sure."

"No," I answered. "No Joe. Joe had the pleasure of my company last night, and Joe must wait for it before he gets it again. The shecret of my shuccess." At this very moment, Joe was nearly invisible, surrounded by a bevy of women. He caught my eye and grinned. Darling boy. I flushed with pleasure.

"Then let's have another drinkie while we decide who's lucky enough to come fetch us," Katie suggested. She flagged our waitress down once more. "Yes, could we please have two slippery nipples?" she said in her sweetest voice. I exploded with laughter.

"You won't be laughing when you taste them," Katie said. "They're gross. But fun to order. Should I call my parents? My dad will come get us."

"No, because then they'll think I'm a bad influence," I reasoned. "And then they won't babysit next time we want to do this. I'll call *my* dad."

"Yeah, right. I can just imagine how happy Big Barnes would be to see his little princess drunk."

"Excellent point. Dad is still a teeny bit overprotective."

"How about Trevor?" Katie named her twin brother, older than she was by eight minutes.

"No, Trevor doesn't like me."

"Oh, come on! He likes you fine!" Katie exclaimed.

"Nope. Not Trev. How about Steve?" I offered the name of another of Katie's many brothers.

"Just married, remember? I don't think Sheila would like him coming out at eleven o'clock to fetch his sister." Our waitress brought the nipples, and they were, as promised, rather gross.

"Sam will come get us," I said, watching as Katie sipped her, uh, drink. "How about Sam?"

Katie's eyes narrowed suspiciously. "Millie," she warned.

"No, no, nothing like that. I've learned the error of my ways. But Sam's sweet, and he won't cop an attitude—get it? And besides, he never goes anywhere. He'd love to come and get us."

"Do you swear you're not trying to fix us up again?" she asked.

"Not unless you want me to," I said innocently, though my eyes may have crossed a little.

"I don't."

"Okay, okay, but let's call Sam. Sam's awesome." I fished my cell phone out of my bag and dialed Sam's number. My nephew answered.

"Hi, Danny, how are you?"

"Hey, Aunt Mil. What's up?"

Not wanting Danny to know I had been overindulging, I spoke carefully. "I'm looking for your father, Dan. Is he available?"

"Sure. Hang on. Dad," he called. "It's Aunt Millie. She sounds trashed."

"Danny!" I said, simultaneously irritated and amused. "The boy can tell I've been drinking," I said to Katie.

"Imagine that," she answered dryly, taking a sip of water.

"Giving up on your nipple?" I asked, and we burst into laughter again as Sam came on the line. He agreed to join us at the Prison, and though it had become increasingly difficult for me to estimate time, appeared at our table a little while later.

"Hey, Millie, Katie," he said, smiling and sitting down. Our faithful waitress, who had put up with us for hours now, took his order for a beer. "I understand you girls need a ride home."

I sighed gustily. "Now who told you that? Danny? He's jushta a child."

Sam laughed softly. "I hope I am here to be your chauffeur, Millie, because there's no way I'll let you behind the wheel."

"What about Katie?" I complained. "She's been drinking, too!"

"At least Katie's not sloppy," Sam said, throwing Katie a little wink.

"Yeah, well, she can out-drink an Irish firefighter at a wake. And here I thought you'd be grateful that we rescued you from another night at home alone," I said.

"Oh, I am, I am," Sam replied. "It's not every night I get to be with the two prettiest women on Cape Cod."

Katie rolled her eyes, but such corn-pone sweetness made me want to weep, suddenly. "Sam, you're the best," I said sappily. "We love you, Sam."

"Hey, guys." Joe Carpenter stood at our table. "How's it going, Sam?"

"Okay, Joe, how about yourself?"

"Never better. You playing next week?" Joe was no doubt referring to the sacred softball league.

"Yup. You guys?"

"That's right. Thursday, I think."

"Danny's looking good. Fielding like Nomar of old," Joe commented affably. I yawned hugely just as Joe turned to me. "Hey, girls, why does Sam get to hang out with you? I thought it was girls only. No boys allowed."

Katie tossed her hair in an efficient shake. "Sam's not a boy, Peter Pan. He's a *man*."

Joe looked startled for a second, but Sam intervened. "I'm here only as a public servant, Joe." He smiled at me, eyes crinkling. I smiled drunkenly back. How I loved Sam!

"Right," Joe said. "Well, I'll let you guys be. Have a good night. See you tomorrow, Millie." He leaned in and kissed me quickly on the mouth, then returned to his stool.

Sam led us to his car a short time later and drove us home. He kissed us each on the cheek, advised aspirin with an entire glass of water and drove off.

"You're a prince, Sam," I called, waving.

"He really *is* a prince," Katie murmured. "Don't look at me that way. I'm just stating a fact."

CHAPTER NINETEEN

THE DAY AFTER MY SLEEPOVER with Katie, Joe dropped by the clinic. Just his walking into the reception area caused a hushed and reverent silence to fall over Jill, Sienna and three female patients ranging in age from eleven to seventy-three.

"Hi, Millie," he said as I came out of an exam room.

"Joe! Hi!"

"Got a minute?" he asked.

We ducked into my office.

"What's up?" I murmured, a thread of uncertainty unraveling in my stomach.

"Oh, I was just driving by and saw your car," he said, coming closer.

"Oh." *Think of something to say, quick.*

"And I missed you."

"Oh," I whispered.

He kissed me then. *Oh, Joe,* I thought, *I can't believe we're really together.*

Ten minutes later, he left the clinic, waving cheerfully to Sienna and Jill, leaving me in a trembling pile of lust after six hundred seconds of glorious necking.

"My God, who was that? Millie, are you sleeping with that guy?" Sienna asked.

"Goodness! That Joe just gets better looking every time I see him," Jill commented. "And *are* you sleeping with him, Millie?"

"Mrs. Doyle!" I said, reverting to childhood formality. "Sienna, that's Joe Carpenter, the sweetest and most gorgeous man in the world."

"He's so…wow," Sienna said, dazed. "He could be a movie star or something."

"I know." I grabbed a pen and wrote out a prescription. I may have been humming.

"I can't believe he's with you," Sienna murmured, still staring at the parking lot. "I mean, you're really great, Millie…it's just that guys like that…uh…"

"*What,* Sienna?" I asked more sharply than I meant to.

She blushed. "Forget it. Sorry."

Giving her a look, I went into the other exam room to see my next patient.

SIENNA WASN'T THE ONLY ONE who was surprised to learn that I was dating Joe.

On Thursday I was in my office dictating cases, getting ready to race home to change, fix my hair and reapply makeup for my date with Joe. Sienna poked her head into my office and I switched off the tape recorder.

"What's up, Sienna?" I asked.

"The cops are here to see you," she whispered.

I glanced out the window and saw an Eastham police car in the lot. "Oh, that's just Sam," I told her. "My brother-in-law."

"He's cute, too," Sienna said thoughtfully. "In an old-guy kind of way." Of course, for Sienna, anything past twenty-five was old, so no doubt Sam seemed close to death. I quickly ended my dictation and smiled as Sam came into the room. Thankfully, the leathery-faced, gravel-voiced Ethel wasn't with him. She frightened me.

"Hey, Sam," I said. "Thanks again for the ride the other night."

"No problem," he said, standing in the doorway. "It was fun."

"Everything okay?" I asked, expecting more news from the Trish front. "You can sit down, you know."

He looked strange in my office, very official and serious. And, let's admit it, a good-looking a man in uniform...*nice*. He sat down, his gun clunking against the chair.

"Are you seeing Joe Carpenter?" he asked bluntly.

"Yes," I answered cautiously. "What about it?"

Sam looked at the floor. "I was, uh, kind of surprised the other night, when I picked you and Katie up, that's all. You know, when Joe kissed you. I didn't realize you guys were dating."

I stared at Sam. "So?"

"I guess I'm just surprised. You didn't say anything about it."

"It's kind of new," I replied neutrally.

"Yeah, sure. It's just...I don't really see you guys together." He shifted in his chair as if he had sand in his bathing suit. "You don't seem..."

That was it. I flung my pen down on the desk. "Don't seem what, Sam?"

His eyebrows rose. "Well, it's just that Joe doesn't seem like your type."

"What exactly *is* my type, Sam?" I snapped. "Do you have any idea? Tell me, since obviously you're an expert in 'my type.'"

"Whoa there, Millie, I didn't—"

"What you really mean is that *I'm* not *Joe's* type, don't you?"

"Millie—"

"Because why? I'm not pretty enough?" I slammed my file drawer shut.

"No! I didn't say—"

"God, I am so sick of hearing people ask why Joe is with me! First Trish, then Sienna and now you!"

"Millie, don't put words in my mouth. I didn't mean anything—"

"Did it ever occur to you that maybe Joe likes me because I'm a good, fun person? And maybe he actually finds me attractive? I might be Trish's dorky little sister to you, Sam, but maybe Joe doesn't feel that way."

"Millie, *stop*. Jesus. You're not Trish's dorky little sister," Sam said, holding his hands up defensively. "It was just a surprise. I'm sorry I said anything at all."

"You should be!" I said hotly. "It's none of your business, Sam. Frankly, I don't care if you think Joe is my type or I'm his. Butt out, okay? You're not my big brother. You're not even my brother-in-law anymore."

Sam stood up, his face stony. "Fine. Once again, I'm sorry. See you later." He left, closing the door quietly behind him.

My heart thumped sickly against my ribs. Damn Sam Nickerson! Of all people to wonder what Joe saw in me! Sam had always seemed to like me, always had time to talk to me, even when I was a fat, geeky teenager with braces. To imply that there was something off balance in my relationship with Joe... Angry tears stung my eyes, and my throat was tight. *Damn you, Sam,* I thought, swallowing hard.

I was still fuming when Joe picked me up a few hours later. The whole night, I fumed. It was hard to pay attention to Joe when I was reliving my fight with Sam every two minutes. But Joe didn't seem to mind, or even notice, actually. He was his usual happy-go-lucky self, and if I was preoccupied, it didn't bother him. When we got back to my house, I went at him with a bit of a vengeance. I deserved Joe Carpenter, and screw anyone who didn't see that.

CHAPTER TWENTY

OF COURSE, THE NEXT DAY, I was wracked with guilt. Had I been, perhaps, a teeny bit hard on Sam? One of us Barnes girls already had the role of harpy-shrew…if nothing else, I was the *nice* sister. Granted, I had been mad, but that last thing I'd said, about not being my brother-in-law anymore…ooh, yes, I had indeed been too harsh. Wicked harsh.

I remembered when I'd come home from college for Sam's graduation from the police academy. I had been trying to look uncaring and French, wearing the all-black uniform and heavy eyeliner that we college students imagined was a statement of intellect and cynicism. When Sam, dressed in his uniform for the first time, had come over to me, I'd said something stupid like, "Well, I guess the world's a safer place now." And he'd just smiled down at me, ignoring my pissy attitude, and answered, "I'll always look out for you, Millie."

That memory had me grabbing the phone. His machine picked up. "Sam, hi…um, I guess I maybe overreacted a little bit yesterday, kind of bit your head off a little…oh, Sam, I'm really sorry. Please forgive me. Pretty please." I started to hang up, then thought better of it. "It's Millie, by the way. Call me. I'm at the clinic. Bye."

He didn't call me back and by the time I got home, I

fretted about, tidying up, brushing my dog. The air was hot and dry, and I didn't feel like a run. It was Friday, and at this moment, I had no weekend plans…. Joe and I were not at the point yet where we automatically did everything together. Joe. The thought of him brought an automatic, if not quite heartfelt, smile to my face. Things were going great, completely in accordance with the plan. As Katie had noticed the other night, he really did seem eager to be with me, something definitely different from what I had observed over the years.

And yet there was something missing, though what *it* was remained unclear. As I folded my meager load of laundry, I wondered if I would ever confess all my stalking and plotting to Joe. No, probably not. I had made a jerk out of myself far too many times over him, and the fact that he remained unaware of this was a definite plus.

Joe and I had fun together—he was mellow and sweet—but what was lacking, exactly? Maybe it was that I didn't know him any better now than I had five years ago. Maybe it was that our relationship seemed to consist of hanging out and sex…nothing deeper. Not yet, anyway. Where was that hidden side of Joe, that heroic, helpful, humble part that I'd seen so many times? That was the Joe I really loved.

It's only been a couple of weeks, I told myself. Sensing my gloomy state of mind, Digger came over and stared at me adoringly, his whip-like tail slicing the air. He nudged my thigh with his nose until I relented and petted him.

"You're such a good pup," I said. "What do you think about Joe? Huh, Digger? He's a good doggy, isn't he?" Digger seemed to agree.

Once again, I glanced at the phone. Why hadn't Sam called me? *He must be furious,* I thought, mentally cringing. Making

Sam angry—or hurting his feelings—caused acid to churn in my stomach.

"I think Sam should call me, don't you?" I asked Digger. I swear he nodded.

I flopped onto the couch. Laundry folded, house clean. Looked like I was on my own tonight. Rubbing Digger's tummy with my foot, I considered my options. Cook? Nah. Eat out? Nah. Not on a Friday night on Fourth of July weekend on the Cape. What was Sam doing? Had he gotten my message yet?

At that very moment, the phone rang. "Be Sam!" I commanded before picking up. "Hello?"

"Aunt Millie, it's Danny," my nephew stated needlessly.

"Hi, honey," I said.

"Can you come over? Right now?"

"What's the matter?" I demanded, fear shooting through me.

"Everything's okay…I just need some help, and my dad's not here."

"Are you hurt?" I thought I heard a strangled cough.

"No, no, Aunt Mil. I'm fine." Something thumped in the background. "I just need you to come over real quick. It's not something for the phone. Can you come?"

"Of course, Danny. I'm on my way."

What could be the problem? I wondered as I zipped down Route 6. He had definitely sounded odd. Something with Trish? I neatly passed a lumbering New York Hummer that took up a lane and a half and flew down to the rotary and onto Bridge Road. Turning onto Danny's street, I glanced at the house. Didn't look like anyone was home. I yanked up the emergency brake, ran up the steps and opened the front door.

"Danny?" I called.

"Surprise!"

I leaped back in terror, my bladder loosening dangerously,

my heart rising to my throat, hands fluttering protectively in front of me. Oh, Christ! It was—

"Happy birthday to you," someone began, and then everybody joined it. My face burned and I slumped against the door.

Jesus. A surprise party. For me!

There were my parents, singing away, right at the front of the crowd. Danny, the deceitful nephew. Katie. Her boys. Her parents. Oh, Lord, there was Joe! And Jill and Mr. Doyle and Sienna and even Dr. Bala with a stunning woman whose exotic beauty marked her as his wife. Dr. Whitaker smiled and nodded hello. The Robinsons, my parents' next-door neighbors and lifelong friends. A woman I didn't know, curly blondish hair, smiling eyes. Ethel, Sam's obscenity-spewing, chain-smoking partner. There was Sarah, Danny's girlfriend. Oh God, Janette, my best friend from residency, all the way from Bean Town, and her longtime boyfriend, Zach. Chris from the Barnacle. Curtis and Mitch! Hooray!

And Sam.

Sam was hosting my surprise thirtieth birthday party at his house, the day after I'd torn him a new...

The song finished and everybody clapped and laughed at me, and then I was surrounded by hugging, giggling, babbling people.

"We got you good, Aunt Mil!" Danny exclaimed triumphantly.

Joe came over and planted a big kiss on my mouth. "Happy birthday, Millie! Surprise!"

I squeezed his hand. "Joe...I'm—I—my God, you bad, bad people!" I said. I had to wipe my eyes, because apparently I was crying a little bit.

"You really didn't suspect anything?" my mom asked, giving me a hug.

"Suspect—God, I had no…my birthday's not till the end of next week…and…"

My dad lumbered over, Coors Light in hand. "Happy birthday, sweetie," he said, giving me a hug that lifted me off my feet and squeezed the air out of my lungs. "Nancy, our little baby is thirty!" he bellowed at my mom.

"Oh, Daddy," I wheezed happily, my ears ringing.

He set me down and kissed me loudly on the cheek. "Got a little present for you!" he crowed.

"Not now, Howard," my mom instructed. They made way as Sam came over and kissed my cheek.

"Happy birthday, Millie," he said a little awkwardly.

"Oh, Sam…can you just sneak in here with me for sec?" I asked. Abandoning my parents and Joe (I guessed my parents already knew we were dating or were about to find out), I took Sam's arm and dragged him into the bathroom off the foyer. I flicked on the light and shut the door.

"Sam, I'm so sorry!" I said.

"No, I'm sorry," he said. "I shouldn't have said anything."

"I was so mean. I feel like crap."

"Don't, kiddo. You were right, I sort of crossed the line there."

"No, no. It just hit a nerve, I guess."

"I understand." He shrugged a little.

"Are we okay, then?" I asked, the muffled booming of the guests and the stereo forcing me to raise my voice.

"Sure," Sam answered, smiling.

"I can't believe this party! My God, Sam! Thank you!" I smiled up at him, and he reached out and pinched my chin affectionately.

"Well, it was Katie's idea, and your mom's. I just offered the house and stuff."

"I've never had a surprise party," I said.

"Well, you'd better get out there and start enjoying it." He paused, his eyes turning serious. "Millie—"

"Yes?"

"All those things you thought I meant about you and Joe…I wasn't thinking them. If anything, I think Joe's damn lucky. And he better deserve you. Okay?"

My eyes filled with tears. "Okay. And I'm sorry again. You know I love you, Sam."

"Love you, too, kiddo."

It suddenly seemed very still as we looked at each other, just inches apart in the small bathroom. Sam's eyes were smoky-blue today, and his lips parted to say something. My breath caught for a second, then Sam seemed to change his mind. Reaching behind him, he opened the door. "After you, birthday girl," he said.

The odd tension of the moment was forgotten as guests swarmed up to me, chatting merrily, laughing in the thrill of secrecy. Sam put an icy Corona in my hand and I smiled gratefully.

"How are you keeping, Millie?" Dr. Whitaker asked, peering at me through his horn-rimmed glasses.

"Very well, Dr. Whitaker," I answered. "Thank you so much for coming."

"You're very welcome. And I think you should call me George, don't you?" He gave me the smile that inspired so much trust in his patients, and I grinned back, delighted. "I'm looking forward to talking about our partnership this fall," he continued.

Wanting to shout *Yippee,* I instead restrained myself and replied calmly, "As am I, sir."

"Wonderful. Enjoy your party, my dear."

Dozens of dishes swamped Sam's kitchen counters,

lasagna and green salad and pasta and lobster bisque so creamy and ethereally pink it could only have come from the Barnacle, quesadillas, buffalo wings (my favorite!), and a beautiful white cake with strawberries on top that must have been made by my mom.

I made my way back to the living room. Most people were in there or out on Sam's huge deck, and for a minute I just soaked it all in, all these great people, throwing me a surprise birthday party. I couldn't keep the goofy smile off my face.

Then the front door opened. "Where's my baby sister?" called that unmistakable voice. "Oh, damn, Avery, we're late!"

Ah, Trish. The queen of grand entrances. There she stood, wearing a black sleeveless knit dress that just cleared her ass, her long, tanned legs bare. Chunky diamond earrings. Hair gleaming like a crow's wing. My guests grew still to watch, as Trish knew they would.

"Hi, Trish!" I called gamely.

"Millie!" she cried, swishing over to me in strappy high heels. "I'm so sorry we're late! Oh, well, happy birthday! Hi, everyone!"

The adoring big sister was a new act, but I decided not to care and accepted her hug. "Thanks for coming."

"Avery," Trish said loudly, turning to the man behind her, "this is my little sister, Millie, the one I've told you so much about."

The only one you've got, I thought. I had yet to meet the man she'd dumped Sam for. A generic-looking man stepped forward and offered me his hand.

"Avery Smith," he announced.

This was the guy Trish had dumped Sam for? He was as bland as beige. Medium height, medium build, medium face, medium aged. The only notable thing about him was his choice in clothes—he wore a lime-green polo shirt and bright pink cotton pants.

"Hi," I said, not shaking his hand. I just couldn't, not in Sam's own house. "Nice pants."

He looked puzzled. I grinned.

"Sam!" Trish continued in cordial ex-wife mode. "Everything looks just great! How have you been?"

"Hi, Trish, good to see you," Sam answered. He dutifully received the kiss she planted on his cheek to illustrate to Avery and everyone else that there were No Hard Feelings.

"And where's Danny? Oh, hi, honey!" Now at least Trish seemed genuine, because her eyes teared up when she saw her son. "God, you've grown another inch, I think! And so handsome, just like your dad."

Sam looked my way, and I rolled my eyes. He smiled back with a little shake of his head.

To Avery, Sam gave a stiff nod. My stomach clenched with discomfort…was this the first time Sam and Avery had met? Avery said something and Sam answered, then gestured to the kitchen. He watched Avery leave the room. His face was neutral, but I felt a sudden rush of anger. How could Trish bring her lover here, to what had been her home with Sam? Did she have any idea how that made him feel? She had to know that Sam would be classy about the whole thing, and it seemed like she was taking advantage of it.

I reminded myself not to judge. Sam and Trish were a mystery I didn't understand, and, as Sam had pointed out to me, I had no firsthand experience of marriage *or* divorce. Trish was shaking hands with Dr. Whitaker, gave Jill a kiss and then hugged our parents, exclaiming over Mom's outfit. She seemed cheerful and relaxed, completely at home, despite the fact that she had cheated on Cape Cod's finest man.

"Hi. I'm Carol."

I turned, grateful for the distraction, and saw the blond stranger I had glimpsed in the crowd earlier.

"Hi, nice to meet you," I said. "I'm Millie, and I'm thirty years old."

"So I gathered. Happy birthday."

She had kind brown eyes and a natural, clean beauty that was echoed by her simple, summery outfit of linen pants and silky pink shirt.

"So…do I know you?" I asked curiously.

"Well, actually, I'm more of Sam's guest. But that doesn't mean I didn't get you a present."

"I knew we'd be friends," I grinned. "Sam's guest, is it? Are you from around here?"

"No," she replied, taking a sip of her Corona. "I'm from Connecticut. But my folks have a place up here that I'm using this summer."

"That sounds nice. How did you meet Sam?"

"He pulled me over for speeding," she said dryly.

My eyebrows rose. "Is this how you're working off your fine? Because I think that might be illegal."

Carol laughed. "No, no, I had to pay. But he called the next day and we chatted a while, and he asked if I'd like to come to your party."

"Well, Carol, I'm very glad you did. Especially since you brought me a present."

So Sam had asked someone out! I guess I shouldn't have been so surprised. It was just weird, thinking of Sam with someone, especially a stranger. Picturing him with Katie was one thing, but this Carol person—

At that moment, Joe walked up. "How's my birthday girl?" he asked, looping a casual arm around my shoulders.

"Great," I answered, "now that the shock has receded. Joe, this is Carol, a friend of Sam's."

"Joe Carpenter," he said, shaking her hand. "Hey, Millie, I didn't know Trish Nickerson was your sister."

I stared at him in surprise. "You—you didn't?" Being Trish's sister had pretty much defined my first eighteen years, and the fact that Joe was oblivious to this was stunning. Then again, Joe hadn't made studying me his life's work, as I had done with him.

"So Sam's your brother-in-law, right?" Joe asked.

"Well," I said, glancing at Carol, "no, not anymore."

"Oh, that's right. Okay. Well, I'm starving. You hungry, Millie?" Joe asked cheerfully.

"Sure," I answered.

"I'll get you a plate, then. Nice to meet you, Carol."

"Nice guy," Carol commented as we watched Joe's lovely, jean-clad backside as he walked into the kitchen.

"As nice as they come," I agreed.

"Pretty gorgeous, too."

"Yes, ma'am." We exchanged a grin of feminine appreciation.

The party progressed as most parties do, with my guests walking idly around, admiring the spectacular view from Sam's deck, eating, chatting with each other. I had a nice long talk with Janette about her practice and the inner-city clinic where she volunteered, and we made plans to meet in Boston. Danny chastised me for not attending one of his softball games, a neglect I swore I would quickly amend. My mom buzzed around happily, urging people to eat more, and Sam and my dad had their heads together in the kitchen. I passed

Curtis and Mitch, who were holding hands and murmuring to each other, smiling.

"Did you see Pink Pants?" I hissed.

"An unfortunate choice," Mitch replied with a grin.

"You have such nice manners, young man," I answered. "Please excuse me, for I, I must, um…"

"Powder your nose?" Mitch suggested.

"That works! It sounds so much better than 'evacuate my bladder.' Thank you." I left them and went upstairs, as the downstairs loo was occupied. Someone was in the upstairs hall bathroom as well, so I went into the master bedroom.

As I passed through, my footsteps slowed. Gone were Trish's jewelry boxes and perfume bottles that had once adorned the dresser. There were no scarves, no slippers, no earrings on the night table. The bed was made neatly, and on Sam's bedside table were some reading glasses, a paperback novel and a picture of Danny. My heart tugged at the lonely picture his things evoked.

And how could Trish bear it? She had lost so much…a husband, day-to-day life with her son, a beautiful home, the comfort and security of marriage…and yet she was downstairs, playing star of the Trish Show yet again. Even though she wouldn't admit it, it must be awful, being back here, outside of the circle that had once revolved around her.

Well, nature was calling my name, loudly, so I went into the master bathroom. As I was tugging up my pants, I heard a voice.

"This room's got an incredible view," said a male voice. "Jesus!"

They were in the bedroom. I paused, waiting to flush, hoping they'd quickly leave, feeling slightly embarrassed about being caught in the bathroom.

"The whole house has a great view," answered a female voice. My eyes narrowed. *Trish.*

"What's the market like?" asked the man, who must be Pink Pants.

"Fantastic. The house's value has doubled in the past four years."

"Well, it's ridiculous that he won't sell it," Avery replied.

"He says he never will," Trish answered.

"Too bad you couldn't get Danny to go to Larchmont. If he'd moved out, you could have had your half in a month."

"Well, I tried, Avery!" Trish snapped. "But Danny wanted to stay. He knows Eastham, he's doing great in school, and really, there's no reason for him to transfer. Besides, I think he feels sorry for his father and didn't want to leave him." I ground my teeth at her dismissal.

"I can't believe you have to wait five years for your piece, Trish. This house is a goddamn gold mine!"

"Oh, for God's sake, Avery. I wanted to get divorced fast. *You* wanted me to get divorced fast. Once Danny doesn't live here anymore, I'll get my share, okay? Can you drop it now, please?"

My heart was pounding, my face hot. So that's why Trish had wanted Danny to transfer. She and Pink Pants wanted some cold hard cash. There was no further conversation for a few minutes, and I risked a peek. They were gone. I flushed, washed my hands, then walked over to the bed and sat down. My hands were shaking. Should I tell Sam, I wondered? Should I tell him that his ex-wife had tried to use their son to get some money?

Of course I wouldn't tell him. It would be one thing if Danny was considering it, but he wasn't. End of story. It still left a bad taste in my mouth.

Joe was looking for me when I came downstairs. "Hey, Millie," he said. "Your mom wants you to open presents now."

"Oh, goodie," I said. He smiled at me and gave me a soft kiss. My insides squirmed…not from lust this time, but because my dad was watching.

"My father…" I murmured to Joe.

"Right." He grinned and kissed my forehead chastely, and I smiled back.

Most of the guests were waiting in the living room, where a lovely pile of gifties sat on the coffee table. I loved my birthday in general, and this one was especially great…the party, the end of my educationally focused twenties, the feeling that the next decade would bring wonderful things…a practice, financial independence, a husband, children… security. Love.

My parents gave me the first present. Dad made a big show of leaving the room and coming back with…a bike! Feeling as if I were twelve again, I jumped up and down.

"Oh, Daddy, thanks! I love it!" The Cape was famous for the Cape Cod Rail Trail, formerly a railroad line that had been paved from Harwich to Provincetown. All year round, bicyclists came to the Cape to enjoy the gorgeous views and freedom from cars, and now, so could I. "Dad, thank you so much. Mom, this is the best!"

My parents beamed. "Your mother thought you were too old for a bike," my dad said proudly. "But I knew my baby girl would like it."

Curtis and Mitch gave me their trademark gift—a huge basket of skin-care goodies that smelled heavenly…almost as good as the stuff they used themselves. From Katie was a matted and framed photo of the two of us at age twelve, standing triumphantly on Doane Rock. Her boys had made me treasure boxes, little white cardboard containers that they'd reinforced with yards of masking tape and then painted. "For your stuff, Aunt Millie," Mikey instructed me seriously. "You know, sand, rocks, stuff like that."

Next, Sam handed me Ethel's package, a slim, rectangular box.

"It's a carton of Camels," he whispered. "Unfiltered. She'll keep it if you don't want it." I stifled a giggle and kicked him on the shin.

The gift was actually a very pretty, very feminine scarf. "Thank you, Ethel," I said, somewhat surprised at the loveliness of her choice.

"Shit," she barked, scratching her head vigorously. "It's nothing."

From Danny and Sam came dangling little earrings in the shape of sand stars. I remembered admiring them at a craft fair we had all gone to last fall, when Trish had just left, and the idea that Sam had somehow remembered this…well. I kissed both Danny and Sam, a lump in my throat.

And then came the gift from Joe…

I smiled into his soft green eyes, my earlier doubts about our relationship now seeming silly. Joe Carpenter was here, he adored me, we had been dating for three weeks, and he was giving me a present on my birthday. The very important first gift. With a mixture of trepidation and joy, I struggled with the packing tape that sealed the box.

"I made this," Joe murmured with a quick grin, kneeling at my side. He broke the tape so I could open the box. What could it be, I wondered? A jewelry box, maybe? I pulled out a large, heavy object and unwrapped the newspaper that covered it.

It was a breathtakingly ugly lamp. Large, bulky, weighing at least ten pounds, it was encrusted with rocks and shells that Joe had apparently glued on and covered with polyurethane.

On the wooden base was carved the words *Cape Cod* and a rough-hewn fish.

"Oooh," I breathed in horror, holding up the lamp. Curtis gave a choked squeak and bolted from the room, his hand clamped over his mouth, while Mitch stared at the ceiling, blinking impassively.

"Do you like it?" Joe asked.

"Oh. Wow," I answered, feeling my cheeks grow warm, unable to pry my gaze from the object in my hands. I dared not look at him, or Sam, or Katie, or my mother. But at the same time as a rush of hysterical laughter wriggled around in my stomach, my heart was sinking. There was no getting around the fact that it was the tackiest lamp I'd ever seen in my life. I wanted to love it, I really did. His beautiful hands had wrought it, after all, and obviously, he thought I would like it. Why, I couldn't imagine.

Aware that some kind of response was required, I managed to say, "You made this, Joe?"

"Yup," he answered. "I thought it would remind you of the Cape."

"She doesn't need reminding. She lives here," Corey said with the logic of the young.

"Oh, yeah, I know…I mean…" Joe said.

"I love it," I lied, finally snapping out of my shock. I forced a smile and kissed his cheek. "Joe, thank you. You're so sweet."

"It's goddamn gorgeous," Ethel growled.

Trish rolled her eyes. "This is from Avery and me," she said, plopping a large, flat box into my lap and mercifully removing the lamp from my hands. It was a cocktail dress. Black, shimmery, expensive, gorgeous, one size too small and with a neckline that dipped toward my navel. Nothing, in short, that would ever leave my closet.

"Wow, Trish," I said. "It's, um, wow. Beautiful."

"It's Calvin Klein," she said smugly.

"Yikes! Thank you. I've never owned anything like it," I said, standing up and holding it in front of me.

"I know. I thought maybe you could use a little glamour in your life," she answered, not unkindly.

"Um, thanks, Avery," I said, my toes curling in discomfort at actually having to thank him. Still, Mother had raised me right.

"That will be gorgeous on you," Mom said. "Joe, make sure you take her somewhere nice so she can wear that."

"You bet, Mrs. Barnes," Joe answered, smiling his heart-stopping smile.

A few hours later, we'd decimated my beautiful cake and the party had dwindled down to just a few of us. I said happy goodbyes to my friends and family and then went to help clean up a bit. Katie left, and then Danny and Sarah went to catch a movie, and finally, only six remained. In fact, just three couples: Joe and me, Sam and Carol, and Trish and Pink Pants. We sat out on the deck and watched the sky deepen and stars come out.

"Remember *my* thirtieth birthday, Sam?" Trish asked, giving him her thousand-watt smile.

"Uh, sure," Sam answered. He began picking the label from his beer bottle.

"Sam took me on a surprise trip to the Caribbean," Trish informed the others. "Remember, Millie?"

"Of course," I said. "I came home from school to stay with Danny."

"Oh, that's right. Well, it was so romantic. Wasn't it, Sam?"

Sam just looked at her. "I guess so," he answered hesitantly. Avery said nothing, just stared off at the sunset, obviously bored.

Trish turned to Carol with a pleasant expression on her perfect face. *Oh, beware, Carol.* "So how long have you two been dating?" my sister asked.

"Actually, this is our first date," Carol said, giving Sam a little grin.

"Really!"

"Mmm hmm."

"How did you meet?" my sister asked.

"I was going forty-nine in a thirty-five-mile-an-hour zone," Carol answered.

"Oh, how typical!" Trish fake-laughed. "Has he strip-searched you yet?"

"Trish!" I rebuked.

"Maybe on the second date," Carol said calmly. Sam smiled.

"I can't believe you two are sisters," Joe said, apropos of nothing, but mercifully changing the subject.

"Why not, Joe?" Trish asked, turning her attention to him.

"I guess I didn't know you *had* a sister, Millie," Joe answered. Trish's smile faded.

"Well, she's much older than I am," I murmured, earning a venomous glare from said sister. I smiled back.

"So how long have you and Joe been seeing each other, Millie?" Trish asked.

"Just a few weeks, I guess," I answered cautiously.

"Really. And how did you hook up?" she asked.

"Huh, let's see," Joe said, taking my hand. "How exactly did it start, Millie? Seems like we've been together forever." He smiled at me.

"Well, we've known each other since high school," I answered.

"That's right!" Joe exclaimed. "I wonder how come we didn't hang out then."

. I closed my eyes with dread. Sure enough, Trish's fake smile grew maliciously genuine. "Well, of course Millie looked a lot different in those days…." she began.

"Oh, yeah? I can't seem to remember," Joe answered. "I wonder how I missed you?"

"That's a great question," Trish answered. "Poor Millie was hard to miss, huh, Millie? You must have been fifty pounds heavier back then! And oh, God, remember those braces? And that perm? Oh, that was rich." She laughed merrily at the memory of my horrible adolescence.

My face flushed as helpless anger rushed through me. Joe looked at me, surprised, and I felt a little flash of fury toward him, too. Did he have to set Trish up so perfectly? Carol politely looked out at the water, and Pink Pants stared at his drink.

"Well," Sam said, rising and taking my empty beer bottle. "I always thought you were adorable. You're a lucky man, Joe." He gave me a grin, and I smiled gratefully back at him.

"I sure am," Joe said, kissing my hand. Trish's eyes narrowed, I noted with satisfaction. I didn't have to be jealous of Trish's high-school success when I had the two nicest guys around defending my honor.

"Avery, it's time for us to go," Trish announced, unfolding herself from the chair. "Sam, we'll be back tomorrow to take Danny to brunch. And if he wants to come back with us to New Jersey for a visit, please don't discourage him. Bye, Millie. Happy birthday."

CHAPTER TWENTY-ONE

THE SUMMER UNCURLED and stretched like a sated, sleepy cat. Day after day, the sky glowed blue, the air was clear and dry. We didn't get much rain, and every passing vehicle stirred eddies of dust along the roads. By the end of July, the leaves were grayish green, the ocean a balmy sixty-two degrees, and Joe and I were a couple. An official couple. We got together three or four times a week, and every time I saw that incredible face smiling at me, I shook myself mentally. It was real. I had done it.

Curtis and Mitch came down from Provincetown and gave him their four-star approval rating. They flirted mercilessly with him, but Joe didn't seem to mind. But when I called Curtis and Mitch later to get the inside skinny, they didn't say much other than to wax poetic about Joe's beauty, leaving me with a slightly empty feeling in the pit of my stomach.

Another night, we went to my parents' house for dinner. They knew Joe, of course, and Joe and my dad had even played poker a few times, so it wasn't as uncomfortable as most of those "meet my parents" situations. Joe happily wolfed down three helpings of ham and scalloped potato dinner, much to Mom's delight. He and Dad talked about potholes and traffic.

"Nearly got sideswiped by a goddamn minivan yesterday in Ben & Jerry's parking lot," my dad said through a mouthful of green beans.

"What were you doing at Ben & Jerry's?" my mom asked suspiciously.

"Say, Joe," my dad said, pretending not to hear Mom. "They're taking bids on the library renovation. Gonna put one in?"

"Oh, yeah, thanks, Mr. Barnes, I did hear about it." I smiled at my guy for his good manners. "But no, I'm not bidding on that one."

"Why not?" my dad asked.

"Well, I'm pretty busy as it is," Joe said. "Plus I'm working on my own place."

"Which I've never seen," I murmured.

"You will, you will," Joe smiled. "But anyway, the library project is kind of a bi—I mean, you've got that whole board to answer to, and there's a ton of paperwork you've got to fill out, cost estimates and schedules and stuff, so I just figured I'd pass. This ham is great, Mrs. Barnes."

"Call me Nancy," my mom sighed dreamily.

"Still, Joe, it's indoor work over the winter," my dad went on. "Guaranteed money, too, working for the town. Seems silly to pass up the chance."

"I guess so," Joe said mildly, winking at my mom. She sighed again.

I didn't want to gang up on Joe, but Dad had a point. Carpentry was seasonal work on the Cape, and it did seem that Joe was a little remiss in not bidding for the library job. Still, maybe he had other projects lined up.

As Mom and I cleared the dishes, the guys went out in the yard to admire the new pile of topsoil Dad had ordered.

"So, Mom," I said as we loaded the dishwasher. "What do you think?"

"About Joe? Not those wineglasses, honey. Those are hand-washables. Millie, he's just darling." She smiled warmly at me.

"Isn't he?"

"Absolutely. And he always was such a friendly boy." She removed a copper-bottomed pot I had recklessly put into the dishwasher and shook a little powdered cleanser into it. "You'll lose the pretty copper shine if you let the dishwasher do all the work," she said.

"I see."

"So, Millie, honey, *are* things serious with you two?" She scoured vigorously.

"Well…we are seeing a lot of each other."

"Mmm hmm."

"And we get along just great."

"Do you, honey? Wonderful, because that's what's important. Once the newness wears off, you need to be able to talk to each other."

"Are you and Dad that way?" I asked.

"Oh, yes," she said, flashing me a quick smile. "We have plenty to say to each other. And we still have a lot of fun together."

I started to put a wooden spoon into the dishwasher, but Mom tut-tutted at me. "Nothing wooden, hon. Especially not those wood-handled knives."

"Right." I wondered why they had the damn appliance at all.

"Millie…" There was that cautionary Mom voice.

"Yes, Mom?"

"Well, honey, I hate to say anything, but, well…"

"What is it, Mom?"

"It's just…well, Joe is a sweet boy and all…but I have to wonder if he's really…enough for you."

I was torn between love and irritation. "Oh, Mom. Joe is great! Don't you think every parent wonders if a guy is good enough for their little girl?"

"No, not always. We always thought Trish was pretty damn lucky to get Sam."

The pot I was wiping slipped out of my hands and bounced on the floor. I looked at my mom sharply, but she was scouring the sink, oblivious to my shock. "Well, there was that little matter of Danny," I said, retrieving the gleaming pot.

"Yes, of course, but still…that's not really the point. We're talking about you and Joe."

"He's a good guy, Mom."

"I know, sweetie. But is he good enough for *you?*"

I didn't really know what to say. Mom wondering if a man, any man, was good enough for me…I'd have thought she'd have been planning my wedding by now. But it was sweet, kind of.

Dad had his turn next. Joe and Mom cleared the coffee cups and dessert plates (strawberry-rhubarb crumble, which I'd had to fake eat, because I had gained back three pounds since dating Joe and didn't want to start the downward spiral into fatness again). From the patio, my dad and I could hear Mom and Joe laughing in the kitchen.

"So, baby, does he treat you okay?" Dad and I were sitting next to each other, and he picked up my hand.

"Sure, Dad. He's great." I smiled in the semidarkness and squeezed his big hand.

"Anything you want to tell your old man?"

"Um, like what, Daddy?" Like, *I'm not a virgin?* Like, *It's still not great but it's getting better?*

"Oh, I don't know, punkin. Are you happy?"

"Sure, Daddy." I squeezed his hand again to reassure him.

"You sure?"

"Yes, Dad. Why?"

"Oh, I don't know. If Joe's good to you, then that's all I can ask, right?"

Why were my parents so…unthrilled? Joe was charming, gorgeous, polite, good-natured and had a blue-collar job. What more could they want?

Their lack of enthusiasm stuck in my mind. Was there anything wrong with Joe that I didn't know about? No, of course not. I had a master's degree in Joe. And maybe it was just natural to wonder about things as the first blush of our relationship wore off.

ONE SATURDAY, JOE AND I went fishing together. We drove up to P-town at the absolute crack of dawn to borrow his friend Sal's boat. Of course I'd had to get up while it was still dark to beautify before Joe pulled into my driveway. On the ride up, I slumped against the truck window, staring out at the fog as Joe whistled softly, his three-legged dog curled between us. We parked on Macmillan Wharf, grabbed a cup of coffee from a nearby shop and walked down to Sal's little power boat. Trying not to spill my precious coffee, I gingerly climbed onboard, failing to notice the dampness of the seats until it was seeping into my shorts. Tripod leaped in beside me, nuzzling my arm so that coffee sloshed out of my cup and into the bottom of the boat.

"Naughty puppy," I said, stroking his head as Joe started the motor.

"You ready?" he said, smiling at me. I smiled back. He really was so delectable. The Cape Cod Tourism Council should feature him in their ads. He adeptly steered us out of

Provincetown Harbor into the choppy bay. I turned and watched the picturesque, weather-beaten buildings of P-town's shoreline grow smaller.

We didn't talk as the boat zipped around Race Point and into deeper waters. Sal's boat didn't have much in the way of navigational equipment, or so it seemed to my anxious gaze. How would we find our way back? Just do a one-eighty? Like a lot of Cape Codders, I rarely went out to sea. That was for fishermen and tourists, not something that ever crossed my mind to do.

As the boat skipped across the choppy waves, I began to know why. If I fell overboard, would I be able to swim to shore? How cold was the water? Were there sharks underneath us? What about giant squid? As we crossed the wake of a bigger vessel, popping over the swells, my stomach rolled, and I clutched the seat.

"Isn't this the best?" Joe called, the wind whipping his hair around his face.

"You bet!" I chirped, clenching my jaw against the bile that surged upward. *Look at the horizon,* I instructed myself. My stomach lurched again, making me grateful I hadn't eaten breakfast. I breathed through my mouth and looked around the boat for flotation devices.

After about an hour, we stopped, and Joe scrabbled about. "Ready to fish?" he asked.

"Oh," I murmured, envisioning the effect of bait on my unsettled stomach. "Hey, let's just sit for a minute and look around." The boat rocked vigorously. Was this really safe? Normal? Tripod and Joe did not appear worried. Joe came over and wrapped his strong arms around me. He felt solid and warm and safe, and my seasickness released its grip somewhat.

"Lie down, Tripod," Joe commanded, and his dog obeyed

instantly. "You okay?" Joe asked me, kissing my hair. I smiled.

"I'm great."

The only sounds were the wind and the waves slapping at the sides of the boat. "You know what?" Joe asked.

"What?"

"This is the longest I ever dated anybody."

"Really?" I answered, remembering to sound surprised.

"It's the truth." He kissed my neck, and my heart swelled. I couldn't be wrong about Joe. We would be perfect together soon enough. Soon, that hidden, heroic side of Joe would emerge once more, and I'd know that I had been right all those years. Pretty soon he'd be saying the L word, buying a ring, and we would be perfectly happy together.

"What about you, Millie? Ever been serious with anybody?"

"Well…" I pretended to muse. The truth of my dating history would never pass my lips, not in front of Joe Carpenter, at any rate. "No, I guess not really serious. Being in medical school and residency and all that…"

"Right." He didn't say any else about our relationship, and I decided not to push for more tender words. We were quiet for another minute, as Joe seemed to have exhausted his curiosity about my love life, and then I asked a question my stalking had been unable to answer.

"Joe, how did Tripod lose his leg?" At the mention of his name, Tripod wagged his tail vigorously.

"Oh, that." Joe stood up and started rummaging in one of the coolers. "Well," he smiled sheepishly, "I hit him."

"What?"

"Yeah, I know. It was pretty bad. He was a stray, roaming around, eating trash and all that. I was driving home, and I guess I wasn't paying attention, had a couple of beers and all, and I just…hit him. Took him to the vet and felt so guilty that I adopted him." Another sheepish grin.

"Joe! You can't drink and drive! You could kill someone."

"I know," he said, then he began baiting the hook with a small fish. I tasted bile and looked away.

"That's how Sam's parents were killed, you know," I said harshly. The memory of Sam, bent in grief at his parents' funeral, punched me in the heart. I had cried myself sick that weekend, and I'd barely known them.

"Really?" Joe's eyebrows raised.

"Yes! Don't you remember? We were in high school, and Sam had just come back from Notre Dame…. It was on the news and everything, Joe. Half the town went to their funeral."

Joe obviously didn't remember. Still, he nodded. "That sucks," he said.

"It more than sucks, Joe!" I snapped.

"Okay, okay, Millie. You can relax, okay?" He grinned, and I looked away. "Millie," he continued in a more serious voice, "don't worry. I learned my lesson. Okay? Forgive me?"

Let it go, Millie. Don't ruin this day. It was a long time ago, anyway. I took a deep breath and looked at the endless blue sea. "Just don't ever do it again, okay?"

"Of course not. Like I said, I learned my lesson." He squeezed my hand, and my anxiety melted a little. I managed to smile at him, and he kissed the tip of my nose. "Here you go," Joe said. He cast into the water and spun out the line, then handed me the pole.

We didn't say anything else for a long time, just watched the water, the breeze ruffling our hair, the waves slapping the side of the boat.

"I can't think of a better way to spend the day," Joe said.

"Being out on the water with my honey." He turned and gave me the full power of his green eyes and gorgeous smile, and whatever concern was in my heart melted. *Honey*. He called me *honey*. I was Joe's honey. Even if he had done stupid things in the past, he called me *honey*.

For the next hour or so, I commanded myself to have fun, to enjoy this lovely day with Joe. Unfortunately, I was undeniably seasick, and of course, I'd forgotten sunscreen. Though it had been cloudy when we'd started out, it was sunny on the water. Joe didn't have sunscreen (it would be so unmanly!), but he found a foul-smelling Red Sox cap, which I dubiously donned, hoping I looked gamine but fearing otherwise.

We trolled around aimlessly, catching nothing. I had only been fishing a handful of times with my dad and had no interest in actually reeling in a cold, flopping creature. Occasionally Joe would check to see if the bait was still attached, then toss the lines back into the frothy wake, where they were carried out to the mysterious depths. I tried not to stand because each time I did, I staggered drunkenly, nearly falling on my backside.

"Joe, how deep is the water out here?"

"Oh, hell, I don't know."

"What if we fell overboard?" I asked. "Are there any life vests?"

"We're not going to fall in, silly Millie," he said, playfully pulling the brim of my cap down over my face. "Even if you did, I'd jump in and save you."

"Thank you, kind sir. But where *are* the life vests?"

"Oh, they're here somewhere. Maybe under those seats." He suddenly looked up ahead at the horizon, then leaped to kill our motor.

"What is it? A tidal wave?" I asked, going to stand next to him, grabbing the waistband of his jeans for safety.

"Shh."

Tripod began to growl. "Shit, Joe," I whispered. "What is it?"

The answer revealed itself as a plume of water exploded into the air. I let out a scream and held onto Joe for dear life.

Not fifty feet from our boat, a whale surfaced. We glimpsed its huge, glistening, barnacled back and massive tail as it dove again. To our left, another whale crested with a spray of water and air. Tripod barked excitedly, the fur on his back standing on end as he hopped onto the seat.

"Let's get out of here!" I yelled, tugging at Joe's shirt. "Come on!"

"Millie, settle down! Look! It's great!" There was a great splash of water just in front of us as one of the whales slapped its tail. We were so close that droplets of water tickled our faces.

"Joe, they're going to tip us over! Please!" Tears of panic pricked my eyes.

"They're not going to capsize us. Just watch." Joe laughed at the display, ignoring my distress. Barking, Tripod jumped onto the bow of the boat.

"Joe, Tripod's going to fall in! Get him! Tripod!"

"Get off, Tripod. And Millie, calm down." Tripod obeyed. I didn't.

We were surrounded by whales, how many I had no clue. Every time I saw a spout of water or heard that whoosh of air, I thought of Moby Dick ramming the *Pequod*. Damn my English professor for making me read that book! We were in the middle of the freaking Atlantic Ocean, and I didn't even have a life vest on! Huge mammals surrounded us, any one of whom could easily overturn our stupid little boat. Tripod would drown. I would drown. Joe would undoubtedly be rescued by mermaids seduced by his beauty.

When a whale actually breached into the air and slapped down, rocking our boat with its power, I began to cry.

"Oh, hey, come on, Millie," Joe said. "We're safe. Don't cry."

"Joe," I sobbed, shaking, "I really want to go home."

"Oh. All right. Okay, we'll go."

Finally, he started up the motor, and with a last regretful glance at the whale pod, he turned the boat around. "Too bad," he couldn't help saying.

Shaking, I sat down and clutched the seat, still crying. Damn Joe! Couldn't he see that I was terrified? Why did he have to wait until they were practically jumping on top of us to leave?

"You okay?" he called, glancing back at me as he steered us.

Go screw yourself, I thought, wiping my eyes with my arm. He did something at the controls, then came back to sit next to me.

"Aw, Millie, don't cry. Come on. Wasn't that great?"

"No, Joe, it wasn't! That was terrifying!"

"They weren't going to hurt us."

"How do you know? Are you a marine biologist? A cetacean expert? We're just in this tiny little boat…"

"Okay, Millie, calm down. It's all right. The big bad whales are way behind us now."

"Oh, screw you," I said, giving him a halfhearted shove. He smiled back. "You're an ass," I added.

"You're cute when you're mad," he said.

"I'm also seasick."

"Very cute."

"Not when I'm puking."

"I guess I'll have to wait and see."

Oh, damn. That smile could end wars.

"I'm sorry," he said, tucking some hair behind my ears.

"Hmmf," I said, pouting.

"I'll take you to my house when we get home," he cajoled. "I know you've been wanting to see it. I'll even cook you dinner. Okay? Don't be mad anymore, Millie."

How could I resist? I couldn't.

BACK ON LAND, I STARTED to feel better. We drove down Route 6, not talking much. I wanted to stop home and shower, feeling sweaty and salty, but curiosity about Joe's house outweighed my need for cleanliness. Digger would be fine, as I'd asked Danny to swing by and let him out for me.

We trundled down Joe's washed-out little lane, locust and bayberry branches scraping along the sides of the truck. At last we pulled into Joe's sandy driveway. As soon as we stopped, Tripod jumped neatly out Joe's window and disappeared into the yard. Joe turned to me, fiddling with his keys.

"Millie, I know you didn't exactly love it out there on the water, but I had a great time with you today. You were a really good sport."

I melted. Warmth began at my toes and flowed upward, suffusing me with love. "Oh, Joe, I had a good time, too. Being with you, I mean."

"Good." He slid across the seat and kissed me, long and slow and hot. The boy could definitely kiss. On trembling legs, I got out of the truck.

Of course, I'd seen Joe's house from the outside, but I had to pretend I hadn't. I exclaimed over the funky shape of the house—not quite a Cape, not a ranch, not a farmhouse—as I followed Joe up the path to the back door.

"Now I wasn't exactly expecting you, so it might be a little messy," he warned me. "But I'm glad you're here." Another kiss. His hands wandered down my back, and more heat threaded through me. I had a feeling that our sex life was about to go from mediocre to unbelievable in about half an hour, and it would be about time.

He opened the door and let me in. The blood drained from my face.

Might be a little messy. A little messy. The words echoed in my head.

The large room I surveyed was under construction. Most of it was framed out, but not in a new, expectant way. In a way that said, "A few years ago, somebody started doing this to me, but I don't know what happened." The wooden studs were grayish-brown, not the creamy-blond of new lumber. Pink insulation sagged wearily between them, defeated. The floor, at least the part that could be seen, consisted of warped sheets of old plywood. A stained, bluish-gray square of carpeting, edges curling and frayed, covered the living-room area. From a liver-colored couch with a tear in the back drifted a very unpleasant damp, moldy smell. I forced myself to close my gaping mouth.

"I still have a lot of work to do," Joe explained, tossing his keys on a…table? No, a giant wooden spool, the kind that holds cable or wire, a big, rough thing lurking before the couch. It was covered with two pizza boxes, a couple of beer bottles and old newspapers. Oblivious to my horror, Joe wandered into the kitchen, a crude area containing a fridge, stove covered in dirty pots, and a huge black plastic trash barrel filled to the brim. Two sawhorses supported another sheet of plywood. The kitchen table, I presumed. It was covered with a half-dozen cereal boxes and some cans, as Joe apparently had no cupboards. A bare lightbulb swayed from a thick wire in the middle of the room. Perched precariously on a stack of crumbling Sheetrock sat an enormous, early-model microwave.

"I don't have too much time to work on it, but it's getting there. Little by little. You want a beer or anything?"

"Oh…uh, no, I'm okay." Dazed, I tried to take it all in. Through a partially opened door, I glimpsed Joe's bedroom: a mattress on the floor, a tangle of sheets and blankets wadded at the bottom, clothes scattered on the floor. Underwear. Socks. Paint-smeared jeans.

There was a metallic clatter, and pain shot through my foot—I had stubbed my toe on a toolbox lying in the middle of the floor.

"So what are you in the mood for?" Joe asked blithely. "Whoops, before you answer that, let me see what I have." He opened the fridge and I smothered a scream. Mold-covered, graying Chinese food boxes. An orange, so old it was no longer round, had sunken in on its own weight. A few grease-stained paper bags held God-knew-what.

"Some of this stuff doesn't look too good," Joe murmured, tossing the Chinese food cartons into the huge trash can. I leaped out of the way. My bladder ached after all day on the boat, but I would kill myself before going into his bathroom.

"Do you live alone, Joe?" I squeaked, wondering if there was someone else to blame for this horror.

"Oh, sure. This is my mom's house, really, but she moved off Cape when she got remarried a couple years ago, so it's just me." He closed the fridge and put his arms around me. "So, okay, it's messy, but what do you think?"

Disgusting. Repellant. Abhorrent. Unhealthful. "Oh, well, I think it's got potential." I swallowed and forced a smile.

"That's just it, isn't it? It's got potential! One of these days I'll finish it up. But right now, you know what I'd really like to do?"

"Move?"

He threw back his golden head and laughed. "No, not move. Be with my Millie." He kissed me, and I was too numb with shock to resist or respond. Taking my hand, he started to lead me to the bedroom. I planted my heels like a mule and stopped. There was no way on earth I was going to lie down in this house.

"You know what?" I said, scrabbling for a distraction. "Um, I—I'd like to see the back. Is that a deck out there?"

"Yup. Sure, let's go outside."

Bravo, Millie. At least the smell wasn't so pervasive out on the deck. I sucked in the pine-scented air and looked around. Joe's scrubby little yard was enclosed by bayberry, cedars and dwarfed oak trees. I stared down at that yard as if it were a lifeboat and I was standing on the deck of the *Titanic*.

"So, Millie," Joe whispered, kissing me on the neck from behind. "Seen enough? Want to go back inside?"

"No!" I whirled around. "I mean, um, let's go down into the yard. It's cute." Looking a little confused, Joe nonetheless followed me down the rickety stairs. *Just tell him that you don't feel like fooling around. Tell him you want to go home and shower. Tell him his house is disgusting.* But somehow, I couldn't bring myself to say any of those things.

In the deepening evening, in the relative privacy of the yard, we could hear the sounds of his neighbors, but we really couldn't see anything. And nobody could see us.

"Let's go to bed, honey," my honey said, wrapping his arms around me. He gave me another world-class kiss, one that I would have enjoyed greatly had I not been so focused on my escape.

"Joe," I murmured against his mouth.

"Hmm?"

"I've never, you know…" He was kissing my neck.

"Never what?"

"I've never made love outside."

He pulled back to look at me, a grin crossing his face. "We can fix that."

Just fix it fast, I thought. I wanted desperately to be in my own house, in my immaculate bathroom, showering off the salt and whale spit.

Joe's hands slipped under my shirt and neatly removed it. Amazingly, as much as his hands knew what they were doing, as beautiful as he was, as long as I had wanted him, I found myself faking it. A few minutes later, we were lying on a small patch of grass under a cedar, and all I could think was *hurry up.* Finally, he moaned into my neck and sagged against me, rolling over so I was snuggled against his side. *Okay, let's go home,* I thought.

"God, Millie, that was fantastic," Joe murmured.

"Mmm." Wondering how much longer it would be till he took me home, I stroked his silky hair for a minute, then turned my head. I shrieked, unbelieving. Joe jumped.

"What? What?"

"Jesus, Joe!" I shrilled, leaping to my feet and grabbing my shirt against me. "Shit!"

Clearly evident in our post-coital resting place was an unmistakably healthy crop of poison ivy.

CHAPTER TWENTY-TWO

THE NEXT DAY, ITCHY, STINGING, prickling, burning welts covered my back, arms, neck and half of my ass. Mercifully, my female parts were spared, and so were my legs. My face, however, swelled red, tight and aching, a victim of sunburn on the boat. The rest of it was Cape Cod's national flower, poison ivy.

Joe had driven me home, sheepishly apologetic. Even in my distress, I hadn't wanted to wash off at his filthy house. I was furious—not just at him, but at both of us. But yes, at him. It was his yard, after all. Granted, I could've paid more attention, but my focus had been on escaping the grime of his house. He should have seen where he was rolling me, right? It was...thoughtless. *He was just caught up in the moment,* I argued with myself. *Isn't that a good thing?*

"I'm sorry, Mil," he'd said, pulling into my driveway. "I'm immune to poison ivy, so I guess I just don't notice it."

Of course he was immune. I was not, I soon discovered. Despite a long, hot shower, the welts came home to roost on Saturday night. For the first time in my life, I'd been stupid enough to get poison ivy.

There was no way I could go to work. On Sunday morning, I phoned Juanita, who kindly arranged for coverage at the clinic for Monday. Then I called myself in a prescription of prednisone, which my mom picked up for me, as I was loath to show my face in public. Joe called me and I lied, telling him I think I got lucky and didn't get anything. He crooned about our day together, and while I was glad that he was happy, I also felt a little irritated. After all, I'd been seasick, terrified, horrified, disgusted, itchy. Not my best day.

At least it was Sunday and I could hide here at home. I gazed at my reflection in the mirror. Did my face look more like an enormous slice of salami or a blotchy Marlon Brando? Brando won. I was very *Island of Dr. Moreau*. I couldn't sit, as my entire back was tender, itchy and sore all at once. I could lie on my stomach, but if I tried to read or watch TV, my neck started to ache. I vacuumed my house and washed the floors, wanting more than ever to be in a nice, clean environment after visiting Joe yesterday.

In a Benadryl fog, I soaked in an oatmeal soap bath, and it was as disgusting as it sounds. Now I was *slimy*, itchy and welt-covered. The steroids would take a day or two to work, and by Sunday evening, I'd only had four doses. I changed into a roomy old Notre Dame T-shirt that Sam had sent me a thousand years ago and some scrub bottoms. Digger was very sympathetic, wagging gently and looking at me with his sweet brown eyes. It was one of those times when animals prove vastly superior to humans. I stroked his pretty head and gazed back.

"Good puppy," I said, grateful for his presence.

The itching began in full strength. Little razor-sharp flashes of hurt, followed by almost psychotic itching, raced up and down my back and arms. Thank God my nether regions were unaffected, or I truly would have been suicidal. I rubbed my arms gently, then a little harder. *Oooh*. The itch flashed into a blaze of heat. "Distract yourself," I said, pacing around my small home. Flash! Youch! *Don't scratch*. "Don't scratch," I repeated out loud, reciting the instructions I gave at least twice daily at the clinic. "Scratching will inflame the area and just make it feel worse."

Standing between the dining room and kitchen, I leaned against the door frame. I rubbed—gently, gently—back and forth. The flames of itch leaped in exhilaration. Oh, man, that felt good! Just one scratch to make the itching go away. The skin on my back sang in searing joy. I stopped, satisfied for two entire seconds, and then my entire torso crawled in a wave of fresh, stronger itchiness. Oh, screw it. Don't scratch, be damned. This was agony.

I stomped into the kitchen and yanked open a drawer. Knife? No, too sharp. Didn't want to draw blood. Spatula? No. Whisk? Ineffective. Aha! Pasta fork! A plastic pasta fork, with those lovely little prongs for grabbing spaghetti. Blessed utensil! I grabbed it and slammed the drawer shut, then reached back and went to work. *Ooooh. Aaahhh. Oh, Mommy.* I scratched maniacally, the razor flashes subdued by the hurt-so-good reaming. Leaning my hot, blotchy, swollen face against the coolness of the fridge, I raked my back in a delirium of Benadryl to near orgasmic satisfaction.

So deeply satisfying was this activity that I didn't notice the noise of a truck pulling into my driveway. Luckily, my dog did and began his frenzied barking. Jumping away from the fridge, I dashed to the window to peek out.

Shit! It was Joe! He got out of his truck with a bouquet of flowers and headed for my door.

It was still bright enough outside that I hadn't turned on the lights. *Pretend you're not home!* Before my mind had even formulated that thought, I was crouched on my living-room floor in front of the wing chair. Joe knocked. Digger's barking became joyful as he jumped up on the back door.

"Millie?" Joe's voice came to me easily through the open windows.

Please, God, let the door be locked. My car was in the driveway, so he obviously assumed (correctly) that I was home.

"Mil?" Joe knocked again. "Digger, where's Millie?"

Digger didn't answer but began to whine and tremble. My legs, too, began to tremble as I squatted. I eased into the kneeling position. My back, now thoroughly ravaged, convulsed in a massive itch-pain, and I couldn't help a little gasp.

"Millie? You home?"

Go away! But no. Joe's work boots thumped on the back deck as he went to peer in the kitchen window. I inched around the chair slightly, trying to keep it between us. If Joe saw me like this—

He left. I waited to hear his truck door open and close, but I wasn't that lucky. Couldn't the guy take a hint? I crawled frantically into the dining room to sneak a peak out the window. He was walking around to the front door, causing Digger to have a brand-new fit. Lurking in the safety of the dining room, I pressed my throbbing back against the wall like a POW escaping from an enemy camp, waiting for the searchlight to pass over.

"Millie?"

Go home! My arms, jealous of the attention my back had received, cried out for the pasta fork. I rubbed them gingerly. Thump, thump, thump went the work boots. Joe, not easily deterred, was coming to the kitchen door again! Damn it! I power-crawled back into the living room and crouched again in front of my chair. Digger, now tired of barking at Joe, thought I was playing a game. Wagging, his ears pricked, he trotted over and licked my inflamed face vigorously.

"No," I whispered. The hall carpet called to me seductively, inviting me to take off my shirt and writhe around on its scratchy nubbiness. Digger barked once.

"Guess she's not home, hey, Digger?" Joe said. There was a rustle, then, finally, blessedly, his footsteps sounded off the deck. His truck started a minute later, and he was gone.

"Thank God!" I exclaimed, clambering up from the floor. Now, what had I done with that lovely pasta fork?

Not a minute later, I heard the truck pull into the driveway. "Jesus! What is *wrong* with him?" I hissed over Digger's barking. I catapulted into the bathroom before Joe could reach the back door. The window in there was frosted, so I would be safe. It was also getting darker, so that was in my favor, too.

"Millie?"

Not Joe! Sam! I didn't have to hide from Sam. I walked into the kitchen. Sam stood in the doorway, holding a bag.

"Hey, Millie. I stopped by the clinic and they said you were sick."

"Look at me!" I flicked on the light and Sam's eyes widened.

"Oh, Millie…Oh, Mil."

"It's poison ivy."

He did *try* not to laugh, for a minute, anyway. And then he couldn't help himself. His laughs progressed to wheezes, and he leaned in the doorway, helpless, tears running down his face. As I stood there watching him, finally the humor of my situation hit me, and I joined in.

"I hope you're here to scratch me," I said finally, wiping my eyes.

"Uh, no," he answered. "But I did bring you some ice cream. And a movie."

Ben & Jerry's Coffee Heath Bar Crunch, my favorite. And a nice romantic comedy. Sweet Sam.

"There are flowers on your porch, you know," Sam said, sticking the ice cream in the freezer.

"Right. Would you grab them?" I asked, retrieving the Ben & Jerry's and prying off the lid. Sam picked up the flowers. I watched, shoveling in cool, deep, dark deliciousness right from the carton, as he put them in a vase.

"Want some ice cream?" I asked around a spoonful.

"No, it's all for you. What I want is to know how you, of all people, got poison ivy."

"The gods are punishing me for making fun of the tourists all summer," I answered, sitting gingerly at the counter. "Mmm. This ice cream is so good, I might bathe in it."

"So, how did you get the poison ivy?" Sam helped himself to a beer and sat down with me.

"Oh, I really couldn't tell you."

"Come on, kiddo."

"Nope."

"Please?"

"Never."

"Well, then," Sam said, grinning, "I'll have to use my police training and guess. Someone brought you flowers, and I'm guessing it was Joe. An apology, perhaps? You. Joe. Poison ivy. I'd have to guess you were fooling around outside. Millie, Millie." He shook his head regretfully.

"You're wrong," I said through another mouthful of ice cream. "The flowers are from the grateful parents of a lost child I rescued today, who, unfortunately, was wandering in poison ivy. The police were involved in urgent business at the Donut Shack, so I had to do their work."

"You wish, kiddo. Next time, watch where you're rolling."

CHAPTER TWENTY-THREE

TRUE TO MY PROMISE to Danny, I went to a baseball game.

The poison ivy had cleared up, just a couple of pale patches not readily visible to the naked eye. On a beautiful sunny evening, Katie, the boys and I went over to the high school to watch the big boys play. We sat on the bleachers while Corey and Mike played in the sand underneath, where Tripod was lying per Joe's instruction. The dog was incredibly well-behaved, wagging agreeably if approached, waiting patiently for his master. Maybe Joe could give me some tips on how to get Digger to stop humping legs.

Despite having a dad who could name every player in every sport and a brother-in-law who had been as close to an athlete god as they come, I didn't really enjoy sports. Too much of a good thing, I guess, since all my memories of childhood weekends involved some sporting event, on TV or live. But with Danny involved, I was excited. And of course, there was my boyfriend, looking rather magnificent in his Bluebeard's Bait and Tackle uniform.

Joe and Danny were on the same team, Joe the pitcher, Danny the shortstop. Very prestigious positions, Katie informed me. Her twin brother, Trevor, was on the same team, in right field, so it was clear where our allegiance lay. Poor Sam. He played first base for the opposing team, Sleet's

Hardware. But my parents were here, so they could cheer for him. Not that they would, with their only grandchild playing for Bluebeard's...

Katie and I chatted, not really paying attention that much, clapping when other people clapped. It was a beautiful night, a breeze just strong enough to keep the bugs away (that and the Deep Woods OFF! we had liberally bathed in). Watching Joe pitch was lovely, however. Apparently, I wasn't the only one who felt that way, for an appreciative murmur went up each time he wound up. There were plenty of high-school girls here, some to watch Danny, who had recently and suddenly gone from awkwardly cute to damn good-looking. Plenty of summer people wandered into the field to enjoy this most American of pastimes.

The game was pretty dull, and not just by my standards. Only one or two players made it to base. Sam hit a fly ball his first time up, caught by Katie's brother. Danny struck out on his first time up, and Joe made it to first but no farther. The fun part was watching the easy grace of the men, throwing, catching, leaning on their knees. Danny looked so...adult out there. He adeptly fielded the balls that came his way and was rewarded with a good bit of applause and appreciative bellowing from my dad.

With two men on in the fourth inning, Sam stepped up to the plate.

"Easy out, easy out," called a woman in the first row. It was Carol, Sam's date from my birthday party. Sam heard her and turned around to grin. He tapped his cleats with his bat and took a practice swing. On the pitcher's mound, Joe squinted at the catcher.

"Carol!" I called. "Come sit with us!"

She turned and shielded her eyes and waved. "Oh, hi, Millie! I'm with my neighbors, but thanks," she answered.

"Oh, okay," I said. "We're going to the Barnacle later. Can you come?"

"Sure. That would be nice."

"Hey, batter, batter," someone else called. "Three pitches, Joe." It was my dad.

Joe grinned and waved the infield in a few steps. Sam laughed easily—ever the good sport—and stepped up to the plate. Joe threw the pitch. Strike one.

"Two more, Joe," called Carol, laughing. Sam smiled again.

"You got the stuff, Joe," a woman called. Might have been my mom.

Another pitch. Sam swung and missed. The crowd clapped, a few feminine voices calling more support for my boyfriend. Poor old Sam! I stood up. "Come on, Sam!" I yelled. "Knock it out of the park!"

Katie and a few other people laughed, and Joe looked at me in surprise. Well, too bad. His fan club was big enough. I gave him a cheeky smile. He grinned back and wound up for the next pitch. Ball one.

"Good eye, good eye, Sam!" I yelled, still standing and clapping.

Katie stood up, too. "Take your time, Sam."

Sam tipped his helmet to us. "Thank you, ladies," he called. Joe wound up again and threw, high and outside. Ball two.

"Got him on the ropes now, buddy!" I yelled.

On the mound, Joe motioned for a time-out. He loped off the field toward us and climbed right up onto the bleachers where I was standing. "You're *my* girlfriend," he said, planting a big kiss on my mouth. "You're supposed to be cheering for me." With that, he turned around and trotted back to the mound as the crowd laughed.

"Come on, Sam!" I called again, undeterred. Joe shook his head, smiling, and Sam waved again.

The wind-up. The pitch. Crack! The ball flew high into the air and over the left fielder, who bounded after it. As Sam raced for first, his helmet flew off. The other runners on base scored, and Sam slid into second. Joe cocked an eyebrow at me, his hands on his hips. I blew him a kiss.

By the bottom of the ninth, the score remained 2–0, Sam's team. Joe came up to bat and made it to first, and I applauded enthusiastically, if a bit automatically. After all, I didn't really care who won as long as Danny held his own. Besides, Corey and Mike were getting tired. Sal DiStefano also got on base. So did Katie's brother. Bases loaded. Danny came up to bat, and my heart leaped into my throat.

The winning run was on first. Joe on third. Two outs. My seventeen-year-old nephew was at bat.

A tense silence fell over the crowd. No more catcalls, no more joking. My heart began to thud. Katie pointed out Danny to the boys, and even they seemed to sense the gravity of the situation.

Danny took a practice swing and stepped up to the plate. The Sleet's Hardware pitcher squinted ominously, nodded, and then wound up and threw the ball. Danny swung so hard he practically spun around.

"Hee-rike!" called the umpire. An uneasy murmur rippled through the crowd. A couple of high-school girls clutched each other's hands.

My dad stood up. "Take your time, son," he said.

The second pitch. Another huge swing, another miss. Strike two. I swallowed hard. "Come on, baby," I whispered. Katie patted my leg.

Danny stepped out of the batter's box and tapped his cleats. He stretched his arms behind him and stepped back in. His shoulders were tense, his face expressionless. The pitcher shook his head at the catcher's first signal, then nodded. My heart was pounding so hard I felt ill.

The pitch blazed in. Danny swung hard. Bam! The ball sailed into the rich blue sky, up, up, up. By the time it landed, Danny was rounding second and Katie's brother was headed for home, and the outfielder hadn't even gotten close to the ball yet. The crowd was screaming, my parents jumping up and down, the high-school girls shrieking. I stood stock-still, speechless with amazement as I watched Danny run to home plate and his cheering teammates. A grand slam. My nephew had just hit a grand slam.

I looked over at Sam, who was applauding into his glove. He glanced over at the stands, and our eyes locked. Then Danny emerged from the crowd of his teammates and loped over to his dad. Sam shook his hand and then hugged him. My eyes filled.

Joe appeared at my side as I watched father and son in their *Field of Dreams* moment. "Great game, wasn't it, Millie?" he said.

I shook myself mentally. "Oh, it sure was," I replied huskily.

"Are you coming to the Barnacle?" he asked, tucking a strand of hair behind my ears. It was tradition for the winning team to buy the losers drinks.

"I think I'll help Katie put the boys to bed first," I answered. Katie was busy packing up the boys' Matchbox trucks and cars into her bag. "I'll stop by later, okay?"

"Okay," Joe answered, kissing my cheek. "I'll see you there." He gestured to Tripod, who leaped up and followed Joe to the parking lot.

Climbing down the bleachers, I went over to my nephew, who was talking animatedly with my parents.

"Aunt Millie! Wasn't that awesome?"

"Oh, honey, it was fantastic! I was so proud of you, I just about peed my pants!"

The lad hugged me, making me feel very short. He was at least six feet tall now. Sam joined our little circle.

"You going to the Barnacle, Dad?" Danny asked, his eyes still shining.

"You bet," Sam answered. "You owe me a Coke."

"Hal!" my father yelled to our neighbor. "Did you see my grandson hit that ball?"

"Looking like Ortiz there, Danny!" Hal called back. My parents said their goodbyes, and Danny went off to join his teammates.

"I can't believe it," Sam said dreamily. "My son hit a grand slam and won the game."

"That must have been the best moment of your life," I said, giving him a squeeze.

"I think you're right," he answered. "And thanks for cheering for me."

"Oh, you're welcome, big guy! I've always been your biggest fan."

Sam laughed and slung his arm around my shoulders. "Remember how you used to come to my football games? You'd sit there, reading a book the whole time, then tell me what a good job I did."

"I watched!" I protested. "Whenever you had the ball, I looked up." It was true—I'd go to the games (attendance was pretty much required, as my sister was dating him *and* held the coveted position of head cheerleader), but I'd always felt a secret thrill as Sam dodged his way down the field or intercepted a pass.

Sam slapped at a mosquito. "Too bad Trish—" His smile dropped.

I studied his face. "You wish Trish were here?"

He tilted his head. "Yeah, I guess I do. To see her son's big moment."

"Well, you can have Danny call her later on, right? Or even right now, before you get to the Barnacle."

"Good idea, kiddo. Thanks."

"You know, dopey, Carol's waiting for you."

Sam jumped. "Oh, right! God, I almost forgot. Okay, I'll see you later, right?"

"Right-o, matey."

I helped Katie gather the last of the boys' paraphernalia and scooped Mikey up. He buried his sticky little face in my neck, and I kissed his silky hair. "Ready for bed, sleepyhead?" I asked.

"I'm not tired," he yawned, closing his eyes.

As we walked across the field, I glanced over at Sam, who was still talking to Carol. Their laughter floated over to us. Then Sam leaned in and kissed Carol, not a huge kiss, but definitely not just friendly, either. My step faltered.

It was just strange, seeing Sam with somebody other than Trish, I told myself. Carol was nice and all, but it didn't seem…normal. Natural. They began walking toward the parking lot. Sam caught my eye and lifted his hand. Carol turned and waved, too.

I swallowed and continued toward the parking lot.

CHAPTER TWENTY-FOUR

AT THE CLINIC A FEW DAYS LATER, Jill informed me that we had a young woman with a chief complaint of "not feeling well." She'd been waiting for a while, Jill said, and had asked for me specifically.

I glanced at the chart as I went into the exam room. There on the exam table was a rather beautiful young woman, tawny hair, tanned, lovely complexion. I checked the chart again. Jennifer Bianco, age twenty-three. "Hi, I'm Millie Barnes," I said, extending my hand.

"I know who you are," she said coolly.

"Have we met?" I asked.

"Actually, yes. And we have someone in common," she said. "Joe Carpenter."

"Oh. How do you know Joe?" I asked. A feeling of dread unfurled and flapped in my stomach.

"I used to sleep with him." She looked at me steadily.

"Ah." My cheeks began to burn.

"And now you are, aren't you? I saw you at the baseball game the other night."

"Well, Ms. Bianco, I don't mean to be rude, but you're here at the clinic, and I have other patients to see. Do you have a medical problem I can help you with?" My neck felt stiff, my mouth like chalk.

"What if I said I had some disease, like gonorrhea or something? Or what if I said I was pregnant?"

"Do you think you are?" I asked, trying to keep my voice steady.

"No. I'm not, but I could be. Your boyfriend's a slut, you know. And an asshole, too." Her voice was husky. She slipped off the exam table. "I thought you should know." She stood in front of me with her fists on her hips, eyes bright with tears...not exactly angry but pretty damn intimidating.

"Listen, Jennifer, are you sure I can't help you with anything?" I asked.

She sighed and looked away. "No. I'm fine. I don't have anything, Dr. Barnes." Somehow her calling me *Dr. Barnes* made me feel sad, as though I were so much older but still obviously clueless. "I just wanted to tell you that Joe sleeps around," she continued. "He dumped me for no reason that I could see.... One day we were doing it in my grandmother's attic, the next day he wouldn't return my phone calls. When I finally tracked him down, he just acted like we had nothing serious, that it was just for fun." Her voice cracked, and she wiped her eyes with the back of her hand. "But it *was* serious, to me, at least. So be careful."

She stepped around me and opened the door, then turned and looked at me again. "You babysat for me once. When I was sleeping over my grandparents' house. We colored, and you let me have ice cream before bed. I thought you were nice." With that, she left.

Legs wobbling, I sat down on the exam table.

Jennifer Bianco. Her grandmother lived in my parents' neighborhood. I had a vague memory of the night she'd mentioned, and now I remembered something else. Joe had fixed Mrs. Bianco's back porch steps a few months ago. Apparently, while he'd been doing his good deed, he'd been doing Jennifer as well.

I knew I could, if I tried, rationalize this. I could find a way to justify Joe's behavior. I could tell myself how different he was with me, because he *was* different. But somehow I couldn't summon the energy. Seeing Jennifer in the flesh was different from thinking about Joe's many past girlfriends.

When I got home that night, I called Joe and asked him to come over. He happily agreed. I made dinner, a simple pasta dish with vegetables that I had perfected, and we ate on the back deck. We didn't talk much. Was it my imagination, I wondered as I picked at my dinner, or did we never really talk? We held hands, we flirted, we went out, we slept together, but did we talk? Weren't soul mates supposed to talk? It seemed like Digger and I talked more than Joe and I.

"Joe," I began cautiously. "Why do you think we're, um, doing so well together?"

Joe looked at me, surprised. "I don't know. I like you." He grinned. "A lot."

I gave a small smile. "I like you, too, obviously. But, well, you know, you've dated a lot, haven't you? And you told me this was the longest you'd been in a relationship. Why do you think that is?"

Joe took a swig of his beer and looked out at the darkening sky. Digger came over and put his nose on Joe's leg, and Joe scratched his head idly. "I don't know, Millie. I guess I feel like you're different."

"In what way?" I asked.

"Oh, shit, Millie, I'm not really good at talking about stuff like this. Are you mad at me or something?"

I reached for his hand across the table. "No, Joe, I'm not

mad. I've just been thinking about the two of us, that's all. And we don't really talk about stuff like this…."

"Talking can be overrated." He gave me a crooked grin.

"Sometimes, definitely." I smiled back but didn't drop my gaze.

He sighed, then kissed my hand. "Okay, I'll try. I guess I like how you don't chase after me, Millie. I mean, we've known each other forever, but you were always just kind of friendly and normal to me. A lot of girls, you know, they kind of…throw themselves at me. And you didn't. You weren't out to get me, and you didn't go crazy picking out wedding dresses when we started seeing each other. You have a great job and friends and you've got this funky little house and your dog…you just seem, I don't know…happy with yourself. There, how's that?"

"Great," I answered, my heart sinking. Because of course, all of the above was exactly what I wanted him to think. While that *had* been the whole point, I nonetheless felt deceitful. To cover my dismay, I made a kissing noise at Digger, who happily left Joe to nuzzle my crotch. "No, no, Digger. Sit. Good boy."

"Why are *you* with *me?*" Joe asked.

"Huh? Oh, well, lots of reasons." I scratched Digger's tummy, causing my dog to collapse in joy.

"Go ahead." Joe smiled in the semidarkness, his perfect teeth gleaming.

"Well, you're cute, there's no denying that. But you're also, uh, hardworking, and nice. You know, kindhearted. And you're cheerful. I mean, happy. Which is good." That sounded a little feeble, but he laughed a little.

"Yeah, well, you can't take life too seriously, right?" He leaned back in his chair and took another swallow of beer.

Digger curled up in a tight circle beside my chair, resting

his chin on my foot. The silence stretched on, the wind soughing in the leaves of the locust trees. It should have been a lovely moment. "Joe?" I asked. "Do you remember the time our class went to Plymouth Plantation?"

Joe frowned in concentration. "Um…not really."

"Sure, you do. All the people were dressed in period clothes and stuff? The blacksmith, the guy who was Miles Standish?"

"Oh, yeah! That was pretty cool." He paused. "You want to go back or something?"

"No," I said, a little exasperated. "I just— Do you remember on the bus ride home, when I threw up?"

Joe grimaced. "Yuck."

I took a quick breath, then pasted a smile on my face so I wouldn't seem like a nag. "Do you remember, Joe?"

"No, not really."

My smile dropped off my face like a rock. "You don't?"

"Nope. Why?"

"You were so sweet to me. The other kids were laughing and you told them to shut up." My voice took on a whining note.

"Oh. Well, that's good."

I forced myself to close my mouth. *It doesn't mean anything, Millie. Joe does that kind of thing automatically. It doesn't matter if he can't remember.*

But it did matter. That moment was arguably the most important moment of my adolescence. It represented every good quality I ever thought Joe Carpenter had. That moment had sustained me through some awful times, reminded me why other men didn't measure up to Joe Carpenter. And he didn't remember.

I BEGAN TO ANALYZE Joe's every word, action and gesture. We'd been together for more than a month now, and everything was great. Except for my brain. I was driving myself crazy with the analysis, but I couldn't help it.

I loved Joe. I did. Right? Aside from his charm and beauty, though, what did I love? He *did* work hard. And he *was* kind-hearted. Sort of. Except that some of the examples that had previously thrilled my heart were not exactly what I'd thought.

"Katie, what do you think about Joe?" I asked one day when we had brought the boys to Wiley Park. They were splashing about happily at the edge of Great Pond, digging to their hearts' content.

Katie looked at me sharply. "Uh-oh. What happened?"

"Nothing, nothing. It's just…well, why do you think something happened?"

"Because," she said, digging her toes into the coarse sand, "you've never wondered about Joe in the past. Ever."

I sighed. "Well, I can't really go into it, but I ran into someone who used to date Joe, and it made me think."

"Well, hell, Millie, if you swing a cat around here, you're going to hit someone who used to sleep with Joe. You know that, right?" She rummaged around in the cooler and handed me a Snapple.

"Thanks. Yeah, of course I know. It's just…" I shifted in my beach chair.

"What are you worried about, exactly?" Katie asked.

"About…I don't know. Do you think we're good together?"

Katie studied the her sons. "Michael, honey, don't dump sand on your brother's head. Thank you. Listen, Millie," she said, "I think you know enough about Joe to make up your own mind."

"That's it? That's all you've got for me?"

"Yup. Sorry." She smiled apologetically.

"Okay, well, answer me this, then, o mighty sphinx. How do you know if you really love someone?"

"Ooh, great question. I have no idea."

"Katie! Come on. Play with me."

She laughed. "Okay, okay. Not that I've had true love, mind you. I've only had Elliott." She thought for a minute, then said, "Okay. Real love would be when no matter how happy you were at any given moment, it would be better with the person you love. Like having that person there would make it perfect."

"That was good," I said. "'You complete me' and all that."

"Sure." She smiled and scooped up her long blond hair under her Red Sox hat. "And when you're with that person, you're showing your best self. Not faking, just at your best."

My smile faltered. Was I faking with Joe? No, impossible. I loved him. I was my best self. I just wished it wasn't so much effort…. To change the subject, I asked, "Don't you ever want to experience that? Some day in the far distant future, I mean?"

"I feel that way all the time," she answered, pointing to her boys. "The best moments of my life are right there."

"I mean with another grown-up, Katie. As you well know."

She smiled, started to say something, then paused. "Well…if you try fixing me up again, Millie, I *will* kill you." I smiled back. "The answer is maybe," she continued. "Not Sam, okay? He's not for me. But lately, things haven't been so exhausting, you know? And so I suppose that yeah, I would be open to the possibility of someday, someone. Just not right now."

"You and Sam—" I began.

"Millie, were you listening to me? Not Sam! Corey, Mike, you need more sunscreen, guys." The boys hopped up and ran toward us.

"I was just going to say, my sensitive little friend, that you and Sam are alike. You both put your kids first, yourselves second," I said, squeezing some sunscreen onto my palm and slathering some on Corey's back.

"Of course we do. You will, too, once you and Joe hatch one." Katie kissed the boys loudly and they ran back to their excavation.

"So you think Joe and I are good together?" I asked, returning to our original subject.

"Honey, do you?"

"Can't you just answer, Dr. Freud?"

"Only you can do that, pal. Mike, do not put that in your mouth. Do not!"

CHAPTER TWENTY-FIVE

ONE OF OUR ADORABLE TRADITIONS here in August was to have an end-of-summer bash for the high-school juniors and seniors, as well as the Nauset High graduates from the past spring. Lighthouse Day was a day-long carnival held at the school grounds, followed by a semiformal dance that night. It was a way to say goodbye to the kids who'd graduated in June and to usher in the coming academic year for the upperclassmen. The dance rivaled the prom in social import, and Danny and his girlfriend, Sarah, had been talking about it for weeks.

I rode my new bike over to Sam's the Sunday before Lighthouse Day to see how my guys were. I'd spent the morning at the senior center, checking in on Dr. Whitaker's patients, and I could use a little fresh air after being inside for three hours. I cruised easily down the level bike path, savoring the deep blue of the kettle ponds and gulping in the fragrance of bayberry, pine and the sharp scent of the salt marsh. Feeling cheerful and energized, I steered my bike down Sam's road. I hadn't been over since my birthday bash, and his yard, as always, was magnificent, bursting with color and fragrance. Sam was out in the yard, dripping with sweat as he reinforced a retaining wall under a cascade of pink clematis.

"Now that Trish doesn't live here, you can let this all go

to seed, you know," I suggested, sitting on the steps next to him.

"Trish, nothing. This is all my doing. How are you, Millie?"

"Oh, good enough. How about you?"

"Fine and dandy." He wiped his brow and grinned.

"Still seeing that nice Carol?" I asked.

Sam grimaced. "Actually, no. We kind of dropped it."

"Oh, no!" I blurted, torn between sympathy and guilty delight. "What happened?"

"Nothing, really. We just kind of hit a wall of pleasantry and didn't seem to want to go any further."

"Summer lovin', had me a bla-ast," I sang. Sam had been in the chorus of *Grease* in high school...my sister, of course, had been Sandy.

"Summer lovin', happened so fast," he sang back obligingly.

I watched admiringly as Sam wrestled another rock into place. His T-shirt was dark with sweat, his hair sticking up in odd places, and he was tan and smiling.... All in all, not too sad about the breakup with Carol. Neither was I, for that matter. "Maybe Carol just didn't like you," I suggested.

"Watch yourself, doc."

"In fact, she said something to me along those lines. 'Millie,' she said, 'I just don't like Sam. He's such a stiff.'"

Sam laughed and swatted me on the leg. "Well, Joe said something to me. 'Sam,' he said, 'That Millie is a real pain in the ass.'"

"Plus, Carol also said, 'That Sam can't play baseball for shit.'"

"Well, Joe asked me if I had ever seen you running, and if so, what was wrong with you."

"Carol also said, 'That Sam is much too sweaty.'"

"Joe told me…oh, forget it. You win, kiddo." He smiled and grabbed another rock.

"Hey, guys!" my nephew said, leaping down the steps and flopping on the grass. "What's up?"

"The sky is up," I said thoughtfully.

"Gosh, you're funny, Aunt Mil. Hey, I've been meaning to ask you something. We need chaperones for the Lighthouse Dance, and I thought it would be cool if you and Joe came."

"Really?" I asked.

"Sure."

"You flatter me, darling. Of course we'll come. It will be fun."

Sam stopped his macho pursuits and wiped his forehead with his arm. "I didn't know you needed chaperones, Dan. I could do it, too."

Danny winced. "Well, Dad, here's the thing."

"You're just not cool enough," I offered.

"Shut up, Millie, or I'm giving you a big sweaty hug. What's the thing, Danny?"

"You're just not cool enough," Danny answered, grinning. I burst into merry laughter as Sam scowled at me.

"No, really, Dad, you're a cop," Danny explained. "You know, you'll make everybody behave."

"You better behave anyway."

"Oh, of course I will. Please. You know I don't do that sh— stuff. Straight edge all the way. Don't worry about me."

"I will anyway." For a tiny second, Sam looked a little bit sad, but then he picked an errant weed out of his garden and tossed it into the wheelbarrow. *Nice cover,* I thought.

"Aunt Mil will keep an eye on me, right, Millie?"

"Yes, of course I will, Daniel," I answered. "And Sam, just because Joe and I are incredibly cool and you're not doesn't mean—"

"Give us a hug, sweetheart," Sam said, opening his arms wide. I leaped up and ran away across the lawn, shrieking with laughter, feeling about nine years old again.

JOE WAS MORE THAN HAPPY to come to the Lighthouse Dance with me. "Great!" he exclaimed when I called him. "Man, those things were fun when we were kids, weren't they, Mil?"

"Actually, I don't think I've ever been to a Lighthouse Dance," I told him.

"Really? How could you have missed out on that?"

Because I was fat and had acne and braces and would have jumped off the Sagamore Bridge before going. Luckily—or not—Joe didn't seem to remember me back then. "Oh, I was kind of shy back then," I answered.

"Well, we're going to have a great time, Millie. You'll see."

I was excited, too. According to the guidelines the Lighthouse committee had sent me, chaperones were encouraged to dress up as well. Jill Doyle was going to be a chaperone, too, and she'd invited Joe and me to have dinner with several other couples before the dance. It all sounded very grown-up and fun.

I arranged to have my hair cut and colored again and had lunch with Curtis and Mitch in P-town afterward. When I got home, I called my mom and threw her the bone she'd been waiting for her whole life.

"Mom, I need a dress."

"Millicent Evelyn Barnes!" she exclaimed in Nordstrom's dressing room later that week. "Look at you! What a figure you've got, honey!"

"Well, I finally managed to lose some weight," I answered modestly.

"But you kept your curves, you lucky thing," she said. "Trish and I are just skin and bones."

"I think *slender* is the word you're looking for," I said, blushing with pleasure.

Mom had me try on roughly a thousand dresses. The one we (she) picked in the end was, I had to admit, fantastic. Creamy-white satin, knee-length, with wide, 1950s off-the-shoulder straps and a curving, graceful neckline. The dress definitely made the most of my light tan and, uh, curves.

"You have such a natural beauty," my mom sighed, looking mistily at me. Then she snapped out of it. "On to shoes. And we're going to need a serious bra for that thing. Hurry up, honey."

I didn't have to work the day of the dance. Instead, I spent all day primping, just as I should have done as a teenager. First, a run for the healthy glow, then a boring but healthful breakfast. I vacuumed the sand out of my car and washed the windows clean of their doggy nose prints. Then I shaved my legs oh-so-carefully. Bubble bath with fantastic-smelling products. A manicure with clear nail polish, two coats. A long chat with Katie, then another with Curtis and Mitch, who cooed simultaneously into the same receiver. They advised cucumber slices for the eyes and lots of water.

"This is fun," I said to them. "I never went to my prom, you know."

"Really," Mitch murmured politely, pretending to be surprised.

"You'll be the prettiest one there," Curtis replied loyally.

At five o'clock, I was ready. Joe pulled in promptly and came to my door, a single red rose in his hand. He looked— oh, *magnificent* didn't do him justice. He'd gotten a haircut and looked more mature, more reliable than he did with the shaggy adorableness he usually sported. He was freshly shaved and grinning, dimples in full glory. He wore a navy-blue suit with a bright white shirt and blue-and-red tie.

"My God," I breathed as I opened the door. "You're beautiful, Joe." I kissed him carefully so as not to mess up the three coats of lipstick I had painstakingly applied.

"You look great, too," he said, handing me my rose. "Ready?"

We drove to Jill's in my car—I hadn't wanted to crawl in and out of Joe's truck wearing the dress of all dresses, after all. Jill clucked and cooed over Joe and me and introduced us to the other chaperones as "the most beautiful people here." I beamed. In fifteen short years, I had gone from fat girl to prom queen.

Jill's dinner party was lovely. No one was ever allowed to be sad or shy around that woman, and her guests were lively and friendly. Except for one...

"Hi, I'm Millie Barnes," I said, extending my free hand to an attractive woman in her early forties.

"Lorraine McNulty," she said, taking my hand. "Fantastic dress."

"Thanks! This is Joe Carpenter," I said, turning to introduce my guy.

"Joe." Lorraine's features turned to stone.

"Hey, how are you?" Joe said. He looked at my full glass. "Millie, need another drink?" With that, he fled. I guessed the reason.

"Nice to meet you," I said to Lorraine and followed Joe into the kitchen. He was gulping down some wine. "I guess you know her, huh?"

"Oh, yeah."

"Old girlfriend?" I asked mildly.

"Something like that," he answered. He finished the wine and then smiled at me. "Don't leave me alone with her, okay?"

"Anything you should tell me?"

"Shit, no."

I tried not to mind. There were too many of them to take offense. I'd always known that, I reminded myself. Besides, it was my very first big dance, and I wanted to enjoy it. I ate carefully, knowing the effect of my dress would be rather less with a big splotch of cocktail sauce on the bodice. I took only a few sips of wine; I was a chaperone, after all.

We settled into our dinner, chatting, laughing, having a lovely time, aside from the granite-faced Lorraine. Joe seemed subdued, speaking in a low voice, carefully not glancing at her end of the table.

"Well, my dears, I believe it's that time," Jill trilled after coffee and cake. We thanked her profusely and headed to our cars.

"So, Joe, you okay?" I asked as we drove up Route 6 toward the high school.

"Sure. Why do you ask?"

"Well, you seemed a little shaken up by seeing that woman…Lorraine?"

He sighed and glanced at me. "She was one of those women I kind of told you about, Millie. I was doing some work at her house, and she put the moves on me, and the next thing you know, she's talking about leaving her husband and—"

"She's married?" I barked.

"Yeah. Well, she was back then. I think she got a divorce."

"Joe! You slept with a married woman?" I couldn't keep the shrillness from my voice.

"Well, yeah, I guess. But she was the one cheating on her husband, not me."

Sam would never do anything like that. The thought popped into my head, taking me by surprise. But it was true.

While I wanted desperately to believe there was a secret, heroic side to Joe Carpenter, there was nothing secret about Sam's goodness.

"That's not how adultery works, Joe," I began, my voice tight. But at his look of confusion, gave up. We were at the school, and I couldn't deal with this conversation right now. As we pulled into the parking lot and got out of the car, the kids were starting to arrive, the girls as bright as exotic birds in their dresses, the boys adorably awkward in their suits.

Joe took my arm and led me toward the school, whistling under his breath. Once again, he was oblivious to how I was feeling. I gritted my teeth and tried to shove my negative thoughts away. *He can't help how women act around him, Millie.* But it wasn't just how the women acted. It was Joe, too.

"Ready, gorgeous?" Joe beamed at me, holding the door.

Forcing a smile, I took Joe's hand. *He's not perfect,* I told myself. *No one is.*

The gym was festooned with streamers and balloons, and strands of multicolored Christmas lights winked. In the middle of the room was a model of Nauset Light, about fifteen feet high, with a real light going round and round inside it.

"Oh, look, Joe! A lighthouse!" It was so charming that I forgot my turmoil.

"Yeah, well, I hate to tell you this, Millie, but they've had that since we were here."

"Oh." My smile slipped.

We wandered around, waving to the other chaperones and kids we knew. Our duties were pretty vague; keep an eye out for drinking and drugs, overly intense making out, stuff like that. Be the grown-ups, in other words.

My nephew and Sarah approached us. "Hi, you guys!" I said. "Oh, Sarah, you look beautiful! Wow!"

"So do you, Millie," she said shyly. "Hi, Mr. Carpenter."

"Hi, Danny," I said, reaching up for a hug. "You're so handsome, my little angel boy," I whispered into his ear.

"Thanks for whispering that," he said, grinning happily. "Hey, Joe."

"Hey, Dan," Joe answered amiably. "You having fun yet?"

"Sure," they answered in unison.

"Well, go have a good time. You don't have to hang around and talk to us." I shooed them away, swallowing around the lump in my throat at the sight of my nephew. I hoped Sam had been able to see Danny and Sarah looking so beautiful. I hoped he'd taken a picture for me.

"She called me *Mr. Carpenter,*" Joe said, jerking his chin toward Sarah. "That girl."

"Well, Joe, you *are* almost twice her age. We both are."

"Yeah, I guess so. Makes you feel old, though."

"Thirty is not old, Joe."

"I guess not." He sighed. "Hey, are you gonna dance with me or what?"

I hesitated. "How about in a little while, when more people are dancing. I don't see any other chaperones out there yet."

"Okay, okay," Joe muttered, looking a bit irked. "I'll be back in a few minutes, all right?"

"Sure." I watched Joe walk around the dance floor to the exit. He might be twice the age of some of the girls here, but that didn't keep them from stealing looks at him. Yes, I was definitely with the prom king. A rather old prom king, but a prom king nonetheless.

Somehow, though, the rush of surprise and pleasure that I'd once gotten from being near him was absent tonight. The voice that usually defended Joe was getting a little quiet these days, and I was having trouble reconciling what I thought about Joe to…well, to how he was.

I glanced around the room, suddenly feeling a little awkward, standing there alone amid all the kids. Maybe I would go to the ladies' room and give my bra a tug. Couldn't hurt. I walked in that direction, careful not to twist an ankle in my high heels. As I glided cautiously, I spied a familiar figure…tall, lanky, graying brown hair. Sam!

His back was to me, and he was talking to another chaperone whose name escaped me, though she had been at Jill's party. I stood politely to the side for a minute, waiting for them to notice me. Just as it became uncomfortable, the woman said goodbye to Sam and gave me a little wave.

"Hi, Sam!" I said. He turned around.

"Hey, Millll…" was all that came out. Sam stared at me like he'd never seen me before, mouth slightly open, looking rather stunned. His eyes traveled down and then up, and I couldn't help giggling. I spun around so he could see the whole dress. His breath came out in a rush. "Wow."

"Did my dad pay you to say that?" I asked, standing on tiptoe to kiss his cheek.

"Millie, my God."

"Thank you. You're too kind." Even though it was just Sam, the thrill of being openly admired washed over me. "Okay, close your mouth. What are you doing here? I thought you weren't cool enough."

Sam gave his head a little shake. "Sorry. Okay. What did you say?"

"Why—are—you—here—Sam?" I asked again, over-enunciating the words as if he were hard of hearing.

"Oh. Randy Lynch got appendicitis. Danny asked if I could fill in at the last minute."

"Oh, great! For you, I mean, not for Randy. I just saw Danny and Sarah. Did you take lots of pictures?"

"I sure did."

We stood there a minute. As the music pulsed, more people ventured out onto the dance floor. It was funny to watch; you could tell that all the girls had practiced for hours in front of the mirror, they moved with such grace and precision. The boys, on the other hand, danced as if they were being poked with an electric cattle prod, sudden, spastic movements of long limbs and jerking heads.

"Did you have fun at your Lighthouse Dance?" I asked, dimly remembering Trish primping much as I had today.

"Oh, sure. Did you?"

"I've never been to one before."

"Really? How come?" Sam asked curiously.

"Because, dummy, I was fat and hideous and awkward and there was no boy on earth who wanted to be around me. Don't you remember?" I gave a sharp laugh, irritated at having to revisit my gawky adolescence for a second time.

"No, Millie," Sam answered slowly, looking at me gravely. "That's not how I remember you at all."

His words caused an odd wiggle in my knees, and I looked away abruptly. My cheeks felt hot as I surveyed the crowd. A chaperone couple joined the dance fray, braving the heaving bodies to do their duty.

"Do you have a date?" I asked above the noise.

"Nope. Just me."

"Too bad Carol dumped you."

"I dumped her, kiddo."

"Of course you did, honey. My mistake." Sam laughed and

shook his head. "So, Sam, what are you going to do next year when Danny's at college?" I asked, hoping belatedly that it wasn't a painful subject.

"Actually, I was just thinking about that myself. I thought I might try to finish my degree. I just have a couple courses to go. Then I'm thinking about getting a master's in criminology."

"Sam, that would be great! Good for you!"

"Well, you know, I'd finally have the time. It would be good to finish, too."

"That is just fantastic, buddy."

Joe appeared at my side. "Hey, Sam!" he said, shaking hands.

"Hi, Joe. Beautiful date you got there," Sam replied.

"You bet. The prettiest. And hey, pretty woman, you want to dance?"

I glanced at Sam, who gave me a wink. "I'll take pity on you later," I called to him as Joe led me onto the dance floor. The DJ was playing a nice slow song by Norah Jones, and Joe pulled me close against his warmth.

"Dancing always makes me horny," he whispered into my hair.

"Joe! Shh! We're chaperones!"

"Hmm. Want to duck into the AV room?"

"No, you dope," I laughed, but it was with an edge. "Behave yourself."

We danced for a minute or two more, and I watched the kids swaying around us. Danny and Sarah were nearby, Sarah's eyes closed, her cheek on Danny's shoulder. So beautiful. I glanced over at Sam, who was standing in the classic cop stance, feet slightly apart, hands clasped behind his back. He glanced at me and smiled, and I gave him a little wave.

At that moment, Joe decided to kiss me—a pretty intense

kiss, too. I pulled away as best I could with his arm around my waist. "Joe! Come on! We're chaperones! We can't make out on the dance floor," I hissed.

And then it came to me. That unmistakable taste of alcohol. Not wine. Something else.

"Joe, have you been drinking?" I whispered in horror.

"Well, I did have a little nip out there in the parking lot." He smiled down at me.

"A nip of what? And why?"

"Jeez, Millie, calm down. Just a little blackberry schnapps, that's all. For old time's sake."

As if I had psychic powers, I glanced to a corner of the room where three boys stood huddled together. One of them pointed at Joe, and then they disappeared out the door.

"Joe." I stopped dancing. "Did you give your schnapps to anybody?" Though my heart had begun to pound in my throat, I forced my voice to stay low.

"What? Oh, yeah, I gave it to a couple of kids who were hanging around. What's the matter, Millie? It's not a big deal."

"Joe, you idiot," I whispered harshly. "It's against the goddamn law to give alcohol to minors! What if one of them is driving tonight? What if they hit somebody? Christ, Sam would throw you in jail for this!"

People were beginning to look at us, standing still and arguing as we were. I stalked off the dance floor and out the same door the boys had left. Joe followed.

"Where are they?" I demanded outside.

"Who?"

"The boys you gave the alcohol to, Joe! Where are they?" I had to stop my hand from slapping his face.

"There." He pointed, and I stomped over to a big maple at

the edge of the parking lot. The boys looked startled. One of them, Kyle, I thought, was in Danny's class.

"Give it to me." I held out my hand.

"Uh, what are you talking about?" one of them attempted.

"Now!" I barked.

Kyle pulled the flat schnapps bottle from his waistband. "Sorry, Dr. Barnes."

I unscrewed the metal cap and dumped the ridiculous drink on the ground. "Do you know that Danny Nickerson's father is inside there? Do you know what he would do to you if he found you drinking? Were any of you planning on driving tonight?"

"Um, well, we were gonna go home together."

"My God!" I surveyed the three of them for a minute, their eyes wide, nervously shifting. "Do you boys happen to know how Danny's grandparents died?"

They shifted uncomfortably. "Uh, no, Dr. Barnes."

"They were killed by a drunk driver. A teenage drunk driver. Those are Officer Nickerson's parents I'm talking about."

To their credit, they looked ashamed.

"I'm calling you boys a cab," I said flatly. "You're going home. Who are your dates? I'll tell them."

"Dr. Barnes, are you going to tell Danny's dad?" Kyle asked worriedly.

I looked them over. "No. Not this time. This time you get a 'Thank God a grown-up caught me and I'm not dead' card. And on Monday, you're coming to the Cape Cod Clinic, and we'll all have a nice long look at drunk-driving crashes on the Internet. And you'll be volunteering at the senior center twice a week for the entire school year. And if you fuck up again, I'm telling your parents, your principal and Officer Nickerson. And I will personally kick your asses into the middle of next week. Got it?"

They nodded miserably.

"Wonderful." I took a deep breath. "Now. Does anyone have a cell phone?"

Ten minutes later, the boys were on their way home in a cab.

My anger at them faded as they drove off. After all, they were just teenagers, and most teenagers are stupid at one point or another. Unfortunately, that particular brand of stupidity often resulted in death. If I had scared them, good. I took a few deep breaths.

Now for the stupid adult I had to deal with.

Joe was sitting on the hood of my car, hands clasped between his knees, looking very contrite.

"I'm sorry, Millie," he said quietly.

Fresh fury raced through my veins. "Joe…I just don't know how you could do such a stupid, awful thing," I said, my voice breaking. He hopped off the car and put his arm around me.

"Millie, I'm sorry," he said earnestly. "I just wanted the boys to have a good time. It was like being back in high school, this whole Lighthouse Dance thing. I mean, I did a little drinking in high school, and it didn't hurt me."

"Joe, shut up," I said harshly, shrugging off his arm. "You can't justify giving those *children* alcohol. Please just shut up." Hot, angry tears slipped down my face.

"Oh, Millie, don't cry. Come on, let's go back in and have fun."

Dumbfounded, I looked up at him, the street lamp haloing him like an angel. A stupid angel.

And then I knew. I didn't love Joe. He wasn't the person I'd thought. He was a very handsome, charming dope. Not malicious. Just…oblivious. All the qualities I thought I'd seen over the years…they weren't there. The Joe Carpenter I loved existed in my imagination only. The man standing in front of me was just some guy who happened to be too handsome for his own good.

I started to cry in earnest.

"Shit, Millie, come on. Don't cry. I'm sorry. Nothing bad happened. You scared the hell out of those boys. It will be years before they take another drink. Come on, sweetie."

"Joe…" I hiccupped. "Are *you* drunk?"

"No, no. I only had a glass of wine at Jill's and just a little hit of the schnapps. I'm fine."

"Good. Because I want you to go. Take my car back to my house, get your truck and just go home. I'll get a ride."

"Millie, come on. Don't be like this."

"I'm sorry, Joe. I'll call you tomorrow."

And tomorrow I would break up with him.

Staring at me for a long moment, Joe finally nodded. I fished my keys out of my bag, handed them to him and tripped back into the school to the girls' bathroom. My face in the mirror looked as if I'd aged ten years. My makeup was ruined. The dress…who even cared? And now I had to go back into the gym and chaperone my nephew's dance and act normal. My eyes welled again.

Don't think about it, I ordered myself. *Just wait till you get home and deal with it then.*

I blotted my face as best I could with the grainy paper towels, blew my nose and fluffed my hair. Danny was having a wonderful time, and I didn't want to make a scene. And for Danny, I would do anything. I heaved a great sigh, blotted my eyes again and went back to the gym. I headed to the punch table and downed a glass of sugary pink liquid, then asked for another one.

Thus fortified, I turned and surveyed the dancers again. There were Danny and Sarah, slow dancing again, just barely shuffling their feet. Jill and her husband were cutting the rug nicely, dancing with energy and symmetry that bespoke ballroom dancing lessons. She waved energetically at me and I smiled and waved back. There was Sam, dancing with a woman I didn't know. He looked happy. The lump in my throat swelled again, aching sharply. I turned away for a minute, fanning my face ineffectively with my hand, tried a few more deep breaths. Hopefully, the dim lights would hide my teary eyes.

Someone tapped my shoulder. Sam.

"What's the matter, honey?" he asked.

I pressed my lips together so I wouldn't start crying again and shook my head.

"Is it Joe?" he guessed, taking my hand as if knowing that a hug would start me bawling. I nodded. Sam looked at the floor. "What can I do?"

"Can you drive me home later?" I squeaked.

"You bet."

I looked around for a minute or two, waiting for the breathless, sobby feeling to leave me. The slow song ended and something livelier started up.

Sam tugged my hand. "Come on, kiddo. You said you'd take pity on me and dance."

"No, not right now, Sam." I swallowed and smiled, bravely, I thought.

"But this is our song," he smiled, bending his knees to look in my eyes.

"We don't have a song."

"Well, we should, and it should be this one." Without waiting for an answer, he dragged me onto the floor and promptly stepped on my foot.

"Ouch!"

"Whoops."

"Did you do that on purpose?"

"Of course not! Come on, kiddo. Don't just stand there. I might step on you again."

"Are you trying to make me laugh?"

"No. Do not laugh. That's an order. Whoops. Sorry. Come on, move those feet."

I gave in and shuffled sluggishly. Sam gave me a quick hug. "It'll be okay," he whispered, twirling me around before I could start crying.

"You're a terrible dancer," I said above the noise, feeling a smile tug my lips despite the tears in my eyes.

"Takes one to know one," he shot back, dipping and nearly dropping me.

"Jesus, Sam, be careful. Precious cargo and all that."

"Right. So. Do you like our song?" he asked. It was awful, a garish, hideous, screeching song that the kids apparently adored.

"I love it. It's so us. What's the title?"

"I have no idea. Hey, Bobby," he shouted to the boy nearest us. "What's the name of this song?"

Bobby looked at us curiously. "'The Unholy,'" he answered.

I MANAGED NOT TO CRY for the rest of the night, thanks mostly to Sam's protection. At long last, the dance was over, and Sam and I got into his truck. I rested my pounding head against the cool glass of the window as we drove home in silence. When we got to my house, Joe's truck was mercifully gone. Sam opened my door and helped me out, then walked me to the door.

"Want me to come in?"

"Oh, no, that's okay." Tears filled my eyes again, and my lips wobbled.

"How about just for a few minutes?" Sam offered.

I nodded, overwhelmed with gratitude at the comfort of his presence. I knelt down so Digger could kiss me, then went straight to the bedroom, unzipped my dress and slid it off. I heard Sam letting Digger out, then water running. I pulled on some old scrubs and went into the bathroom to wash my face.

Joe and I were done. I leaned over the sink and rinsed the tears away along with the soap, then went back into the kitchen. Sam had made coffee.

"It's decaf," he said, handing me a cup.

"Thanks," I said, reaching for a tissue and blowing my nose. We both sat down at the kitchen table.

"Do you want to tell me about it?" Sam asked gently, stirring his coffee.

"Well," I said shakily. "It's just that…I'll be breaking up with Joe tomorrow." I took a breath that was actually a sob and held the tissue up to my eyes.

"I'm sorry, Millie."

"I guess…I guess sometimes people aren't exactly who you think they are, you know?"

"I do."

Yes, I guess he would. We looked at each other, and he reached out and covered my hand with his own.

"I'm sorry, Millie," he said again, very softly. My mouth wobbled again.

"Well, Sam," I said, suddenly feeling as if I had weights tied to my limbs, "I think you can probably go now."

"You sure? I can stay if you want."

"No, I think I'm just going to cry it out for a while."

"Okay, kiddo. I'll call you tomorrow." He rose and kissed the top of my head, and that small kindness squeezed another sob out of me.

"You were really great tonight, Sam," I whispered. Unsurprising, that.

"Take care, honey."

I looked at him through watery eyes. "Thanks."

He let the dog back in and then left.

CHAPTER TWENTY-SIX

I HAD INVENTED the Joe Carpenter of my dreams. For sixteen years—more than half of my life!—I'd been in love with an imaginary man. All the effort, all the time, all the *love* I'd poured into Joe had been like shoveling the tide. There was no payoff, there was no happily-ever-after. There was just nothing. Just a sweet, not-too-bright guy whose looks I had used to construct an impossibly perfect man.

God, I was so stupid.

Self-loathing twisted through me, making me toss and turn in my bed. Stupid, stupid, stupid. Whom might I have met if I hadn't been so hung up on my imaginary Joe? Would I be married to some imperfect but real man by now? Over the past six months, I'd turned myself inside out to get Joe…for what? For nothing, because there was no Joe, not the way I'd thought, anyway. I was like some poor adolescent girl who was in love with a movie star or singer, assigning all kinds of qualities to a pretty face. "And then, someday, our eyes will meet at a concert, and we'll just know that we're right for each other…."

And what about the real Joe? What would I say to him? "Oh, sorry, but I made you up. We're not really breaking up, because the person I thought you are doesn't exist outside of my head. Have a good day!"

When morning finally hauled itself to Cape Cod, I sat up.

My head still hurt, my eyes were gritty from too many tears, my body ached as if I had the flu. The high heels I'd worn the night before caused my calves to cramp, and my hair was tacky from all the goop I'd slathered in it to make it behave.

I drank some orange juice, threw on my sweats and went for a run, needing to purge my mind of the recriminations screaming there. I turned my iPod up loud and trudged along in my trademark trot, Digger plodding beside me, his joy of the outdoors undimmed by my mood. My shoulders cramped, my stomach ached, my calves burned. I didn't care. In fact, I welcomed the discomfort. It distracted me from the ache in my heart.

When I got home, I showered and brushed my teeth and sat on the porch for a while, feeling hollow and numb. Digger licked my face, but I barely noticed. After a while, the phone rang. Thinking it was Sam, I answered it.

"Millie, it's Joe."

My stomach thudded to my feet. "Oh, hi, Joe."

"Are you okay?" He actually sounded a little scared.

"Yeah, sure."

"Are you still mad at me?"

I sighed. "Maybe you should come over, Joe."

"Now?"

"Now would be good."

When Joe got to my house, I saw that he'd brought his dog. Tripod leaped out of the truck, and he and Digger went chasing each other merrily through my yard, just as I had always imagined they would. I winced. All my plans seemed so stupid and shallow now.

Joe stared down at my kitchen table and declined a glass of water or cup of coffee. When I sat down across from him, he looked at me directly.

"Can I just say something first?" he asked.

"Uh, sure," I said.

"Okay, Millie. I know I screwed up last night, and I can see why you're so mad at me. It was a really dumb thing to do. I was just thinking about when I was in high school and how sneaking a drink seemed like so much fun. I guess I wanted to seem kind of cool, you know? Because I've got to tell you, being back at Nauset High, being called Mr. Carpenter, it kind of freaked me out. All of a sudden, I felt wicked old. Do you know what I mean?"

I shook my head.

"Oh. Well, it was stupid, and I'm sorry. Please don't be mad anymore, Millie."

I swallowed. "Joe, it's actually kind of more than just last night."

"It is?" His eyes were wide and confused.

I traced the design of my tablecloth, grateful for somewhere to look other than at Joe.

"Well, the thing is, Joe," I said, needing to whisper because my throat was so tight. He leaned forward to hear me better. "The thing is that I guess I've been thinking…I think maybe we're just not right for each other." I swallowed loudly.

"But Millie…" Joe said, taking my hands across the table.

"No, Joe, I'm sorry." I pulled my hands free. "This is mostly on me, not you. Last night was just…just an example of what's been going on."

"What are you talking about?"

With effort, I raised my eyes. "I haven't been honest with you, Joe," I said. "The truth is, I'm one of those women who went after you, just because you're so…gorgeous."

"You didn't go after me," he countered. "You didn't. That

was one of the things I liked about you. You didn't seem to be so...desperate."

"Well, I was. I've had a crush on you since freshman year of high school, Joe. I've always wanted to go out with you. I even..." I swallowed again.

"What?"

"I kind of, well, stalked you. For a long time. To find out what you liked. I knew where you went and who you were with and stuff like that. And then when I moved back here, I tried to make myself into a person that you'd want."

He ran his hands through his hair. "Millie, what are you talking about?"

"I wanted you to notice me. I lost weight. I made sure I bumped into you when I was at the senior center. I'd figure out when you went to the post office and go at the same time. I started running on roads I knew you drove on. I got a dog because you had a dog. There. Now you know."

Joe stared at me, then leaned forward and smiled. "Well, okay, I guess you definitely had a thing for me. So what? It doesn't matter."

"But—"

He cut me off. "I like lots of things about you. Like how funny you are, and smart. You always seem to be having a good time. And how you were with me...you don't seem to care about what was outside. You like me, you know, just for me."

I looked down. I had never felt so ashamed of myself in my life.

"Well," I said very, very quietly, "I'm afraid you're wrong. I mean, no, you're not wrong, Joe. I have a lot of...affection for you. But I also just assumed a bunch of things about you, and I didn't really bother to get to know the real you."

Joe sat up straighter.

"And now that we *have* gotten to know each other a little more, I think that we're just not right for each other." The last sentence came out in the barest whisper.

"So what you're saying is, now that you know the real me, you want to break up."

The wind sliced through the yard, making the kitchen screens rattle, and the dogs yipped as they played. "Right," I whispered.

"And this is not just about me screwing up last night."

"No."

We sat there another minute, then Joe closed his eyes and pinched the bridge of his nose. "Okay. I guess I should go, then." His voice was husky. He pushed back his chair and got up to leave.

I looked up at him, this beautiful man, standing for the last time in my house. "Joe, I'm very, very sorry."

He drew in a shaky breath. "I just want to say one more thing, Millie. I love you."

Then he left, calling his dog more harshly that was necessary. Tripod clambered into the truck, and Joe drove away.

HOW COULD I HAVE BEEN so blind/stupid/foolish?

It became my theme song. I agonized over that question. How could I have done this? How could I have not seen? How could I have let it get so far?

I ached for Joe, knowing that I'd hurt him. I'd gone after him with a vengeance, manipulated him into thinking he loved the facade I'd constructed. Joe Carpenter was not a bad person. He had done a stupid thing, of course, but no one deserved to be told he wasn't good enough, yet that's just what I'd done.

Shame pressed down on me. I was drowning in shame. I

was afraid to go for a run, in case Joe should drive by. I didn't want to go to the Barnacle. I didn't want to talk on the phone. I didn't want to garden, ride my bike, see my friends or my parents. I told them, of course, though nobody seemed to be too surprised.

"I'm sorry, Millie," Katie said about a week after the breakup. "But I'm sure it's for the best."

"Did you know about this?" I asked, reaching for a tissue. "Did you know that I was making him up as I went along?"

She sighed. "Well, kind of. I mean, I hoped that you were right, of course, but I never really saw all that wonderfulness that you did. I mean, Joe's not a bad guy or anything, and yes, he's gorgeous, but he always seemed like a big kid to me."

Curtis and Mitch took me out to dinner at an expensive restaurant and ordered me to drown my sorrows. "He was just a pretty face," Curtis consoled. "You'll find someone else. Someone with a little more upstairs."

"Absolutely," Mitch echoed, finishing his martini.

Even my mom and dad weren't that upset. "Well, honey, someone will come around who really is right for you," my dad consoled. "Joe's a nice guy and all, but…"

"But what?" I asked, needing the validation and hating myself for it.

"But he wasn't the sharpest knife in the drawer, punkin."

It didn't help.

In addition to the self-recrimination that was running rampant through my veins, I simply missed Joe, too, his sweetness and his happy-go-lucky ways. I missed the thrill of seeing him, the sweet shock of his beauty, the physical closeness. And even more than that, I missed the days before I'd been involved with him, when thinking of Joe had sustained me. Let's face it. I'd lost my lifelong hobby.

Once, I'd been so sure that Joe would be a huge part of my future. The truth was, I never really imagined myself with anyone else. My thirties suddenly yawned in front of me, and I pictured myself with only Digger and his irritable bowel syndrome to greet me each night, no person to interrupt the relentless quiet of my house.

Only when I was seeing patients was I remotely normal, but the clinic's business was slowing down, and I had too much time on my hands even there. The new wing at the senior center was nearly finished, and I took to visiting patients twice a week, sometimes just dropping in for a visit. If Joe's truck wasn't in the parking lot, that was. The folks there all knew me by now, and it was comforting to be in my Dr. Barnes persona rather than full of self-beratement. I'd stay as long as possible in my patients' rooms, reading to them, asking them questions about their lives before creeping through the halls, praying that I wouldn't run into Joe.

SEPTEMBER BROUGHT IN EARLIER evenings and chillier days. The ocean seemed to have less green in it and more gray, and the wind was cool enough that I brought a hat when I went to the beach at night. The poison ivy was edged with red, the tourists left and the kids went back to school, and in the quiet of my home, I couldn't avoid the thought that had started to ring the loudest in my head.

For years, I'd thought that Joe was a wonderful amalgamation of kindness, decency and dependability. But I only knew one man that terrific, and it wasn't Joe.

Joe Carpenter was no Sam.

For the past several weekends, Sam and Danny had been visiting colleges throughout the Northeast—Williams, Wesleyan, Colby and Penn—and I hadn't seen much of them lately. It was just as well. My head was muddled enough without me dwelling on the fact that my sister's ex-husband embodied all the qualities I'd wished on Joe.

CHAPTER TWENTY-SEVEN

DR. WHITAKER GAVE ME the chance to snap out of my funk.

"Millie," he said over the phone one day toward the end of September, "I'd like to discuss the partnership with you, now that the clinic will be closing…when exactly is that?"

My breath caught. "We close the week after Columbus Day," I answered calmly.

"Right. At any rate, you've done very well at the senior center, and I'm very pleased with your work at the clinic. If you're still interested in joining me, we should work out the details, don't you agree?"

I bolted upright. At last. At last! "I'm absolutely still interested, Dr.—George. Thank you. I'm honored," I smiled.

"Excellent. Why don't we meet next Thursday for dinner here at my house?"

"That would be lovely," I answered.

"There's something else I'd like you to do, more of a favor, actually," the doctor went on.

"Of course! What is it?"

"The high school has a career day for the seniors. Professionals from the community come in and talk about what they do, how they got interested in their work and the like. I've been doing it for years, and I thought it would be beneficial for you to tag along."

"Sure," I said. "I'd love to come. My nephew's a senior this year."

"That's right," Dr. Whitaker replied. "Such a fine boy, young Daniel. We'll attend Career Day, I'll give my little presentation, and then later in the week we can nail out the details of our partnership. How does that sound?"

"It sounds wonderful."

The night before Career Day, I laid out my seldom-used suit and polished my shoes. Then I took an hour or so to jot a few notes on index cards, just in case Dr. Whitaker asked me to add anything to his little spiel. He was a formal, precise man, and I didn't want to be caught unaware. Katie, too, would be speaking, representing the world of restaurant management, and several other people I knew. It might turn out to be a really fun event.

The next morning as I drove into the high-school parking lot, my heart sank. Joe's truck was there…apparently he'd been asked to speak at Career Day, too. I hadn't seen or spoken to him since our breakup.

"Go down to the teachers' lounge. You remember the way, don't you, Millie?" asked the secretary, who had been at Nauset High for decades.

As I walked down the hallway, I heard an undeniably angry (if somewhat muffled) voice coming from the janitor's supply room. The door was closed, but I could recognize the voice easily. It was Katie. My footsteps slowed.

"…in the first place!" my friend was saying. Having been on the receiving end of that iron tone, I cringed for the recipient, freezing in the horrible thrill of someone else's reaming.

"For God's sake," Katie continued, "you sit there night after night, crying into your beer, and for what? You make a good living, have a lot of people who like you, Joe—"

Joe!

"—but you're wasting your life. You screw anything with a pulse, break hearts all over the place, just float through life without thinking of anyone but yourself. I'm not surprised Millie dumped you. She's way out of your league."

Oh, my God.

"So there you have it, okay? You asked, I answered. Now stop whining, grow up and act your age."

Realizing their conversation, for lack of a better word, was ending, I leaped down the hall to the teachers' lounge and yanked open the door. Several people were already assembled: Dr. Whitaker, Maeve McFarland, an attorney; Bobby and Sue Schultz, who ran the Atlantic Winds Motel; and my dad, sultan of sewage. I scampered over to the coffeepot and smiled breathlessly.

"Millie! Good morning," Dr. W. said.

"Hello," I answered. "Hi, Dad."

"Hi, punkin! Doc here and I were just talking about you." My dad placed a heavy arm around my shoulder and gave me a squeeze.

The door opened, and Katie, looking like a tourism ad for Norway, came in, her face serene and lovely, blond hair swinging in a silken curtain over her shoulders. "Hi, Millie," she purred. "Hi, everyone."

I went over to her side. "Why were you yelling at Joe?" I whispered.

"Oh, did you overhear that?" she asked blithely.

"Yes! I certainly did. Why, Katie?"

She smiled. "He asked for it."

"Did he?" Was anyone so foolish as to ask for the Wrath of Katie?

"Well, he wanted to know if I knew why you broke up with him. So I told him."

She looked as sated as if she'd just had a night of world-class sex, her cheeks slightly flushed and glowing, her eyes sparkling. "Did you have to enjoy it so much?" I asked.

"That Peter Pan routine is pathetic," Katie murmured. "High time someone told him." She sighed contentedly and floated away. I turned around, bumping right into Joe.

"Hi, Joe," I said, feeling my ears grow hot. "How are you?"

He didn't look nearly as healthy as Katie. "Fine," he answered.

"So, um, I guess you're here for Career Day," I said, feeling my stomach contract with discomfort.

"Yup." He continued to stare, unsmiling, a look that was foreign to his usually cheerful face.

"Okay! Well. Um, see you later." I scurried away like a cockroach. Apparently, Joe hadn't gotten around to the "no hard feelings" stage. Or he was still shell-shocked from the Katie grenade that had just been launched.

At that moment, the door opened and in came Mrs. Deveau, who'd been principal when I was a student here. "We're all set, people, if you'll follow me," she said. We made our way en masse to the auditorium. A number of my former teachers still taught here, and one or two waved as we passed through the halls.

"Hey, Millie," Sam said, appearing at my side. "Representing the medical world today, are you?" He looked handsome in his uniform, brawnier with the radio and gun clipped to his belt. Downright…well, actually, quite…

"That's right. And you're discussing…what is it again that you do? Dog warden?" My banter was automatic because of the strange, hot…

Sam laughed, and my innards contracted in a warm

squeeze. "That doesn't sound too bad. Actually, most kids ask me about playing football in college." He smiled at me, his hazel eyes crinkling, and there it was again, that…that…

Okay, okay. Sam was a looker, I knew that. Sure I did. But suddenly, I seemed to be feeling…things. For my sister's ex-husband. For the father of my nephew. *Of course you love Sam,* a voice in my head soothed. *But only in a platonic way.* Right. So why was adrenaline spurting into my bloodstream, urging me to flee? And why did he suddenly seem so…delicious? I shuddered at the mere thought. Sam, delicious? Oh, God, he was!

"Okay," Mrs. Deveau said. "Why don't we have you go first, Mr. Barnes, since you've done this before. Everyone gets ten minutes, give or take, and then the kids can ask questions. Are we all set?" She didn't wait for an answer, in typical principal fashion, and led us onto the stage. The kids were already in the auditorium, shuffling and chatting, but they quieted as we filed on and sat in the chairs lined up for us.

I did not feel well. Was I sick? I wished I was! *Do not feel this way, Millie. Isn't life complicated enough?* Dr. Whitaker sat on one side of me. Sam sat on the other, his leg brushing mine, causing my nerve endings to leap.

Oh, no. No. No. Sam was off-limits. Do Not Enter. No Trespassing.

My palms grew clammy, and I tried to wipe them discreetly on my skirt. Mrs. Deveau was giving the introduction. A cramp pierced my abdomen. Dr. Whitaker leaned in close to whisper something, but I only dimly heard him over the roar in my ears. "Okay, sure," I whispered back when it seemed an answer was called for.

Oh, this was bad! My knees were humming and weak

with terror, and my pulse must have been at least one hundred and twenty. Maybe more. *Breathe deeply, Millie.* I obeyed myself, causing Sam to glance at me.

"Nervous?" he whispered with a grin.

Oh, shit. This was not what I needed. This was awful.

"It's not so bad," he continued. I could smell his nice Sam smell, soap, starch from his uniform, shaving cream. *Oh, please, please—*

"…Howard Barnes," Mrs. Deveau said. Dutiful applause rose from the kids.

"Hi, kids!" my father bellowed. "I'm Danny Nickerson's grandfather, and I'm the owner of a septic service company…or, as I like to say, the King of Crap." Warming to his fecund subject, Dad launched into a lurid tale of a pipe erupting during a storm several years ago, causing sewage to flood our fair streets. The kids were hooked.

Concentrate on Dad. My carotid artery throbbed sickly in my neck as I stared straight ahead. God, these lights were hot! Was anyone else hot? My fellow panelists looked composed and relaxed. In the audience, I spotted Danny, sitting next to Bobby Canton. There was Kyle and another boy from the Lighthouse Dance.

"Your dad is so great," Sam whispered. I didn't turn my head, just nodded mutely, staring at my father's gleaming bald spot. My stomach churned with acid, and a light sweat broke out on my forehead. Beside me, Dr. Whitaker chuckled at something my father said. The kids applauded.

Joe was next. As he spoke somewhat shyly about his apprenticeship, I stared at his flannel-clad back. My mind refused to shape the words that buzzed around in my head like a swarm of mosquitoes. *No. Absolutely not. Stop.* Sam turned to me again, and I whirled to face Dr. Whitaker.

"Do you…um, do you talk about anything in particular?" I whispered as the kids applauded for Joe.

"Not really. You'll be fine." Dr. Whitaker smiled reassuringly.

I would be fine? What did he mean by that?

Now it was Sam's turn. My heart rate accelerated even more, my pulse thudding wildly in my ears, and I closed my eyes for a moment, dizzy. This was a nightmare. In fact, the whole scene was a textbook panic dream…sitting on a stage, terror racing through my limbs, heart hammering my chest. Unfortunately, I was wide awake, and in more ways than one. Sam said something that made the kids laugh…. He turned back to smile at us grown-ups because whatever he'd said apparently involved us. His eyes stopped on me for just a second.

Oh, damn it all.

The sandbags in my brain dissolved and the river came roaring over the banks.

I was in love with Sam Nickerson.

Sam. My brother-in-law!

No! my brain hollered. *It's practically incest! Completely wrong! What about Trish? And Danny! You can't!*

But I did.

My mouth was tacky, my throat coated in sawdust. My intestines rolled, my face practically shimmered with heat waves. I opened my dry mouth with an audible clack and sucked in a shuddering breath. Dr. Whitaker looked at me oddly. I stretched my mouth into a smile and blinked stupidly.

"…time to hear from Dr. Barnes."

Dr. Barnes. That was me. Sam walked back toward me. Could he tell? Did he know? Why was he looking at me like that? Oh, God, he knew—

"It's your turn, kiddo," he whispered. "Knock 'em dead."

My turn? My—oh, Christ. "You want *me* to do this?" I whispered to Dr. Whitaker.

"Is that all right?" he asked, his bushy gray eyebrows coming together in concern.

"Sure! Just…sure!"

Clenching my jaw against the urge to throw up, I smiled wildly again at Dr. Whitaker and wobbled to the podium. I glanced at Joe, who was staring at the floor. Poor Joe. *Don't look at Sam,* I warned myself as my eyes found him. He winked at me, and my stomach clenched as a wave of warmth rolled over me.

"Hi." My voice came out as a slight gasp. I looked at the kids, squinting against the stage lights. "Uh…I'm, um…I'm Millie. Millie Barnes. A doctor." *A doctor with shaking legs, about to puke on you.* I giggled, but it morphed into a slight dry heave. "Sorry. I think I have a little stage fright." I gripped the podium, my palms slick, and swallowed. Stage fright. Better than looking at Danny and blurting out the truth—*I'm in love with your dad!* I gave a slightly hysterical laugh.

Dr. Whitaker is sitting behind you, Millie, a rational voice in my brain called against the internal din. I swallowed again. "Okay. Down to business." I cleared my throat. "I'm a doctor, which I just told you. Um, I work at the clinic in Wellfleet…but pretty soon, I'll be working for Dr. Whitaker there."

What else was I supposed to say? They all knew what doctors did! Everyone knew! What was the big mystery? Why did they want a doctor for their stupid Career Day? And where were those stupid note cards? In my stupid pocketbook, under my stupid chair, next to Sa—

"Well, in medicine, there are a lot of fields…um…like uh, orthopedics, which treats…um…uh, it's from the Greek, *ortho,* meaning—" What *did* it mean? Ortho, ortho…My mind was empty. *Oh, Sam.* "Okay, and there's, um, well, gynecology…no, let's not talk about that one. How about pathology? Pathology's fun. That's the one with dead people. Autopsies. Cause of death. Stuff like that. It's fun. Well, not fun…I meant interesting. It's…interesting."

This wasn't going well. "Okay, lots of fields. You choose what you want in med school. Any questions?"

The students were supposed to save their questions for the end, but I couldn't go on like this. Thankfully, a girl raised her hand.

"What kind of doctor are you?"

"Me? Oh. I'm a family practitioner. I treat everybody, kids, adults, you know. But if you have a real problem, like heart disease or something really bad, we send you to someone else." Well, that made us sound *completely* incompetent! "We're the family doctor," I backpedaled. "You get strep, you come to us. Um, need to lose weight, we'll tell you." I glanced at the audience, searching for inspiration. "Acne? We can help."

Jesus, deliver me from this stage. "Next question?"

Danny took pity on me. "Millie, why did you become a family practitioner?"

Gazing at my nephew, I felt my terror ebb a bit. I took a deep breath. "Well, um, as you know, Danny, it's because I— I guess I really want to get to know my patients. Sometimes, when people go to their doctor, it's just routine stuff, like earaches or rashes or fevers. But patients let their family doctor into their lives, you know? They trust us to help them. There's medicine out there that's probably more exciting, like reconstructive surgery or emergency medicine, but in this field, I get to help you in your everyday life. And that's what I always wanted to do."

Danny's smile affirmed that I had—finally—constructed a sensible sentence. *Danny, you're such a good person,* I thought. *Just like your dad.*

DESPITE HOW IT FELT, Career Day did finally end. I fled as quickly as possible, grateful that I had to be at work to cover the late shift. I squashed my thoughts of Sam and concentrated on the several patients who came in, taking as long with them as possible, trying to avoid any downtime. When I finally got home around ten, I grabbed Digger's leash and walked with him to Nauset Light Beach. There, listening to the roar and shush of the waves, I gave in.

I was in love with Sam. I didn't know when it had happened, but it had. Looking back over the past few months, I had to close my eyes. The evidence was all there, but I'd never put the pieces together and made the diagnosis. Until today. I loved Sam Nickerson. It was so starkly true that I couldn't believe a whisper of it had never entered my conscious brain.

Everything I had wanted Joe to be, Sam was. And always had been.

A slight breeze brought the scent of a fire somewhere, the salty, rich smell of the ocean. Digger nudged my hand with his eager nose, and I bent down and rubbed his head before letting him off the leash. I watched as he raced joyously down the beach, his white splotches glowing in the darkness. Then I sat on the damp sand, staring out at the rollers, counting the seconds that it took the beam from Nauset Light to sweep across the ocean.

If I thought I'd been miserable about Joe, I had been kidding myself. That had been choppy water. This was a tidal wave. I was in love with the one man, aside from my dear old dad, who was absolutely off-limits. But hey! If I loved Sam, maybe I *should* take another look at Dad! After all, I clearly had my head up my ass.

Digger returned, panting and smelling of the sea. He flopped down beside me, his fur sandy and wet. I stroked his ears and watched the sky go from black to navy. In a few hours, it would be morning. When my legs went numb from sitting so long, Digger and I got up and returned home. There was a message on the machine. From Sam, of course.

"Hey, kiddo, just checking in, wanted to see if you were okay. You were pretty funny at the school today. Come for dinner some night this week, okay? Bye."

Yup. Loved him.

Shit.

CHAPTER TWENTY-EIGHT

THE FIRST THING I DID WAS nothing. Aside from going to work and taking care of Digger, I didn't do a damn thing. A whole week passed, and all I could do was reach out and touch the new sore spot in my heart. But then, as I got over the shock of my revelation, I turned to my closest friends.

Katie and I drove up to the Pink Peacock one evening for dinner. Curtis and Mitch had converted the third floor into a spacious, elegant apartment with sweeping views of the long stone breakwater and small lighthouse that stood on Provincetown's final spit of land. Over grilled striper, I gently broke the news, saying the words gingerly.

"It seems that I'm—um—I'm in love with Sam." I waited for their alarm, their sympathy, their words of wisdom.

Curtis and Mitch glanced at each other. Katie was silent for a moment, then nodded. "I know," she said.

"You know?"

She gave a little smile. "Yeah, Mil. I'm sorry to say, it was kind of…obvious."

"It was?" Mouth hanging open, I turned to Curtis and Mitch. "Did you know, too?" I asked, blinking rapidly.

"Well, no, not exactly," Curtis answered. "But it does make sense. Sam really is true blue, isn't he? Definitely more your type than Joe was."

"Curtis, he's my brother-in-law!" I yelped.

"Well, technically, not anymore," Mitchell murmured.

"So what am I supposed to do?" I asked.

"Tell him?" Katie suggested, taking a bite of her meal.

"Right, Katie. He thinks of me as the sister he never had. I'm not going to tell him." I flopped back in my seat. No more advice was offered.

THE CLINIC WAS WINDING DOWN, and things were already pretty slow. After we closed, Dr. Whitaker was giving me two weeks off before I'd start with him. We'd worked out the details of our arrangement…. He'd cover half my malpractice insurance for the first year, and any new patients would be mine. Although I'd initially be making less than I had at the clinic, it was a good, solid offer, exactly what I'd always wanted. Professionally, I was all set. Personally, I was struggling.

Though it was easy now to see that I had never really loved Joe Carpenter, I nonetheless missed that old image of him. My obsession had unknowingly motivated me to do a lot of things that I might not have done otherwise—embarrassing, slightly humiliating, but true. For so many years, I'd dreamed of a life with Joe.

As for dreaming of Sam, forget it. My friendship with Sam was one of the best things in my life, and I wasn't about to ruin it with a declaration that he'd never be able to forget.

The thing was, of course, that aside from apparently being the love of my life, Sam was also part of my family. I couldn't avoid him. And aside from the awkwardness I knew I'd feel, I missed him. So when my mom called and asked me to come over for dinner with Sam and Danny, I said yes.

My heart was thumping as I pulled into my parents'

driveway. Sam's truck was already there. I wiped my palms on my jeans and went in.

"Hello, darling," my mom called, hunching down to check the roast.

"Hi, everyone," I said. Sam was leaning against the fridge, nursing a beer.

"Hey, kiddo," he said, leaning over and giving me a one-armed hug. "How's it going?"

"Fine, fine," I said, quickly extracting myself.

How many times had Sam hugged me in my life? A hundred? Two hundred? More? And now suddenly my mouth was dry, my stomach fluttered and my cheeks grew hot. I scurried across the kitchen and hugged my nephew.

"How are you, tall one?" I asked, grateful to be with someone for whom my emotions were still pure.

"Good, Aunt Mil. Hey, sorry to hear about you breaking up with Joe. He was nice." Danny gave me a sympathetic grin.

"Thanks, honey."

"Hey, Mil, remember that, um, project you said you'd help me with?" Danny asked in a low voice.

"The midwestern project?" I murmured back.

"Yup. Got any time this week?"

"Sure. Want to come over one day after school? How about Thursday, around four? You can stay for supper."

"Great. Thanks."

Sam was watching us, a smile crinkling his eyes. An almost painful tightness wrapped my heart. *Get used to it,* I admonished myself.

Dinner was fine, I was fine. I told everyone about my arrangements with Dr. Whitaker, and they were thrilled. We talked about Danny's school year. Dad talked about work. Mom talked about the upcoming local elections. I acted normally throughout, and it wasn't actually too hard. I just couldn't look at Sam for more than a second without that ache coming back, my throat tightening up and my hands shaking. Otherwise, no problem.

"Well, I've got to go," I said the second I thought I could make a run for it.

"Let me make you up a plate, Millie," my mom said, leaping for her Tupperware.

"Oh, no, that's okay, Mom. It was fantastic, but, um, no thanks. Send it home with Danny and Sam."

I kissed my parents and waved to Danny. "Bye, Sam," I said, grabbing my purse.

"I'll walk you out," Sam said, rising

"No, no, that's okay." Heat rushed to my face as I fumbled for my coat.

"Don't be silly." Sam caught up to me in the hall and put his arm around my shoulders, his familiar height so unbearably dear to me that I almost cried. Mutely, I let him escort me down the walk and to my car. My heart thudded in my chest, and I seemed to have forgotten how to take a breath.

Sam leaned against my car door, blocking access to the escape pod. "Everything okay, Millie?" he asked.

"Yes! Everything is great!" I exclaimed, looking skyward.

He squinted at me, cop-like. "You're acting strange."

"Really?"

"Is it breaking up with Joe?" he asked. "Because I know you guys were pretty tight this summer. It must be tough."

"You have no idea," I said. "Literally no idea."

"Well, why don't we go out for a bite some night and you can tell me about it?"

"Um, sure, Sam. That would be terrific. Listen, I have to

go now, though, because, um, I have to call a patient back at nine o'clock, and—"

"Oh! Sorry, Millie. I'll let you go." Ever the gentleman, he opened my door for me. "I'll call you this week, okay?"

"Bye!" I stretched my mouth into a smile and nearly backed over his foot.

CHAPTER TWENTY-NINE

A NEW CHAPTER OF MY LIFE was unfolding. Unfortunately, it wasn't any better than the previous chapters. More pretending. More faking. And the fact that I was avoiding Sam, who'd been so good and kind to me for decades, killed me. I dodged his invitation when he called later in the week. Dinner together? How about if we drown me instead?

Danny was the bright spot. He came over with his Notre Dame application and we pored over it as if it were a missing book of the New Testament or the newest Harry Potter.

"'What is the best book you've ever read and why?' Brutal!" I said. "I guess we can't say *Goodnight Moon.*"

"Why not?" Danny laughed. "You haven't read that to me in about six months."

"Don't get me started. My baby nephew is going off to college. I'm going to bawl. Now what *is* the best book you've ever read?" I asked, getting up to give him more meat loaf.

"Hmm. I guess that would be *The Iliad.*"

"God! Mine is *Bridget Jones's Diary.* Somehow, I think your choice is a better answer."

We roughed out his essays, me murmuring encouragingly as he talked his way through the sections.

"Okay, what are you going to put down for your preliminary major?" I asked, going through the easier questions.

"Pre-med."

I looked up, startled. "Really?"

"Yup. One of my favorite people is a doctor, and I want to be just like her when I grow up." He smiled at me and started packing up his papers.

"Danny…" I said, my eyes wet, "you're already ten times the person I'll ever be."

"Well," he said modestly, looking so much like Sam it just about broke my heart. "We'll see about that."

He gave me a moment to blow my nose and dab my eyes, tolerated a kiss, and then shrugged into his jacket.

"Have you heard from your mom?" I asked.

"Oh, yeah. Every night at ten. I'm going down to New York City to spend the weekend with her. Gonna go to some museums, maybe see a show."

"That sounds like fun. Give her my love." My feelings had softened a bit toward Trish lately. I'd even called her a couple of times, listening without censure as she described Avery's latest car or the restaurant that had just opened in SoHo.

Danny gave me a hug. "Thanks for the help, Aunt Mil. God, I hope I get in."

"Danny, you have a 4.0 average, you got 2380 on your SATs, you volunteer for Habitat for Humanity, you play varsity baseball and you have very straight teeth. You'll get in."

I STARTED RUNNING AGAIN. If Joe passed me, I planned on waving, but he never did. He'd finished at the senior center, so I was safe when I made rounds there. Katie insisted that I get out and dragged me to the movies. Curtis and Mitch called almost daily. I went to work, but I didn't really have that much to do. I stopped by to see Danny once or twice only when I was pretty sure Sam was working. Sam called me a few times and asked me to go out, but after the third time I gave him an excuse, he backed off.

It would just take time, I rationalized, to get used to this and be able to deal with it gracefully. One day, things would be back to normal, and Sam and I could be friends again. We would talk on the phone and maybe go for a run together. He would meet someone, and the three of us would have dinner together, and I would be happy for him. You betcha. One of these old days. Until then, I planned a campaign of evasive maneuvers.

I hadn't counted on Sam pulling me over for speeding one night. When I saw the flashing lights in my rearview mirror, I cursed. Pulling over to the side of Route 6 by the Visitors Center, I watched Sam unfold himself from the patrol car. Officer Ethel got out also, but she just leaned against the cruiser, lit up a cigarette and sucked deeply, her cheeks hollowing. She tossed me a careless wave.

"Hey, Millie. Looks like this is the only way I get to see you." Sam leaned down and smiled at me. My heart squeezed painfully.

"Oh, Officer, please don't give me a ticket. I'm a doctor and I have a medical emergency." I tried to find the old groove I used to have with Sam. It fell flat.

"Oh, yeah? And what's that?" He waited expectantly.

I sighed. "I don't know, Sam. Are you really going to give me a ticket?"

"Nope. You were only doing forty-four. I just saw your car and wanted to say hi. Seems like you've been awfully busy lately."

"Yes, yes, very busy," I said, looking straight ahead, hoping the darkness hid the tears that pricked my eyes. "Lots to do."

He looked at me another minute, his smile fading. "Okay, Millie. I'll see you around."

I glanced quickly at him and took a quick breath. "Okay, Sam. Thanks. Good to see you."

I zipped away, safe for another day.

OCTOBER'S COOLER WEATHER seemed to come overnight. The poison ivy flashed brilliant red, the maples and locust trees glowed with yellow, the oaks a solemn brown. All of a sudden, summer was over. It was a bittersweet time. Never had I felt so in tune with the seasons…. My summer brightness had faded, and I felt a long winter of the soul coming on.

But I was determined to get on with my life. I would keep running and trying to eat right, since I didn't want to lose my newfound health. It was funny, though. All that time spent trying to lose weight, and now I found eating to be a bit of a chore. But I plugged along resignedly, chewing food I didn't much taste, staring at the kitchen table a lot.

Thank God for Digger. I appreciated his company more than ever. In the evenings, I taught him silly tricks, like collapsing to the floor if I pointed my finger at him and said, "Bang." He learned to crawl, toss a cookie off his nose and catch it midair, and sneeze on command. "I'm sorry, Diggy," I said the night that he failed to learn to dance on his hind legs. Still, I was grateful that he entertained me, even if it was at the cost of his personal dignity. For his reward, I started letting him sleep on my bed.

I tried to read. Medical journals were the only thing I could get through, which was lucky, since I wanted to be on top of things when I started with Dr. Whitaker in a few weeks. I thought about taking a quick vacation, going off-Cape for some of that time, but I didn't think I could afford anything far enough to be worthwhile, and frankly, I didn't have the energy.

I tried not to think about Sam.

ON COLUMBUS DAY WEEKEND, we had a party to say goodbye. Dr. Bala and his family came, as did Jill and her husband, and Juanita from the hospital. Sienna brought a boyfriend, a sinister-looking man in leather and metal who actually was quite sweet and friendly, Satan-worshipping garb aside. Jeff, our dear college student, couldn't make it, as he was back at Tufts, but we generously forgave him. Pizza and soda were passed around, and we all felt a bit nostalgic.

"Do you remember the man who unfortunately put the nail through his hand? Goodness, that was a nasty one. It reminded me of a crucifixion," Dr. Bala reminisced.

"And the lady who fell asleep naked on her deck? Poor thing! I have never seen such bad sunburn!" Jill chuckled.

"What about the newlyweds with poison ivy?" Sienna hooted. (I had to fake-laugh on that one.)

"What are your plans, Dr. Balamassarhinarhajhi?" I asked, the now-familiar syllables rolling effortlessly from my lips.

"You can call me by my given name, you know, Millie," he said in his lovely, lyrical accent.

"Well, actually, Dr. Balamassarhinarhajhi, I don't know your given name." Dr. B. had always signed his name in trademark doctor scrawl, and we had no nameplates around our seasonal clinic. I had only seen his first name listed as J.

"You do not? Oh, dear, dear. Well, it's John."

I stared at him. "You're joking. It's really John?"

He smiled. "Oh, you Americans are so funny. So culturally stifled." His beautiful wife joined in his merry laughter.

"Your plans, *John?*" I repeated, grinning in spite of myself.

"I will be heading up another clinic in New Hampshire, a permanent position close to my son's university, so I will not return to Cape Cod except for vacation," he answered.

"I hope you'll call me when you're back," I said, meaning it.

"I certainly will, Millie. It has been a pleasure working with a young doctor of your competence and good humor."

"Well, thank you very much. I've learned a lot from you, sir."

Because Dr. Bala was headed north, I offered to take up his last few shifts. With Jeff back in college, I also answered the infrequent phone calls after four and did the small amount of paperwork necessary. It meant working until ten at night, but I didn't care. Jill came in for a few hours during the middle of the day, but we were pretty much finished. I only saw a few patients over the last week, spending most of the time reading or sending falsely cheerful e-mails to Danny and my off-Cape friends. Most days, I brought Digger with me so he (and I) wouldn't have to spend the whole day alone.

I was waiting. Waiting for work to begin with Dr. Whitaker, waiting for the next chapter of my life, waiting for the ache over Sam to subside.

CHAPTER THIRTY

ON THE VERY LAST NIGHT that the clinic was open, I sat in my office, packing up a few papers and deleting some files from the computer. Jill was long gone, and the silence of the empty space echoed, the clock's ticking very prominent in the quiet. Digger and I reviewed his repertoire, but it seemed like his doggy eyes were begging for reprieve, so I gave him a chew stick and rubbed his back with my foot as I let myself steep in melancholy.

I would miss the clinic. It had been a very pleasant place to work, and it had been safe, with the strength of Cape Cod Hospital behind us. While private practice would be more rewarding, no doubt, it would also be a lot scarier. I'd miss working with Jill and Sienna, miss the fun of our girl talk in the back room.

Tomorrow the hospital people would come to reclaim the cardiac monitor and X-ray equipment, pack up the medical supplies and drug samples, the computers and files. The clinic would sit empty until next April, when some other doctor would staff it. It wasn't my place anymore.

Nine o'clock found me in my office, trying to finish an article on a new heart valve prosthesis. A half-eaten cup of yogurt sat abandoned on my desk, and Digger lay twitchily dreaming on the floor. I vaguely heard a siren, but it didn't register at first, not until it became louder. Digger leaped up, startled. I got up, too. When I saw the blue light flashing and slowing in front of the clinic, I ran outside.

An Eastham police cruiser came screaming into the parking lot. Ethel jumped out from the driver's side.

"It's Sam! He's hurt!" she called, adeptly sliding across the hood of the car like Starsky or Hutch. My heart stopped then surged at her words even as my feet carried me over to the car. Sam was sitting in the passenger's seat.

Ethel yanked the door open and Sam got out. He was holding his right arm across his stomach and couldn't seem to stand up straight.

"Calm down, Ethel," he said. "I'm okay, Millie."

"I am fucking calm. It's just that my goddamn partner is fucking hurt!"

"What happened?" I asked. My voice was tight and high.

"I'm fine, all right? Stop panicking." He was obviously in pain.

"Some butthole hit him with a tire iron, Millie," Ethel said, running ahead to open the clinic door. "Jesus Christ, he almost got hit in the fucking head!"

I had never seen Ethel so emotional. Her leathery face was scrunched tight, and her hands were shaking slightly.

"Okay, let's get you in here, buddy," I said, taking his good arm. Ethel grabbed Digger, who was leaping ecstatically at the sight of Sam, and put him in the office as I led Sam to an exam room. "Can you get up there, Sam?" I asked. He awkwardly scootched onto the table, apparently unable to use his arm, and I felt my eyes grow wet.

"For God's sake, don't cry, Millie," he growled.

"We were just doing a routine traffic stop down by the rotary," Ethel rasped, coming in to join us. "One of these asswipe kids was stoned, and Sam asked him to open the trunk. And before we even knew it, the kid was swinging a goddamn tire iron, Millie! Fuck me! The little shit swung it right at Sam's head, and Sam turned just in time, and bam! The goddamn fucker slammed him right in the fucking shoulder!"

"Ethel, for God's sake, settle down." Sam said, rolling his eyes. "Millie, I'm fine. Can you just x-ray this and be done with it? Eth, why don't you go out to the cruiser and radio in, okay?"

Ethel looked at him. "Okay, Sam." She took a rattling breath. "Take good care of him, Millie."

"I will." I closed the door after her and looked at Sam. His face was pale, and he was favoring his right side. His expression was grim. "Did she get it about right?" I asked him, writing something—I know not what—on a paper. My own hands were shaking.

"Yeah, yeah, that was it. Not a huge deal. Just a punky kid."

"He hit you with a tire iron?"

"Yup."

I swallowed loudly.

"Millie, if you start crying, I'm going to strangle you. Just get the damn exam over with. The union says I have to be cleared by a doctor before I can go home. Can you just do that for me?"

"Why so ornery, Officer?" I asked, hoping to get a smile.

"Because my shoulder is killing me, damn it!" he yelled.

"All right, all right. Settle down. Jeez, you sound like my dad."

"Is this your bedside manner, Millie? Because it sucks." A ghost of a grin slipped across his face. I smiled back, though the smile wobbled.

"Okay, Officer," I said. "Let's get that shirt off and have a look." I sounded like a porno movie.

"You sound like a porno movie," Sam said, fumbling with his uniform buttons.

"Here, you jerk, let me help you."

"Now that's my Millie."

Those words caused my throat to close with a muffled click. Eyes stinging from tears, I undid the buttons and gently tugged the shirt tails out of his pants, hoping that Sam didn't notice my flushed face.

"Please stop crying," my patient sighed.

"Sorry." I slipped the shirt off his hurt shoulder, wincing as I did. White scars crisscrossed his skin from the surgery he'd had in college.

"I forgot this was your bad shoulder," I whispered, biting my lip.

"Millie! Snap out of it and get me out of here."

I jumped. "Right. Okay. It's just that…you know, Sam. It's you. I don't like seeing you hurt."

"Well, fix me up and get me home, then. For God's sake."

I was grateful for his irritation because if he hadn't said that, I'd probably have sobbed out my love for him. I did snap out of it, gently examining his shoulder, moving it carefully to test for range of motion, extending his arm.

"Did you get hurt anywhere else?" I asked as I took his blood pressure on his good arm.

"No," he said, looking steadily at me. We were only an inch or two apart, and suddenly the air seemed very thick.

I stepped back fast. "Okay. I don't think it's broken, but let's x-ray you to be sure."

I helped him off the table and over to the X-ray area, had him lie down in the appropriate positions. I didn't usually do this part of an exam, but I knew how. I went through the steps and tapped a few keys at the computer. Sam sat up on the table and waited for the verdict as the images came up on the monitor.

"Nothing broken. Got a nasty bone bruise, though. And your old fractures are stable. See the screws there? You got lucky."

"So what do you do for a bone bruise?" he asked.

"Motrin, a sling, no work for a week. I'm going to write you a scrip for Vicodin in case the Motrin isn't enough." I scrounged around the desk, looking for the prescription pad.

"Okay." He groped at his shirt, trying to get it around him and onto his right side.

"Here, let me help you with that." I reached around, slipping the sleeve gently onto Sam's hurt arm, then buttoned him up carefully. My fingers seemed to be having trouble getting the job done. I eased the sling onto his arm and tightened the strap so it would be comfortable. Sam had grown very still. I glanced up at his face.

He was looking at me. Not over my shoulder, not at his shirt. At me. Then his eyes dropped down to my mouth. And then, very slowly, Sam leaned forward and kissed me, a gentle, soft kiss as if I were the most precious thing in the world. And when I didn't pull back, he kissed me for real.

His good arm slipped around my waist, under my white doctor's coat. His mouth was so warm and soft and fit against mine so perfectly that my knees softened in a rush. My brain stopped registering everything but Sam, his kiss, his warmth and his lean solidness, his arm pressing me closer against him.

"Holy motheragod!"

I leaped away as if I'd been electrocuted, jostling Sam's bruised shoulder in the process. He winced, I winced, Ethel winced.

"Oh, shit on salad, I am so sorry! Fuck me! I'm leaving. Sam, don't worry about anything, not that it looks like you are. Everything's called in. Wellfleet PD caught the kids up near Moby's. Lieutenant says just go home and he'll call you tomorrow. Crap! I guess you don't need a ride. Shit. Sorry." Ethel gave a meaty cough and left. We listened to the cruiser squeal out of the parking lot at about thirty miles an hour.

Which left just Sam and me. His face said it all. He looked like a baby harp seal, freshly clubbed.

"Millie—"

I drew a shaking breath and pressed my fingers to my mouth. I tried to say something, but I couldn't.

"Oh, Millie, I'm so sorry." He, too, was breathing rather heavily. "Mil, say something. Please."

What could I say? I was speechless, maybe for the first time in my life.

"I didn't plan that, Millie. I'm sorry. I never should have— I'm really sorry." He got up from the table and started to come over to me.

"We—we—we—we should go. Right? Let's go," I babbled. "Just sit here and let me finish up. Because it's the clinic's last night, and I have to just make sure everything's done and turned off and all that."

"Millie, I'm so sorry. I didn't mean to—I'm sorry. Please say something." He looked miserable.

"Um, let's just, let's, let's just pack it in here. Okay? Okay. Great."

I ran, literally ran, into my office and closed the door. Digger snuffled my hands, but I barely noticed.

He'd kissed me.

And he was sorry. So sorry. Sorry, Millie. Please. Really sorry.

My legs shook almost uncontrollably. I took a few deep, heaving breaths, and looked around. *Do what you have to do to get out of here,* I commanded. Like a robot, I shut down the computer, scratched the words *Police officer assaulted, bone bruise, right shoulder, full range of motion, no fracture* on the chart and grabbed my bag. Going out to the X-ray area, I breezed past Sam and made sure his file was in the queue to be read by the radiologist on call at Cape Cod Hospital. Then I ripped off the prescription and handed it to Sam, who looked as if his dog had just died.

"Here you go. You have an orthopedist, right? Reardon? Call him tomorrow and make sure you get an appointment. I'll let him know you need to be seen. Danny can bring the scrip down to CVS in Orleans if you need it, but try the Motrin first, six to eight hundred milligrams every six hours. Do not use the arm. Use ice for the first forty-eight hours, heat after that. Any questions?"

He just looked at me. "No."

We went outside and I started to lock up.

"You forgot your dog, Millie," Sam said quietly.

"Right." I went back in and got Digger, apologized and let the faithful beast into the back seat.

"Need help?" I asked as Sam opened the car door with his left hand.

"No, thanks."

I got in and started up the car, studiously not looking at Sam. After a minute, he tried again.

"Millie, can we talk about what happened there? Please?"

I took a deep breath, but instead of steadying my nerves, it came out as almost a sob. "Not right now, okay?" I squeaked.

Sam looked at me another long minute. "Okay. But I'm sor—"

"Don't apologize! Just forget it."

"I think we need to talk about it, Millie."

"Not now! Not right now! Okay, Sam? Not now." Digger, sensing my distress, poked his head between the seats and licked my ear.

Sam didn't say anything else until we pulled into his driveway. Danny, obviously having been contacted by Ethel, came leaping down the stairs.

"Look," I commented. "It's Danny. Your son. My nephew."

"Oh, Millie," Sam said softly.

"Dad! Dad! Are you okay?" Danny ripped the passenger door open, and Sam got out, turning to his son.

"I'm fine, Dan. Just a bruise."

"Oh, Dad…" Danny wrapped his arms gingerly around his father and grimaced as he tried not to cry. I rested my forehead on the steering wheel, hot tears flooding my eyes.

"Aunt Mil, will he be okay?" Danny asked, his voice breaking a little. I wiped my eyes, opened the door and got out, but I didn't step away from the car.

"He's going to be fine, honey," I said, my voice sounding normal for the first time all night. "He got hit in the shoulder with a tire iron. He can tell you all about it. Call me if you need anything, okay? But right now, just get him inside, give him four Motrin and put an ice pack on his shoulder."

"Come on, Dad," Danny said. Sam glanced at me but let his son lead him inside.

CHAPTER THIRTY-ONE

"MILLIE, I'M SORRY. I don't know what came over me. I didn't mean to kiss you, and I'll never do it again."

"Millie, clearly that was a huge mistake. Can we forget it ever happened?"

"Millie, I'm sorry. Sorry, sorry, sorry."

I said the above phrases out loud into my bathroom mirror all the next day, trying to thicken my skin for when the shoe dropped.

How could my life go from ridiculous to idiotic to just plain awful so fast? The man I loved had kissed me, but that clearly wasn't a good thing, not when he was so sorry, sorry, freaking sorry. Now I would have to pretend that it didn't matter, that I had forgotten all about that little whoopsy-daisy, and that Sam was just the father of my nephew. We wouldn't be friends. We would be awkward and horrible together, and I would miss him for the rest of my life.

"Crap," I whispered tearfully, banging my head against the mirror. I wandered around my house, muttering to myself. Most of what I could make out was "Stupid, stupid, stupid." Over and over, I revisited the stricken look on Sam's face. How many times had he apologized? At least six, as I recalled. He was sorry. And so was I.

Oh, the kiss had been unbelievable. That was the problem.

The best kiss of my life, from the man I loved from my bone marrow on out, and he was sorry it had happened.

The phone rang at nine. I stood tensely next to the machine, eyes burning, fists clenched, heart thudding dully in my ears.

"Hi, this is Millie. Leave me a message and I'll call you as soon as I can!"

My chirpy voice sounded idiotic. No wonder Sam was sorry. *Beep!*

"Millie, it's Sam. Pick up the phone."

"No," I said to the machine. Sam sighed as if he could hear me.

"Millie, please call me. I'm home all day, except at two, when I'm going to see Dr. Reardon. I should be back by three. Okay? Call me."

Ten minutes later, the phone rang again.

"Hi, this is Millie. Leave me a message and I'll call you as soon as I can!"

"Aunt Millie, it's Danny—"

I snatched up the phone. "Hi, honey. How's your dad?"

"He's okay. I don't think he slept much last night."

"Uh-huh." No mystery there. "How's his shoulder?"

"He says it's okay, pretty sore, though. Want to talk to him?"

"No!" I yelped. "I mean, no," I continued more calmly. "I'm just running out. Let me know what Dr. Reardon says, okay?"

"Okay, Aunt Mil. Bye."

Sam called again, around four. "Hey, Millie. It's Sam." He paused for a second. "Millie, we can't…listen, I really, really want to talk to you. Please call me. Thank you."

I didn't call. I just couldn't listen to him tell me what a mistake he'd made, how sorry he was, how we should forget it, put it past us, blah, blah, blah. Nor did I want to talk to anyone, not Katie, not Curtis or Mitch. It was one thing to have this big, aching love. It was another to tell people that you'd been rejected.

Danny called again later and filled me in on the doctor's visit, which had confirmed the diagnosis of bone bruise. Sam had taken a Vicodin and gone to bed. Sadness and sympathy flared at the idea of Sam sleeping uncomfortably in his big bed. Danny told me the sling could come off in another day or so, and I told him that I thought that would be fine, too.

"Is everything okay, Aunt Millie?" my nephew asked in a low voice.

"Sure, Danny. Everything's fine. I just…I'm just distracted. We closed the clinic yesterday, and I start my new job in a couple of weeks…." My voice trailed off. I didn't want to lie to Danny.

Sam called the next day, but only once. "It's Sam," he said. He stayed on the line for a minute, waiting. "Okay, Millie," he said quietly. Click.

I cleaned my already immaculate house. I baked cookies, then brought them to the senior center. I went for a run. I showered, e-mailed, organized my closet, polished my shoes, but the day refused to end. My skin felt stretched too tight, trying desperately to hold my secret in. Finally, I grabbed my keys and drove into Orleans, heading for the Barnacle. Hopefully, it wouldn't be too busy and Katie could take a break. I needed my best friend.

I burst into the restaurant and then lurched to a stop. For the first time in my life, I hadn't noticed Joe Carpenter's truck in the parking lot. He was sitting next to Katie at the bar, some papers in front of him, their heads close together.

The bar was quiet, only a few tables taken now that the tourism season was finished for the year.

Walking up to the bar, I cleared my throat. "Hi, guys," I said.

Katie looked up. "Hey, Millie!" she smiled. "Guess what? Joe's getting Tripod certified as a therapy dog!"

Joe looked up. "Hi, Millie," he said, his voice neutral.

"Hi, Joe," I said. There was an awkward pause. "That's great."

Joe looked down. "Yeah, well, he's a good dog. You know."

"And if Tripod does well, then Joe can adopt a puppy and train it to be a therapy dog, too," Katie announced, beaming like a proud parent.

"That's great, Joe," I said.

"Katie's helping me with the application."

"Great." I glanced at Katie.

"Ask her," Katie whispered, nudging Joe's arm.

Joe took a deep breath. "Would you give me a reference, Millie?"

My mouth fell open. "Sure! Of course, Joe. You're great with dogs. Tripod is so well-behaved."

"Thanks." He smiled then, a little shyly, and I found myself smiling back. "I heard Sam got hurt by some punk," Joe said, taking a swig of beer. "How's he doing?"

"He's fine." My ears burned at the mention of Sam's name. "Thanks for asking. Um, he just got hit pretty hard, but he's good." Again, I glanced at Katie.

"Listen, Joe, you finish filling that out, okay?" she said. "I have to talk to Millie for a sec." Katie and I went to a table in the corner and sat down.

"So what's up?" she asked.

Suddenly feeling uncomfortable, I stalled. "What are you doing with Joe?"

She laughed and pulled her hair over one shoulder. "Oh, he just needs a little…guidance. I don't know. Remember I told him off at Nauset High that day?"

"Sure." The Wrath of Katie was not easy to forget.

"Well, he came in last week and asked for some advice, can you believe that? On what I thought he should do to get himself on track. Whatever. So I told him to volunteer for some worthy cause, and he showed up tonight with all the paperwork and stuff." Katie smiled, clearly pleased. "Anyway. What's going on with you? You look whipped."

I took a deep breath and launched into the whole story, ending with Sam's endless apologies.

"Huh," said my best friend. "Hmm."

"Can you do better than that?" I asked, more caustically than I intended, glancing at Joe, who was still immersed in his paperwork.

Katie grimaced. "Gee, Millie, this is a toughie. I guess you're just going to have to talk to him and get it straightened out. But still, he did kiss you, so he must have some feelings there."

"Which he's sorry for! You should have seen his face!"

"Oh, sweetie, I don't know." She squeezed my shoulder. "And you're not going to know until you talk to him." Chris called Katie's name and she looked up. "I'm sorry, Millie, I need to get back to work. Just talk to Sam. Sorry I can't help more. Call me tomorrow. I'm home all day."

So much for the advice of a best friend. Nonplussed, I rose to leave. Joe jumped up. "Millie!" I stopped. "Hey, Millie," Joe said, coming closer. "Listen, it was…" He paused. "It's good to see you, Mil." He gave a small smile, and tears pricked my eyes.

He was forgiving me.

"It's good to see you, too, Joe," I whispered.

CHAPTER THIRTY-TWO

THE NEXT DAY, THE BEEPING of a storm warning scrolled across the bottom of the television screen. Huh. A tropical depression was rolling up the coast. Could grow into a hurricane. Well, that would be fun. Storms were fantastic on the Cape. Lots of drama, lots of wind. I didn't have anywhere to go.

At some point the night before, I had resolved to call Sam. I couldn't just lie around drooling anymore. He deserved to hear from me, and I had been acting like an ass, avoiding him. I would let him say his piece, assure him that I'd be fine and pretend to have no feelings for him for the rest of my life.

Thus steadfastly determined, I decided to procrastinate just a little bit longer. I dragged the porch furniture into the cellar in case the wind got too rough later on, taped the living-room picture window and made a pot of soup. Glancing at the scudding gray clouds outside, I decided to take advantage of the fact that it wasn't raining yet and go for a run. Digger stood stock-still as I put on my running shoes, breathlessly hopeful that his dream might come true.

"Let's go, pal," I said, and he leaped joyfully for the door.

The wind was growing stronger, and the smell of rain was in the air. Every once in a while a gust would shove at Digger and me, or I'd have to run around a small branch in the road. The wind was cold, and occasionally I could hear a rumble of thunder as the front came closer. It was getting darker by the minute. Perhaps this had been a mistake.

It was. Just as I reached the halfway mark, stinging rain began to pelt down from the black clouds. I had no choice but to run faster. I rounded the turn onto Ocean View Drive, hearing the waves well before I saw them. Sand blew across the road, slicing into my skin, and I opened my stride as much as I could.

By the time I was finished, I was exhausted. My legs ached, my ears burned and I was completely drenched by rain and salt spray. Even Digger was subdued, fur soaked through.

As I plodded up the driveway, I saw Sam sitting in his pickup. He got out, bent to pat my wet dog, then straightened and looked at me, shielding his eyes from the rain. "Hi."

"Hi, Sam." I managed to smile a little. "Believe it or not, I was going to call you the minute I got home."

"Uh-huh." He didn't smile back.

"Um, how's your shoulder?"

"It's fine." He waited until I sighed. It was time.

"Come on in," I said, opening the back door. Turning on some lights, I grabbed a towel. Drying off Digger meant that I didn't have to look at Sam. Digger moaned joyfully at the brisk rubdown. When I released him, he immediately went to Sam's leg for a little romance.

"No, Digger." Sam bent to remove Digger's front legs from his shin. "Millie—"

"Is it okay if I just grab a quick shower? I'm not trying to stall, I'm just afraid the power's going to go out."

"Sure," he answered a bit tightly, taking off his jacket. "I'll, um, I'll make some coffee."

I showered and washed my hair as fast as I could. The sky was downright black now, and the house shook periodically from the force of the wind. I pulled on some jeans and my comfy old Holy Cross sweatshirt and went to face Sam. The minute I stepped into the kitchen, the lights went out.

"Well, this gives us a sense of foreboding, don't you think?" I asked cheerfully, though my stomach was in knots.

"At least the coffee's done perking." Boy Scout that he was, he'd rooted out a few little votive candles while I'd been in the shower, and now lit them, placing them around the kitchen. Their warm, gentle glow flickered in the drafts. Sam handed me a cup of coffee, cream, no sugar, just the way I liked it. "I filled up some pots with water in case we're out for a day or two," he said, and I could hear his nervousness in his voice.

"Thank you."

Sam cleared his throat and leaned against the counter.

"Do you want to sit down?" I asked, suddenly dying to delay this awful moment.

"No, I'd better do this standing up," he answered. Dread rose in the bottom of my stomach and trickled into my arms and legs, leaving a path of cold behind. It was one thing to imagine this conversation, but it was another to have it here and now.

"Okay, Millie," Sam began. "I just want to say this and get through it, and then you can have a turn, all right?"

"Okay," I said, my voice catching. Digger, sensing my sorrow, came over and put his head in my lap. I stroked his ears for a second, then said, "Go lie down, boy." He obeyed, disappearing into the gloom of the living room.

"You know I think you're great, right, Millie?" His voice was so gentle and soft that it caused a physical ache in my throat and chest. Tears, my constant companion, stung my eyes. I nodded, unable to look at him. A gust of wind rattled the windows and slapped sheets of rain against the shingles.

"Over the past year, you've been a really good friend to me, and I can't tell you how much I appreciate it. You're important to me, Mil. I want you to know that."

I swallowed loudly and looked out the window.

Sam took a deep breath and rubbed his palms on his jeans. "At the clinic the other night, I…I didn't plan on that. I don't want you to think I'm some lecherous creep who's been sniffing after my wife's sister all this time. Okay?"

"Okay," I whispered. A tear slipped down my cheek, but hopefully it was too dark for Sam to see.

"So, Millie, I'm sorry. I'm sorry I took you by surprise like that. I surprised myself, too. And I'm sorry you felt so uncomfortable that you couldn't even call me. I mean, I understand, believe me. But the last thing I wanted to do was ruin our friendship. You're probably the best friend I've got, and if you didn't want to see me anymore, Millie, I'd miss you more than I could say."

I nodded and pressed my fingers to my lips to hide the fact that I was crying. My hands and legs were shaking, and it felt as if a steel band were crushing my chest. So this was heartbreak. It was living up to its reputation.

Sam shifted, putting his coffee cup on the counter. As the candles flickered, I sneaked a look at him, then quickly looked back at the table. "It's okay, Sam," I began, my voice rough with tears.

"I'm not done." His voice was almost sharp. "Millie, I need to tell you this because I can't lie to you." He gave his head a little shake, then took a deep breath. "See, Millie, while I'm sorry I surprised you, I'm not sorry I kissed you."

It took a minute for those words to reach my heart. When they did, I turned and stared at Sam, dumbfounded. He was looking right at me, his fists shoved into his jeans pockets, clearly scared. He winced a little.

"Something changed, Millie," he said, his voice shaking. "I don't know exactly when it happened, but somewhere along the line, I…I fell for you."

The roaring in my ears had nothing to do with the storm outside, and my heart felt like a seagull soaring up on the ocean breeze. Sam was still talking.

"I didn't want to admit it, because of Trish and all that. I mean, I've always cared about you, of course. But at the Lighthouse Dance, you looked so beautiful, and then, at the clinic I just…I just couldn't pretend that I don't have…that I don't…ah, shit. Please, Millie, say something."

I tried to answer, but no sound came out. Sam obviously misread my silence, because he looked down at the floor and his shoulders sagged a little. I wiped my eyes on a napkin, went over to him and put my hands on his shoulders.

"Sam," I said. "I think I've loved you my whole life."

His eyes widened, his lips parting slightly. For a moment, we just stared at each other, the only sounds coming from outside. "You… Say that again?" he said.

"Oh, Sam, I love you. I'm in love with you. I'm crazy about you." A laugh hiccuped out of my mouth.

"You love me."

"Yes."

And then suddenly Sam was kissing me, his hands in my damp hair, his mouth hot and sweet against mine, and nothing had ever felt so right in my life. He pulled me closer, and I could feel his heart thudding. He was such a thrilling combination of familiar and new. His hair was surprisingly soft, his ribs solid under my hand.

Then Sam pulled back. "Millie Barnes," he whispered, and

a smile tugged at the corner of his mouth. "Let's sit down, okay? I guess we should talk." He picked up a candle, and I was gratified to see that his hands were shaking. We went into the living room and sat on the couch, the single candle casting just enough light for us to see each other. Sam reached out and touched my cheek, and the way he was looking at me, with such intent, such softness, made my heart squeeze.

"So," I said, blushing.

He smiled. "So. When did you, uh, realize you felt like this?"

I cleared my throat. "Career Day," I admitted.

He threw his head back and laughed. "So that's what was going on."

"It wasn't funny."

"Oh, it was." He took my hand. "So what are we going to do, Mil? How do you want to handle this?"

I took a deep breath. "I don't know, Sam. I guess it's a little weird, dating your ex-brother-in-law."

"Yeah. I guess we should be discreet. Take things slow." He paused. "Maybe we shouldn't tell Danny or Trish or anyone before we...I don't know. Get settled."

"Sure." I grinned suddenly. "At least my dad will be happy."

"I know I am." Sam smiled back, his eyes crinkling, and a warm tug of desire pulled in the pit of my stomach. His hand slid up my arm to my neck and pulled me closer. His lips were warm and firm, and we fit together as if our sole purpose in life was to kiss each other. His hands slid down my back, and I kissed his neck, his skin as sweet as chocolate.

Sam Nickerson. I was kissing Sam, and he loved me. Life was unspeakably kind.

"Millie," he whispered a little hoarsely, "I want you to know that this is not some passing thing. I look at you and I see the rest of my life."

Who wouldn't feel like swooning? My knees went watery, and when he kissed me again, I found that I was clutching a fistful of his shirt. I could feel his heart thudding hard against my breast, feel the heat of his skin. Apparently his shirt came untucked—okay, I pulled it out—and I slid my hands over the warm skin of his back, so incredibly happy and stunned and thrilled that I felt like laughing and crying at the same time.

"About this discreet and slow thing," I managed to say, my limbs tingling with that odd combination of weakness and desire. I pulled back to look in his eyes and ran my fingers through his hair.

"What about it?" His breathing was ragged.

"I'm all for discreet. But maybe we could rethink slow."

Because I had known Sam all my life. I knew his goodness and kindness and I knew that I loved him with all my heart, and really, why on earth should we wait?

"I love you, Millie," he whispered, tucking a strand of hair behind my ear, and I actually felt dizzy at the words.

"I love you, too," I breathed.

And I disentangled myself from his arms, stood up and led him down the hall. To bed.

THE AFTERNOON DARKENED, the storm growing weaker as it blew out to sea, and Sam and I were still in bed. The occasional gust of wind and the rain drumming on the roof reinforced the feeling that we were the only two people around, and the only thing that mattered was the two of us, together, alone, at last. Except for Digger, whose cute little head popped up next to the bed. "Hi, buddy," I said. He jumped on the foot of the bed, curling himself into a tight circle.

"If he wants my leg, he's got it," Sam murmured, pulling the blanket up over my shoulder. "I'm too tired to move."

"It's only fair," I agreed. Sam laughed, but Digger, unaware that he had carte blanche, fell promptly asleep.

For a long time, we lay wrapped around each other, my head on his uninjured shoulder, his fingers playing in my hair, my hand over his heart. "I really love you, Millie," Sam whispered.

I sneaked a peek at his face. His eyes were closed, a smile on his generous mouth. I'd never noticed how long his eyelashes were, or the little scar on his chin. "I love you, too, Sam," I said, and my heart swelled at being able to say the words.

"You better. This is going to be a little tricky, when we tell your family. Especially Trish."

"Maybe we can just run away," I suggested.

"Elope. That's not a bad idea," Sam said, still smiling. I snuggled back down against him, kissed his shoulder. The wind scraped against the sky, rattling the screens. It was the happiest moment in my life to date. Here I was snug at home with the man I loved, and he loved me right back. I didn't have to pretend with Sam, didn't have to try to get him to notice me or make him love me, because he already did. The feeling of safety and utter contentment made my heart ache with fullness.

There was a crack as a branch or something fell in the yard. Digger jumped off the bed, barking at the window. "It's okay, Digger," I said. Less than reassured, Digger raced into the kitchen and continued to bark. "Crazy dog. Doesn't know the difference between a branch and a burglar." Sam chuckled.

But it turned out that I should have paid more attention to Digger because if I had, my sister wouldn't have walked in and found me naked in bed with her ex-husband.

CHAPTER THIRTY-THREE

THERE SHE STOOD, DRENCHED to the skin, face glowing white in the dark afternoon, her eyes like black holes. "Oh, God," Trish choked. "Oh, Jesus."

Sam and I were frozen in horror. I don't even think I drew a breath. She backed up, then turned around and fled. The kitchen door must have caught in the wind, because it banged repeatedly behind her.

"Trish!" Sam called, unfreezing and sliding out of bed. He glanced at me. "This is not good." Pulling on his pants and shirt, he glanced out the window as I reached for my bathrobe. "She shouldn't be out in this weather. The roads are probably a mess." Ever the cop. He went into the kitchen, me trailing uncertainly behind. Trish was already peeling out of my driveway, mud flying from her tires as she sped away.

"This is really bad," I stated needlessly.

Sam turned to me. "Millie, I better go after her. It's still pretty rough out, and she's upset. She shouldn't be driving."

"Right. Yes, go ahead." I was too shocked to say anything else.

"I'll see you later." He started to leave, then came back and planted a kiss on my mouth. "I'll see you later," he repeated.

"Okay," I said, giving him a tight smile. The rain blew in as he opened the back door and ran to his truck.

The candles had long burned down. It was almost completely dark outside. I went into the living room and sat in the darkness. Digger followed, wagging, and curled up at my feet. The wind howled and the house shook.

If I could just erase the past five minutes, there would be no doubt that this afternoon had been the best of my life. Being with Sam, loving Sam and knowing he loved me, feeling that sweet, absolute bliss... It was overwhelming, a warm wave of happiness that I could not turn away.

But neither could I turn away the image of Trish's face. I winced, my toes curling in discomfort. I hadn't even realized she was back on the Cape, and I'd bet that Sam hadn't, either.

I found my hurricane lanterns in the cellar and lit them, feeling very *Little House on the Prairie* in the warm, flickering light. Going to the dark refrigerator, I grabbed a Corona—not what Laura Ingalls would have done, but hey. A little alcohol was called for. Drinking in my bathrobe, alone. Not the most auspicious start to a new relationship.

I wondered where Trish had gone, if Sam had found her.

I didn't have to wonder for long. The phone rang before I'd taken two sips of beer.

"What's going on, Millie?" It was my mom, using a voice I hadn't heard since adolescence, a voice full of fury, eager to punish. I could hear someone sobbing in the background, and I didn't have to guess who it was.

"Um, what did Trish tell you?" I asked.

"That she found you and Sam together, Millie! In bed! How could you?"

"Well, okay, Mom, I seem to remember that Trish left Sam, quite some time ago."

"That is beside the point. Oh, here's Sam now. Sam, what is going on?"

Sam took the receiver from my mother. "Millie? I'm hanging up now. I'll call you later."

"Bye," I said gratefully.

Anger at Trish quickly replaced my momentary pity. It hadn't taken her long to go crying back to Mommy. And my mother! Trish had cheated on Sam, had left him—and Danny!—to go shack up with that jerk from New Jersey. She'd been gone for more than a year, but Mom instantly took her side.

The sickening thought occurred to me that Danny might be with my parents. My heart, so mobile of late, sank to my knees.

The phone rang again. "Hello, princess!" Curtis sang. "Want to come to P-town and sit out the rest of the storm? We're having an impromptu little party, just cocktails and some little treats, maybe some dancing later—"

"Curtis, you will not believe what's happening down here."

"New York minute, honey. I've got guests. Go."

"Sam got hurt and came to the clinic and he kissed me and it turns out that he's in love with me, too, and then Trish found us in bed."

"Mitchell! Leave that and come here! Millie shagged the cop!"

Thank God for my friends. My family might be in turmoil, but my friends were on my side. I called Katie next, giving her the quick version, wanting to leave the line clear in case Sam called.

I got dressed, then gently remade the bed. Obviously, things had just gotten very complicated, but I had faith in Sam. He'd calm everyone down. Everything would be okay. I sat at the edge of the bed—on the side where Sam had lain—and smiled, touching the pillow. It had been perfect.

The way we were together, the way he made me feel so beautiful, so safe—it was perfect. Everything would be fine.

Later that evening, my dad pulled into my driveway. He lumbered into the house holding his raincoat over his head with one hand, a flashlight in the other.

"Hi, punkin," he said, hanging up his coat.

"Hi, Daddy."

"So." He sat down at the kitchen table and mopped his face off with a napkin. "What's going on with Sam?"

"Do you want a drink or anything, Daddy?"

"No, thanks, hon. Just the story."

I sat down, too. "To tell you the truth, Dad, it's kind of between Sam and me."

"Your sister was crying her eyes out, practically hysterical. Said that you've always hated her and now you've slept with her husband."

"Youch!"

"So? Any of it true?"

I scowled at my father. "I just told you, it's private, Dad. I'm not really comfortable talking about it with my father."

My father grimaced. "So that's a yes?"

"Look, Dad." I stopped, then sighed. "Not to be rude or anything, but Sam is not married to Trish anymore. She took care of that when she left him for another man last year. I'm not sure why I'm the bad guy here. It's not like I crept into the marital bed or anything."

"Spare me the details, baby. But tell me this. Are you going after Sam to hurt your sister?"

"No! Daddy! Come on. You should know better. And Trish is going to have to accept that everything is not always about her."

"You're right, you're right. I'm sorry, punkin. You're not

like that. And your sister does like to make a scene. But still, Millie. There are a lot of guys out there. Why pick Sam?"

I reached for my father's hand. "I didn't really pick him, Daddy. I wasn't even going to tell him how I felt. But he's the best guy in the world. You know that."

My dad gave a little laugh and squeezed my hand. "I guess there's some truth in that. Okay, baby. Back to the war."

"Is Sam still over there?"

"No, he took Trish back to their house. Danny was pretty shaken up by his mother carrying on."

"Shit, Danny was there? Did she have to do that in front of Danny?"

"Watch your mouth, young lady. And yes, apparently she did. It was a big shock, honey."

We sat in silence for a minute. "Well, thanks for coming, Daddy," I said.

"Sure, sweetheart. Anything you need? Got enough oil for your lamps? Enough food?"

"Yes, I'm fine. Thanks, Dad. Thanks a lot."

"All right then. Call me if you need to."

He kissed me on the cheek and went back out into the storm.

Digger and I had a cold supper, and I played solitaire for a while. Finally, I took the phone into my room so I'd hear it. I wanted to call Sam, but he'd said he'd call me, and I had no doubt his hands were full right now. Digger jumped up next to me, spoiled hound, and I petted his head. Within minutes, much to my surprise, I fell dead asleep.

CHAPTER THIRTY-FOUR

THE POWER WAS BACK THE NEXT day, the sky blue and crystal clear. I barely noticed.

I was dying to hear from Sam. I also wanted to call Danny, but to tell the truth, I was a little nervous about that one. I hadn't really thought about Danny in terms of Sam and me being together. Hell, there hadn't been time! Was it just yesterday that Sam had told me he loved me? It seemed like an age ago. The hours ticked past with agonizing deliberation.

When the phone finally rang, I leaped to answer it.

"It's Sam." His voice was low.

"Hey! How's it going? Is everything okay?"

"Listen, Millie, I can't talk right now. I just wanted to give you a quick call and let you know that right now, things are kind of, um, crazy."

"Is Danny there?" I asked.

"Yeah."

"Is he upset?"

"Yup."

"Oh, Sam. I'm sorry."

"Me, too, Millie. I have to take care of a few things, but I'll call you when I can. Okay?" His voice was tight.

"Can I do anything?"

He sighed. "I don't think so. I've got to run."

I was hoping that his call would reassure me. It didn't.

Unwilling to sit and fret anymore, I went down to the cellar and brought back the deck chairs and table, then started picking up the branches that had fallen during the storm. The air was rich with the scent of cedar and salt. Birds celebrated their survival, squawking and chirping loudly in the trees. As I was dragging a particularly large branch across the yard, the Digger alarm went off. Trish's BMW was pulling into my driveway. My pulse thudded sickly in my ears.

What does one say to one's sister in a situation like this? Where was Mitch when I needed him? I called my dog to me as Trish got out of her car and stood for a moment. She was wearing jeans and a yellow shirt, and she looked younger and more natural than she had in years.

"Hi," she said neutrally. "Got a minute?"

"Sure," I said, dropping the branch. A small blob of sap remained on my palm, and as I looked at it, I saw that my hand was shaking.

"Do you want to come in?" I asked.

"No, let's just stay out here." Trish pulled a chair out from the table and sat, folding her hands before her as if in prayer. Hesitantly, I sat across from her. Digger stood beside me like a bodyguard, ears pricked, eyes fixed on Trish. I reached out and patted his head.

"I won't waste your time, Millie," my sister began, gazing into the backyard. "I broke up with Avery, and I came back here to get back together with Sam."

I drew in a sharp breath. "Oh."

Trish tapped her French-manicured nails on the table. "Look, Millie, I know you have a crush on Sam. He said the thing with you guys was brand new. I want you to back off. It really would be best for everybody if you'd just drop it."

"Well, golly gee, Trish, if you think so." My casual tone was belied by the fear that leaped to life at her words.

"Don't be sarcastic, Millie," Trish snapped, sitting back in the chair, glaring at me from her dark chocolate eyes. "Think about things. Sam and I have been together for eighteen years now—"

"Except that you divorced him—"

"—and we have a son together. A home. A whole life. There's a lot of history there. You can't just dismiss that."

"No, you're right, Trish, I can't. And I won't try. But, Trish, you left him more than a year ago! You cheated on him, you divorced him, you moved in with someone else! You broke his heart."

"Yes. I did. It was a mistake."

Somehow I hadn't imagined Trish saying that. It was hard to counter.

"Millie, Sam is a wonderful man," Trish said slowly. "I know you two have been spending a lot of time together, and I don't blame you for falling for him. But can't you just see that it's not real? It doesn't compare to what he and I have together."

I clenched my teeth. "Trish, you dragged his heart through the dump. I hate to be the one to tell you this, but he's over you."

"Are you sure about that, Millie?" she asked gently. Uncertainty flickered through my heart. I didn't answer.

"Well. Whatever the case may be, let me just say this," she continued, pausing to adjust her sandal strap. "I've never asked you for anything, Millie. But I'm asking now. I want my husband back. I want my son back. I want you to drop this thing with Sam. It's so new you won't even miss him, and things will go back to normal."

Her casual dismissal was like acid. "You don't know

anything about me or my feelings for Sam, Trish," I snapped. "You have never given a damn about anyone but yourself. I won't drop Sam, as you put it, just because you want me to. I love him."

"Millie, you have *always* been jealous of me," Trish spat. "You've *always* wanted what I had."

"You know what?" I barked, standing with my hands braced on the table. "You're absolutely right! You, Trish, are the only one who's *never* wanted what you had. And you had everything. A great guy who married you when you tricked him by getting pregnant. He loved you and did everything to make you happy. You had a perfect baby boy who's grown into a wonderful kid. A beautiful home. But you just crapped all over that and went off with that asshole from New Jersey."

"Well, as I said, I was wrong," Trish said coolly, standing also and looking at me. "You're making a mistake, Millie. I feel sorry for you." She walked to her car and drove away. I went into the bathroom and threw up.

THERE WAS MORE. OH, YES. The fates weren't done with me yet.

I called Digger and got into my car. Where I was going, I wasn't sure, but I wanted to be out of the house. I stopped by Katie's, but she and the boys had gone to the mall, according to her mom. I was still peeved at my own mother for instantly taking Trish's side, so I didn't want to go there. I looked at the car clock. It was half past two. High school was just letting out.

I knew Danny's schedule pretty well. He had basketball practice today, if I was not mistaken.

I was not. I went into the gym and watched the boys until one of the kids pointed me out to Danny. My nephew hesitated, then said something to the coach and walked over, the ball tucked under his arm.

"Hi," I said, trying for a light tone.

For the first time in his life, Danny wasn't happy to see me, and it was like a knife in my chest. He stared at the floor, bouncing his basketball a few times. "What do you want, Millie?" he asked flatly.

My face attempted to scrunch up in crying formation, which I tried to convert by contorting my lips to a smile. "I just wanted to see you, see how you're doing."

"I don't think I want to talk to you right now."

I took a quick, sharp breath. "Oh."

"What did you expect?" he said, glancing back at his team.

"I don't know, Dan." My voice cracked and Danny grew blurry as my eyes swam. He turned to rejoin the others, and I turned blindly toward the door.

"Aunt Mil, wait. Coach, I gotta take a break." Danny's voice was defeated as he loped over toward me. Without a word, we went outside and walked over to the split-rail fence that circled the parking lot.

"Mil, what do you want me to say? I mean, come on. How am I supposed to feel good about this?"

"Oh, Danny, I don't know. Everything is going way too fast."

He sat on the fence and hung his head. "Mom wants to get back together with Dad," he said.

"I know. She told me."

"You gonna mess that up?"

I looked at the ground. "I think…I think your parents' marriage should sink or swim on its own, outside of anything I do."

"Mom says she's learned a lot, that she and Dad could be really happy together now that she knows what she had."

There it was again. The new and improved Trish, Trish Mature. "What do you think, Danny?"

Danny sighed and rubbed his hand over his eyes in a gesture that echoed Sam. "I don't know, Aunt Mil. But this thing with you and Dad…I don't know. That's…I don't know."

I swallowed. "I, um, I really love your dad, Danny. I know it's uncomfortable for you to hear it, but it's the truth."

He responded by peeling a shard of wood off the fence and meticulously splitting it.

"Danny, do you *want* your parents to get back together?"

He tossed the splinter on the ground and looked at me. "Shit, Millie, of course I do. Doesn't every kid with divorced parents wish that? That Mommy and Daddy would kiss and make up and live happily ever after? I mean, if they could pull that off…sure. Of course I want that."

"You told me they hadn't been happy for a long time…."

"Well, what if this is their big chance? What if you're messing that up?"

"I don't know." My throat thickened at the misery on Danny's face.

We were silent for a minute, the only noise from the crows croaking in the trees. "Aunt Millie," Danny began slowly, concentrating on peeling another slice of wood from the fence, "what if I asked you, as a favor to me?" He looked up, sadness and confusion making him look about six years old again.

"Asked me what exactly, Danny?" I wanted to push his hair out of his eyes, but I had a feeling those days were gone.

"Asked you to step aside and leave my dad alone. For me. To give me the chance to have parents who were happy together. Would you do it?"

My heart sat like a cold stone in my chest as I regarded my nephew. "I guess I would. Yes."

"You would?"

"Yes."

"Why?"

"Because I love you more than anything else in the world, Danny. And you don't deserve to be involved in this mess. So, yes, if you asked, I'd step aside. I wouldn't do it for your mother, but for you, the answer stands."

Danny looked at me for a long time, and I met his gaze steadily, even if my eyes were wet.

"Well, fuck it," Danny said quietly. "I won't ask you, then."

I let out a breath I hadn't known I was holding. "Thanks."

"You guys are like a soap opera," he muttered dejectedly.

"I know." I whispered. "I'm sorry, Danny. I...I love you, and I'm sorry."

"Yeah." He slid off the fence. "I gotta go."

"Okay."

"I'll see you."

"See you, Dan."

The tears spilled over as I watched my nephew walk slowly back into the gym. He looked like an adult, shoulders sagging, feet heavy. Not like a kid anymore. We grown-ups had taken care of that.

WHEN I GOT HOME, THERE WAS a message on my machine.

"Millie, it's Sam. Look—" Pause. "We need to talk. I—" Pause. Deep breath. "I stopped by about a half hour ago, but you weren't home. I'll call you later."

I sank into a chair as my legs went rubbery. That did not sound heartening. No, not at all. *We need to talk* never bodes well.

For one afternoon, I'd had a glimpse of what love could really be like. What loving Sam could be like, and for that afternoon, I had been truly, deeply happy to the very roots of my soul. I'd been with the man I loved, and he'd loved me, and we were on the verge of the rest of our lives.

Tears spilled out of my eyes and onto my cheeks, but my face felt carved from stone. God, I was so damn tired of crying. And waiting. I'd been waiting for years now for my life, my real life, to begin. Waited for things to happen, for people to notice, to call, to invite, to love.

We need to talk.

If Trish got Sam back, there was no justice in the world. But I knew Sam, and as Curtis had said, he was true blue. Faithful, loyal, dependable. If his ex-wife, who had left him just over a year ago, begged him to forgive her and take her back so they could be a family again, what would Sam do? If Danny asked him to give Trish another chance, wouldn't Sam do exactly that? Wouldn't it be easier to turn his back on one afternoon with me instead of a lifetime—Danny's lifetime—with Trish?

I didn't move out of the chair for hours. I barely even blinked. My ass grew numb, my stomach growled, but I sat there still. Digger put his head on my lap and I stroked his silky head automatically. The sun began to set, the room grew dim, but I didn't bother to turn on a light.

The phone rang. My heart immediately began pounding with sickening intensity. Without consciously thinking about it, I answered.

"It's Curtis." His voice was low, and I could hear the murmur of voices in the background, some music.

"Hi."

"Mitchell and I are at the Forge," Curtis said, naming a charming restaurant in Wellfleet. "It's the tenth anniversary of our first date and—"

"Curtis, that's great, but I've got a lot going on here. I can't really talk."

"Princess, I don't want to be the one to tell you this…" The sympathy and hesitation in his voice caused a wave of dread to wash over me, and my hands grew clammy.

"What is it, Curtis?"

"They're here," he whispered. "Sam and your sister. They have a table near the window. They're in a very heavy tête-à-tête."

My stomach cramped. "Oh."

"I can see their table. Our friend Bart is a waiter here. You met him last Halloween, he was dressed like Barbra Streisand, remember? Anyway, he's helping us. I'm sitting at the bar with Bart. Mitch is two tables away from Sam and Trish with his back to them and he's called Bart on his cell, and Bart is right here…what? What did she say?"

"No. Curtis, don't. I don't want to know. I'm not spying anymore. Please don't."

"Shh!"

"Curtis, no! Please stop." The idea that the guys were going to relay Sam and Trish's conversation made me nauseous.

"You don't want to know what they're saying?"

"No! It's private. Please don't."

Curtis paused. "Oh. Oh, all right. It's okay, Bart, she doesn't want us to." My friend sighed, irked with my lack of cooperation. "Well, Millie, do you at least want to know what they're *doing?* It is a public place and all. It's not like we need binoculars or anything."

I hesitated and pressed my palm against my aching forehead. Sam was with Trish at a beautiful, expensive, romantic restaurant. *Yesterday, you were in bed with me, Sam.*

You loved me yesterday. How can you be with Trish now?
"Okay. Go ahead."

"Great. Let me take a peek. Well, they haven't eaten much. Trish is talking…. She's wearing a yellow dress, some chunky topaz jewelry, very nice shoes, I think they're Jimmy Choo…. She's leaning forward, very intense, talking, not smiling— Hi, Mitch, hon, no, Millie pulled the plug, but thanks, you make a great spy—okay, now Sam is talking." Curtis's voice grew softer. "He's taking her hand. Now he's…okay, she's crying, is she laughing a little, too?"

I felt as hollow as an abandoned mine shaft, echoing, empty, dark. "Curtis, that's enough—"

"He's kissing her hand. Now she's really crying. He's going around to her side of the table, got his arm around her. Oh. Oh." Curtis drew a sharp breath. "He kissed her, Millie."

"I think that's enough," I whispered.

"Yes. Right."

My chest was tight and my head throbbed with every beat of my heart. I kept the phone to my ear, listening to the restaurant where Sam and Trish had made up.

Trish would be living on the Cape again. I would see them all the time. And now, unlike just thirty-six hours ago, everyone *knew.* I loved Sam, and he, Trish, my parents, Danny, everyone knew. Things with my nephew would never be the same. I'd have to smile at Sam at Thanksgiving and buy him a sweater at Christmas. Maybe they'd have another baby.

"Millie? Are you still there, honey?" Curtis's voice was horribly gentle.

"Do you think I can come up and stay with you guys for a couple of days? Before I start work?"

"Sure! Of course. Stay as long as you like. You can even bring your dog."

"I'll just throw a few things together...."

"Fantastic. And Millie...I'm so sorry."

CHAPTER THIRTY-FIVE

CURTIS AND MITCH GREETED ME as if I were a delicate cancer patient, holding my arms gently, talking in hushed voices.

"You can stay for as long as you like," Curtis said staunchly.

"Thanks, bud, but I think it'll just be for a couple of days at the most. I just…I just wanted to be somewhere else."

"Of course! And what about dinner, Millie? Would you care for something to eat?" Mitch asked kindly. I tried to remember the last meal I'd eaten and couldn't, but my stomach seemed to have a bocce ball in it.

"I think maybe I'll just go to bed. I'm sorry I ruined your anniversary."

"No, don't be silly! It's just the anniversary of our first date! We'll celebrate our real anniversary next month. Don't worry."

They carried my bag upstairs and, like the innkeepers they were, showed me the amenities of Dry Dock, my suite. It was hard to pay attention. Sam and Trish. Trish and Sam. Their names had been linked together for so long that they still sounded normal. Now, Sam and Millie…that just sounded dumb.

My large suite had lavender-scented sheets, a huge arrangement of bright flowers on the bureau and a view of the water. I made a quick call to Katie, as I hadn't wanted to talk to my parents, and told her briefly what had happened and where I was. Then, so tired I ached, I climbed into bed without even washing up. Digger came over for a little reassurance, and I petted him weakly until he gave up and went to lie before the fireplace. The only sound was the wind and the slap of the small bayside waves. Alone in the dark, my misery curled up with me, and a heavy weight seemed to press me into the mattress.

"Oh, Sam," I whispered, and the endless spring of tears spilled over again. How would I do this? I asked myself. How could I handle this incredible sense of loss? That time with Sam was like a cruel trick. It was bad enough to love him, but to have heard those words from him, to have felt the way we felt, to have that incredible rightness taken away, was unbearable.

In the morning, Curtis and Mitch made me a huge breakfast. I ate the food, but chewing was such an effort. The boys tried to distract me by chatting about the Peacock. They were getting ready to close for the winter and had to do a final cleaning of all the guest rooms, paint a few rooms, make some repairs and the like. They would spend the winter tucked away on the third floor, happy and cozy and together. Not that I begrudged them that…it was just hard to see the contrast between their happy couplehood and my solitude.

Digger and I took a long walk out to the very end of Provincetown, where the huge rocks of the breakwater stretched into the choppy bay. Digger trotted along happily, sniffing at crab shells between the crevices, returning to nudge my hand with his nose. I felt dead inside, as flat and lifeless as week-old roadkill, my eyes barely seeing the lovely houses of Commercial Street, hardly noting the raucous calls of the gulls as they wheeled and glided above me.

The boys cooked lunch and dragged out an old game of Trivial Pursuit and even took Digger to the dog spa for a little pet pampering. And while I knew I couldn't hide out here forever, I was glad for this little reprieve. Instead of waiting around for other people to decide how my life was going to turn out, I had at least taken action.

That night, as I lay listening to the sounds of the ocean, I tried to make peace with my situation. Digger crept onto the bed and licked my tears as I sobbed quietly for the love that I'd very nearly had, for the humiliation I felt, for the empty, hollow days that were waiting for me back home.

Somewhere in the night I resolved to go back to Eastham and face things. Sam would probably come over to break the news to me, and I'd have to be dignified and strong and somehow let him know that I would be just fine with everything. I'd start work and engross myself there. And someday, I'd find someone else.

But for now, I gave myself one more cry in the dark over Sam Nickerson.

THE NEXT DAY, THE BOYS PUT ME to work. In the morning, we draped and taped the salon, which was a vast room featuring a Steinway grand piano and a wall of French doors that led to the small beach. The boys had decided to go from hunter-green to royal-blue, and we donned our painting clothes and set to work. Actually, their painting clothes were on par with my best stuff, but that was just their way.

It was good to be focused on something as mundane as painting. It didn't take a great deal of mental effort, but I had to pay attention, too. The guys gossiped about friends I didn't know, taking great pains to tell me the whole background story so I wouldn't feel left out. Dipping the brush in the pure white paint I was using for the trim, I wished my whole life could be repainted the pure, empty color.

"You know, princess, sometimes things really do happen

for the best," Curtis said rather abruptly, interrupting Mitch's dialogue on a friend's terrible taste in men. He gave Mitch a meaningful look.

"Yes, you're right," Mitch replied blithely. "Millie, don't you agree?"

"What exactly are you talking about?" I asked, dragging my brush along the baseboard.

"Maybe you and Sam weren't meant to be," Curtis said rather smugly.

"I guess," I said, my chest aching dully.

"He wasn't good enough for you, anyway, dearest," Mitch murmured gently.

I gave a choked laugh. "Not good enough for me? Sam—"

"He broke your heart, after all," Curtis put in.

"He's a good man," I said, my throat closing up on the words. "Very, very good." I dipped my brush back into the bucket and swallowed.

"Oh, I don't know. I always thought he was a little dull," Curtis said.

"No, he—" I started to break in.

"Yes, rather unremarkable in conversation. You're right, darling," Mitch agreed lovingly. "He may have looked good in uniform, but aside from that, he was rather ordinary."

"Hear, hear," Curtis sang. "Not like that arm candy you were seeing earlier this summer, Millie."

I straightened up, bewildered. "Sam's—"

"And of course, Millie, if he left you, then he's obviously very stupid," Curtis said almost gleefully.

"And he probably couldn't kiss worth a damn. Officers of the law never can," Mitch added, his lips twitching.

"Stop it," I ordered. "Sam is the best man I know! He's kind and smart and funny and thoughtful, and if he dumped me for my sister, then he's only doing what he thinks is best for his family, which means he's also unselfish and decent. And he's a *great* kisser, not to mention fantastic in bed. So shut up." I tossed my paintbrush on the drop cloth next to me and glared at them.

"There's something else he is," Curtis said, more gently.

"And what's that?" I snapped.

"He's here."

I froze, staring at Curtis and Mitch. My heart stopped, then surged almost up my throat. I swallowed. Swallowed again. Very quickly, I sneaked a peek behind me. Yup. Sam. Standing in the doorway.

"He's got flowers," Curtis whispered. "And he's smiling."

I tossed Sam another quick peek. It was true. But still I stood with my back to him, my knees trembling violently. I folded my arms across my chest to hide my shaking hands.

"Hi, Millie."

At the sound of Sam's quiet voice, my eyes flooded with tears and I put my hand over my mouth. Curtis reached for Mitch's hand.

"Fantastic in bed. That's good to hear." There was a smile in Sam's voice. I heard his footsteps coming closer.

A bouquet of yellow roses appeared in front of me. Sam stood so close behind me that I could feel his warmth. "Turn around, Millie," he whispered.

"What about Trish?" I managed to force out, my voice choked and squeaking.

"Turn around and I'll tell you."

I looked at Curtis and Mitch for courage. They were teary-eyed, too, clutching hands as if they were about to meet Russell Crowe on the set of *Gladiator.* Curtis gave me an encouraging nod.

I turned around.

Sam's arms went around me and he kissed me hard, fast, and then just crushed me against him. He dropped the flowers to hug me tighter, and my heart flew so high and fast that I could actually feel it move in my chest. I heard a shuddering intake of breath from the other side of the room. Apparently so did Sam, because he looked up.

"Guys, come on," he said. "A little privacy?"

"Oh! Of course. Terribly sorry." Mitch, smiling a wonderfully huge grin, led a happily sobbing Curtis from the room.

Sam kissed my forehead and then stared sternly at me. "I've been looking for you," he said, a little smile creeping onto his face.

"You must be a lousy cop," I said a little breathlessly. "I'm not that hard to find."

"I had to take care of a few things first," he answered. "Come on, let's sit down."

He led me to a sheet-covered couch and sat, pulling me down next to him. "This has been a hell of a week," he said, running a hand through his graying hair. Then he sighed and gave me a smile that was half sad and half relieved, and my heart lurched. He took my hand and grew serious.

"In answer to your question, Trish is now over the Atlantic, on her way to Paris."

From the kitchen came a muted whoop. Sam grinned and shook his head. I smiled back, still dazed at his presence. I was here with Sam. My mind couldn't seem to get further than that.

"Millie, I'm sorry you were hiding out up here, thinking what you must have been thinking. But I had to straighten things out with Trish before I could take care of you. I mean, she did get a pretty big surprise, finding us like that. And she's Danny's mother…"

"I know."

"That asshole Avery dumped her, and she panicked. She didn't think she had any choice other than coming back to the Cape. So she convinced herself that we should give our marriage another try."

At that moment, Curtis came scurrying in with a beautiful tray of Brie and crackers, grapes, a bottle of wine and two glasses. "Pretend I'm not here," he whispered, expertly pouring the wine. He flashed a brilliant smile and scurried back out.

"Good friends you've got there," Sam said, watching him retreat. I picked up my glass and took a long sip.

"Curtis and Mitch saw you at the Forge—"

"Yes, we went there for dinner. It was too hard to talk about things at home, with Danny around, and we wanted to go somewhere where no one knew us. Your friends are crappy spies, by the way. Too bad they weren't listening. They could have saved us a lot of time." He smiled at me, and I cringed, remembering how I had ordered my friends *not* to eavesdrop. "Katie told me that you came here, and what you were thinking."

"Well," I said, looking down at the Persian carpet, "one does draw conclusions when one hears that one's boyfriend is kissing his ex-wife, who also happens to be one's sister."

"Um, right. And I did kiss her. But I kissed her goodbye." Sam leaned back against the couch and ran a hand over his face. "Trish said she wanted to get back with me, and I told her two things. The first was that I just didn't buy it. I'd never made her happy before, and there was no reason to think that I would now. And after she'd calmed down, I think she could see that, too." Sam sat back up and took my hands in his. He looked at me, his gentle eyes sad. "She just didn't know where else to go. She's never been on her own before."

It was true. My sister, at age thirty-six, had never lived alone. A sudden stab of pity for her pricked my heart.

"Then there was the other thing I told her." Sam's voice broke my reverie.

"What was that?"

"I told her that I loved you." His eyes were steady on me. Even as my heart leaped at his words, a trickle of sadness tempered my joy.

"That must have been hard to hear," I whispered, looking down. Poor Trish. It was the first time in my life that I'd ever thought of her that way. Alone. Confused. Rejected. I took a deep breath. "So what is she going to do now? Is she really headed for France?"

"Yes. She's always wanted to go there, always wanted to see more of the world than South Bend and the Cape."

I nodded, thinking of Trish's many tirades about how there was more to life than sand and salt.

"I sold the house, Millie," Sam said quietly.

"Sam, no! Not your house!"

"It's done," he answered. "I sold it to the bank, not quite for market value, with the promise that Dan and I can stay until he leaves for college next year."

"Sam," I whispered, my eyes filling.

"No, it was the right thing to do," he said. "Millie, don't cry."

"You love that house," I said. "It was your parents'...."

Sam smiled, then pulled me back against him and kissed the top of my head. "Of course I love it. But it was Trish's house, too. In a way, it was hers more than it was mine. And she deserved half of it, no matter what the divorce papers said. So now she has plenty of money, hopefully enough to last a good long time, and she can find something that makes her happy. And I can put some more in Danny's college fund, too."

"You're too good," I whispered, wiping my eyes.

"Millie, this thing with us…" He turned to look at me and cupped my face with his hands. "We started out fast, but I think we should maybe slow down. It's not your average relationship, being with your ex-sister-in-law. But I love you, Millie, and I want to be with you. Be patient with me, okay?"

"Okay," I whispered, my heart so full of love and happiness that it didn't seem there was enough room in my chest to hold it. "Oh, Sam, I love you."

He kissed me, a slow, sweet kiss that was new and home at the same time. When I opened my eyes, Sam was smiling at Curtis and Mitch, who were peeking around the kitchen door.

"We get to be bridesmaids, right?" Curtis asked.

Sam laughed. "Come on, Millie," he said. "Let's go home."

EPILOGUE

A YEAR AND A HALF LATER, I was once again being harbored at the Pink Peacock, hiding from the man I loved. But this time was very different. Today, in roughly forty-five minutes, I would be marrying Sam Nickerson.

There had been some bumps in the road. Things hadn't been perfect. Danny had had a bit of a hard time with the thought of his dad and me together. Neither Sam nor I had wanted to cause him any unnecessary discomfort, so we'd been very discreet, dating as if it were the 1950s, with him picking me up at my house and bringing me back with a kiss good-night on the front porch.

But with each passing week, the rightness of Sam and me grew stronger. The strangeness of dating my sister's ex-husband faded, both for us and for other people. My father was the only one who had no adjustment problem whatsoever, and in that way, he paved the road for us. In the spring, he took Danny away for a weekend of fishing, and when they came back, Dan took Sam aside and told him it was okay if he wanted to marry Aunt Mil. My father never told me what he'd said, only that some things in life were just right, even if they were a little weird.

Then came the sale of Sam's house, and despite his brave words, Sam's heart had been a little broken. Three weeks after

Danny went to Notre Dame, Sam left his home and moved to a little house near the salt pond. He'd wanted a place of his own, at least for Danny's freshman year.

It was a smart move. It was good for him to live alone, as it had been good for me. We saw each other at least a few times a week and talked every day. Then one night a few months ago, after we'd eaten dinner at my house, we took a walk up to the lighthouse, and there, while the beacon swept across the ocean and the wind gusted and Digger frolicked, Sam slipped an engagement ring on my finger.

So here I was, sitting at a dressing table, looking at myself in the mirror, daydreaming. Curtis poked his head in. "Princess, are you ready?" Katie had temporarily abdicated her responsibilities as my maid of honor, saying that Curtis would do a much better job with hair and makeup. He looked at my not-quite-finished state and clucked. "The guests are here, everyone is downstairs, and look at you! I leave you alone for two minutes…" He came over and knelt next to me. "Are you nervous?"

"No." I smiled at my buddy. "Have I thanked you and Mitch for my wedding?"

"Honey, if it were up to you two, you would probably have eloped, and we couldn't have that. Here, don't forget this."

I let Curtis fasten a bracelet on my wrist. "Come on," I whispered. "Let's spy." Snickering, we tiptoed into the hall and took a peek downstairs.

Garlands of roses twined around the railings of the staircase, and candles glowed warmly in the elegant salon. Everyone was there. Mitch, dashing in an Armani tuxedo stood with Katie, who was stunning in her simple, rose-colored sheath dress. They laughed and talked with Jill Doyle and her husband. My mom was elegant and beautiful, bustling about like any good mother of the bride. My dad had Dr. Whitaker cornered, no doubt fascinating the good man with tales from the septic world. Corey and Mikey scurried around, adorable in their tiny suits. Ethel, Sam's partner, looked quite different out of uniform, actually female, though she seemed a bit on the murderous side, probably because the Pink Peacock was nonsmoking.

A few of Sam's pals on the police department clustered around the bar. Janette, now pregnant, stood chatting with Zach. Several patients I'd become close with were also here. Not too many people, but everyone we cared about. I couldn't see Sam, but I heard him laughing. There was my beloved nephew, giving my aunt a kiss and laughing at something she said. Today, in a tuxedo, Danny looked like an American prince. He was Sam's best man.

There was one more guest, the only one who happened to turn and catch me peering over the banister. Joe Carpenter. He smiled and raised his beer bottle in a silent, affectionate toast. I waved at him fondly.

When Katie had asked me if she could bring him, I must admit I'd been a little stunned.

"As your date?" I'd asked.

"No," she'd said dismissively, but her cheeks had turned the slightest bit pink. "Not really. Well, we're just friends right now, okay? Can he come?"

Joe had changed in the past year or so. He'd become head carpenter for Habitat for Humanity on the Cape and had started teaching a woodworking class for the adult education program. Once in a while, our paths would cross at the senior center, where Tripod visited as a therapy dog. When I saw him at the Barnacle, Katie always seemed to be busting his chops in a casual, almost affectionate way. Then one day I'd stopped by and Joe was fixing something at her house, patiently showing Corey how to find a stud in the living-room wall. Who knew? Maybe someday soon, Katie would let a man into her life. If so, it seemed as if Joe would be waiting, because it was clear that he was smitten. They'd certainly have beautiful children.

I took another long look around, trying to press the beauty of this evening into my memory forever. With brimming eyes, I turned to Curtis.

"The Peacock looks beautiful."

"Thanks. And speaking of beautiful, let's hope this mascara is waterproof. We don't want raccoon eyes on your wedding day, do we?"

"How did Sam look?" I asked, standing up and returning to the dressing table in my room. A final glancing at myself in the mirror assured me that the mascara was holding up.

"Nauseous and terrified. What do you think? He's probably checking his watch every five seconds. Are you ready, honey? The photographer is here."

Curtis turned me around and took a long look.

"Oh, Millie," he sighed, his own eyes filling with tears. "You're…"

"Don't start," I said, my throat instantly clamping shut with tears. We laughed shakily.

"I'll go get Katie and your dad," Curtis said, wiping his eyes on a monogrammed hankie. He left, and a second later, Katie came in.

"Hi!" I chirped. "I'm almost ready."

"Yeah, great. Uh, listen, Millie…" Katie looked worried, not a reassuring expression to see on one's maid of honor. "There's someone here to see you," Katie whispered, tucking a wisp of my hair behind my ear. "Scream if you need me." She gave me a quick hug and hurried out, her dress swishing softly. Before I could wonder who my visitor was, there was a quiet knock, and the door opened again.

Trish.

I hadn't seen her since she'd ordered me to drop Sam.

A month after landing in France, she'd enrolled in Le Cordon Bleu, where she'd been ever since, studying to become a chef. At Christmas, my parents and Danny had gone to Paris for the holidays. Trish and Sam had been to Notre Dame twice together, to see Danny off and for Parents Weekend, but Trish had not been on the Cape for a year and a half. I'd spoken to her on the phone a few times, and we'd been very cautious and cordial with each other. Of course, she'd been invited to the wedding…she was my sister, after all, but she'd been vague about coming.

She looked, as always, stunningly beautiful. Her hair was quite short, very French, and she wore a navy-blue dress, very Coco Chanel, very Juliette Binoche. She looked closer to twenty-five than forty.

"Hi," I ventured, unsure of her purpose here. I gave her a stiff hug, which she returned with equal uncertainty.

"Hi. Sorry I didn't let you know for sure…" Her voice trailed off. "Listen, have you got a minute?"

"Well, actually, we're about to…sure," I answered, my palms growing clammy. *Please, please don't let her ruin this day,* I prayed.

"I'll make it short," Trish said. She came over to the edge of the bed and sat down, crossing her legs and making me feel, as she always did, a bit like a frump, even on my wedding day. I fluffed my dress out so it wouldn't wrinkle and looked at my sister expectantly.

"Um, Millie," she began, suddenly looking at her perfect manicure. "I'm sorry that I didn't let you know I was coming. It was kind of a last-minute decision. In fact, I kind of sneaked in the back door. Nobody else knows I'm here, just Katie."

"Oh," I said.

She twisted a silver ring. "Anyway, I just…well, it's not every day your ex-husband marries your sister. I wasn't sure if you really wanted me here."

"We invited you for just that reason, Trish," I fibbed.

"Well, I guess you'd have to invite your sister," she said. I didn't say anything, just watched her fidget. It was so unlike her.

"All right, listen, Millie. I'll say my piece, then I'll fly, because you do have other things to do, right? I wanted to see you today. You're my only sister, it's your wedding day, and I just wanted to see you and wish you the best. I hope you and Sam are very happy together. Okay?"

I stared at my sister. She had always been so beautiful, so supremely confident, and yet here she was, babbling and nervous, and I suddenly felt a wave of…something. She stood up as if to leave.

"Is there something else you wanted?" I asked gently.

Trish turned around, quickly, took a breath as if to say something, then sighed. "Yes. I'm sorry I was such a crappy sister."

"You weren't—" I began automatically, then stopped myself as the shock of her words hit me.

"I was. I have been." She sat back down. "Millie," she said, taking a big breath, "I've done a lot of thinking lately. Since I left the Cape, I mean. I've thought about the two of us a lot. Not just because you were with Sam, but…well, we've never really been close. And since I was older, I guess it was my fault."

"Trish—"

"No, it was. I mean, when we were kids, that was one

thing, sisters fight all the time, right? But when we were older…I should have been nicer to you, Millie, but to be honest, I was just so jealous."

An incredulous snort burst out of me.

"I was," Trish protested. "You were always the smart one. Mom and Dad were always so proud of your grades and your advanced placement courses, and your college and on and on. And I was just the pretty one." She stopped, her face flushing pink. "Whoops."

"Well, it's true. You're still the pretty one, Trish."

"No, Millie. Take a look in that mirror. You're beautiful." Her gentle words brought tears to my eyes. It was the first time that I could remember Trish ever saying anything so nice to me.

"I've made a lot of mistakes, Millie," Trish said slowly. "I shouldn't have pinned all my dreams on Sam. I was just a kid back then, and I was so afraid he was going to have this wonderful, glamorous life without me, so I got pregnant. I was too scared to see if he'd stay with me otherwise. And then, when I left him for Avery, that was even worse. The same mistake, thinking a man could make me happy, and that time I was old enough to know better."

She paused, looking down at her sleek shoes, and when she spoke again, her voice was husky. "But I think the biggest mistake has been keeping you at arm's length, Millie. At the end of the day, if your own sister doesn't love you, then what kind of a person must you be?"

"But I do love you, Trish."

As the words left my mouth, I realized they were true. Sure, there were plenty of times when I hadn't *liked* my sister, but underneath the irritation and jealousy and rejection that I'd always felt, there it was—the rock-solid love you could only feel for a person who shared your gene pool.

"And I've always been jealous of *you*," I went on, reaching out to hold her hand. "Not just because you're so beautiful, though I have to say, it wasn't easy being the dumpy sister of the swan princess. But also because you were always so together, so confident. You were always so sure of yourself, in a way that I never was. And you...you had Sam."

"Well, now it's your turn," Trish said, cracking a smile.

"I guess so," I said, smiling back. I grabbed a tissue and wiped my eyes, smearing my so-called waterproof mascara.

A knock came on the door, and Curtis stuck his head in. "Millie, Mitch saw the evil queen! She's—oh, sorry!" he said, stunned, popping back out. "Sorry!" he said again through the closed door. Trish rolled her eyes.

"I should let you finish getting ready," Trish said. "I'm glad we talked, Millie."

"Me, too, Trish," I said. "I'd like us to be closer."

Trish's big chocolate eyes filled with tears. "That would be great," she whispered. She wiped her eyes (her mascara didn't smear) and stood.

"Here, let me fix your makeup," she said, picking up a compact and frowning at its label. "I should really send you some better stuff. Oh, shit, sorry." She grinned sheepishly, then dabbed some powder under my eyes. "We're about to have a lot in common," she went on, opening the mascara for a re-application. "Sam will get on your nerves, you know. He's always right, and that gets pretty irritating. And he sulks when he's mad. Well, you'll find out, if you haven't already. You can call me to complain. I'll know just what you're talking about."

I laughed as she finished repairing me. She stepped back for a closer look. "There. Perfect. And Millie—"

"Yes?"

"Sam's the best guy in the world." Trish flashed me her

brilliant smile, and I stepped up and hugged her hard. After all these years, my sister had come through.

"You have to stay, Trish," I said.

"Oh, I…I don't know," she murmured. "I don't want to…"

"Upstage me?" I suggested. She gave a shaky laugh. "Really, Trish. If you're okay with it, I'd really like you to be here."

She smiled, took a breath and nodded. "Okay. Absolutely."

I went to the door and whispered to Katie, then returned to Trish.

"Nobody knows you're here?" I asked.

"Just Katie and your friend there."

Just then, Danny came in. "What's up, Millie?" he asked. Then he saw his mother.

"Mom!" He bounded over to her and enveloped her in a huge hug. "Good for you, Mom. I knew you'd make it." He murmured something to her, still hugging her tight, and she kissed his cheek soundly, her eyes bright with tears once more. "Come on, Mom," Danny continued. "We'll definitely nail the award for 'Best Adjusted Family Members.' And at least we can dance. Have you seen Millie and Sam? Total car wreck."

"I resent that," I said, laughing.

Trish looked at me, her eyes hopeful. "Are you sure, Millie?"

"Positive. Danny, why don't you take your mom downstairs, then send Grandpa up so we can get this show on the road, okay?"

"You bet," Danny said. "And, Mil, you look really pretty, by the way. Aunt Stepmother. It's so freaky." He pretended to shudder, then turned to Trish and took her arm. "Mom, I'm so glad you came. Let's go surprise Dad."

"Thanks, Millie," Trish whispered.

"No problem." I smiled wetly as Curtis came back in.

"Sorry about that, Trish," he muttered.

"Which one are you again?" Trish asked. She flashed me a grin and I felt a rush of affection for her as she left with her son.

Curtis and I followed them to the landing, then hunkered down.

"What's going on?" Katie hissed, kneeling next to us.

"Shh. Look." We crouched down low enough to see as Danny and Trish entered the salon. We saw Sam do a double take when he saw Trish. Then, as a huge smile lit up his face, he went over to Trish and kissed her on the cheek, hugged her. We couldn't hear what they were saying, but we didn't need to. The best guy in the world, indeed. He looked up suddenly and our eyes met, and for a second, it was just the two of us, hearts full, ready for the rest of our life.

My dad lumbered up the stairs.

"I'll get our flowers," Katie said, zipping into the bedroom.

"You ready, punkin?" my dad asked as I stood up and smoothed out my dress.

"You bet."

"Let's get going, then. It's time for Sam Nickerson to steal another one of my daughters."

Katie reappeared with our bouquets. Glancing up, Curtis nodded and gave the string quartet the high sign. The music started, and I went downstairs to marry the love of my life.

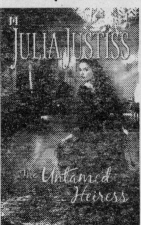

REQUEST YOUR FREE BOOKS!

2 FREE NOVELS FROM THE ROMANCE/SUSPENSE COLLECTION PLUS 2 FREE GIFTS!

YES! Please send me 2 FREE novels from the Romance/Suspense Collection and my 2 FREE gifts. After receiving them, if I don't wish to receive any more books, I can return the shipping statement marked "cancel." If I don't cancel, I will receive 4 brand-new novels every month and be billed just $5.24 per book in the U.S., or $5.74 per book in Canada, plus 25¢ shipping and handling per book plus applicable taxes, if any*. That's a savings of at least 10% off the cover price! I understand that accepting the 2 free books and gifts places me under no obligation to buy anything. I can always return a shipment and cancel at any time. Even if I never buy another book from the Reader Service, the two free books and gifts are mine to keep forever.

185 MDN EF3H   385 MDN EF3J

Name	(PLEASE PRINT)	
Address		Apt. #
City	State/Prov.	Zip/Postal Code

Signature (if under 18, a parent or guardian must sign)

Mail to The Reader Service:

IN U.S.A.	IN CANADA
P.O. Box 1867	P.O. Box 609
Buffalo, NY	Fort Erie, Ontario
14240-1867	L2A 5X3

Not valid to current subscribers to the Romance Collection,
the Suspense Collection or the Romance/Suspense Collection.

**Want to try two free books from another line?
Call 1-800-873-8635 or visit www.morefreebooks.com.**

* Terms and prices subject to change without notice. NY residents add applicable sales tax. Canadian residents will be charged applicable provincial taxes and GST. This offer is limited to one order per household. All orders subject to approval. Credit or debit balances in a customer's account(s) may be offset by any other outstanding balance owed by or to the customer. Please allow 4 to 6 weeks for delivery.